THE W

Judi James was a
model before running a school of modelling in
Chelsea, discovering and training such super-
models as Naomi Campbell. She then became
a management consultant and now lectures to
businesses on presentation skills, as well as writing her own column for *You Magazine*.

She lives in North London and is the author
of five novels, including *Carmine*, *The Devil's
Own Boy*, *Supermodel* and *Naked Angels*, and
also *The Office Jungle*, a non-fiction book on
how to survive office life.

JUDI JAMES

The Wedding Suit

HarperCollins*Publishers*

This novel is entirely a work of fiction. The names, characters and incidents portrayed in it are the work of the author's imagination. Any resemblance to actual persons, living or dead, events or localities is entirely coincidental.

HarperCollins*Publishers*
77–85 Fulham Palace Road,
Hammersmith, London W6 8JB

A Paperback Original 1997
3 5 7 9 8 6 4 2

A catalogue record for this book
is available from the British Library

ISBN 000 649865 5

Set in Sabon by
Rowland Phototypesetting Limited, Bury St Edmunds, Suffolk

Printed in Great Britain by
HarperCollinsManufacturing Glasgow

CHAPTER ONE

ZG

LONDON 1998

VICUNA

*On tall mist-shrouded mountains, high above the
clouds in Peru, live small goats with fleeces so fine
and delicate the fabric spun from them is known as
The King of All Cloths. Softer than cashmere and
therefore six times as expensive, it will take as many
as forty fleeces to make one vicuna overcoat. In its
natural state vicuna is either fawn in colour or a rich
cinnamon brown, and wearing it must always be
considered a privilege.*

THE MURDER

Abusing that privilege through neglect or misuse should rate
as a criminal offence – though that was not the reason why
the police had been called out on this particular evening.

The suit must always fit the man – the man must never
be expected to fit the suit. This suit fitted like bespoke
rattlesnake skin. All the best suits reflect the character of
their wearer, and this garment – both cut and finished
by hand with a minimum of five hours' work in the
buttonholes alone – delineated an exacting perfectionist,

1

traditionalist and consummate purist who was, above all else, outstandingly, overwhelmingly and nauseatingly rich.

Even a detective swathed in a high-static blend of Bri-nylon and crease-resistant polyester could bend to pay homage at this altar of style and expert workmanship and, as he fingered the cloth reverently, he felt a twinge of resentment for the suit's wearer – even though the man was obviously dead.

The corpse was clad in a double-vented jacket with notched lapels and working cuff buttons. The stain was a shame, though, running as it did from chest to crotch with a particularly dense concentration around the stomach and the waist. The blotch would have been crimson, edged with a pie-crust frill of dull rust where the blood had dried, but it was night and so it lay dark and saturating, like wet ink.

He was a once-handsome man, though not young, tall and well-built in the Armani manner, with a meringue of dove-white hair crowning a face of nicotine-coloured, Continental skin. It was impossible to tell the shade of his eyes because the eyeballs had been removed by the murderer and the lids carefully stitched, along with the mouth.

'Gimp,' the SOCO noted. 'A special thread used for stitching buttonholes.' He turned to the young policeman beside him. 'My grandfather was a tailor,' he explained. 'Those stitches are professional, see?'

The policeman began to careen slightly.

'Tell me what's in the bag,' the detective-in-charge asked, dusting his knees as he rose from an unsteady crouch. The tone of his voice told the others they should guess rather than look. A great, waddling, whale-bellied man in an edge-

2

to-edge shirt and Roadrunner socks, Malcolm Abberline was noted for the large black-and-white picture of Robbie Coltrane he had tacked to the cork-board behind his desk, alongside the snap of his dead collie Roy, and he didn't care who bloody saw it. As he pointed towards the ground a Man. United solid silver memento cufflink slithered slyly out from beneath the sleeve of his Hugo Boss jacket.

Beside the corpse lay a Gucci handbag – a six-hundred-dollar job, brand new and fresh off the catwalks, puffball-shaped in gleaming mint-green patent. The bag appeared to be heavily full. The policemen made bets on its contents:

'Money. The guy was a mugger who took off with some rich tart's coffer – maybe her bodyguard caught up with him and took a little revenge.'

'In that suit? No fucking way, José. No way is a suit like that going round on a fucking bag-snatch, no siree.'

'So how come a suit like that in an area like this, then?'

They all straightened together like a pack of meerkats and looked around, sniffing the air. The question was valid. The body did look poetically misplaced in that turbid, crap-carpeted street. Off to their left somewhere lay the dreaming spires of Spitalfields. To their right a small army of Japanese on a walking tour of 'The Undiscovered London' gawped from behind a length of fluttering blue-and-white tape.

Six pairs of policemen's eyeballs glinted suddenly in fanciful unison – for it was at that precise moment that the first whiff of a major scandal rounded the corner and doffed its cap by way of introduction. They scented big-league. A spread in the *Screws* at the very least. At best a *Crimewatch* reconstruction: '... and in tonight's show actors replace

3

the victim and his family, but the police involved will be playing themselves...' A line of looping smiles spread across their faces like bunting.

'Heroin?' one of them asked, looking back at the bag.

'Leather-gear, pervie-wear. Thongs and stuff.' A nervous laugh ran round the group.

'Intestines,' said Detective Abberline finally, silencing the sniggers in an instant.

And as it happened he was right; glistening greasily in the spanking-new Gucci bag lay a fat wine- and elderberry-coloured mound that appeared almost to writhe with life as it lay pinned in the lights from their torches once the faux-gold, logo-bearing zipper was gingerly pulled back.

THE PARTY

Imagine this: an abandoned urban tower-block earmarked for demolition, standing ghastly black and cavernous on a howling bitter night. Raddled and scarred by scorchmarks and sun-bleached graffiti, partially blinded by nailed-up chipboard hoarding, the place retains a strange gothic dignity while at the same time scaring you shitless.

Packs of mongrel dogs race and skitter around the building's shabby, urine-marinated legs. Your taxi abandoned you at the perimeter of the estate, refusing all inducement to venture further. The wind whips around the hem of your snazzy Versace and you realize you are gripped in the gruesome bowels of your own worst nightmare, clutching nothing more substantial than a gilt-edged invitation to ward off the terrors that lie beyond.

At this point you wish to be anywhere else on this planet,

but sweet-Jesus, there is no multiple choice involved here. This very venue on this particular night is the hippest place in London – and you are aware that if you aren't hip then you may as well be dead.

And so you teeter on your heels across meadows of undulating tarmac, past rusted, char-grilled Vauxhalls, through dripping dark alleys where green lights gutter over a sorry line of wind-blasted plaques erected in the memory of various policemen who fell in countless age-old battles.

There is the scent of Special Brew and cat's pee in the air. You come to a dead end and you feel the muscles of your heart begin to pucker in genuine fear.

There is a lift. The doors part noiselessly and, pulse pounding a gay rhumba beat, you step inside on gelatine legs. There is no apparent motion, but when the doors slide open again you are blinded by light so white that you feel actual heat from it and have to shield your eyes before you can begin to advance.

You are in the very crotch of the tower-block, then, but you are also somehow in a gilded and scented cathedral to style and chic. Someone has gutted out twenty floors above you so that there is no apparent ceiling, only row upon sick-inducing row of walls and balconies, all swathed in lengths of shimmering opal fabric.

When you look up the roof is so high you get vertigo and you pitch like a drunk. There is music so violently loud it slaps against your eardrums, making them smart. Others swarm around you; beautiful people or uglies, you can't really tell – A-list guests, anyway, bug-eyed with chemical mood-enhancers, all gazing opaquely while French-kissing the king prawns-en-croûte they have lifted from the finger buffet, while the roar of Bach's 'Toccata' buzzes busily about their lacquered heads.

There is womb-like warmth and there is the smell of a thousand hot scents. A white catwalk descends slowly from the heavens in clouds of dry ice and suddenly there are stilt-legged models upon it, around twenty or thirty of the most emaciated British faces, plus a couple of pouting celebs and ex-royals prancing ridiculously among them for good measure.

The theme of the show is evasive, though its title is 'The Divine Comedy', but the audience roars anyway because the alcohol quota has erred on the comatose side of adequate.

Laser lights cut through the dazzle overhead as the music builds to a crescendo. They spell out initials: ZG entwined. There is applause and you laugh, near-hysterical with relief. You have made it. You thought you might die en route but instead you are here, at the party of the season, held in honour of Gabriel Zigo's triumphant return to British Fashion Week after four years of showing in Paris or Milan.

Voices crow nearby: '. . . there are few things worse than sleeping alone and Michael is definitely one of them.'

'. . . if you enjoyed Tarantino then you absolutely *must* hoof it down to Camden to see the little Mongolian pic we caught last week . . . very arthouse and so minimalist it reads like a home movie . . . all hand-held and everything . . . Jean Paul swore the murders were real but it was in *Time Out*, after all, and I can't see them giving a rating to a snuff movie . . .'

'. . . would somebody please find out if this is soya in the pastry, only I'm on gluten-free and I already carry a loaded syringe in my bag in case I catch as much as a sniff of a peanut . . .'

'. . . did you say Paul McCartney? Who? Oh, *Linda's* husband. I seeeee . . .'

'. . . and you know one bee sting can put me into a fucking coma – remember that shoot in Provence where I had that complete collapse in that field and it was only because the stylist had studied basic first-aid on his aromatherapy course that I'm here to tell the tale today, so I have numbers always in my bag here where people can get help. I can never travel alone, never . . . shit, I brought the wrong bag out tonight, anyway, just ring this chap at the allergy clinic in Harley Street if I begin to turn blue. Where are you going? . . .'

There is a surge around the buffet. Hester Zigofsky pushes past, lost in a fog of Givenchy and utter confusion. Her children are vanished and her ears pop and sizzle from the speed of the lift. Only the very young are tolerant of such things. She peers at someone's heaped plate and clicks her tongue: marinated cheese-hearts, egg-size truffles and wild mushrooms in vine leaves, braised sweetbreads and fresh beetroot meringues – nothing kosher, she notices. Was this worth such a scrum?

Her son Burgess hares past but fails to stop when she hails him. Or perhaps he just doesn't hear. All the rest of her brood are there somewhere, of course – China, Kitty, Nula and, of course, Chloe, who organized the whole ghastly event.

There is a life-size Hockney portrait of them all in one of the anterooms. It took ten men or more to carry the vast canvas into the building at dawn that morning and

7

then the frame had broken, which sent Chloe off into a spontaneously-combusted breakdown, not just for the glass, which could be replaced, but for the very occurrence itself, which she claimed was an omen of impending disaster.

The portrait is good – weirdly surreal but good. What is wrong is the way the whole group looks. Functional, that is the word that springs into Hester's mind, they look functional. A functioning family. She smiles, but more to air her teeth than from any genuine pleasure.

Gabriel is seated in the middle of the portrait, of course, his face no more than a few swipes with the palette knife, but very alive for all that. He appears god-like among them, as he does in real life, his prematurely whitened hair a halo around his strong, broad, classical head. Kitty is shyly but adoringly at his side as always, her well-honed features a virtual mirror of her father's. Burgess is smiling, which is deeply unlikely. He is behind his father, straight-backed and in awe, with his eyes fixed on Gabriel's head. The son and heir, so ambitious and yet so painfully in need of praise and approval from the parent who eclipses him. Chloe is sprawled in an effort to attract maximum attention, while China's leaden-featured face is turned slightly away. She wanted her husband in the portrait but Gabriel said not, and his word is law and always will be.

Hester peers at her own portrait – a blur beside the others, like a shadow dressed in yellow – smudged and indistinct as a thumbprint, as though the artist had not really seen her there at all.

She touches the picture with her finger. The paint of her husband's suit still feels wet. She gasps and draws her digit back quickly. There is a crimson stain on the tip. Mesmerized, she stares at it in some horror.

A camera crew appears alongside and she is momentarily confused by the lights in her face.

'A success?' a voice asks her. She turns, alarmed, her expression distraught.

'The party?' the interviewer prompts. 'A success?' He is young and he is nodding encouragingly. Hurry. Speak. They are wasting good film.

Hester straightens and smiles the smile of the Sphinx. The smile she uses for *Hello!* and *Harpers*. 'Of course a success!' she trills, her eyes sparkling. She puts her hand to her face and a fistful of diamonds glints like a glitterball.

'Is your husband here? We don't seem to find him.'

Hester shrugs and her smile widens. 'You know Gabriel!' she laughs. 'Always the workaholic. He's bound to be in his cutting-room right now, putting the finishing touches to a new design. He forgets what hour it is when he's in a creative mood – I'm sure he'll turn up later.'

The scorching light disappears as quickly as it arrived, leaving her feeling like a cooling, fresh-baked roll. A woman clutches at her hands and she is air-kissed, solemnly and ceremoniously.

'Wonderful, magnificent!'

'*Marie-Claire*,' a voice whispers in her ear. It is Deeta, the company PR, a minuscule but muscular girl who looks no older than twelve in a Minnie Mouse dress. She's been circling Hester all night. Her hair is citrus-yellow with orange tips to the knotted peaks.

'Italian *Vogue*,' the girl adds, as a woman in gleaming pvc looms.

Hester feels a shriek forming somewhere inside. Mumbling apologies, she finds a door marked 'Exit' and thrusts herself through it, waving blindly, then up some stairs, like a mole towards the air of the lawn. The atmosphere outside is shockingly cold, like a vapour of iced water. She has tinnitus from all the noise. Where is her husband? She needs him. She can't handle all this on her own. She slips a Prozac from bag to mouth and swallows it dry. The outside world smells funny; musty old smells of her childhood – boiled food and the pungent smoke from burning coal.

She turns her face to the east and sees the shimmering tower at Canary Wharf flashing like a lighthouse in the darkness. Maybe there are still ships out there to be warned off the rocks – the same ships that brought her family and her husband's family to this country many years before. What had their thoughts been, those wretched souls? Did they see this party from hell mapped out in their future ambitions?

Between there and here lay ancient streets: Commercial Road, Radcliffe Highway, Brick Lane. Lost in a dream, Hester feels the heat from the pressing irons and hears the zip of French chalk making deft marks down a yard of navy suiting; the hum of ancient machines and a stench of old oil and cloth-dust; the phantoms of old noises ring in her ears. She shudders suddenly and rubs her pimple-chilled fat arms twice over with her hot hands.

A car approaches warily across the tarmac. She has never seen a police car drive so slowly, only when ... Maybe someone has complained about the noise. She fumbles for cigarettes, glancing back at the tower-block. Only it has been soundproofed – no noise, no trouble. Maybe a form of lowlife still haunts the old estate. Perhaps there has been some disturbance. Heroin-hawking. Window-smashing. But she is aware at the same time that that's not it.

Hester knows before she hears the car doors thud and she knows before she sees the expression on the policemen's faces what it is they have come to say to her.

'He's dead,' she tells them helpfully, once they are standing before her. It really is the only option. Her mind is suddenly totally lucid and logical. Strange that – the police thought they'd come to break the news to her, not the other way round. Sixth sense perhaps, or maybe the look of gravitas they put onto their youthful, kebab-fattened faces. They wonder at the sight of such a rich-looking woman, standing in this steaming piss-pit.

'My husband.' Hester's voice sounds patient.

'Mrs Zigo?'

'Zigofsky,' she corrects them. 'Zigo is a trade name. It is from the old family name, Zigofsky. My husband's family emigrated here many years ago. Like many Jews with names that were too complicated for the English ear and tongue, they found it was abbreviated on the immigration lists, hence Zigo. Zigofsky – Zigo, it sounds so much better, don't you think? So English? Ha!'

And then they tell her what she already knows, almost as though she had never spoken. No one offers her a chair, no one asks if she would like to go inside.

'I'm afraid Mr Zigo ... Zigofsky ... has been found dead,' they tell her. They don't say it was murder, not yet.

11

It even crosses their minds that she might have done it. It could explain the way she already knew, before they'd told her.

Then Hester slides to the ground before they can stop her, a great buttery mountain of slithering embarrassment, laddering her eight-pounds-ninety-five-pence Harvey Nichols stockings at the knee as she does so. And they think that maybe she didn't do it after all, or if she did she's a bloody good actress, what with all that snot coming out of her nose all of a sudden and the way all that screaming suddenly starts emerging from her Chanel-painted mouth. Very Helen Mirren, that – or maybe Diana Rigg *après The Avengers*, after she went all arty.

They look at the woman lying shrieking at their feet like a run-over rat and as it starts very suddenly to rain – and rain hard at that – the policemen realize reluctantly that, despite her considerable size, they have little option but to carry her inside.

1889

We are a million miles from anywhere and sick with all the delay. I miss Papa so badly that each night I cry until the others complain angrily.

The sea makes a terrible sight – pitching and grey by day, while in the crimson skies of sunset it becomes boiling sulphur – so that I would not be surprised to see the devil himself rise from its bowels and take us all to hell with him in his fist.

It is a miserable thing to be frightened and alone, and the stories I am told of the country we are travelling to for our stop-over make me wonder whether I should ever have left The Pale of Settlement.

We are saving the meagre candles for *Pesach*, so at night we sit in the dark, and Kaspar the cutter's wife – a huge, dark-eyed peasant from the Ukraine – has taken it upon herself to tell us stories. There is much shrieking at what she has to say and last night four women swooned right away and had to be carried up on deck to recover.

According to the presser's wife there has been a murderous fiend stalking the streets of London preying on young women, cutting out their entrails before they are even killed, and cooking and eating them once they are dead. They call him The Ripper, she says, and he guts the women just as cleanly as a fishmonger guts a fish.

The picture she paints is so vivid that it has me quaking beneath my blanket, though I will not scream out as I want to, for fear that it will give her even greater satisfaction.

She tells me his victims are whores so I had better beware. I catch her staring strangely at my belly and pull my shawl tighter. I reply haughtily that I am certainly no whore and never will be, but then she laughs, saying I might not be so full of myself once I am on the streets without money and my gut is growling for food.

I fear now that I have left bad for worse and that I shall be killed for certain, if not by the Ripper then by the sea itself, for we have lost twelve to the sickness already and more will die daily if we do not reach land soon.

At dawn I stand hidden by fog so dense it plasters my hair to my face, and watch the sailors slipping corpses over the side of the boat and down into the pitching grey water. In my silent terror I imagine one of the shapes cries out as it falls but the men mock me, saying it was a gull that screamed. I count five bodies altogether – one of them a child, by the size of the sack.

Then tonight I think my time has come to join the dead. I wake in such pain that I have to bite my lip to avoid crying out. I dreamt that I was being butchered by the Ripper and that he was cutting at my vitals. When I wake I feel wetness beneath me on my little straw mattress and I am more scared than ever before in my life.

'I am killed!' I cry out at last. 'He has butchered me in my sleep!'

The women gather around, hissing and shushing, stuffing cloth into my mouth to silence me, so that I now fear suffocation more than the pain that tears through my belly. In my head I scream for my mother, though God knows she is too far away to hear and would be little enough help even if she were.

Many hours go by in this way as, full of pain and terror, I slip in and out of strange dreams. Then one of the women whispers angrily into my ear: 'You have a child, girl. A baby.'

She takes the gag from my mouth and mops my brow with it. I look at her ugly old face in disbelief at such a strange miracle.

'Let me see it,' I say, for I still imagine that she must be lying to me.

They hold the bloody little package up by its hind legs like a skinned hare for my inspection and I can see very little of it in the dark, apart from its face, which catches some of the yellow light from the candle they shield with their hoary old hands.

14

I see one thing, though. I see the mark on its face – the tiny red, thumbnail-shaped impression between its minute brows. In an instant the pain and hot aches leave my body and I am chilled like ice through my veins, instead. I fall to quaking then, and the shakes become so violent that even the old crab at my side looks alarmed.

'Stop that, now,' she says.

'Why doesn't it cry?' I ask. 'The child – it makes no sound.'

'It's dead,' the woman tells me, 'and better off, too, the bastard.'

I cry bitterly then, though no one gives comfort for they all think me damned for the shame of my terrible situation.

'Forget the baby,' they tell me, 'forget you ever gave birth. Lead your life. Do the best you can.'

At dawn I am discovered again shivering at the side of the ship, only this time I watch as my own child is dropped into the sea. She is wrapped in my vest, which I have stitched quickly but carefully into a suitable shroud, for I could not stand to look at even such a poor thing put out to sea in a filthy sack.

As I sat stitching by the light of the one meagre candle they allowed me, I was reminded of my father stitching my wedding suit, and how joyous it was to watch him, and I saw what a miserable sight I must make now as I sew for my own child.

I wish I had time to embroider a little message onto the fabric. I think of my father in his workroom, sewing delicate flowers in Indian-dyed silks onto the waistcoat of the wedding suit.

I am thirteen years old. The following day will be my fourteenth birthday. The sun is so beautiful as it rises, swollen huge and blood-red from the sea-mists. I watch the spot where my dead child was swallowed by the water. My eyes ache but they will not leave that point, even long after it is gone on the distant horizon.

CHAPTER TWO

ZG

LONDON 1998

ZEPHYR
A fine, lightweight woollen fabric.

The room was dark, apart from a candle that burnt day and night, filling the room with the warm, rich scents of tallow and beeswax.

Murmuring visitors materialized and evaporated and Kitty barely knew who they were, for their whispered regrets all sounded so similar; but after they were gone, like the tide, the family alone remained as stubborn as pebbles on the beach, sitting face-to-face in silence, though not one of them could look into the eyes of another.

Who did it? The low chairs made their legs ache. Who was it? Kitty rubbed at her temples in an attempt to separate overwhelming grief from suspicion and revenge. Her father had been murdered. When she looked in the mirror she saw his face merged with her own. Of them all it was she who most resembled him. 'Who killed me, Kitty? Who did it?'

They observed the traditions at that time: a family

then for the seven days of *shiva*, not a board meeting or collective. A mother, four daughters and a son, all mourning the passing of their famous husband and father, a proudly dominating man who had them all reined in so tight they had scattered like drops of oil on water at his death.

What they had in that room was the end of an era, for as they sat in silence they were aware that out there somewhere a business empire was crumbling. It could never have survived the death of Gabriel. A principled, honourable and – to them – heroic man, he was central to their very existence and, in their view, the rays of the sun literally shone from his arse.

What a group they made! You would have known their faces, each of them, for they had stalked the pages of the press for a decade, slithering from Fashion to Gossip, to Finance and on to Reportage and Crime with all the oily ease of a butterpat on a hot plate.

They were the Family Zigofsky, but you would have known them only by the name Zigo, which was the brand-name of the fashion group and had been for many years. You would also have known their trademark: Z̶G̶. If you were a person of substance, style and taste you would have it etched on your luggage, while the children of the family had it tattooed wittily on their ankles, each of them branded with the corporate logo long before they were old enough to complain.

There was the mother, made quite mad by her grief, but struck with such a quiet and polite type of insanity that the only outward symptom was that her stockings didn't match. One leg was tan and the other the colour of putty,

18

but nobody dared mention this in case other, uglier crazinesses should well up from inside somewhere and start to spill out.

Hester Lucille. Her face was never terribly well known to you for, like her son, she was eternally eclipsed by her husband's dazzle. She was a large woman but appeared small. Her skin was the colour of marmalade and her hair treacle-black. Her husband had told the children so many times that she was beautiful it was only once he was gone and the magic spell broken that they discovered that she was merely unremarkable.

Chloe, however, had beauty to an inordinate degree. Gorgon-haired and flame-eyed, she was the bogeyman of Kitty's childhood and still capable of terrifying. Sparks had been known to fly from her; Kitty would flinch when she spoke and become paralysed with terror when she moved. The inactivity of the *shiva* threatened to prove fatal to her. Kitty sat in readiness, aware that her sister would combust spontaneously sooner or later.

There was no continuity with Chloe, apart from her height. She was thin but strong and had had three noses in the previous two years. She picked up accents and buzzwords faster than she picked up her men, but through each and every sea-change she had always found a place on the published list of the world's most beautiful people.

Her hair was currently dyed chartreuse and her skin had been laminated against wrinkles or ageing. Her eyes were like dragonfly eyes and her mouth was stained tangerine. She appeared to survive on a diet of lychees and breadsticks and so the kosher food was causing great internal anguish.

Chloe had bullied Kitty remorselessly as a child. Ghosts

of long-faded bruises rose up to haunt the younger sister with pains again when she walked by.

Burgess was Lizard Man – the brother who never blinked, farted or fucked. An ex-alcoholic who dried out via cocaine to discover a loathing for any abusable substance short of pure oxygen, Burgess looked like the most un-hip man in the universe as he pursued his eternal crusade to disprove the theory about still waters always running deep.

Kitty carried a photo in her wallet of Burgess at his Bar mitzvah and would pull it out every time she needed reassurance that he was in fact of human extraction. She used to love the boy in the photo, with his geeky grin and his skinny legs in the long pants, but that was before the drugs ate away the cute part and left just a smile in a suit. Then he became Corporate Man, a virtual reality of what used to be, with his pink, pinned-back ears and his helmet of cropped black hair.

'Who killed me, Kitty?'

She had that childhood photograph with her now. She needed it badly. She needed to remind herself that Burgess, with all his impatience and his cold calculations that made business a boardgame, could never have wanted his father removed from the field of play.

The timelessness of the *shiva* was anathema to her brother as well. God created the world in seven days, but Burgess would personally have done it in four and sold it knock-down to the Japanese by the fifth. He had glanced at his watch forty-three times before the first hour was over. Then he discovered some internal focus and sat hunched in the dark, dank womb of his family instead, his eyes glazed in corporate contemplation as his mind grazed through the pastures of exotic far-off lands like Hang Seng and Dow Jones.

China, the eldest sister, was the most like their mother and was married to Stephano, who would bite the heads off babies for fun. On the day that she married China shaved off her hair, following ancient traditions, and ceased to speak – allowing Stephano to do the communicating for her via some form of advanced telepathy. When asked a direct question she would turn mutely to her husband, and signals would seem to come out of her head, which Stephano was capable of translating into answers of such indifference and arrogance that you would have thought they had emanated from his brain in the first place.

Nula, the youngest, was perfection: pretty, shy and talented, she was as sweet as Chloe could be sour and they all cherished the very bones of her for being what they couldn't be – sensitive, modest and quiet.

Nula had the round face of an overstuffed cherub and an earthy, herbal smell. Her hair was short like soft fuzzy moleskin and she wore cellophane fabrics and hand-knits.

China, Chloe, Burgess and Nula – and not forgetting Kitty, of course. And their ages? Twenty-two, nineteen, twenty, fifteen and eighteen respectively. Fashion is a young business, at least that's what their Uncle Leonard kept saying and he should have known, for he was the greater side of ninety.

Kitty looked around at the circle of shocked faces that were frozen in grief, like masks of a Greek chorus. Ghosts spoke to her via voices in her head. 'Who was it?' She heard

Gabriel, his voice coming in snippets and half-remembered phrases; it was like flicking through the pages of a talking-book photo-album.

His face had already slipped from her mental grasp. Did this happen? Would she start to forget how he looked? And so soon? How little had she dared to stare at him when he was alive – even she, who was his own cherished darling. Sometimes when he worked she would watch. She concentrated on his frown as he spent time on his sketches. A black cashmere roll-neck. The glasses with the half-rimmed frames that he never wore outside the studio. Music. She could hear the stuff he would play while he drew. Ella Fitzgerald. Billie Holliday. She would stuff her fingers into her ears and howl like a dog because to her it was off-key, and he would laugh – though he didn't laugh now in her memory, she had lost sight of his face altogether . . .

She saw his back as he bent over the cutting-table. Why was he being so elusive? Why was he turned away from her? She wanted to call out, to make him show her his face again.

'Kitty.' She heard his whisper in her head, along with other, unfamiliar voices. 'Who was it?' She opened her eyes quickly. Was he to be turned away from her until she discovered his murderer? Was that her task? Was this shunning to be her punishment if she failed him?

Time and again she looked across at the other members of her family. Their misery should have united them, but a sense of fear held them apart. They were wealthy – powerful even – but most of all they were terrified, each in their own way.

22

When God created Gabriel he must have made Kitty from the off-cuts. She too was darkly handsome with the same graphite eyes and hair thick enough to make even regular combing painful. To her father she was a peach of a child; quiet and sunny, with the same disposition as the family dog – loyal to the point of stupidity, ferociously loving to anyone dumb enough to show a kindness, and effortlessly comical.

Now she was none of those things. Since his death she had become humourless, simmering in the darkness, waiting for the fan of air that would cause her to burst into flames of anger and resentment.

This was her own family, her blood. And she believed one of them might be a murderer. Her father had been killed and his death was symbolic. They had stitched his eyes and they had stitched his mouth, using tailor's thread to do it. It was a planned slaying, full of hatred and irony.

'Inevitable,' a voice whispered in Kitty's head. 'His death was inevitable.' She blew her nose hard to make the voice go away.

'Watch me, Kitty.' Her father was teaching her to sew. 'Watch the needle. See the way my hands work. Don't let your fingers stiffen, keep them strong but supple. The smaller and sharper the needle the less the mark it will leave on the fabric and these are the finest cloths, Kitty. Feel them against your cheek. Angel's breath, eh?'

He had designed less in recent years, as the job had become more a desperately-salvaged business than an adored obsession. Yet as a child she had watched him

23

pinning fabric onto a dummy, marvelling as it took shape, guessing at his thoughts, trying to follow his creative path and maybe sometimes jump ahead, although she never could. She was not an artist.

The only tragedy of Kitty's young life until now had been that she had shared Gabriel's passion for the business, but not his talent – at least not for design. She could be a useful spectator, though. As she grew older she would be allowed to sip at the brandy her father always drank prior to launching a new collection, making useful comments, keeping the day-to-day problems of running the place off his shoulders when he was busy.

The voice was right; her father had had to die, there was no question of it. The wheels of evolution and development must grind on relentlessly, and anyone who stands in the way will fall and be crushed.

Despite herself, Kitty loved them all – Chloe, Nula, China and Burgess. How could it have been otherwise, for they were of the same blood and they were her family, and there lay the two lynch-pins of her very existence: Family and Business. Blood ties and the clothing industry. They were all that was important in life, it had been drummed into her from birth.

She chewed at her fingernails. Soon she would have a new family. She was marrying Freddy. Starting a new life. Leaving the business, except for retaining a place on the sidelines. Her cuticle started to bleed. She could have managed a glass of her father's brandy right now.

'Who *was* it, Kitty?' The voice was becoming insistent, angry even.

'Okay, Daddy, okay.'

'Who will run the business now, Kitty? Who will take over from me?'

'What you worked at was dying too, Daddy. You saw the figures. We were going under. Let it go.'

'It's family, Kitty, a family firm. It has a history. It must be inherited, not bought.'

Her culture, her birthright. Tradition. Continuity. How many times had she and Chloe groaned or laughed at all that crap?

Family – her family.

'*Kitty!*'

'Okay.'

The wedding would have to be postponed.

THE BUSINESS

The real heart of the British rag trade is not sited – as many would believe – in the swanky climes of Chelsea and Mayfair, but in the busy, dusty network of narrow roads around Great Portland Street in the West End, and the rather more feisty area around Mile End Road, in the East. These are the places where the work gets done, from the orders being taken in the wholesale showrooms of Great Portland and Great Titchfield Streets, to the sweatshops of the East End, where many of the garments get made.

There is very little glamour in either of these locations and they are not the haunts of top models or wealthy clients.

Immigrant labour is exploited to full capacity in the sweatshops to keep the making costs of each garment down. This tradition has a long history and is the main reason why so many of the businesses are sited

The four greatest memories of Kitty's childhood were:

1. Being towed, screaming, up a Milan catwalk aged two years and five months, by a model with hands so pallid and cold she could have been made out of frozen pastry. Until the time of her father's death this was still Kitty's most *awful* and *traumatic* memory, too.

This had been *rehearsed* terror – before the show had started she had been trawled the length of the runway many times, just in case, and each time her screams and yelps had been enough to drown out the music.

Look at Chloe's face, though. Wreathed in dimpled smiles she is the all-perfect model infant. Her baby hair is sculpted into a neat chignon, her tiny legs move in time to the beat with immaculate precision, and her eyes! She is loving it, just adoring the whole whorey nature of the event, being stared at and photographed; this is her moment.

2. The faces around her cot. Real or imagined, they are there in her mind. What expectation shone from all their eyes! What did they want? Swaddled in French silk with a huge Chanel velvet bow stuck to her bald little head, Kitty would lie there for ages trying to work this one out. Her father wanted an ally. Her mother wanted peace from her nanny's demands. Her uncles wanted cute. Her sister Chloe wanted a toy. Each day she would reach out and squeeze Kitty's arm, just to see how she was coming along,

staring at her, sizing her up, seeing if she would bounce.

One day she painted lipstick on Kitty's mouth – three months old and with a port-wine pout. This was Chloe's disappointment, then, because Kitty never wore make-up in the rest of her life. Neither did she dye her hair. Nor resculpt herself with plastic surgery. This Chloe could never understand. Even now she would paint Kitty's toenails with varnish while she was sleeping.

3. The day she realized her father was *somebody*. This was not a gradual realization, but sudden. This was the day of her fifth birthday, when her father had booked a table at the Ritz for a whole dozen of her little friends, and when they had walked in dressed up like the cast from *Les Miserables* the maitre d' had pointed them towards a large table – a beautiful table, dressed in fashion fabrics and trimmings – laid with party gifts and crackers and balloons, and Kitty's father had just said, 'No,' in a quiet voice.

'No,' he had told the maitre d', 'that one.' And he had nodded towards a larger table, an even more beautiful one right next to the fountain. Kitty had nearly peed her little Swiss-lace-trimmed knickers right there on the spot for fear the maitre d' was going to throw them all out onto the street, dressed as they were, in the middle of Piccadilly on a cold afternoon.

But he hadn't. Instead he had smiled and said, 'Naturally,' and they had been given free fizzy orange, while the changes had been made like magic. Even so, being the sort of child she was, Kitty had still felt the need to say a whispered, 'I'm sorry,' to the maitre d' and gave him her party gift to make up for the aggravation when they were leaving.

4. Then there was the moment – only this wasn't early in her life, but later – about *now*, in fact – when Kitty had first been given the wedding suit.

As soon as Kitty was grown-up enough to walk, her father took her to work with him like a sweet little mascot, teaching her every aspect of the industry: couture, ready-to-wear, the high street short-order, and even the cabbage. She saw samples being pinned, shaped and sewn, and jumped like a flea as the steam rose when the final garments were being finished.

Gabriel focused his expectations for her like this: what he needed from her he saw in her. Our earliest self-belief is founded by our parents' opinions and perceptions. What Gabriel perceived in Kitty was something that passed for genuine talent – an honest interest that mirrored his own – and he took it upon himself to nurture that imagined spark until it became reality.

His passion for exquisite fabrics, therefore, was her birthright, and his eye for design and cut came to exemplify all she ever wanted in life. Uncle Louie, Uncle Benjamin, Uncle Leonard and her father – the Business was their Family and their Family was the Business.

It was Gabriel who saw the Dream Merchants appear on the horizon long before most people; that smiling army of grey financiers and suited money men – polite, quietly-spoken hordes – who were to hold out the hand of assistance only to take the rag trade businesses by the throat once they were within grip, and choke the vital essence out of them.

Or maybe the great houses would have destroyed themselves eventually anyway, for the internecine scraps between Kitty's family members were savage and relentless – and had been since long before Kitty was born.

When the seven days of *shiva* were ended, right down to the very exact minute, if not the second that they were finished, there was a banging downstairs and all action resumed in uproar as limousines arrived at the door of their mother's vast mausoleum of a house and they were shrouded in coats and spirited away from St John's Wood to the new heart of the ancient city and the magical Palace of Chrome.

Kitty travelled with Chloe, noting that her sister's foot had become a metronome, tapping out each second and minute that had passed since their father's death. Did she still remember Gabriel? It had been a whole two weeks since he died. Chloe's attention-span was as fleeting as a gnat's. Time heals all and Kitty expected Chloe's wounds would mend much faster than most.

Chloe excelled at excess. It is what she was best at and she used it to great advantage in the business. What the big names did, she would have to do better. If Versace hosted a party then she would outdo him. When Lacroix dressed actors for the Oscars, she would sniff out the winners and bribe them with wardrobes both larger and more extravagant. When she saw the Armani Wall in the via Broletto – the five-storey-high painting of his newest collection – she would not rest until the cream of their own

29

designs were displayed in laser along fifty floors of the tower at Canary Wharf.

Hence the party on the night of their father's death. Hence the codfish-cold shutters that had slithered across Chloe's eyes like a third lid when the police had staggered in carrying their mother clumsily between them, signalling a premature halt to the evening's activities.

To get her own way Chloe would cajole, flirt, bribe and, ultimately, threaten. She was an acknowledged diva of the fashion circuit, a celebrity sans cause. Their father loved her too, of course.

To reach the Palace of Chrome it was necessary to travel via the East and hence the Streets-That-Throng-With-Poor. Chloe had the door-locks on sharply – urgently – before the dispossessed rose up to prise the car wide open like a sardine can and have the Rolex off her wrist.

'Don't look,' she insisted to her sister, as though skewering the oppressed with eye contact would inspire serious insurrection.

For maximum irritation Kitty let her window down an inch, savouring the patchouli and cardamom and dust smells that were a fragrant relief to her sister's fifty-pound-a-squirt scent. She didn't want a conversation, she didn't want to set her sister off talking, because Chloe currently had a fad for peppering her speech-patterns with unspeakably aggravating New-Age words. She would say wrong things and then they would argue in the sort of hissy, spitty, snake-style language that sisters often indulge in. Kitty desperately wanted silence. Her brain had turned to mush in the heat.

They rode to the twenty-first floor of the Palace of Chrome in a lift made of molasses-tinted glass that treated all on the bustling mezzanine to a view of Kitty's Calvin Klein knickers. Chloe still scorched and sizzled with suppressed urgency. The lift was so speedy their faces contorted with G-force, but still it was too slow for Chloe and she pummelled the controls like an astronaut set for Warp Nine. The button for the third floor had no number, just the logo 𝗭𝗚, on its dial.

There was 𝗭𝗚 on the glass doors that they passed through and 𝗭𝗚 on the gum wrapper that Nula was flicking into the 𝗭𝗚 aluminium waste-bin. Household goods was one of the newer additions to the Zigo Empire, acquired in a blind panic after Versace and Ralph Lauren had made lucrative forays into that end of the market.

The boardroom had been transformed. No longer a place of minimalist sterility, it hummed and glowed with electronic life like the Harrods gift hall at Christmas. A dozen small desks had been strategically scattered and on each desk winked the eye of an ever-vigilant VDU screen. Nula gawped at the magical effect; it was an Aladdin's cave of on-line digital technology.

Stephano and China came up behind the others so fast they almost forgot to brake.

'Fucking shit!' Was that from Stephano or did China's words come out of his mouth? And who was the magician in charge of all that wizardry? Burgess appeared on cue, arms akimbo, Master of Ceremonies, the Unsmiling Host of the afternoon's celebrations.

Behind him, half-concealed in the slatted shadows by the Venetian blind-draped windows, a figure rocked back and forward gently in a grey leather chair. It was Nicky Kofteros, Burgess's own little superhero, the western face of giant-size eastern corporations; polite, well-mannered and handsome.

His suit fitted too perfectly, Kitty noted. Pretension. It was a class thing – ghastly, but a fact of life. A way of telling real earthlings from alien invaders. Kofteros looked like a being with a human outer skin that he would shed at night. Underneath would be a grinning Robert De Niro shelling hard-boiled eggs with long fingernails, like he did in *Angel Heart*. Kitty felt Nula shudder beside her.

'Where are they?' Chloe asked Burgess. 'Where are the others?' Her brother snapped his fingers and the dozen VDUs speckled about the room flickered with life.

At first each screen seemed to display an identical image: a gleaming, bland, oriental face in a suit, beaming and full-frontal. Mesmerized, Nula bent to peer.

'He blinked,' she whispered in awe, 'this one's alive! It blinked!'

'We are on-line live,' Burgess told her with a sidelong glance at Kofteros and a voice as flat from embarrassment as a stale, unbuttered croissant. 'We are video-conferencing on the global network. Take seats, please. You are watching and you are both watched and heard. Translation will be instantaneous. Please reserve questions until the end, when you will be expected to register a voting tendency.' One of the identical screen faces fell to chattering on cue and a virtual-reality oriental woman of air-hostess proportions and garb appeared in their midst to umpire the verbal ping-pong.

'Mr Hutchai of the Korean Waika Retail Group wishes

to bid you all welcome and to beg your kind attention while he outlines the proposed intensive globalization programme for the esteemed Zigo International Fashion and Wholesale Group,' she began. Burgess beamed.

Fazed as she was by all the technology, Kitty was still able to recognize the name of the woman's masters. Gabriel had sold certain merchandizing and licensing rights to Waika long ago in the Days Of Darkness, when liquidation loomed and injected capital was vital plasma.

Since then Waika had bought up the rest of the world, stamping desperate-looking, poor-quality tack from here to Timbuktu with their once-prestigious ZG logo.

'In an initial three-point-five million pound expansion programme,' the woman continued, 'Mr Hutchai and his board envisage the current twelve per cent year-on-year rise in first quarter sales to be raised a minimum thirty per cent, with margins up forty per cent from their current seventeen per cent position.'

With this tempting *hors d'oeuvre* on the table the translator began to assail them with details of the main course. Kitty watched the face on the screen in front of her in fascination as it flickered and chattered amicably. The face on Nula's screen just blinked, and not often at that. The face on China's screen was so still it might have been that of a hologrammed corpse. Stephano cracked about looking for knobs as though chasing horizontal hold on his ancient television set at home.

'. . . pre-tax losses for the group in the year to December totalled three-point-nine million pounds and the current forecast for the following year stands at seven-point-four million . . .'

Burgess gasped politely like a netted guppy. His etiquette always was impeccable, even when he was drunk, and it was appropriate to feign shock at hearing they were so totally and completely up to their necks in debt.

The Zigo empire was a lumbering, complex creature, founded financially on its mail-order business – which had since been sold – and currently consisting of three main segments: Couture, which is where the company made its name but lost its money; Ready-to-wear, and Diffusion. It was the couture side that was dearest to Gabriel's heart and – therefore – to Kitty's.

The couture name had been lent to various items of upmarket merchandise throughout the fifties and sixties, but always under licence. Gabriel's own name was also applied to a range of shoes and – for a brief while – cosmetics. But it was the perfume and handbag market that proved the most lucrative, and it was this that Gabriel sold to Waika to keep the salon afloat during the late seventies.

The Ready-to-wear and Diffusion ranges were marketed from the showroom. These garments sold to a world-wide market, both in small boutiques and the better class stores.

In the eighties the trend for concessions within stores became rife and Gabriel was forced to open several of these 'shops within shops' to avoid losing business. He was further encouraged to open half a dozen small retail outlets of his own in Britain – a move that proved to be a costly mistake.

The boutique in Beauchamp Place was expensive to rent, and for much of the year, even though business was good, the rental and overheads far exceeded the sales. The shop in Bond Street was only bought after pressure from Chloe, who concluded that they could not afford *not* to be seen there. Clients expected personal attention and pampering. Chloe's bill for champagne for one famous customer outstripped the cost of their purchase by three pounds. Most celebrities treated the place as a lending library, borrowing frocks for big events and then returning them the following day.

The wholesale showroom in the West End handled what Gabriel had called the '*schmutter* trade', which was the cheapest, and therefore most accessible and also most lucrative side of their business. For Chloe this side did not exist, yet it supported their largest factory, a state-of-the-art place in Wales where fabric was cut by laser and designs logged into computers.

The business as a whole had also supported many other outworkers – until Gabriel had been forced to make cutbacks, that was . . .

'. . . with an initial injection of up to thirty million into the parent company, the Korean Waika Retail Group envisages a massive reorganization programme to ensure Zigo are at the forefront of the market as we move towards the Millennium . . .'

Kitty began to twitch in her seat. Her acute allergy to techno-speak was making her itch.

'. . . the constant utilization of International Trend Forecast Consultants to keep us abreast of trends, styles and market intelligence . . . the deployment of the current market and showroom methods of sales presentation and a turn to 3D CAD images in fashion runway mode to display on a local or global scale, with the potential for virtual reality as a point-of-sale technique . . .'

35

In a moment of great sanity and enlightenment Kitty leant forward and pressed the button to the right of her screen, banishing Mr Hutchai to the dark outerspace of the Internet hinterlands.

'That was wonderful.' Kitty had been forced to take the great ride back down to the ground floor in the flying glass coffin with her youngest sister, Nula the gum-chewer.

'Did you understand any of it?' she asked her sister. In the silent void that constituted Nula's answer Kitty took it upon herself as a kind of sibling duty to explain.

'No more fashion shows, Nula, no more clothes in shops, no more sitting at the board designing a new model, no more trying garments on and – later – no more shops,' she said in a flat voice. 'In future you just plug in and go. Throw a 3D model of yourself on screen and dress it up before ordering up. Swap a virtual reality helmet for the shopping mall. Hell, who even needs to wear the damn things? Programme your little 3D image in the chosen outfit and watch it go off to the party instead of you!'

Kitty was fulfilling a sorely-felt need to see someone else as hacked off as herself with all this blasphemy. She started punching the lift buttons for dramatic effect, much in the aggressive style of Chloe.

Nula stared out from the lift in gummy silence. A little puffball of mist appeared where her breath met the cold glass. She wiped the condensation with her sleeve and then Kitty could see in the reflection that there were tears coursing down her small pudgy cheeks, and she turned her and hugged her while they both wept.

'It's a lot of fucking money, though, Kit,' Nula croaked between tears. Kitty nodded because there was no arguing with that statement.

'But you voted *for* . . .' Nula began, 'when Burgess asked you said yes . . .'

'I voted to think about it,' Kitty corrected her. She had voted to live. She had voted not to wake up to find her guts in a Gucci bag. 'It's okay, Nule,' she whispered.

'No.' Her sister's voice sounded weird. 'No, it's not okay, Kit,' she said, 'don't tell me it ever can be, not now, not again.'

They clasped one another in an embrace that was nothing less than pure unadulterated schmaltz. Kitty had voted not to stand in front of the wheels, like her dead father had done. She'd voted not to make the same mistake. She'd voted not to get killed. She was getting married. Soon. Despite the voices in her head. She was out of it. Safe, not dead, like Gabriel.

Kitty had popped into the off-licence on the way back from the city. A new experience, she discovered, standing at the counter, pointing to a stylish-looking bottle of Hine. The brown paper bag it came in made her feel guilty. She couldn't even find the right glass in her father's office, she had had to use a tumbler. The first sip was so full of nostalgia it made her head spin.

The workroom was empty and dark. The police had been through the entire place, inch by inch, but they had been amazingly careful and – apart from small patches of white powder around the safe door and desk drawers – very little looked different.

37

Kitty's feet made a padding noise on the thick wool carpet of the salon and then tapped across the bare boards of the studio one floor above. She wasn't ready for this yet. She would go home right now and forget about anger and revenge. This wasn't *The Godfather*. She wasn't about to go out blowing people's heads off until family honour was satisfied. Yet the voices were still there in her mind: 'Find out, Kitty. No one else can.'

The police will, she thought as she snapped on a desk lamp. They'll find out who did it.

She'd phoned them three times. What she got each time was patience, sympathy and weary politeness; an offer of victim support; counselling. She wanted to know what they knew, to find out how far they'd got. She'd tried to sound rational, intelligent and intensely sane on the phone. There was someone coming to interview her: Detective Abberline. He'd already spoken to Burgess and her mother. Maybe they worked in some sort of dynastic pecking order: her mother, Burgess, China, Chloe. What was she? Fifth in line to the throne?

She sat at her father's computer, staring at the blank screen for a full five minutes before she could summon up the courage to switch it on. The tears had been a problem, starting as they did the moment the screen lit up and her father's codes appeared, but she had wiped them scruffily out of the way with the back of her hand and she could see enough to get the information she wanted.

Gabriel had kept files on everyone. A compulsively tidy man, he had liked his friends, family and colleagues to appear in some type of order, even if they ran a disorganized lifestyle. He had told Kitty that his records were the secret of his social success; when he was introduced to anyone new he would always be sure to open a file on them, containing all that he'd discovered, even in a short space of time. Tastes, family, interests. If they met again they would be charmed by his recollected knowledge of them.

Kitty had laughed inwardly about this habit, but never to her father's face. He even had photos to go with most of the files. It was an unusual hobby but her Gabriel was an unusual man. He had been called a genius during his lifetime and so occasional lapses into eccentricity were always indulged.

Kitty saw her own face come up on the screen – a smiling shot, curiously dated and taken when she was still at school, but she beat the temptation to stop at that page. Instead she pulled up all the other major players in Gabriel's life and printed each sheet, one at a time. In the end she had a fair-sized bundle on the desk in front of her.

When she got home the apartment was empty – Freddy was working late at a trade fair – and she was able to sort the papers into two piles, excluding passing acquaintances and lost contacts and bundling the rest into one stack for 'close' and the other for 'unlikely'.

She pulled on her reading glasses and poured herself some more brandy. There were noises from the apartment upstairs. Freddy said the block – she'd bought new – reminded him of Japan, with paper-thin walls. The couple above were having sex. Kitty yawned and slid off her glasses to massage the bridge of her nose.

'Oh, dear God,' she sighed as the squealing and pet-name-calling started. She slipped a CD onto the player: Manic Street Preachers – one of Freddy's. She'd thought it might shame her neighbours into silence, but instead they barely paused a beat before picking up the rhythm with gusto. Kitty forced a smile and took a large slug of brandy before focusing again on her task.

She laid each sheet out in front of her: family first, then close friends, enemies and other business acquaintances.

About thirty in all. She had created a circle of paper around herself. She rotated slowly, the drink making her dizzy.

'Who?'

'*Who?*'

She pulled out the ones she wanted it to be.

Business rivals.

People he blocked.

People he sacked.

People who wanted him out of the way. The whole of the buy-out corporation. An Italian designer her father had slagged off in Rome last season. The press had made a thing of it but it was all hype and publicity. A chauffeur he had sacked last year for being drunk at the wheel. These were the ones she didn't mind hating.

But there were others.

Burgess: washed and scrubbed, with his hair plastered down like a little boy's. He wanted the buy-out so badly, but would never have stood against Gabriel while he was alive.

Stephano? But he was a joke baddy. And China never left his side, which would mean she was in cahoots . . .

She stared at Chloe's face. Gabriel was running the

business into the ground through his own stubborn pride and sense of history. A family-run business, as it was and as it had always been. A dinosaur in the fashion world.

'Your family suffered to create this empire, Kitty.' That was her mother's voice now. Generations on and she was still harping on about what they owed to the past.

'So if our ancestors were coalmen you'd still expect us to be humping sacks of the stuff around?' Chloe would joke. You couldn't joke about the past with their parents, though. The suffering that had gone was sacrosanct.

Freddy had found her sitting clutched into a miserable ball in the middle of her paper circle.

'Rogues' gallery?' he'd asked.

'Something like that,' she'd replied.

He'd hugged her and fed her coffee until the tears stopped. She loved him. Of course she loved him. She was marrying him. Only not yet.

'You know this has to stop, Kitty.' His eyes were large, sane and sensible. 'Right now. Before you hit paranoia.'

But because he said that, she just started to suspect him, too. Why else would he want her to stop hunting down her father's murderer? Was he scared she might guess? He'd been so keen for her to see a doctor, too. Did he want to see her drugged up and out of it?

Then she smelt his normal, lucid smell and felt his lips on the side of her face and knew she had to hold on or she would be losing it. Freddy? Kill her father? She drank more of the strong coffee he'd given her.

'*Caffe latte*. Double shot. The Seattle Coffee Company,' she said. Freddy grinned, nodding.

'You looked at the paper cup.'

'No. Absolutely not. Not even a peek.'

It was a game they played. Guess the take-away coffee. Freddy was good but she was better.

And then he'd given her the package. 'It came this morning,' he told her.

It was a photograph, taken from an old newspaper. A wedding shot. Her parents' wedding. Gabriel was smiling. Hester looked nervous and very very young.

'I hadn't seen this before,' Freddy said, looking over Kitty's shoulder.

There was no letter with the picture.

'Jesus, look at those outfits,' Freddy whispered.

Hester was in ankle-length crushed velvet with ribbons around the neck. Gabriel wore a suit from what looked like the same fabric, with an elaborate waistcoat underneath. Kitty had seen the shot before, of course. But not properly. Parents' wedding shots are something you see but don't look at, like your own face in the mirror each morning – familiar but unstudied. Until one of your parents dies, of course. Then you start scanning in properly.

Anonymous photos. Kitty's hands went white. Was this supposed to be a message? Was it some kind of a warning? Was it from the killer? Did they already know she was trying to piece things together? Did they see her as some sort of threat, like her father?

Kitty had been brought up to be happy, not brave. Her father would not have wanted her put in any danger. But even as she restacked the computer print-outs with shaking hands and placed the wedding shot carefully on top, prior to throwing the lot into the rubbish, she heard the voices again in her head.

'Who, Kitty? Who killed me?'

And another voice now – a woman's voice, old and heavily accented: 'Two things, Kitty, two things, dearest. Never be poor and never grow old. Learn from your past. And never, ever forget.'

CHAPTER THREE

ZG

LONDON 1954

BOMBAZINE
*Bombazine is a twilled fabric of silk and worsted, and
its name is said to derive from the Greek word for
silkworm. Dyed black, it became very popular years
ago as a fabric for mourning clothes. In Victorian
times the Jews called death 'God's kiss', while to the
Gentiles it was known as 'The Great Secret'.*

ROSA'S STORY

Dearest Kitty,

When I was dead they bore my coffin the entire length
of the Commercial Road and there was much wailing and
gnashing as I passed, though in truth I doubt there was
one Jew present not secretly relieved that I had gone. 'She
was dead three days when they found her,' Rabbi Fleish-
man whispered, sucking the moustache of his yellowing
beard. 'I saw her with my own eyes, face bloated and white
as the belly of a toad. The skin flaked so much you could
have pared it off yourself with the nail of your smallest
finger.'

'I could never eat fish again in my life because of the

way she smelt,' Leon Bloomberg muttered into his chest, and old Ada Markovitz at his side overheard and passed out cold.

Kitty, they were wrong, of course. I am beautiful in death, not plain as I have been all my life. My skin is iridescent and fine-veined, like the petals of lilies, and my blind eyes are milk-white, like rare opals. My lips are the colour of irises. When I was discovered my hair lay spread and webbed with dew and hung with spangles of frost. There is no ugliness now. I am transformed.

I chose three woods for my casket: pine for its sweet fragrant scent, oak for its strength to see me against the worms, and mahogany for its richness of colour. The lining came from a bolt of silk spun by the old Huguenot in Whitechapel. Not mere China silk, either, but the finest faille, dyed a regal scarlet by a gentleman in Bow and then stitched into a thousand pin-tucks in my own workshop.

How those same machines must have hummed each night to ensure the quantity of new costumes that are displayed today. A sea of seal-black bombazine parts before my coffin. All the mourners bought new, supposing death cancels all debts. They reckoned without my employees though, who have a detailed and accurate list of each penny that is owed. Your father is there, Kitty – a young child, dressed smartly in black. He is bored by the event and why not? Old women are daunting creatures. He called me Bubba but I doubt he understands that I have gone at last.

For my shroud I have the finest outfit I ever wore or made. I stitched it myself in secret, a black marocain tea-dress in the old-fashioned style. It has a ruby georgette bodice with long circular ruffles that fall in soft folds at my bare wrists, and a beaded jacket of the best rayon faille.

Next to my skin is a foundation bodice lined with heavy taffeta that rustled like leaves as I was lifted into my casket. There are bust pads made of soft black crepe padded with cotton wool, and a zip fastener stab-stitched into position by my own hand runs from the bodice to the narrow Petersham waistband.

How can I describe the perfume that each fabric has always had for me, Kitty? The faintest acrid, metallic tang of the taffeta; the sharp-edged aroma from the Petersham; the soft fat muskiness of the crepe? What of the scent that flies screaming from the outfit as its seams are steamed? Or the delicate sweetness that hangs over the swatch of fresh rayon when it first arrives?

Did you ever in your life smell a garment before it has hung in a shop or been perfumed by its owner? I could always select fabrics blind by scent alone; maybe even tell colour by sucking at the taste of the dye.

If you know of cut and seam you will already see the old-fashioned skill in my death-dress, but even a novice would find much to wonder at in the more showy detail of the elaborate revers. There could be less work on a cardinal's robe: gold and silver embroidery in twisted wire braid; ruby glass beads forming delicate, gleaming flowers, with diamante on a raised twist of silver between each bloom; and precious hanging pearls along the edge of each lapel, with gold bobbles sewn top and bottom to gleam and sparkle in the unseen light.

You may laugh at me for my vanity now, dear, for I was an old and ugly woman. I would take pleasure in your humour, though, and even welcome it. The *Chevra kaddisha* may have me later to wrap in their plain linen and seal in a bare box; until then I will travel in style, and the grander the better!

There are those who would say that a life spent on the creation of garments is a wasted life, Kitty, and yet where would society be without clothes to define its parameters? Where would rich or poor stand if both dressed alike? Who could tell judge from criminal or duchess from whore if all bought from the same source? I am proud of my grand obsession. I know of no more worthwhile occupation.

So what of my life, now that I am discovered in death? Who are my mourners to arrive at my home and sit on their low chairs burning a candle and reciting Kaddish through the *shiva*? How many heads will be bowed for me? Or shall my soul wait alone, listening for its prayers in an empty room?

My tale is simple to tell, but full of lies and secrets. We are each of us the hero of our own life story, but my story is not my own. I share it with millions and it is therefore without ending. I am the ghost of my ancestors and will haunt the generations of the future.

I am *your* ghost, Kitty. You cannot hear me or see me but I am here nevertheless, watching you and your destiny. You are like my own child, for even though more than one generation separates us my blood still runs in your veins. I beg you to remember that, dear. You are *my* future and my own destiny, just as much as I am your past.

We were all of us the children of history, blown like

smoke across many oceans to strange lands: moving spirits, drifting and homeless.

Seventy-nine years old at my death I was, and yet now in my dreams I am a child again, studying the sulphurous clouds that amass daily in the purple skies above our steamship that will bring us to England. How many of us have left Russia for the new country? We stand there on deck, miserable and grief-stricken but at the same time aching with such hope for the new lands. When we arrive in England, our eyes brimming with dreams, we are called, 'The offal of the earth'. Such a welcome!

1889 is the year, Kitty. I am fourteen years old and have left Russia for America, and my only ambition right now is to stay alive. Can you imagine that, dear? I have no beauty, either; if your taste is for elegant heroines such as yourself you had best turn away. My face is full of bitterness at what has been my misfortune and my legs as thin and bent as a wishbone. The clouds have grown the colour of albumen and the snow has begun to fall . . .

I am three years old when I catch my first snowflake. It falls into my lap, surprising me immensely and filling me with wonder, and I fold it carefully into my apron like a precious gift and trot into the house to show it to my mamma. She, of course, laughs at my tears when I see it has vanished. She is an astonishing woman: tall and strong and, for the most part, insane.

Papa – your great-great-grandpapa – is a fine-looking man, and a master tailor, which is to say he can make a suit complete from start to end. At home we speak only Yiddish, but Papa is fluent in the master tongue, which is

48

Russian, as well as having a little English, too. Papa is an intellectual while Mamma is illiterate, for she cannot read Russian, only Yiddish that is written phonetically in Hebrew characters.

Papa spends his evenings locked alone in his study poring over the Talmud like a scholar, to discover the meaning of life. So far he has uncovered two things for me:

'Never be poor, Rosa,' he tells me, 'and never grow old.' I swear solemnly to obey him. Wealth and youth throughout my life, such easy things for a child to promise. My father calls me Rosa, even though my name is Bertha. Bertha Cecilia Zigofsky. Thank God for simple Rosa.

A lifetime ago we lived well in Moscow, in a great house that I loved. Papa was originally a travelling tailor before the business expanded, and would often work for goods in lieu of money, so that the cellar at our house was full of cheeses and salamis that his grateful clients had paid him with. The smell as you stood on the basement stairs! He was a generous man, too, and often gave much of the produce to the needy.

But then we were moved on to our new home here in Vilna, in The Pale of Settlement, to live alongside our grandmother, who we call Bubba, and the other Jews, and it was then that Mother began to plan the terrible thing and Papa started his quest for the truth.

I am happy enough in Vilna. Bubba has seven children other than Papa and we all visit together at her home and she bakes *kichels* to eat with the sweet wine and I sit with the aunts while they talk, though they all become quiet when it is my mother's turn to speak.

Our mother's name is Ernestine but she answers only to

Rintzi, which was her mother's family name. Rintzi has views on many things, and most of them angry. When she speaks her face becomes flushed and the aunts smile strangely and turn their eyes to their feet.

'Where is the history of Jewish women written?' Rintzi shouts. And, 'Why are we the nameless ones? Eh? Why should we be segregated in the synagogues and why are we ineligible to be counted in *minyan*? Who can tell me? Why?'

Rintzi has large pink hands and smells of the sour vinegar she sprinkles about to rid us of the scent of Bubba's many cats. Her face is large and handsome with thick brows set over wild, darting eyes. Those eyes miss nothing. Sometimes they see what is not even there. Before she married her hair was black and long enough to sit upon and she tied it into two long plaits that she bound across the top of her skull. Now her head is shaven and she covers it with scarves, which is the custom.

Rintzi is the best-dressed woman in the *shtetle* because my father makes her clothes. There is an old Yiddish saying, *Ale shuste geyn borves*, or, 'All shoemakers go barefoot', but that was never true in our house, for we are all dressed well. There are more tailors and shoemakers in Vilna than there could ever be buyers, and yet still people come from miles to purchase my father's suits.

I hide happily in the fabrics in his workroom and Papa pretends to have lost me. He is a thick-built man with a fine set of whiskers that ice up in the cold. His business in Moscow employed ten other workers but here the room is small and here there is just Papa. At night he nails wooden boards to the windows in case they get smashed. Some nights he will sleep here, on guard.

The great rolls of cloth are more home to me than my own house. It is gentlemen's cloth; dark flannels and gabardines, soft undyed cottons and rough gluey calico for the stiffening and interfacings. I wrap myself in the end of the roll. The room buzzes like a hive and the steam makes my little nest warm. I hear the hiss and thud as the hot iron hits the padded sleeveboard. Sometimes I sleep here, knowing that I am safe. I know you love fabrics every bit as much as I, Kitty. Close your eyes now and imagine the scene.

Gregory is Rintzi's favourite. He is her son and her eldest and her love for him is intense and exclusive. She adores him and she fears for him. Her life revolves around him as the moon revolves around the earth. That is the way of the world and also the way it has always been, therefore Papa and I cannot mind.

I love Gregory, too – it is impossible not to. He is quiet and earnest and pale and very beautiful. His speech is slow, like his thoughts, and next to him I am like an ugly little monkey with a flea in its fur.

Gregory should be studious, like Papa, but he does not have the mind for study. His hair is brown, like mine though a little lighter, but his eyes are paler and have a dreaminess that mine do not. When he smiles you can see that his teeth are crooked.

Bubba takes us to the store to buy us pickles and the old woman who was Bubba's friend in Odessa rolls up the sleeve of her dress and plunges her fat arm into the barrel

51

of cucumbers. The sourness of the pickle makes Gregory's eyes water with tears but he always eats it all because he knows it makes Bubba happy.

When Rintzi was a child herself her beloved brother Isaac was kidnapped for the army. She never saw him again, though for years she lived in hope. Jewish boys were taken at the age of twelve, though some were younger, and they served twenty-five years each.

One day ten years later, when she and Papa had just married, Rintzi was hurrying through snows outside the town when she saw a long crocodile of small children making its way somewhere off to the east. She stopped to watch as they passed; tiny, whey-faced Jewish boys, some as young as eight, all in too-large uniforms and all with faces of such misery and terror and despair that she was on her knees, trembling and shaking from pity, before half of them had stumbled by.

There was a guard with them, a man with a face as round as a loaf and icicles on his moustache.

'Where are you taking them?' Rintzi shouted out, wringing her hands in anguish.

'To Kazan,' came the reply, and then Rintzi knew that the boys she watched were mostly doomed, because Kazan was miles and miles away and they would never survive in all that snow.

'Isaac,' was all she could think, for she had now at last realized her poor brother's fate. Papa searched for her when it became dark and found her by the woods and carried her home, more dead than alive. The rabbi even tried to make her recite the Shema, but for two days she was unable to speak.

Rintzi recovered from the exposure but her mind never really did. When Gregory was born she became happy again, but the happiness turned slowly to terror with each year of his life as it passed. Now she often argues with Papa in his study, begging him to pay the authorities to watch her to keep her son at home and out of the army. I listen at the keyhole and always it is the same thing: 'Pay them the money, Dovid! Three hundred roubles! It's not so much – find it, find it, I beg you . . . look, I am begging!' She always falls to the floor then, and clutches at my father's knees. Papa is crying too, and it would be a cruel hard man who could not, for her voice is so full of sadness and desperation.

'I don't have the money, Rintzi,' he tells her.

'He'll die,' she says, her voice full of hatred. 'Gregory will die like all the others, like all those other little boys!'

Papa tries to hold her but she scuttles away from him across the floor.

Gregory is twelve and I am seven when Rintzi decides at last to do the terrible thing. There has been a burning of the shops the night before and Papa has left early to see to his workroom. Outside is a swirling tangled mist of snow, and a hammering echoes through the small house as Uncle Levin nails planks to the windowframe to protect us from the gangs that night.

There is one window still bare. I press my tongue against it to taste the ice that has formed on the inside.

I am wearing an overall Papa made for me: plain blue ratine with my initial, 'R', embroidered in pink silk on the handkerchief pocket. Rintzi is in the kitchen crying and she has been there for the entire morning. Gregory pretends to be bored, but in fact he is full of fear, we both are.

Rintzi is quiet suddenly and that is somehow worse than the crying. We hear her boots on the bare wooden floor and then suddenly she is inside the doorway. She must have washed her face because it looks dry and calm now.

'Put on your coat, dearest,' she tells Gregory, and he rushes off to fetch it obediently. She appears not to have noticed me. While Gregory is gone she paces the room, pressing her scarf to her head with her hands, and when he returns she smiles. She takes his arm when he is dressed. I see they are prepared to leave and so I run for my cape too, because Uncle Levin is finished now and I don't care to be left alone in a boarded house.

Rintzi pulls Gregory across the street and his legs are going two steps for her one. The road bends towards the left but she strides out towards the open country as though hurrying off to the shops. I follow but I cannot catch up and neither do I wish to. Afraid as I am of the forest and the snow, the expression on Rintzi's face fills me with a far deeper dread. Also, I have noticed what Gregory has not, that she has the knife from the kitchen – the biggest one that we are always told never to touch – tucked into the back of her belt, so that the silver tip of it peeks beneath the fur lining of her grey wool jacket.

I lose them now in the whiteness. When the flakes clear again they appear miles away, like two scurrying beetles in the distance, one grey and one black. Gregory's coat is whipped up by the wind and lifts out behind him like dark, shiny wings.

I run behind them, following their footprints, envying

my brother his cap because my own head is so cold now.

'Mamma!' I see her turn and Gregory turns with her. He is smiling, he thinks it is a game. He is just happy to be with his beloved mother after all her tears of the morning. His britches are wet to the knee but he is still happy. They turn and walk again, only now I am nearer.

Are there wolves in the wood? Papa said so and we sometimes hear them howling at night. Perhaps Rintzi has the knife to kill a wolf. I run without appearing to move. My legs are tired. I am pleased when I see them halt.

Gregory is standing still now, his arms and legs rigid with indecision. I am close enough to see his face, so I stop running. I can't go any closer. The snow has eased a little and I look around for wild animals.

Rintzi takes Gregory gently by the hand again and at first I think they will walk some more, but she removes his glove before clutching him to her body and kissing his head. She pulls him down until they are sitting right there in the snow and then she pushes his bare hand into the ice and holds it down, staring at his face all the time.

Gregory doesn't squirm at all, which is peculiar to say the least. I push a fingertip into the snow to see just how it feels for him. After a few seconds it becomes unbearable, but still Gregory is obedient and doesn't move one inch. Rintzi is his mother and what she does is right.

Which is why he sits, still and upright, as she lifts his now-blue hand from the ice and pulls the knife out from her belt. Maybe he is even smiling because he trusts his besotted mother and knows she would never harm him.

She splays his fingers carefully and then uses the knife quickly, like an axe. Chop. Nothing happens. I stuff my hands into my mouth and the sky begins to spin about me. Rintzi looks at Gregory's face but it holds no expression, unlike her own, which is a mask of agony. She looks down at his little hand. And then she lifts it slowly and Gregory's fingers remain in the snow.

Four little pink-blue-and-white sticks, all in a neat row.

Gregory moves now, at last. His legs kick out frantically, like a beheaded turkey's. His feet find the ground and somehow he stands up. His mouth is smiling but then the smile splits wide and his whole face falls apart and his mouth is now open larger than I knew a mouth could go. He is silent, though; the scream I hear comes from my mother, followed by a louder scream from me. We set off crows which rise, flapping, from the bare black trees, shrieking their own mad cries. And then the blood comes at last, trickling in four sad little ribbons onto the white ground.

Rintzi forces the hand back into the snow to freeze the pain and then binds it quickly with some cloth. Gregory's legs kick and twitch but he does not make a noise. Rintzi takes off her scarf and ties it about his head, which would normally have been a treat, and she tries to embrace him and kiss him again, but he struggles to get away from her, so she folds him under the wing of her cloak and drags him back towards the house once again.

I walk to where they were. My teeth chatter and I make a noise with my mouth: 'Zee-zeee-zeee-zeee.' It is a noise of cold and fear and shock. The fingers are still there on the ground. They are Gregory's fingers, I know them, I recognize each one. His nails were dirty. Rintzi was always telling him to wash them. I kick snow over them and I say a short prayer, but I don't cry because I can't, because my tears will freeze my face.

The army won't want Gregory now. Rintzi did it to save him. She is the bravest woman I know. I pray that Papa will agree.

CHAPTER FOUR

ZG

THE SEASON
Seasons are meagre in the fashion trade: four weeks in spring, when the winter orders are taken, and four more in autumn, when the summer styles are sold. A range of sample garments is hawked about to the buyers from home and abroad, first at the fashion exhibitions and later at the showrooms themselves. Unlike the couture ranges, which will be modelled profession- ally in front of wine-swilling clients, the business in showrooms is often done on the rails by buyers clutching tea and a biscuit.

Everybody in the business knew that couture was dead; a lost leader at best, a dinosaur at worst. Which was why Kitty sat in the Zigo-owned wholesale – or 'down-market', as Burgess would call it – showroom in Newman Street watching the buyer from The House of Fraser tapping on a laptop before calling out her order to the showroom manager. Kitty didn't mind downmarket. Kitty didn't mind any of it – up, down, cabbage, *prêt-à-porter*, diffusion, couture – it was all the same business and it was all part of her life.

It was difficult not to hover. Kitty had never learnt the art of diplomacy in the way most of her siblings had. Also, people were looking at her as though she was some sort of freak because of her bereavement. Things were leaking into the newspapers; every day a new fact – it was like a simmering pot waiting to boil over. Death is embarrassing enough, people run out of conversation after the initial condolences, but murder? She walked about the business in a miasma of self-conscious hush. She knew she was like the Ancient Mariner to the business right now, haunting the showrooms with her grim-faced presence, but it was hard to keep away at such a vital time.

She checked her watch. The buyers were onto their third lemon tea and looking about for sandwiches. If the girl was sent out to the little Italian place on the corner it would mean she'd be unavailable to model the range. There was silence – plus the muffled tap-tap-tap of the laptop keyboard.

The buyer paused for thought and air. There was an expectant rustle of pure silk dupion suiting. Kitty leant across. 'Would you like some lunch?' Food meant a pause, a respite. Kitty had to be at the Chelsea barracks for a show in fifty minutes. Lunch spelt disaster. Small triangles of granary interleaved with cos and smoked salmon signalled the end of all hope.

The buyer shook her head. Oh joy – she must be on a diet.

The Chelsea show was high-class crap. The models were quite blatantly smoking something-or-other backstage, and were subsequently turned out by a new stylist to look like tramps. Many were pale, starved and bruised, like elderly fruit. They contrasted painfully with the gleaming, fit and sporty types that Ralph Lauren had been parading the week before in the US. Or the older and quietly elegant models that had been so well-acclaimed in Milan.

This was the opening show of British Design Week. The silent groans from contributors reached a vacuum-like crescendo during the retro sequence, where students from the leading art colleges had been asked to participate as a come-on to new talent of the future.

In a moment of supposedly highest camp satire one of the students had dressed a live cow in a kilt and sent it out on stage. They'd sprayed it liberally with Chanel to get rid of the farmyard smell and the result was an intriguing bouquet that had fashion hacks in the stalls fishing into their Prada bags for hankies to press to their noses like Regency fops.

As the placid, pongy animal lumbered past, Kitty peered through the spotlights to the faces seated opposite her. Once reserved for the top journalists from *Vogue* and *Elle*, the little gilt seats that made up the front-row now tended to be filled with bemused-looking sponsors in flat-arsed suits. These were the same dull faces that occupied other front-row seats at all the top sporting events and concerts. Nervously poised and silent, eyes glazed and fully aware that they had barely a nut-size speck of knowledge or interest in the event they were attending, they smiled politely and clapped as the cow was led round and, udders swinging, made its way back up the runway.

Kitty glanced at the press photographers, who were penned in like battery hens on tottering tiers of lightweight, aluminium ladders, at the far end of the stage. Hadn't they lost the will to live yet? Did they honestly want to clamour for shots of a heifer clad in tartan lycra?

'This is a fucking travesty!' someone said next to her, but not with enough feeling or pitch to constitute a 'scene' that might make the front pages the following day, and Kitty noticed that the hacks continued sketching and scribbling in their notebooks regardless.

Kitty had notes of her own, but they weren't about the show. She was busy compiling a list of names. At the top of the list was one name that had been underlined several times – Nicky Kofteros, one of the major players in the financial market. One of the Dream Merchants, henchman of the Waika corporation. One of the men-in-suits who sat opposite her right now. She wanted him dematerialized. She looked across at him. He smiled back. She underlined his name one more time. He was poised to take all that was important in her life. She wanted him gone.

There was a crush in the reception area as journalists fought to be the first out to file their copy. Kitty moved to the side of the tent, closing her eyes to the hum of the voices. Maybe what she had just seen had all been a dream – a nightmare. Maybe she would wake up any minute and take herself off to the real show, where fabrics would hang like liquid around the sylph-like shapes of smiling, healthy models. Maybe she'd see bias cuts and faultless seams and shapes that flattered and styles so innovative she would wonder why no designer had conceived them before.

The photographers found her leaning up against the ropes and, judging her expression to be one of unutterable personal grief, started snapping mercilessly. Kitty opened her eyes in mild surprise. Ten paparazzi. No matter. She'd lived with them for years now. Two were currently camped outside her apartment, tailing her since her father's murder. She'd got into the habit of buying take-away coffee for them, too. In fact, she'd miss them if they weren't there. They rarely used the shots they took, anyway. Kitty was attractive but hers wasn't the sort of beauty that worked in print. Chloe was the one the cameras fell for. Subtlety didn't exactly pan out in newsprint.

'Miss Zigofsky?' She opened her eyes onto Kofteros's wide, smiling, clean-featured face. Almost humanoid. Maybe a little too chiselled. He took her hand and shook it. His flesh felt amazingly life-like. The photographers continued to snap away. Oh joy, a chummy shot for the city to brood over.

There was not a trace of a crease on the man's suit, despite the cramped heat of the fashion theatre. Not a linen man, then.

'We met in your brother's office,' he said. His handshake was just right – not too strong, not too weak. His eye contact was straight out of the training manuals – focused but not overpowering, forceful but with the hint of a twinkle to imply an underlying sense of irony.

His tie told of Pall Mall clubs and his suit was pure Jermyn Street, although the narrow leather wrist-thong, just visible below the sleeve of the Turnbull and Asser shirt, smacked of a sense of native, ethnic cunning. He was slobber-inducingly good-looking. The sort of looks that had moral standards tripping off down the street with a wave of adieu. The kind of man that made you realize you were wearing tights and knickers *plus* a lycra bodysuit that joined at the crotch with noisy velcro – and that you'd somehow pulled them all up in the wrong order on your last trip to the loo.

Kitty found him nauseating.

'Might I buy you a drink?' he asked.

She looked at her watch. 'I have to be at the factory by three-twenty,' she told him.

'Then perhaps I can accompany you?'

Kitty smiled then. 'Oh yes,' she said. Why not? Dressed as he was he'd go down a storm in Mile End.

When they got to the car park she discovered he had a brand new, virginal Bentley and her happiness was complete. She could hear them sharpening sticks and coins even now in the Commercial Road. With a bit of luck the wheel-removers might be on duty – or even the gangs who liked to pee through the sun roofs of flash cars.

Her mood was good, then, as they hit the Marylebone Road. Maybe it was time for Mr Kofteros to see the less prestigious side of the business that he was so keen to buy into.

CHAPTER FIVE

ZG

RUSSIA

Fashionable Parisian society responded to the bloodshed of the Russian Revolution by developing a taste for Russian embroidery on its dress designs. The demand was so great that Grand Duchess Marie Pavlovna, daughter of Grand Duke Paul, started a lucrative business employing ex-patriate women to embroider traditional peasant designs onto clothes. The houses of both Chanel and Patou were customers of this business.

Kitty,

It is wonderful to see the whole family assembled in Bubba's house. Grandmother is, of course, the oldest person present and therefore is allotted the great wooden chair in the centre of the room. The chair is huge and Bubba is tiny, but she more than fills the space through presence and bearing alone.

The room is small and lit by flickering candles, in whose warm and golden light I watch the stony faces of my bear-like uncles and their cheerfully-gossiping wives. When I look from the small, wood-framed window I see the peasants walking home across the fields in the scarlet light of the dusk. They sing as they walk, great booming Russian harmonies that I will remember the whole of my life.

We eat before business is done. There is no table big enough and so planks have been found and laid with white cloths. We sit in lines with the planks resting on our knees. The women are on one side and the men facing them, so that the planks tip unevenly, but that is how it has to be, according to Bubba. When someone moves the 'table' rocks and we all grab at the bowls to save them, and Bubba lectures the unfortunate person who moved about the sin of fidgeting while the rest of us laugh out loud.

Uncle Leopold is the youngest of Bubba's eight sons, yet his moustache is the longest. Uncle Sergei has hands as big as anvils and can eat a whole loaf at one sitting. Uncle Reuben repairs watches for a living, and Uncle Levin makes cabinets when not nailing boards over the windows of our houses.

This is the last time we will all be present in one house, for soon four of the brothers will be leaving to make great lives for themselves in America. The room is as warm as an oven, apart from a knife-like draught from beneath the kitchen door, which makes me wish I had worn boots. When the wind blows I lift my feet, careful not to make the planks wobble.

We eat hot beetroot soup that leaves pink-purple stains on all the beards, and pickled fish with potato. Bubba's house is bare in style, but full of fine things from the old days. Grandpa's picture hangs on the wall in a painted wooden frame behind his sons' heads. He looks small, like his wife, and yet he would terrorize his strapping boys and beat them with logs of wood if they misbehaved.

When the food is finished and the planks cleared and

put away the chairs are pushed into a circle and I am banished to the kitchen to eat sweet cakes while the business of the evening commences. I nibble at one cake and then kneel to peer through the crack in the door.

Papa sits with his hands on his knees and tells the tale of Gregory's fingers simply and with as little anger as possible. Bubba listens but her eyes do not leave Rintzi's face. My mother sits beside my father, her back as straight as a soldier's and her eyes fixed on a spot somewhere close to the ceiling.

When Papa has told of the terrible thing that Rintzi did there is silence and then Uncle Andrei, the eldest brother, clears his throat to speak. His job is a difficult one because, although he is the eldest brother, he is far from being the cleverest, and he is aware of the fact that his judgment of the problem will require more wisdom than he is able to muster, even with three beakers of vodka inside his belly.

'Is the boy well again now?' he asks. The aunts nod approval. He has things in the right order of priority. He smiles broadly with relief.

My father looks at my mother. 'He is well again now,' he says. He loves his wife and he pities her, but he will never forgive her for cutting the fingers from his only son's right hand. Gregory was to be a tailor too, Papa was training him for the trade. They would have worked together, and Gregory would have taken over the business once he was old enough and Papa's eyes too worn from all the fine stitching . . .

Bubba interrupts. 'Ernestine, why did you do this thing?' she asks. Mother's eyes are like lakes, full of water and far

66

away. Gregory will no longer approach her. When she enters a room he scuttles out in fear. When she attempts to touch him he screams. Her hands are pale and composed in her lap. She did this thing to keep her son, yet now she has lost him anyway. She has been outrageously selfless. I admire her more now than ever before in my life, but she scares me, too. Her courage and single-mindedness are terrifying.

Bubba sits back in her chair and folds her arms across her chest. She nods as though she has had an answer, although my mother has not yet spoken one word.

'Gregory should come here to live with me,' Bubba says, quietly. Her face is perfectly round and there is not an inch of unlined skin on it. Her nut-brown eyes peep out from two cracks among a sea of tanned leather crinkles.

Rintzi's fixed gaze drops down from the ceiling. 'No,' she says, clearly.

There is a pause that hangs around this one word, trapping it in empty air like a bird in a cage.

'Well then!' Uncle Andrei claps his hands on his thighs and then shrugs a little, beaming around the room as though something has been settled.

Perhaps it has. Gregory will remain at our house where he will continue to refuse to even look at the mother he once adored so much. Papa will try to teach me the tailoring trade instead of his son – at least until his patience runs out – and the aunts will take turns to smother us with care and concern.

And, most importantly, no one ever tries to tell poor deluded Rintzi that the cruel policy of child recruitment had died along with the old Czar many years before.

CHAPTER SIX

ZG

LINEN

*Taken from flax, which is widely thought of as one of
the oldest fibres known to man, linen is famous for its
natural, uneven look. For many years a sign of wealth
has been the well-pressed, uncreased suit, but recently,
in a trend of reverse psychology following the glut of
cheap, crease-resistant man-made fibres, linen and all
its wrinkles has come to signify money and taste.*

I am thirteen years old now, Kitty, almost a woman. Rintzi
has employed a marriage broker to match me with a husband and we are to ride out of the *shtetle* to the town on
a borrowed sleigh to meet the man she has found. If all is
well Papa says he will begin to make the wedding suit for
my husband-to-be.

The boy's name is Aaron and we first met as children,
when the snowdrift cut off the *shtetle* and his brothers
bravely brought fabrics in by cart for Papa to sew. I have
not seen him since, but I know he is handsome and clever
because Papa says so, and I am happier than ever before
in my life.

The uncles are all gone away now, and Bubba died last
spring when her stovepipe blocked in the night and the
smoke filled her room and killed her in her sleep.

Rintzi plaits my hair like her own used to be and we all don our best coats and take thick blankets for the ride into town. When I look in the mirror I would like to be prettier, but perhaps I am not too bad, and Aaron will be pleased anyway.

My skin is my best feature; it is pale but not white and I swear it will never have wrinkles like Bubba's, no matter how long I shall live. My eyes are like Rintzi's, dark and never still, and I believe that if you could find Papa's mouth beneath his whiskers, it would be thin-lipped and curved, like my own.

My forehead is too short and my hair too thick to lay flat. My ears are peculiarly large, like a boy's, so that other children at school would sometimes nickname me 'Rabbit', but Rintzi has combed my hair in such a way as to take care of that.

What else is there to say of myself? I am small but, like Bubba, I put up a good fight. I am thin just now, but there are signs that I might inherit my grandmother's figure, which was round with a tiny waist. My legs are more peculiar than my ears but long skirts solve that problem for me. If Aaron likes lively girls with a quick mind and strange looks, then I am the one for him.

That evening we ride back to the *shtetle* again and, whereas we travelled out noisily, with much excitement, the return journey is taken in silence. I watch the frost glittering like diamonds in the moonlight. Rintzi goes home but Papa takes us on to the workshop, where he sits me down on a bentwood chair.

I watch him go round the room, measuring cloth, picking up scissors. Putting them down again.

'Well, Rosa?' he says at last.

'Well, Papa?' I ask him. He picks up his chalk now and studies it like a precious stone.

'I thought maybe Aaron was a little quiet,' he says. In fact Aaron said not one word all evening.

'Yes, Papa,' I agree. He puts his spectacles onto the bridge of his nose and studies some patterns.

'Maybe I was a little optimistic when I described him as handsome, Rosa,' he says quietly, stroking his beard.

'I think he looks very well, Papa,' I say. My father looks surprised and perhaps relieved. In fact Aaron is not at all handsome but then neither am I, so we should make a suitable pair. 'I think he is very dignified,' I continue, and this is what I have told myself on the journey home: when he speaks it will be worth waiting for. Only fools talk when there is nothing to say. I have decided Aaron will make the perfect husband. I smile with excitement while Papa kisses me on the cheek.

Papa spends every spare hour on the wedding suit. He works without measurements for he has a good eye for such things and can even tell how much Aaron will grow by the time we are married. I watch him in the workshop and I can see this is the best suit he will ever make. The fabric took two months to arrive because he ordered it from special weavers.

'Feel it,' he says. It is too soft and fine to feel properly with my fingertips so I press it against my cheek, instead. It smells buttery. When I touch a little against my tongue it has a beautiful, sour-almond flavour.

70

'Can you smell the spices, too, Rosa?' Papa asks. When I try again I can. The fabric has been made in the East. It is black enough to be invisible.

He cuts the first pattern from bleached calico and pins it to the dummy, spinning the thing around quickly many times to tell shape and fit. I wonder if he will swallow any pins, for he has so many in his mouth, but he never does, although I once saw him lose one in his beard.

He lays out the dark wool on the cutting-table and marks it with his chalk before slicing it with a pair of the sharpest scissors ever seen. If they were not so sharp the fabric would move, but as it is he doesn't even have to rest his hand on it to keep it still as he cuts.

I love the noise the scissors make. Small fringes of black fluff fall from the cutting-table to the floor and I sweep them up quickly, being careful to keep out of Papa's way as I do so.

I will not speak while I watch, for fear he will lose concentration and make a mistake. Sometimes I fall asleep with my head on the tailor's ham, but when I wake Papa is still working as before, quickly and deftly. His hands are skilful and swift, like a conjurer's. If I studied for a thousand years I could never create such magic.

In the corner of the workroom is a large copper urn filled with constantly boiling water heated by a charcoal fire. On top of the urn is a teapot and there is a small dripping tap at the bottom. I fetch glasses and pour tea from this samovar, which I press my father to drink. When he finally pauses for a break we sit on either side of the urn and sip the strong tea through lumps of sugar which we suck in our mouths.

When the suit is on the dummy Papa starts work on the waistcoat, which will be worn underneath. The suit itself is a masterpiece, but the waistcoat is little short of miraculous. Papa is an artist when it comes to embroidery and this waistcoat is to be a sample of the finest work he can create. He spends weeks on the intricate designs alone. The silks must be dyed by hand to get a certain depth and richness of colour, even though the overall effect is to be a subtle blend of rouge and maroon.

I forget how many weeks or months pass before the suit nears completion, but when it is I am banished from the workroom because Papa wishes to surprise me with the finished garment. I am so excited I can barely wait. Rintzi tries to share my excitement but I know she is sad, too, because the wedding suit should have been made for Gregory, not Aaron. We all know Gregory will never marry, though, because he has grown a child's heart – his mind seemed to stop maturing after the shock of the thing Rintzi did to him.

Papa works all night to get the suit finished. I am up with the dawn, full of excitement and, when I can stand the waiting no longer, when I am making poor Rintzi's head ache with my continual questioning: 'When? Now? Yet?', I set out to walk from home to the workroom to surprise him.

It is a cold, sun-lit morning and I see people hurrying down the street, away from me. I take large, quick steps, like a man. If my legs would move faster then I would make them. But I don't wish to run. Walking is the nearest thing to patience that I can muster. The air puffs from my hot mouth like steam from a samovar. I feel nine-foot tall and smile at my neighbours as they pass. Don't run, Rosa. Walk. Run and the suit will not be finished when you get there. Only patience gets its reward. My muscles ache from all the effort.

Someone grabs me by the arm, making me spin round in surprise.

'Rosa Zigofsky?' It's the old woman from the laundry. I wonder why she asks my name since she has known me well all my life.

'They burnt the shops last night,' she says. I stare at her face. Suddenly we are strangers. I try to think but nothing comes. I am stupid and dull, suddenly. Shock has made my wits as blunt as Gregory's.

I have my legs, though, if not my brain. Now I begin to run until the stamping of my feet begins to rattle my little brain within its own skull. Run and you will find there is nothing, no problem. Walk now and all may be lost. I can smell the first oily sweet aroma of burnt wood now, and my eyes begin to sting from the drifting pall of smoke.

When I turn the corner I think things don't look so bad, and stop to draw breath into my lungs, bending double with my hands resting on my thighs. Waiting until my ribs stop heaving. A couple of the buildings have windows that are broken but Papa's place appears to be untouched. I have been stupid, racing about like an old horse. My fingers fly to cover my mouth and I let out a laugh. Papa will be waiting to tell me how stupid I am to have galloped about in such a way. I hope he did not see me. He tells me I am a woman, nearly, and I know he would like me to act like one at last.

When I get to his doorway there are three men sheltering inside.

'Rosa,' the biggest man says. I know him, of course, as I know all who live in our village. He worked with Uncle Reuben sometimes. I smile at him but he doesn't smile back.

'They tried to burn the workroom, Rosa,' he says. I think at once of the wedding suit. Papa's best work, all gone in the flames. 'Your father stopped them, though,' he continues. I have never seen him before without a smile on his face. I would barely have recognized him with this solemn expression. 'They got angry, Rosa. They were only kids, but a couple of them were drunk. They nailed your father into one of Lucien Binstock's huge barrels and then they rolled him down the street for a joke. When we opened the barrel your father was dead, Rosa. It broke his bones. I'm sorry. It's a terrible thing.'

I push past them suddenly and run up the stairs, two at a time. Papa will be working there, as usual, and he will smile at me and take off his glasses and rub at his eyes, because he has been working all night . . .

The suit is there, on the stand. It is almost finished. I inspect it carefully, turning it, barely wanting to touch it, and it is so beautiful that it makes me sad. The waistcoat is the most wonderful garment I have ever seen in my life. It makes me realize how little beauty there is here in our poor *shtetle*, where things are drab and bare.

The embroidery is so intricate it seems impossible to think it could have been done by a human hand. Papa's glasses lie on the cutting-table. Perhaps he took them off when he heard so much noise outside. His first thought must have been for this suit. Maybe he smelt the burning as I did and ran out, scared that his life's best work might go up in the flames.

I put his abandoned spectacles on and peer, and every detail of the pattern of stitches is instantly magnified. I inspect it carefully and slowly. Now I can see my name stitched among the flowers and exotic creatures there: *Rosa, the daughter I love.* He has stitched the words there, right amidst the pattern, all but invisible to the human eye. I am so proud my eyes well with tears. The copper samovar lies on its side in the corner of the room. Did Papa knock it over in his struggles with the boys? Tea has stained the bare boards like blood.

'Papa,' I whisper. The suit is not quite finished. There are buttons lying, waiting to be sewn on, and then the whole delicate garment must be pressed.

I thread up a needle, even though my eyes are too wet to see properly and I have to blink hard to make them clear enough to see the silks.

I sew the buttons carefully by hand, using the best stitches I can, so that Papa will be proud of me. The fabric is so soft that I know there must be no mistakes – if I unpick bad stitching the needle will have left holes and the entire garment will be ruined by my clumsiness.

Papa worked quickly but I am as slow as a snail. When the buttons are done I heat the iron and carry the suit, one piece at a time, across to the board. My hands shake from the grave importance of the job that I have to do. To make a mistake would be unthinkable. I pray that I will not burn the delicate cloth, telling God that I will do anything –

anything! If only the suit can be pressed without mistake . . .

When every crease is gone, and every seam flattened into its rightful place, I hang the suit carefully back onto the dummy and then I am so relieved and pleased that I begin to speak to it.

'You are to be my husband's wedding suit,' I tell it, 'my Papa made you. You are the finest outfit in the world.' I reach out and touch the special place on the embroidery: *Rosa, the daughter I love.* Papa guarded this suit with his life.

Only then, when the precious thing is finished, do I sink back onto my little bentwood chair and allow myself to weep for my dreadful loss.

We can't exist here, the three of us. Rintzi barely speaks and the shock of Papa's death has left her exhausted, so I have to fetch and carry for her all day. Gregory is terrified that there will be another pogrom, and that we will all be killed in barrels, like Papa. There are no men here to look out for us. Gregory would be hopeless in a fight, because although he is tall enough in stature his mind is as useless as a child's.

At night I feel that the wolves from the wood are circling closer and closer to the house. I look out into the darkness for the sight of their yellow eyes, that Bubba used to say would be lit up like coach lamps, and my ears ache from listening for their howls.

We each sit at windows, waiting. Rintzi waits for Papa to return, Gregory for the men with the barrels, and I wait for Aaron, for I believe he will get to hear of our plight

76

and somehow come to save us, as he saved Papa's business in the time of the great snowdrifts.

We live like this for many months before I make an important decision: I will ride instead to the town and fetch Aaron for myself. We must have a man in the house again. Once I have decided I know I must go at once, while I have the courage, even though the weather is bad. I am so scared and excited it is as though I have a fever.

We can marry earlier than planned – no one will mind.

I hire a sleigh from the local school, and then have to pay double when they complain that the snows are too bad and there is a risk that the pony could be injured. Rintzi tries to stop me packing but then she suddenly gives up and sits down on the bed instead, with her face in her apron. Even she understands the sense of this thing. She knows this journey has to be done.

I leave at midday, when there is a little pale sun in the sky and the snows have eased to a delightful sprinkling, as though flour were being sifted from above. The pony is as keen to reach town as I am and we are several hours out of the *shtetle* before I realize this is the furthest I have been on my own in my life. I whistle a bit, like Papa used to do, but when we finally see the first shacks of the town I am dearly relieved.

Aaron's house is a two-storey wooden building with a green tiled roof. I wonder if he has seen me from the window and I pat my hair into place, in case he is watching. Now I will hear him speak at last: 'What on earth brings you here alone, Bertha Zigofsky? Don't you know the danger involved, riding alone?' I will tell him our troubles and he will arrange things. When his mother's face appears at the door I am a little disappointed.

'Bertha?' She looks shocked. She is a small thin woman and her hair is wrapped in a black shawl. I wipe my nose on my hand in case it is running and step up to greet her.

'I've come to get married,' I say, smiling politely, holding out the square leather case for her to see. Inside is Aaron's wedding suit. I packed it carefully in the workroom, with paper and lavender between each fold. Aaron will be delighted with it and I will be more proud than I can say when he wears it.

His mother looks confused. 'The wedding has not been planned yet, Bertha,' she says. So far she has not invited me into her house, despite the fact that the wind is making our cheeks pinched and our noses blue.

'I know,' I say, 'but Papa has been killed and we cannot manage. We need to start the plans right away. Aaron must come and care for us.'

Her eyes drop to the floor at my sad news. She turns at last and walks into the house. I follow her inside and she offers me a seat in the parlour. When she disappears I think she has gone to fetch her son, but she comes back with tea. My hands are so cold I can barely hold the cup and I'm embarrassed when my clothes begin to steam in the heat from the stove.

'Bertha, you are so young, still,' she says. I laugh, a little nervously. Of course I am young but then these are exceptional circumstances and I feel she should understand that. Who can wait for the niceties of age when death is a reasonable option? If I do not marry her son now there

78

will be nothing for him to wed but a corpse. But surely she is not stupid? I look at her again.

'Aaron isn't here, Bertha,' she says, after a while. At first I think he is dead, but then I see she looks nervous, not sad. 'He left two months ago, before *Pesach*.'

'When is he coming back?' I ask. I sip some tea and it burns my mouth.

'He left to go to America,' she replies simply. I can only stare. After a while I remember to shut my mouth. The room seems too hot now – the tea has made me giddy.

'We are going to be married,' I whisper.

She shrugs and looks at her feet. 'Maybe,' she says. 'Aaron is a clever boy. He wanted to do well. It was his decision, Bertha, he wouldn't have his mind changed. I would have written to your parents. I'm sorry about your father.'

'When did he decide to emigrate?' I ask.

'Soon after you came,' she says, blushing despite the cold. So he left after he had seen me. Aaron's mother is an honest woman, but I would rather she had lied. I can feel my mouth begin to tremble. I don't want to cry, it wouldn't be dignified. I straighten my back and rub my chin with my finger, pretending to be thinking.

'So he'll send for me once he's made his mark?' I ask her. I have to put the cup down before I break it with my shaking.

She shrugs again and tries to smile at me. 'I'm sorry, Bertha. Who knows? Young men these days – ach!'

Anger and distress fall upon me on the journey home. Aaron's mother begs me to stop when she sees the snows begin again, but I would rather drive to hell and back than stay a night in that house. The pony snorts and complains when I turn him around in the darkness but I shout and yell so much that he takes off like a shot from a gun.

I am the stupid one, and ugly, too. I will never marry now, that is for sure. My face drove Aaron off to America! I spare a hand from the reins to run a finger over my features. Can anyone be that plain? No – Aaron must have gone to make our fortune. He will send for me, I know it! Not all women are beautiful yet all women I know of are wives. I have a quick mind, too – Aaron would know that my conversation would never have bored him and that is more than most husbands can claim! Papa was always entertained by my talk, even when he was working. At the thought of my father a new pain slices me through to the bone.

I am too angry to be afraid, even when the sleet begins to blind me and the wind screams about my ears. The sleigh rolls down off the path. For a moment I think it will tip but it slowly straightens and I jump out to pull it back onto the track, complaining bitterly to the wind for blowing us there.

Despite all that I have said to myself inside my head, though – all the time I am shouting and jabbering to myself – I think of Rintzi and Gregory and wonder why I am even going home, when all I want to do is lay down there in the snow and die of shame and self-pity.

My skirt tears when the sleigh lurches and lands on top of the hem. I am wet through, and dirty, and now my clothes are torn, which makes me thoroughly miserable. We start off again, more slowly and carefully this time, and I promise the pony I will not scream at him again, if only he will get us back to the *shtetle* in one piece.

We ride on a little way with peace restored, and are only half an hour from the village when I first see the dark shapes of a small troupe of men and boys on the road.

The snow has cleared and I can count around half a dozen of them. At first I think they are men from the village, and that I must therefore know them, but when I pull nearer I can see they are strangers. Their faces are wrapped in mufflers, from which their breath rises on either side like steam from a samovar.

I try to pass in silence but one of them puts a hand out quickly and the pony rears, and another catches the reins and we are pulled to a stop.

I climb down from the cart with a mixture of fear and anger, clutching my case with the wedding suit in it to my chest. The men circle me and it appears they have little idea what to do next. Then one walks nearer.

'Are you a Jew?' he asks. I can tell from his voice that he is older than the others. He pulls his muffler down, and his face looks as harsh as his words.

'I asked if you are a Jew,' he insists. His lips are blue and there are spots of yellow pus dotted around his chin. He has the sulphurous eyes of a wolf and a scar in between the brows, like the mark of a thumbnail.

I look round at the others with him, who appear happy to let this older man do all the questioning, and then I stare back at him with what I hope looks like arrogance. He spits at me, which is shocking.

The younger boys laugh.

I spit back noisily, and there is a loud gasp from the

group. The pony rears up and its eyes roll in terror. What did you do, Rosa? You spat back! You should be on your knees begging for your life, but instead you spat back!

The man in front of me stares in disbelief. 'Jews can't spit!' he sneers. He hates me deeply now, I can see it in his eyes. He has lost face in front of his friends. A girl and a Jew has dared to spit at him. I wonder whether he is the one. I wonder whether he killed my father.

They are peasants, I can tell from their clothes. The man looks round at the others but they make no move to help him. He is going to hurt me now – he has to, I know that, I'm not completely stupid, only a little mad.

He takes a step towards me and he grabs me by the arm, staring into my face. He tries to kiss me. I pull away and this time he snatches me harder. I turn to run and manage to drag him with me a few steps up the track. He swears at me in Russian but the circle of friends parts to let us through.

When he slaps me round the face I am shocked, because it is the first time in my life that anyone has hit me. He has cut my lip, but I am so frozen I barely feel the pain. We begin to struggle together and I fall onto a large drift of snow. I look up and a boy is staring at me, his eyes as wide as coach lamps.

'Gunter,' the man calls to the boy, 'get on with things, lad.'

The boy is young – maybe younger even than me. He tries to smile at the older man who holds me, but his eyes are full of terror.

'Move, son!' the man growls. 'It's colder than a witch's teat out here!'

The boy moves to his side dutifully. His features are similar though less unpleasant and when he raises his cap I see he has the same birthmark between his eyes.

The man pulls the boy down to his knees and pushes him onto the ground between my legs. I try to move but he has me pegged out like a pelt drying in the sun. I stare into the boy's eyes. He begins to unbutton his little trousers and the other men watching laugh.

'Come on, son, she's a Jew – you don't have to woo her!'

'Where is all this time going? Didn't your father teach you what you have to do? Hurry up, for God's sake, at this rate she'll be too old before you get started!'

'You were the same at *your* first, remember? That whore charged your father twice for all the time you took snuffling about!'

The boy looks scared. He starts to push at my skirts and petticoats and I struggle so hard I hurt myself with my twisting.

'Ah, he has the scent of her now! That's it, son. Look, now he's got the idea! Like a hound after a rabbit, eh?'

All is quiet while the boy lies on top of me. I close my eyes, awaiting the worst, listening to the groans and whistles of disappointment that slowly build up. After a while I feel his weight leave me and when I look up he is lifted in mid-air by his father, his lifeless little member still dangling from the flap of his britches.

The father curses and throws the sobbing boy into the snow. The other men pick him out, dusting his clothes down and slapping him jovially about the face. I laugh to shame him more but a vile smack on the cheek takes the wind out of me for a while.

'Look at her, she's a whore!' the father says. He is a tall man and heavily built. He would kill me right now, but he has the honour of the family to restore. Instead his hand is upon his trousers and I begin to say my prayers.

My legs are exposed like two bare pink pegs in the snow but I barely feel the cold. I am terrified and full of shame to be seen in such a way. I fill my lungs with air and scream so loud that it would seem the sky could shatter with the noise.

When I can scream no more, when I am gasping to breathe, the man stretches my legs apart again with his hands and falls onto me like an ox, and I feel burning and a tearing inside as he pushes and finally enters me. I am silent with shock at such a thing. My eyes bulge and a line of spittle runs down the side of my chin. There is a pain inside me, like fire, but I will not scream again.

The man makes plenty of noise as he works away: 'Umph! Ungh!' He works so long the others get bored again.

'Hey, Jaspar, it is freezing out here, you know!'

'Let's move! Hurry, hurry!'

'He's no better than his son, you know! No wonder his wife always has such a sour face!'

'It's *her* face, the girl's,' another laughs, 'a face that ugly would put a ram off its stride! Shall I cover it with my coat for you, Jaspar? Would that help, eh?' And my head is suddenly covered by a sweat-smelling jacket. I am in darkness now, blind and in pain.

With their shouts goading him on the father reaches a point where his body is twitching like a dying horse. He lets out a cry of victory that would shame the armies of Peter The Great and then, as he rolls back with a groan I pull away suddenly from the one that is holding me and his coat comes away from my head and he falls back in surprise.

In my terror I am onto my feet like a cat, grabbing my suitcase and thrusting it up at the weapon that still hangs between the father's legs, like an axeman felling a tree.

His scream sounds greater even than my own. He curls up in agony, clutching at himself and vomiting, his feet kicking out in his pain.

I stare round at the others.

'Well?' I scream. 'Is there anyone else that wants me?'

They stare at me in silence.

'Please,' I shout, 'take your turn. After all, what does it matter, I am only a Jew!'

I spin in a circle, my suitcase catching some of them on the hands and the knees. One boy studies his grazed knuckles and another looks at his companion on the ground and shrugs. The others look away. Most of them are just boys, I realize. Perhaps Gunter's father brought them into the woods to learn how to hunt.

Maybe they are too drunk or stupid, or maybe they are a little scared now that their protector is felled. Either way, I watch, panting, as they walk off slowly. A mad girl, that is what they are thinking, and they are right.

I look at the father who has raped me.

'I know your name!' I scream. 'Remember that, I know it! My father will have you killed! He will come with my

85

fiancé and you will be a dead man! Jaspar! See, I have it in my head!' I look at the expression on his face and I can see my madness scares even him.

There is blood on the snow – my blood, from between my legs. I ache inside and out but the shame hurts worse. I am alive, though, I am not killed. I tell myself this many times on the journey home: 'You are alive, Rosa, you are still alive. Alive. It is a miracle. That is all that is important.' I know I am lying, though. My father is dead and somehow I wish I, too, had been killed.

When I get home Rintzi looks at my torn dress and begins to cry. I say nothing of what happened on the road, for fear she will do something terrible. When I tell her Aaron isn't coming her tears get profuse enough.

I watch a while from the window, terrified at my own stupidity of threatening the man with revenge, but mercifully no one comes for me, and I say a long prayer of thanks in my bed that night for that. I must be strong, it is the only way.

Terrible thoughts start to scratch at my head. My shame is unbearable. What has happened is the finish of me. I have been taken before my marriage, and by a non-Jewish man, at that. Does it matter that I was taken without consent? There are teachings on these matters. I quake with fear at the thought that my entire life may have been ruined by the attack. If I marry Aaron now I will be thoroughly wicked. Yet how else can we survive? Should we all die from this one vile act? Should I never be married because I have been touched by that man?

*　　*　　*

86

A month has passed, Kitty, and I begin to make plans now. When the snows have gone I will take myself off to America and I will find Aaron and bring him back. It's the only possible thing if we are all to stay alive. I have his wedding suit. No one else knows what has taken place. The terrible thing lives only in my memory and I know I can forget it if I try hard enough. When each snow of winter is melted it is gone – and so can this be, too. When I have forgotten it will melt and vanish. Is this so bad? Aaron and I were matched to one another. I will find him wherever he has gone, and one day he will wear Papa's suit, I promise myself.

No one knows. No one *will* know. We will be married, and then everything will be all right once again.

CHAPTER SEVEN

ZG

LONDON 1998

VELVET
*A soft, rich fabric that has been used in Europe since
the Middle Ages, velvet would have originally been
made from silk, though more recently it will more
likely be made from a less costly blend of acetate and
rayon. The name is taken from the Latin vellus,
meaning 'tufted hair'. Some of the more exotic forms of
velvet carry the beautiful names of: cisele, panne
and nacre.*

The sex was neither good nor bad. It was satisfying in the
way that anything ending in orgasm has to be by definition
– but he knew at the same time that it was not the end of
his search, merely a stop-off point on his hunt for the Holy
Grail.

Everything that needed to be sucked had been sucked
and every kissable niche had received unstinting attention
from her lips. There had been damp shuddering moments
and wet gasping bits, and even one fleeting, unpursuable
split second when he had found himself on the brink of
crying out – but what? A name? Her name? (Now that

would have been ludicrous!) A word? Something from the dimmest reaches of his childhood, perhaps?

The woman had been – what? Beautiful? Of course. He had selected her from his own ideal. Good company? She had said what needed saying at all the appropriate moments. Innovative? A lot of what she had done to him had been pre-selected by the manufacturer. This added, of course, a rather hit-and-miss spin to the whole procedure, but there had been more hits than misses, so nothing to question there.

The name she had given was crass in the extreme: Vanessa Velvet. Whore-sounding. The sort of stuff you saw printed on cards in telephone boxes. The kind of pseudonym that meant a girl – and even a hooker, at that – would have to be either dangerously witless or desperately tired of the whole bother of the life-thing to assume.

Vanessa had not been a whore, though. Her names had been chosen for storage and filing purposes, rather than cheaply-manufactured thrill. She had emphatically instructed him, in fact, to call her whatever he pleased. This was part of the deal, along with her eye colour and hair length. If he had asked she would have arrived with a cleanly-shaven scalp.

In the event she had arrived wearing a brilliantly-engineered swathe of Yamamoto silk. He always found Japanese designs seductively sterile and deceptively simple. In fact he had been rather disappointed when she had taken the outfit off, and there were a few moments of dull, throbbing temptation when he had found himself torn between bending to examine the garment in more intimate, lingering detail, or allowing Vanessa to perform her first act of oral stimulation on his cock.

Burgess removed the visor from his head with a sigh of boredom and threw it down onto the chair beside him. Cybersex with Vanessa Velvet. Until the program was right he could see no point in making the kind of investment the software house was suggesting.

Maybe if a new strain of virulent sexually transmitted virus escaped from some laboratory or other . . . he tapped his fingers against his chin. And, of course, it would mean the sensory-immersive program would have to come to long-awaited fruition.

What if the whole set-up could be marketed as a health item? He inspected the Vanessa Velvet program notes. Then his eye hit upon some hand-labelled software that lay beside it. His father's name was written in his own, neat print.

Burgess pulled the head visor on once again. There was darkness around him. A huge black void. A glimpse of space as empty and vast as death itself. Emptiness so profound that its infinity made him fearful. Then someone appeared in the distance, walking towards him. And that sight made him more fearful than the emptiness. The figure headed towards him at speed, walking purposefully. Gabriel. His father. Only he was smiling, which had not been his usual expression when he was alive – not when he regarded his son, at least.

Burgess had programmed the smile himself, to see how it would have looked. He smiled back. The two men smiled at one another. Burgess's face felt strange with all the effort. Gabriel strode up beside him and clapped a hand on his back. 'Well done, Burgess,' the anthropomorphic image said, 'well done, son. That was a great deal. I'm proud of you. You make me happy. Where shall we go to celebrate? I think you have earned a glass or two of malt.'

Enough. Burgess ripped the visor off this time. His face and body were drenched in sweat. He checked his pulse with his own fingers and leant back in the seat while its rhumba subsided. Then he rose shakily to his feet and went off in search of a shower.

CHAPTER EIGHT

ZG

AFTER THE POGROM
*In 1881 massacres in Russia led to mass immigration
of Jews from that country. Many of them came to
Whitechapel. The Spitalfields ghetto was acclaimed as
the site of 'solid, sodden poverty', with three thousand
poor souls to an acre.*

Rintzi is excited. After all the wailing that first accompanied my announcement that I would be going to America she has finally realized the sanity of my decision and has set about making plans for my departure.

She leaves the house many times a day and I wonder where she goes off to, in her tired brown coat with the sleeves that she has left torn, now that Papa is no longer here to mend them for her. Her madness appears to gather force and builds like a whirlwind, with Gregory and myself at the eye of the storm.

For many days after Papa's murder Rintzi would barely move. Now it is difficult for her to sit still for a split second. Every morning she is up before dawn, cleaning the house. I ask if she expects visitors but she just taps the side of her nose and her eyes look like the eyes of a bird.

All the activity frightens Gregory so much that he scarcely eats. He watches Rintzi constantly with the fingers of his good hand shoved into his mouth, and I wonder if he worries that she will set about him with the knife again one day. It is as though we are both holding our breath, Gregory and I, waiting for something to happen. And all the while Rintzi darts about hither and thither, throwing buckets of foul, lye-smelling water over the floors and scrubbing the wood until her knuckles bleed.

Then one day there is noise outside the house. Rintzi is up like a colt and I am at the window, peering through the snow. The sudden movement makes my head spin and I clutch at the doorframe. There is a man outside, tall and dark. I think maybe it is Jaspar come for his revenge at last and the fear is like an explosion inside my head. Everything becomes black and I fall to the floor.

When I wake again I find Rintzi bending over me, clucking like a demented hen, and a large man pulling at my arms, trying to get me upright. They sit me in a chair. Rintzi is smiling now, wiping her hands on her apron.

'Rosa,' she announces, 'this is Menachem Kluchersky. We are very fortunate. Menachem has agreed to be your landsman.'

She looks so proud of her own achievement. Her eyes gleam and there is a smile that threatens to split her face. I look at Menachem Kluchersky. Of course I know him, he is the son of the local butcher. Only today he looks like a clown, with that expression of haughty self-importance painted all over his great red face.

'Well,' Rintzi says, almost bursting with conceit, 'what do you say?'

I say nothing and she looks across at Menachem. 'My

clever daughter,' she sighs, rolling her eyes in mock disgust, 'lost for words. Not even a thank you.'

Menachem clears his throat in a noisy process that involves the use of his hand and two grey linen handkerchiefs.

'Are you sure she is strong enough for the journey?' he enquires finally. He looks at my mother. He has not yet looked at me. 'She fainted,' he says.

Rintzi flaps her hands about as though to say the whole event was nothing.

'You understand the role of a landsman, Rosa?' she asks me. 'Menachem is making the same trip as you and he will look out for you on the way. You will be safe with his protection, Rosa. Your poor mother can sleep at night now, knowing you will not be killed en route. Then when you get to America, Uncle Reuben will take care of you. So now I can rest a little in my mind, eh?'

I look up at the butcher's son, whose eyes have returned to the well-scrubbed floor. 'I don't need a landsman,' I tell my mother. Rintzi laughs.

Menachem rises to his feet. There is not much to see of him, he is so wrapped against the cold, but his eyebrows meet in the middle and the skin around his eyes looks raw.

'I'll be here for her in twenty days,' he says, addressing my mother. 'Teach her to lie about her age. Tell her to say she is twenty if anyone stops us. No one will look close enough to notice.'

Rintzi is angry with me once he has gone.

'You don't know how hard it was for me to find you a landsman!' she cries. 'I had to meet with him many times before he would agree. Then you are so rude I would not be surprised if he left without you! How can you go alone, Rosa? You would get no further than the next village! The journey is dangerous – there are guards to bribe and the threat of attack! I had to tell the landsman you are seventeen years, by the way, so act like a young woman, Rosa, for pity's sake!'

I scoff at this. 'Menachem has a sister at my school,' I tell her, 'he would have seen through that little lie straightaway.'

Baile Kluchersky is, in fact, two years above me in school, and much hated by me for all her gracious airs, but Rintzi no longer listens, her agitation is too great. Her large hands flap about before alighting on a broom that is lying near the doorway. She throws the door open and attacks the snow on the step with great energy, sending clouds of the stuff billowing into the house. She now believes the butcher's son will abandon me and that I will be left to the mercy of the Jew-baiters and bandits.

I am more worried at being left to the mercy of the butcher's son's stupidity.

When I have packed my belongings I find Rintzi staring at the bags. She picks them up herself, judging the weight by pacing up and down the room with them.

'If I give you string you can tie this smaller one to your back,' she tells me. 'But this leather one looks too good. What is in it? It will attract robbers from miles around.'

I take the case from her. 'It's the suit,' I tell her quietly, 'the suit Papa made.'

She is on the floor in an instant, kneeling before the case, fiddling with the clasps. 'It's locked, Rosa.'

I give her the small key that I have on some cord around my neck. I watch as she opens the lid and I nearly cry as she rips at the tissue that I have taken so long packing.

Shards of dried lavender fall to her well-scrubbed floor. 'The wedding suit,' she says. She has to be pretending. She could never have forgotten Papa's greatest work.

'It's for Aaron,' I tell her.

She has the waistcoat in her hands. The embroidery is so fine and so beautiful in such an ugly setting as this that I feel like weeping. I can see the back of Papa's head as he bent over his table, sewing it. His neck was pale and clean. He was stitching my name in silks, to surprise me. Of course it is the wedding suit. Like Papa, I would die before I would be parted from it.

'For when you find him,' Rintzi says.

'Who?' I am confused.

'Aaron,' Rintzi says gently, 'it is for when you find Aaron.'

'Yes.'

'Rosa,' she says, 'how will you find him in America? I'm scared for you. You don't know where he is.'

I smile, even though I know she is right. 'They'll have records,' I tell her. 'There will be authorities, like here. Everyone will be monitored and I will only have to ask. Besides, I have the address of one of his cousins, who went there three years before. Aaron is bound to have looked him up. You know how things are. I will have no trouble. When word reaches him that I have arrived I dare say it will be he who contacts me first! I'm sure I will find him, with or without a search.'

'Of course,' Rintzi says, smiling.

And something in her voice tells me that she doesn't believe I ever will. I watch her fold the suit again, as softly as if she were covering a sleeping child with its blanket, and I watch two tears fall from her face onto the tissue.

CHAPTER NINE

ƵG

LONDON

PEAU DE SOIE
*This heavy satin is popular for wedding dresses and
ornate evening gowns. The word 'satin' is taken from
Zaytoun, in China – the place where it was first made.
Satin is still considered a luxurious fabric, despite the
fact that these days it is more likely to be made from
rayon and other synthetics than from its original silk.*

Kitty sat in her parents' vast, polish-scented lounge, trying
hard not to look at the brigade of gilt-framed photographs
displayed on top of the grand piano. 'Dead Man's Gulch'
was what Nula had once labelled this ghastly array of
long-gone smiling faces that Hester so cherished. Even the
cleaner was not allowed to touch them, and sully their
memory with her can of Pledge. No, Hester would dust
these herself, lovingly. Like the TV, which was also cleaned
by her, these things were sacrosanct.

It was a strictly posthumous Hall of Fame. To get onto
the lid of the piano you had to die first – that was an
acknowledged fact. Grandmothers, second cousins, uncles,
rabbis, stars, royalty – rank didn't matter, but the death-

rattle did. Kitty didn't want to look. Not now – not today. She was too afraid of seeing her father's photo there, smiling out with all the other ghosts.

When she did look, which *had* to happen, as sure as eggs is eggs – no brain can avoid the stimulation of being told *not* to look at something for very long without being forced to take a peek – it was worse than she'd imagined, and that was bad enough. All the old platoon had been removed. Nothing had been cleaned, so their previous positions remained obvious from the thin rectangular holes left in the dust. In the middle of this greying landscape sat a particularly obnoxiously-posed and formal portrait of Gabriel, with a large vase of white funereal lilies looming over it.

When had this shot been taken? It was the sort of thing high street photographers who knew no better did: blue, out-of-focus background, foreground so fogged to be flattering that it looked as though he was smiling through a muslin-like hue. He wore a god-awful suit which Kitty had never seen before and a grin that was completely alien to his features. Was it taken after death, or something? Surely Gabriel would never have permitted it otherwise.

Hester entered the room, followed by a servant with a tea-tray. There was cake on the tray, as well as tea; good, home-made vanilla cake that would forever remain untouched. Hester was diabetic and Kitty had no sweet tooth. The cake was therapeutic, though. Mother and cake. This was how Hester liked to be thought of.

'I phoned the Savoy.' Kitty watched her mother smooth her skirt as she sat down. Today her clothing was especially idiosyncratic: dress, jacket, hat and socks. No shoes. The socks, like the stockings before them, did not match. In fact they were Gabriel's socks – one grey and one russet.

'Ah ... I ... phoned the Savoy, Kitty. *Not* to *cancel*, I told them, but to *postpone*. They understood, of course. They read the newspapers like the rest of us. In fact I believe they were *expecting* my call? Perhaps they had already put us on *provisional*?'

Hester's speech-patterns had changed. She spoke slowly now, accentuating certain words carefully, like a drunk.

Mother and daughter looked across at one another. Of course the Savoy had been expecting the cancellation of the wedding reception. Hester had phoned them three times about it already, only her depression made her forgetful. Kitty hoped the sales team were people of enormous tact and patience, for she felt sure it was not the last call her mother would make.

Kitty's head ached. She felt bone tired. Her afternoon with Kofteros had not gone well. He had maintained a polite, cheerful expression during the entire visit to the East End. He had cheerfully drunk three cups of the disgusting, evaporated-milk tea that they made in the factory – and which Kitty herself loved – and he had spoken fluent Turkish and Bangladeshi to the workers there. Even his car had been left untouched by the local miscreants, who must have been on some council-sponsored awayday to Clacton-on-sea.

'How is Freddy?' Hester asked, licking the tip of one finger and dabbing at an imaginary stain on her skirt.

'Fine,' Kitty told her, 'he's fine.'

'He should have been in touch.' Hester's voice sounded reproachful.

'He has been,' Kitty said quietly, 'he was there at the funeral and he has phoned you each day since. Remember? Look – these are his flowers.' She pointed, not to the lilies, with their overpowering scent, but to a bucketful of hybrid blooms that was acting as a doorstop.

'He's always so busy.' Hester sighed.

'He has his own business,' Kitty reminded her. Freddy Jacobs was the young heir-apparent to Jaycee Outerwear, owners of the Right O! and Muira labels. Their marriage was to be the merging of the two fashion dynasties. Only now it had to wait. Kitty felt a shiver, as though a breeze had just passed through the huge room.

'Time, Kitty, you're wasting time,' the voices murmured, 'don't dither, dearest. Things are moving so very quickly without you.'

She thought of Freddy. He had been everything he should have been about their loss. He had held Kitty while she wept and comforted her daily with gifts, calls and food.

She had noticed something lacking in his father's eyes, though. A certain shuttering against the on-coming tornado. Murder. It was an indigestible word. 'Murder in the business' could cause mild heartburn. 'Murder in the family' would be responsible for acute colic and colitis.

'I have something for you, Kitty,' Hester was smiling now. A secret. A secret gift. She left the room, as regal and sweeping as a galleon. Kitty did not want to be left alone. She badly needed company there, in her parents' house, even for the few minutes that her mother was gone. While Hester was not there Kitty was forced to forget Gabriel

101

was dead and her mother made half-deranged. While she was alone she started to imagine that none of it had happened. That she could smell her father's cologne and hear Hester talking sanely. It was too much to bear, like the photograph. Too sad.

When her mother returned she was carrying what looked like an ancient attaché case. Rotted with age, it left a powdering of leather across the top of the piano, where she placed it. Something placed on the piano. This act was unheard of. Gabriel's photograph got knocked aside by the case but Hester did not even move to right it and Kitty could not bring herself to touch it.

The object had a smell about it. Mould? Not unpleasant. Maybe even evocative. But of what? Kitty sniffed lightly. Age: it smelt of old things. She looked at her mother.

Hester was smiling – the first broad smile since Gabriel's death. Not a 'Thank you for your concern' smile of the sort she had pulled during the *shiva*. Or a 'What else can you expect from life such as this?' smile, of the sort she had pulled when friends and business colleagues put a hand on her arm and told her how tragic it all was. This was a mysterious smile. A 'Wait till you see this' smile. It also, to Kitty's eyes, at least, looked like a broken smile. A wrong-in-the-head sort of smile. Like something vital was missing inside.

There was a lock on the case, ochre with rust. Hester had a key, though. Its metal was as thin as a pin but she still worried the clasp until it opened.

Kitty leant across to study the contents. There was tissue – new-looking tissue, and inside that was some clothing.

'The wedding suit,' Hester said in a whisper. Her fat

hands riffled among the paper and pulled the top garment out.

It was a jacket. Dark wool, faded in parts with age. Very old. Incredibly old, maybe. Something for a museum or flea-market. Kitty winced as her mother flapped it about like a sand-covered towel on the beach.

'Look!' she said. 'Look at that fabric!'

Kitty fingered the stuff gingerly. It was soft. She rubbed it between thumb and forefinger. Soft and deceptively light. Quality stuff. She bent her head to smell it.

'Well?' Hester asked.

'What is it?'

Her mother rooted once more in the case. There were trousers first, and then a waistcoat. 'Look at that stitching!' she said.

The embroidery was well-preserved and most of the colour was still left in the silks. Kitty took the waistcoat from her mother and sat back down on her chair, squinting her eyes against the minute detail of the designs, turning her head one way and then another, holding the garment first at arm's length and then closer, to see.

'It was Gabriel's,' Hester told her, 'and now it's yours. Your father kept it in its own little wardrobe but this is the case it came in and I put it back in there so you could see it as Gabriel did on the day it was handed down to him. It was made by your great-great-grandfather in Russia, Kitty. It is for your husband to wear at your wedding. That is tradition. Each generation has worn it once. Apart from . . .' her voice trailed.

Kitty found herself starting melt-down, and oozing inwardly, too.

'I've seen it before,' she said quietly, 'I've seen this waistcoat. In the wedding photo . . .' she nearly mentioned the photograph that had been sent to her in the post. For that was where she had seen it. Gabriel had been wearing it beneath a different suit. It was the first time she had noticed it. Fear: the emotion returned in a rush.

'Of course,' Hester told her, 'you saw the waistcoat in our wedding pictures. I never thought you paid them too much attention, either. You and Chloe were always too busy screaming with laughter at my own outfit. You would groan when I got the album out. Gabriel would have worn the entire suit but it was too small for him, of course. So he settled for the waistcoat instead. I believe it was only ever worn once before, by your grandfather, although it's so old. Gabriel always claimed his own grandfather hadn't worn it at his wedding – I believe he was a huge man, much too big, even for the waistcoat.'

'But China should have it,' Kitty said, 'or Burgess?'

'No,' Hester told her. 'This is yours. Gabriel always said so. Could he have seen Stephano in it? Do you think Burgess would ever wear it? Your father always knew it was you who inherited his love for the business. You all have equal shares now, Kitty, but it is you who must carry the business on.'

Kitty shook her head slowly.

'It's yours,' Hester continued, 'like the suit. He knew you would be the only one to truly understand and value them both. You might laugh and sneer, Kitty – you're young, I remember how that feels – but I know you understand the importance of family traditions.' She looked back at the suit. 'Freddy is slimmer than your father was. Perhaps you could alter it to fit?'

Kitty had no words to speak. Hester's eyes looked full of pleading. 'Of course,' she managed to get out. 'Of course I can fix it.'

Hester nodded, relieved and pleased. Kitty watched her mother as she folded the suit again lovingly and placed it back in the case. One last embrace of the waistcoat. Perhaps it smelt still of Gabriel on his wedding day. How could Hester think it would ever fit Freddy? It had been made for someone a very different shape. Even the fabric looked too frail to wear. Choked with emotion, Kitty took the case from her beaming mother and placed it beside her chair. It was like the vanilla cake, really – a comfort gesture from mother to daughter. One would never get eaten and the other would never be worn.

CHAPTER TEN

ZG

RUSSIA 1889

CABBAGE

A long-established perk of the rag trade, 'cabbage' is the name given to any surplus garments created when a cutter, who has been asked to get, say, fifteen items from a roll of cloth, will lay the pattern up in such a way as to create seventeen. The extra two garments will be made up and often sold on to street-market traders.

I tell Gregory that I am leaving. His reaction is astonishing. His eyes fill with more terror than I have seen in a face before.

'NO,' he tells me. What good does he think I can do staying there with them? Does he imagine I can fight like a man when the time comes? Does he think I could save him from the sort of fighters that killed Papa? I touch his hand – his good hand – but he pulls away.

'Take me too, Rosa,' he says.

'No, Gregory,' I tell him, 'I can't. It's impossible.' He starts to cry then, and I am glad Rintzi is out of the house.

'Gregory,' I whisper, 'you have to look after Mamma.

You are all she has when I am gone. Besides, I will be back once I am married and then Aaron will take care of us all. It's the only way, Gregory, can't you see that?' His crying becomes louder and I try not to listen. He has to stop. When he clings to me I think of the boy in the forest and push him away, staring at the ceiling to avoid his beautiful, cabbage-white, shocked face.

I feel ill and angry and as old as Bubba.

When Menachem Kluchersky finally calls – and call he does, for Rintzi is paying him, of course – the old women of the *shtetle* turn out to see me off.

I am wearing a full black coat of Bubba's and my hair is plaited and hidden beneath a large cap of Papa's. This is Rintzi's game plan – if men attack us on the way they will take me for a boy and shoot me instead of rape me. How could anyone but my mother be so devious! I would share in her delight at this cleverness, but unfortunately for her I really have no wish to die. And what if she knew that the worst had already occurred? What if she knew that I am already defiled? What of her poor, innocent little Rosa then?

So I stand in my hat and coat with my tears forming ice on my raw pink cheeks and the old women hand me presents that load me until my knees begin to buckle.

There are dried meats for us, and dried meats and jars of pickles to use as bribes for the *grenitz* who guard the borders en route. Then just as I think I can carry no more, one of Bubba's oldest friends, a blind woman who must be over one hundred years, is led up and, with shaking hands, presents me with my grandmother's samovar – a glorious brass object at least twice as old as the woman who holds it and which, to my utter dismay, weighs about as much as four large cats.

Weeping profusely now, Rintzi wraps the thing in brown paper and ties it with string, which she ropes around my neck. I smile but I can barely breathe. My face turns red as beet and my poor eyes water with the effort. Can't she see the string is choking me?

I turn then, gasping like a landed fish, and who do I find myself staring at? None other than Baile Kluchersky, sister of my able-bodied landsman. (I will tell you now that Baile was an extremely beautiful girl, though it has taken me sixty-odd years to admit it.)

'Bertha Zigofsky?' she asks, though she knows that is my name. I wonder how she can look so well in this weather. Her light-brown hair looks polished like the brass of the samovar and her eyes gleam with a perky confidence.

Did I tell you how much I hated this girl at school, Kitty? Not for her face or her figure, of course. While the boys watched Baile with codfish eyes we girls considered her face too white-cheeked and her figure a little too vulgar – a fault she tended to exaggerate with a rather affected-looking walk. No, it was Baile's priggishness that generally made her unpopular with her colleagues. Like her brother, she seemed to think she was a little above the rest of us. I just hope Menachem has informed her that I am to marry Aaron in America.

Baile smiles, showing her white teeth to perfection. She holds her hand out towards me. 'Hello Rabbit,' she says, 'I hear you are coming with us on our journey.'

The train journey to the coast is a kind of enforced hell because the seats are hard and Baile has not stopped complaining from the moment we left the *shtetle*. Had I known she was to accompany us I believe I would have defied Mamma and insisted on travelling alone.

Can I describe the terror I felt when I saw my first train, Kitty? I thought it a steam-belching monster come to kill us all. The sight of it on the track filled me with dread enough, but watching it come to a halt! Sparks flew from its wheels just as a scream flew from my mouth! It skidded and slithered to a standstill on the iced tracks, Kitty, *right alongside where I stood*! Fortunately its whistle drowned my yells and Baile did not hear me, and neither did her precious brother. For then I would never have heard an end to it, for all the dry comments they would have made.

Baile is a bad traveller – the motion of the train makes her sick. Menachem, meanwhile, has spoken not one word, either to me or his beloved sister. His eyes remain fixed on the view from the window, which is, in the main, only of snow – though I feel him looking at me when I pretend to sleep.

Baile insists on calling me 'Rabbit', which was my hated name from school. I warn her many times, nicely at first, but she is deaf to my words and will not stop. When she is finished being sick I remind myself that I will kick her.

My buttocks ache and my ears are ringing from the sound of Baile's voice. Did I mention her mouth has a pink, pursed look, like the end of a small pig's snout? Her features appear painted onto her face and her eyes register permanent surprise. She looks like a doll but is less stupid than she appears. Why did all the boys at school blush so much when she was around? Are men such idiots that they can see no further than all this primping and head-tossing?

The view bores me. I decide to stretch my poor legs by walking down through the carriage. There is a queue for the water-closet and the stench is so bad that I walk on further, rubbing my aching back.

There is an empty mail carriage near the front of the train and, although the place rattles me about like a dried pea in a tin and the noise of the engine is deafening, I am relieved to be alone for once and sit down upon my leather case.

I am desperate now for the water-closet and regret not joining the sorry-looking queue that waited outside. Maybe I can relieve myself here. After all, there is no one about. No sooner do I begin to adjust my coat, though, than I believe I hear footsteps coming my way and so am forced to sit rocking in agony instead. To divert my own attention from the subject I pull off my gloves and blow onto my frozen fingers before stuffing them beneath my armpits to thaw them.

The sight of my own reflection in the window amuses me. There outside, flashing by on the endless drifts of snow, goes Papa's big black cap and underneath it the sorriest-looking young monster you could ever hope to see! My face is white, apart from the nose, which is bright crimson. With my hair hidden under the cap my ears stick out like the handles of the samovar. Would I pass for a boy? Only a sickly and idiotic one, I decide. Perhaps I should pass myself off to the other travellers as Baile's young beau – now that would be enough to silence her mouth, for sure.

Laughing, I pinch at my cheeks to pinken them and rub

110

my nose furiously to get rid of the red. When I look up again in the glass there is another face behind my own – huge and red with raw-looking eyes.

'Menachem!' I gasp. What a fool he is! I all but pissed in my clothes at the sight of him!

The idiot just gawps at my reflection. This is the first time he has deigned to look at me and even now that is just via the glass. His silent staring irritates me. If he is comparing my beauty to that of his sister then he had better wait until we pass through a tunnel and the glass is black!

I listen to his breathing and tooth-rattling and wonder what it is that makes men's noses incapable of taking a silent inhale. They snuffle and snort like great boars while women breathe silently, like cats. Then I feel Menachem fingering the cloth of Bubba's coat and I freeze. He says nothing, neither of us does.

I know Menachem of old, and not just from the synagogue. When I was younger and with the other girls in the *bod*, which is the communal Turkish bath in the *shtetle* that we all used once a week, we would hear the men's laughter from behind the wooden partition that separated us. Anna Klowinski and I climbed the partition to see who was peeping and guess who? Menachem Kluchersky, the butcher's son, no less.

He was naked, what's more. When we squawked and fell down Anna was shaking her head from side to side. 'If that great lump of meat is what it's like, then I will never ever marry,' she said. 'The thing was as big as any donkey's.' We have never spoken about it since. And now here is Menachem Kluchersky the landsman and he is fingering my grandmother's coat.

I can stand it no longer. I rise to my feet as suddenly as is possible with two legs frozen by the cold, and turn to face the oaf. He looks away quickly but still his hand rises again and this time it is making its way to my face.

I grab my case and, in a lather of spiralling arms and shaking legs, make my way out of the carriage and back towards the water-closet. Menachem shouts something after me. I cannot hear it exactly, for the steam engine is too loud, but it sounds something like: 'Aaron will never marry you, you are far too ugly.' So be it. But Aaron has something that Menachem has never possessed, and that is a brain. He is clever and quick, and recognizing those same qualities in me he will find them more valuable than a mere sugar-face, like Baile's.

I am so irritable by the time I have returned to my seat that I begin to bicker with Baile and we do not stop, even when the train journey is over and we are marching through the snow on the way to the border.

Menachem has been walking in silence but suddenly he halts and when he turns we see he has a snow-covered beard. I laugh at this and even Baile lets out a snort.

'You will stop these arguments!' Menachem shouts. His voice is incredible when he is angry, it rises to the pitch of an hysterical girl's. I open my mouth to argue and so does Baile, which surprises me, for I didn't think she had the backbone.

'Stop!' Menachem yells, raising a hand in the air. He is close enough now for us to smell the breath that issues in steam-clouds from his mouth.

'You go alone from here,' he says. I feel my insides turn to water.

Baile looks at me and then back at her brother. 'You can't leave her here,' she says.

'Both of you,' Menachem tells us, and I almost laugh again, despite my personal fear. Baile's face must be a picture.

Menachem waits, hands on hips. 'You will stop this ridiculous gibbering, then?' he asks. Baile nods and I join her. I don't believe Menachem would abandon us both, but he is stupid enough for anything and I do not want to push him. 'Come on then,' he says, and I hear Baile sob with relief.

She is still crying when we reach the border which annoys me, though I say nothing, just in case. Menachem talks to the *grenitz* and there is much arm-waving. Then he comes across to me.

'Give them the meats and the pickles – all of them,' he says. I do not consider this the best way to barter but I hand the precious packages over anyway, for I am tired of carrying them.

The *grenitz* look at the bribes and begin to laugh. One of them spits tobacco onto the ground by Menachem's feet.

'It's not enough,' the butcher's son says, and I note that this is the first time he has looked me in the eye, which tells me how desperate he must be.

Smiling hard, I turn to his sister. 'Baile,' I whisper, 'I know you have money. Give it to him.'

Baile's eyes widen but she is not a good liar. 'I have no money,' she tells me.

I move closer. 'I know you have money,' I say, 'it is stuffed into your boot. Don't pretend it isn't, I saw you

113

put it there when you thought I was asleep. It is the reason why you keep limping.'

Her eyes meet mine and I see a stubbornness there to match my own. 'I have no money,' she says. Her little pink hands have formed fists. We would have fought there and then and I would have had the boot off her foot, had Menachem not been watching.

'Give them your samovar,' she says.

'While you have the cash?' I ask. We are forced to whisper. If the *grenitz* hear they will take the samovar and the money.

Baile grins. 'Give them the old thing,' she says, 'you know you didn't want it, I saw the look on your face when it was given to you. It's been hanging around your neck choking you and now's your chance to get rid of it. It's money we'll need when we reach the ship, not cups of tea.'

I grit my teeth and narrow my eyes, but Baile is not intimidated and, in a way, I know she is right. With slow, reluctant steps I approach the *grenitz* and hand over the precious object that has been in my family for generations.

By the time Baile and I have jostled our way through the border and found the road to the docks we are fighting again and Menachem, thank God, is no longer within earshot.

There is a pitiful-looking queue waiting to board the ship. When we stand in line an old man in a threadbare suit takes our tickets and pins labels to our chests with our names chalked on them. I look at Baile and she looks at me and we both think the other looks ridiculous.

'How long do you think we'll have to wait out here?' she asks. I shrug.

'Until we have died from the cold,' I tell her. Her teeth are chattering. Women in the queue ahead are crying and children they carry have started to scream. I can't see Menachem but he must be in the men's queue somewhere.

We wait for an hour. A sailor comes down the line, counting us.

'How long?' Baile asks him. His reply is a curse, which shocks her.

Another hour passes. I think perhaps I was right, that maybe they will leave us all to die here – after all they have our ticket money, so why should they take us?

Baile nudges me in the ribs. A tall young man in expensive clothes walks past us, making his way to the top of the queue. All eyes are upon him as he approaches one of the sailors. We, miserable wretches that we have become, watch as he pulls a wad of notes out of the pocket of his overcoat. The sailor smiles and waves him onto the ship. There is a collective groan from the queue. Money. That is what it is all about. I look at Baile's boot but she turns her head away. How much must we suffer before she undoes those brown laces and hands over the cash?

'Who do you think that was?' a woman beside me asks. I study her face. There is no resentment there for the man, only admiration. 'Maybe he is an actor, or a businessman.'

'Maybe he is a crook,' I tell her harshly. 'The money was probably thieved.'

To my horror I hear the woman take this tale as the truth and I listen as it is told and repeated all the way down the line. I think of stopping her but wonder why I should bother. So they think the man's a crook? Good.

Perhaps he will be less inclined to bribe his way in front of honest folk again in the future.

After another two hours the queue begins to move and there is much wailing as people try to move their frozen limbs. The sailors shout at us to hurry, now. Baile's name is called first and then mine. We hear nothing of Menachem and Baile begins to fret.

We huddle on deck like cattle and eventually the gang-plank is drawn up and steam belches from the funnel and we are on our way to America, at last!

CHAPTER ELEVEN

ZG

RUSSIA

NANKEEN

*Originally woven by hand in Nanking, China,
this yellow-coloured cotton cloth was popular for
lightweight summer wear during the mid- to late-
nineteenth century.*

The boat is so crowded that half a day has passed before
we realize Menachem is not on it with us. Baile turns
hysterical: 'He has been killed! They must have shot him
on the shore! How many grown men do you see here,
Rosa? They must have rounded them all up while we
queued and murdered them! What will become of us now,
eh? What hope can we have without my brother to guide
us? We are young girls, Rosa! We will die now for sure!'
Suddenly she is clinging to my arm. 'Don't leave me, Rosa!
Promise me we will never be split up!'

So now I am 'Rosa' all of a sudden, and not 'Rabbit'! I
watch her in silence. I have my own ideas about Menachem's disappearance, for with him has gone some of our
belongings and most of our cash. He took our things before
we reached the dock, saying they were less likely to be

thieved from a grown man than two whey-faced girls, despite my boy's disguise. He even persuaded Baile to part with her boot-cash, on the grounds that he might need it to get us comfortable cabins for the journey.

The anger in me surfaces during the terrible journey. 'You should know your brother is a thief!' I tell Baile. She looks at me with shocked eyes. 'He has run off with our money, Baile – look, he would even cheat his own sister.'

Baile makes a few noises of disagreement, but even those noises begin to lose conviction once she has had time to think the whole situation through. Then she comes up with a new plan of attack.

'You were rude to my brother,' she tells me on the second day. 'You shamed him, Rosa, that is why he left us. He couldn't bear to spend the journey in your company.'

'And just how did that happen?' I ask her quietly.

Her face puckers like a child's. 'He told me he paid you attention,' she whispers, 'but that you insulted him with your arrogance. Menachem took pity on you, Rosa Zigofsky, he would have proposed had you played your hand right! It's your fault we are in this predicament, you should learn your place in life and know when to be grateful!'

I turn on this spoilt child like a cat. 'I am marrying Aaron!' I tell her, noting that crowds are beginning to gather now. 'What do I have to be grateful to your brother for?'

'Hah!' I watch the spite build in her face now, making it ugly. 'Everyone in the *shtetle* knows Aaron left Russia to avoid marrying you, Rosa, it was the talk of the place for days. "Poor Bertha Zigofsky," they would say, "it is her face that has driven young Aaron out of the country."

He ran off to America to get away from you, Rosa – only a fool would not have realized that!'

I catch Baile by the hair and she screams. The crowd parts suddenly and I see the tall young man in the good clothes who bribed his way aboard pushing through with some authority. He takes my wrist and holds it so hard I am forced to let go of Baile's hair.

'What's this about?' he asks. He has straight, light-brown hair and large, gleaming eyes. Angry as I am, I notice his clothes are not of such good quality as I first thought, though they fit him well enough and are clean and pressed. He looks at me and his eyes narrow.

'A young lad attacking a beautiful young lady?' he asks. 'Where's your manners, boy?'

Baile was all set to fight back, but the sight of this man's handsome face has her patting her hair back in place and fluttering her lashes.

I pull off my father's cap quickly, tugging at my hair as it falls so that it goes part-way to covering my rabbity ears.

The young man sees his mistake and begins to laugh.

'My apologies, miss,' he says, when he can talk again. 'I thought this fight was too one-sided but now I realize my mistake. Please, continue. I'm sorry for the interruption.' His eyes are mocking me. I don't imagine he has ever looked serious for too long in his life. I stare across at Baile. The crowd begins to get restless at the delay. It had been looking forward to a good show. We begin to square up to one another but I know our hearts are no longer in the fight.

Baile raises an arm gingerly and makes to punch me on the shoulder.

119

'What if . . .' the man begins, interrupting once again. 'What if we make the fight more interesting? Eh? After all, no one likes to watch a bloody scrap, especially between two well-mannered young ladies. What if we follow a tradition from my part of the country? A way of fighting that ensures neither woman gets hurt?'

I can see this appeals to Baile and the crowd is so keen at this new suggestion of fun it can hardly wait for it to get started.

I watch as the man calls to an amused sailor to bring us some rope, then he pulls us back to back and binds us together around the waist.

'There,' he says, smiling, 'that should do it.'

The ship pitches and we stagger together to keep our balance. The crowd moves obligingly and the sniggering begins.

Being mocked in such a way makes me mad again. I pull at the rope but the man has tied it too firmly. The audience sees my struggle as the prelude to a scrap and begins to shout encouragement. Some old crone has remembered all the insults we traded and starts to yell them out loud. This sets Baile off, and I feel her arms flail as she tries to land a punch. I begin to retaliate, knocking her on the side of the ribs while she kicks at me backwards, like a mule. The audience roars approval, but within minutes of all this squirming we are both panting and exhausted, with neither of us having landed any damaging blows.

'Wait, Baile,' I shout at her. 'We look ridiculous, don't you see?' I can feel she is pleased to stop.

'Finished, then?' the young man asks. His teeth are white as he grins at us. 'Honour settled? Friends again?'

Baile nods. I feel too sick to reply. The rope is cutting into my belly and I would agree to anything to get it untied.

'You must shake like true ladies,' the man announces once we are free of our shackles and face-to-face once more. Baile holds out her lily-white hand and I take it, though I would prefer to break her arm. The audience's reaction is one of acute disappointment. Then the smell of cooked food wafts up from the galley and people begin to disperse quickly.

'So,' the young man says, smiling at us both, 'you must allow me to invite you to tea. You must be thirsty after such a show.'

His idea makes me laugh. Tea? You'd think he was on a pleasure trip instead of crushed in with a hundred other poor unfortunates. I decide to hate him at this moment. His arrogance and *joie de vivre* are quite unbearable under the circumstances.

He sees my face. 'Anything is possible,' he smiles, 'you should learn that in life, if nothing else.'

'I mean to learn a good deal more than that,' I tell him, 'and I suppose you mean that anything is possible if you only have the money to pay for it.'

He nods. 'Of course,' he says, ushering us away from the main mass of hungry peasants, 'money is a key, that's all, so what's the harm? Just don't ask where I acquired my stash, that's all. I may have to confess to my villainous habits that are the talk of the ship.'

He looks at me as he says this and I am childish enough to blush. So he knows who put the rumour around about his thieving.

The young man's name is Max Warkofski and he is

121

journeying to London to start up business as a photographer. This impresses Baile, I can see – as does the tea-tray he has somehow bribed a sailor to have delivered to our table.

The smell of the tea calms us down and the taste of it is so good and fresh on my tongue that I nearly weep, for our food has been poor since we left the *shtetle*.

'Do you two sisters really hate one another?' Max asks as he pours a second cup.

Baile is offended and shocked by the idea that anyone might take us for sisters.

'We aren't related,' she tells Max. 'We might have been sisters but she refused my brother Menachem, who is known to be a great catch. It is because of that we fell out. I felt obliged to defend the family honour.'

Max looks across at me but I can only stare at Baile's face.

'The best cure for an argument is time spent apart,' Max says, seeing our expressions. 'What if I arrange for you to switch berths so that you don't have to live in one another's pockets – for the duration of the voyage, at least? Are you both off in England?'

I shake my head. 'No. I'm going to America,' I tell him.

'By yourself?' He looks surprised.

'Since her brother changed his mind, yes,' I tell him.

'So that's it, then,' he says.

We return to our cramped berth and Baile packs to move because my journey is the longer. I am pleased to see her go, but then frightened once she is gone.

* * *

122

I was delivered of the dead child some three days after this. How amazing that I could not have known! Yet my body is still skinny and what weight I put on around the waist I put down to the fact that Rintzi was mad to fill me up with as much fatty food as possible prior to the journey, to stave off the cold and other deprivations.

I am still sickly from the birth when our ship sails from sea into river and we are travelling up the Thames on our way into London.

There is much excitement, of course, though I cannot see cause for any celebration, save to mark the fact that we are all still alive. Youth has strange priorities, though. Hard as I try to remain groaning in my little bunk I cannot help but grow curious when I hear all the shouting and excitement from up on deck and eventually, wrapping a blanket about my body to keep off any cold, I walk feebly down the passage to join the others.

Baile, of course, is up there waiting with a smile. She knows nothing of my situation and shows no alarm when she sees me, despite my white, haggard little face.

'Rabbit!' she exclaims, as though surprised to see me.

'Don't you wish your journey were ending here too?'

I look around at the grey buildings looming out of the fog like ghosts. 'With the Ripper waiting to pick you all off?' I say. 'I should think not, Baile.'

I watch her expression turn to one of shock and fear and find myself feeling sorry for my own unpleasantness. The rivalry can end now – we will never see one another again.

'Wait there,' I tell her, 'I'll get dressed and see you off properly.'

*   *   *

Pulling on my grandmother's coat I find I am in better spirits than I had thought. I splash some water on my face and comb my hair for the first time in many days and, even though the experience is difficult and painful, I am pleased that my body feels whole again and that I can button my skirt now that my stomach is no longer swollen. If I had been older and wiser I would have known I was with child, but I am still just a child myself and Rintzi had told me very little of such things.

When I reach the deck again the fog has cleared a little and people are leaning over the rail, stretching their eyesight to make sense out of all the gloom. Baile has met up with Max Warkofski and she is smoking a cigarette that she must have been given by him. Max smiles as I approach.

'How are you, Rosa?' he asks, lifting his hat. I start to pick at my hair with my fingers but I see Baile watching me and my arm falls to my side, instead. 'Are you going to Liverpool?' Max continues. I regard him with as blank an expression as I can muster.

'Max says you will have to change ships,' Baile tells me, her eyes watering from the smoke. She has taken a glove off to avoid staining it with the nicotine. 'You have to get off in London and travel north to get the ship to America,' she tells me, quoting her companion, 'so you may meet with the Ripper after all, Rabbit – won't that be exciting?'

I look around me in a panic. Everyone is disembarking.

'You didn't think you could travel west from the east side of England, did you Rabbit?' Baile asks. She throws her head back and laughs for Max's benefit. I look at her thin, pale throat and know I would have contemplated throtttling it had I not been consumed with terror at what she had said.

Forgetting my recent infirmity completely, I push my way through the crowds and run back to my billet for my things. The day is cold but I am sweating as I sink to my knees and scrabble on the wooden floor to find the case with the wedding suit inside. I had hidden it at the foot of the bunk for safety and it is wedged so hard I cry out with the effort of lifting it.

By the time I am back on deck the ship has docked and Baile is a white dot on a lower deck, waiting her turn to be name-tagged by immigration. I call out to her but my voice gets lost in all the clatter of feet and cases. I clutch my own bag to my chest.

'Baile!' I am sadly in need of her, now she is going. Without this irritating girl I am alone in the world; I realize that with a start.

'Baile!' I would even be grateful for Menachem's company right now.

It is an hour before I reach the steps to the lower deck and by then people are pushing and jostling with irritation that comes from exhaustion. Their children are screaming and it is that sound I can bear least of all. I stand tall in my grandmother's coat, denying the desire to join in the wailing and falling to the floor in a welter of wretched self-pity.

I have never seen so many shadows as those I see on the shore. Everywhere is the colour of wet grey flannel and every wall throws a shadow that envelops the next.

There is a stench of sulphur in the air. The river slaps against the hull and looks like black treacle. I clamber down dank wooden steps with the aid of a rusting chain handrail and at the foot of the steps I slip on sea-slime, clinging so hard to the wet rail that I graze my face. I think I might tumble into the sea and I cry out, 'Papa!'. When I regain my balance I am deeply ashamed of myself. I must be stronger. I clutch my case to my chest again and lift my chin. There is no sky here in England. No sky to see and no air to breathe. The shadows are enveloping us all. I cannot wait to see what I imagine will be the cleaner skies of America.

CHAPTER TWELVE

ƵG

GREENERS

Immigrants to Britain were nicknamed 'greeners' by the local population. When they arrived at the docks many fell prey to the organized bands of robbers, known as 'crimps', who set themselves up to defraud them of any cash they might have brought into the country. Many of the greeners were afraid to report the crimes, as they feared the British police would be as bad as the dreaded Objescik, which they had left behind in their own country.

We are at Irongate Stairs, Kitty – do you know it? I overheard one of the sailors telling another, and this charming place is the point where Baile is to set dainty foot upon her new homeland for the first time. How excited she must be to find herself the guest of so much stink and soot!

We sit on the lower deck now, exhausted and bewildered, each clutching baskets or bags to our chests while various officials board the ship to check out our suitability for integration into this shadowy land.

Most of us have not changed clothes since the day we boarded ship and many have existed on stale food brought from the homeland. What must these officials think as they gaze on us? I do not need to ask, though, I can read the contempt in their eyes.

They are, in the most part, wearing suits, as are the relatives who wait miserably on the quayside, stamping their feet with the cold and waving sullenly at any face that is visible on the upper deck. Their clothing fascinates me. Their British style of dress may appear vastly superior to the peasant styles sported by most of those aboard, but I am proud to note that nowhere do I see handiwork close to the standards of that produced by my own father.

An elderly gentleman is helped on board and we are told he is a doctor, and that we must all prepare for an examination. This sets off much caterwauling among the women, who are appalled at the prospect of being examined in the raw air. In the event the man's disgust at our state is so acute that he barely touches us. By the time it comes to my turn he has a cologne-soaked handkerchief tied around his chin. He looks into my eyes and feels the side of my throat before declaring me 'fit'.

A younger man carrying a ledger walks behind him asking us each how much money we have. He speaks Yiddish, but with such a poor accent that many find it hard to answer. I reply that I have nothing, which is almost true, since Baile's wonderful brother now has most of my money tucked into the seat of his pants and what little I do have left I intend to keep to myself. I make sure to reply in English, carefully pronouncing some of the words I learnt before leaving Russia, which seems to surprise the man.

'I am bound for America,' I tell him. 'Could you please tell me which line I should join?' Amazed, he walks away without answering.

The queue moves on. I can see now that they have rigged a makeshift desk up on the deck and a man sitting behind it is examining everyone's tickets. As I draw close I notice his cuffs are frayed and that he has skin as pink as a pig's. Do all Englishmen have this same soft pink skin? As I approach the desk he looks up at me through a fringe of thick white lashes.

At least Menachem left us with our tickets. I place mine on the desk in front of the pig-man, then watch as he stamps a word onto the front of it before laying it on top of a large pile to his left. I smile pleasantly.

'I need the ticket back,' I tell him.

'Why?' he asks.

'I need it to take me to America. I can't travel without it.'

I watch as he pulls the ticket from the pile and pretends to read it slowly.

'This ticket terminates here,' he says. He looks at my face for a while before turning to his interpreter, a middle-aged Jewish man dressed in an expensive black astrakhan coat.

'Your ticket is for England,' he tells me in Yiddish. 'Look, it says here . . .' He points to some words on the front of the paper, speaking slowly, as though I am stupid.

'I *paid* for America,' I tell him. He is wrong, they both are. There has been some mistake.

The men look at one another and the pig-man shrugs. 'Where did you buy this ticket?' he asks, and the second man interprets.

'From an agent back at home,' I reply. I am beginning to feel sick. Apart from my weakness after giving birth, I have been sitting still for hours without food or drink inside me.

'You paid fifteen shillings for this ticket?'

'What?' I ask. I do not understand the currency. When it is translated for me I shake my head. 'More than that,' I tell them. Rintzi and I were sewing many nights to make up the money.

The man sighs and throws my ticket back onto the pile. 'Then you were taken for a ride,' he tells me. 'You paid for a through ticket but bought steerage to London only. It happens all the time. One day someone will have enough wit to check before paying and I will call myself a China-man when he does.'

So Menachem has feathered even more of his little nest than I had imagined, and from the sweat of my family! If only I had inherited one half of Papa's wits! He would weep if he were alive to see how stupidly his beloved little Rosa is behaving! To think I was always known for my cleverness! I need time to stop and plan but the queue behind me is naturally impatient.

'How old are you?' the interpreter asks.

'Eighteen,' is my lie. He shrugs and they let me through.

Fear and hunger are making my head spin so that I cannot see what I should do. The money I have on me would never buy a ticket to America. There is so much noise around me I can barely know my own name. I look about for Baile but I am shorter than most of the crowd and so can see little, even when I stretch onto my toes.

I see a space near a wall and head for it, sinking down onto my case beside an old woman who, by her colour, expression and smell, could well be dead. I close my eyes and press my hands against my ears to concentrate my thoughts. What would Papa have done? Be clever! Be clever!

Someone touches my arm and I let out a cry. There is a man in front of me, wearing striped trousers and a faded *yamulkh* on his head.

'Do you have relatives here?' he asks. His teeth are yellow, like singed kindling. I look around for help but the crowd has moved to another part of the quay. I must have been asleep. I look to the old woman beside me but even she has either moved or been dragged away.

'Are you waiting for family?' the man asks again in Yiddish. 'If you are alone and penniless there is the Jews' Temporary Shelter, in Leman Street. Would you like me to take you? They will give you shelter for several days.'

Could this be the famous Ripper? If it is then he is smaller than in my imagination because when I scramble to my feet I find I am a good inch taller than him. He still scares me, though.

I pick up my case and push unsteadily past him. 'There will be a hot meal each day and water for bathing,' he calls after me. My feet echo as I run up a sooty alley and out into a narrow cobbled street. To my relief there is a man with a small black carriage waiting beneath one of the gas lamps.

'Cab?' he asks. When I make no answer he repeats the word in Russian.

'Could you take me to the Jews' Shelter?' I ask him, almost crying with relief as he touches his hat and smiles.

'Get inside,' he tells me.

The interior of the cab is dark but it is warmer than the streets and I feel safe enough inside its confining walls. I pull Bubba's coat around my body like a blanket and lean back against the grease-stained headrest. The streets are so narrow I could stretch my arms out of the windows and touch the houses on either side. Do the English hate light so much that they have built everything in shadow?

I am tired right through to my bones but too excited and fearful to sleep. We drive through dank streets for an hour before the road starts to widen and the houses fall away to either side, revealing what I take to be fields or even marshes. The shelter must be in another town, for we pass by many barren stretches before the landscape becomes spotted with dwellings again.

I am so tired my eyes are rolling in their sockets before the cab ceases its rocking and we pull up outside a large, two-storey house.

The cab driver calls out, 'Leman Street,' and jumps down to help me with my case, but I refuse to part with it, a little rudely, I think afterwards.

When my feet are safe on the pavement in front of him he smiles again and touches his hat.

'Two hundred and thirty miles in total,' he says, 'that will be two pounds and fifteen shillings.'

I stare at him dumbly. 'But that is far more money than I have,' I tell him.

His smile fades a little. I watch him studying my clothes and my case. Perhaps he thought I was one of the wealthier immigrants.

'So how much are you carrying on you?' he asks. I turn out all the coins in my right pocket, praying he will not ask me to empty the left one as well. The coins are Russian, of course. The cab driver holds one of them up in the light. I think it looks rather handsome but his expression becomes angry and he says a word I do not understand.

'You owe me twice this much,' he tells me.

'It's all I have,' I say, trying to keep my voice calm. Will he have me arrested for a thief?

As we stand staring eye-to-eye the door to the shelter opens and a shaft of golden light envelops us, making us both jump.

'Is there trouble out there?' a voice calls out. It is an elderly woman with hips as wide as the flanks of the gelding that pulls the man's cab. I watch as she emerges from the doorway, wheezing at every cumbersome step her slipper-clad feet are forced to take. 'Did you pay him?' she asks me, pointing a thumb towards the cab driver.

'I gave him all I have . . .' I begin. 'I owe him double, though. I'm not a thief. I will pay him back if he will wait a few days.'

'How far did he take you?' the woman asks. 'One hundred, two hundred yards? Eh?'

'Two hundred and thirty miles,' I tell her, 'all the way from the docks.'

'The docks?' she says, laughing. 'You mean *those* docks?' She turns me around to face the other end of the street. In a gap between the houses I see the tall iron gates that led out of the quayside. When I turn back, my mouth open in disbelief, I see the cab driver climbing back into his seat and flipping his reins to get the gelding moving.

'I don't understand . . .' I say, 'we drove for two hours, maybe more . . .'

'Two hours going round in a circle.' The woman laughs. 'They try it all the time with you greeners. Lucky you didn't have more on you, or he'd have had it all.'

I drop my bag and run towards the cab as it pulls away,

but Bubba's coat wraps around my ankles and I am forced to stop before I end up sprawled across the cobbles. Frustrated and angry I pick up a stone instead, hurling it with all my strength towards the driver. I hear a shout and to my great satisfaction, watch as his hat flies into the air and goes tumbling off down the street.

Barely has the smile of victory crossed my face, though, than a smaller stone hits the back of my coat, followed by a second stone and a third. I spin round, thinking the old lady is attacking me, but find myself confronted by a group of young boys not much older than I am.

'Greener!' they shout in unison. 'Jew!'

Mad as hell and still buoyed up by my victory with the cab driver's hat, I run straight towards them with arms circling and such a blood-curdling cry issuing from my mouth that they disperse in a rush, dissolving back to the shadows that spawned them.

The old woman watches them hurtling about like chickens, then looks back at me. 'Don't be too smart,' she says, 'they don't mean no harm.'

'They threw stones at me,' I tell her.

She sighs. 'They think the greeners steal their jobs.'

'What's a greener?' I ask her.

'You are,' she says, simply.

CHAPTER THIRTEEN

ƵG

MOIRE
*Watered silk was popular during the late nineteenth
century and is currently used almost exclusively for
evening wear. The effect, called moire, is achieved by
applying heated, engraved copper rollers onto the
delicate fabric.*

Hester telephoned her daughter in the middle of the night.
Three o'clock. It is a magic hour. A time when sleepers
can no longer discern dream from reality. Her voice had
a scratchy quality to it – not tired, not at all drowsily
hushed and night-timey, but full of mid-afternoon
impatience.

'They're saying it was suicide,' she yelled. Kitty cupped
her hand around the earpiece of her phone but it was too
late, the ringing alone had been enough to wake Freddy.
She watched him rise silently from the bed and walk out
of the room, arse-naked, like a sleepy child. When he
returned he was clutching a bottle of iced water and two
mugs. One mug said 'Dick' and the other 'Head'. For an
intelligent, sophisticated man Freddy suffered from a
severely under-developed sense of humour. He thought the
mugs were funny. He had bought them himself on his last

trip to New York. Every time he used them he laughed – in fact he was smiling now, but then he didn't know who it was on the phone yet. There were other things Freddy didn't know yet, too. One of them was about the wedding. She hadn't told him she had postponed already.

Kitty laughed at different things to Freddy. He would split himself apart over someone walking into a lamppost on the street. His favourite comic was Jim Carey and he laughed so much at the burglars in *Home Alone* that he had to be taken out of the cinema to recover. And that had been on their first date, when Kitty was still at school.

Kitty laughed at cleverer stuff, like satire. Fortunately she also laughed at Freddy laughing, or they would probably never have got engaged. Only she didn't laugh in bed at that moment because her mother's tone was worrying.

'Suicide!' Hester repeated. 'How can they say such things?' She sounded angry, not upset.

Kitty sighed. There had been very little information passed to the press about Gabriel's death, and so they had had to resort to speculation, which gave them much better sport. Kitty had tried to keep the papers away from her mother.

At first they had guessed a heart attack. Then it was suicide. The news that he had been disembowelled put paid to that theory quite quickly in all but one of the tabloids. This particular one was made of sterner stuff, though. Their showbiz hack had been quoted in print as saying Gabriel had killed himself over the failing family business – and so suicide it still had to be in the minds of at least a third of the public. The current issue even contained an interview

136

with a 'leading exponent of Eastern martial arts', explaining the technique of Hara Kiri.

'Kitty, you have to take over,' Hester said, her voice dropping.

'What?' Kitty asked. She'd forgotten to recharge her pone batteries and the line was breaking up into hiccups. Hester sounded as though she was talking under water. 'You . . . have . . . tooo . . . take-overrrr.' It had a ghostly quality in the darkened room, at that time of night. Kitty shivered and rubbed her arm. She preferred the scratchy tone.

Freddy stared at her when the call was finished. 'What is it, possum?' he asked.

'My mother says I should save the business for us. She thinks I'm some sort of anointed, chosen one. She says it's what Gabriel would have wanted.' She looked away. 'I expect she's been saying the same things to Burgess and Chloe. She's desperate, Freddy.'

Freddy whistled through his teeth. 'Do you have to save the business tonight or can it wait until the morning?' he asked.

Kitty shook her head and her hair shone burnished silver in the moonlight. 'She means it, Freddo, even though she's confused,' she said. 'Please,' she begged, the smile fading from her face, 'I have to talk. My head's so full of terrible stuff.' Stuff like murder and violence and who would run the business. Stuff like revenge.

Freddy put down the mugs and looked at her. Kitty was silent. When her fiancé went quiet he was thinking business. Like Burgess he had a computer-compartment in his brain that could be activated at will. Thank God he was most-part human, too. His flesh smelt good, like freshly washed socks. He ran a hand through Kitty's hair as he thought.

'*If* your season is a blow-your-pants-off success you *might* find another investor willing to pick up the tab,' he said, slowly, 'although the likelihood of discovering anyone willing to part with the sort of financial injection you must be needing to stay intact, *and* willing to keep on the little lost leaders like your father's precious dream of *haute couture*, could well be as rare as hen's teeth –' Kitty stopped him by placing a hand over his mouth.

'I couldn't do it, Freddy,' she said. 'Even with all that. Burgess wants to sell. Let him pick the bones out of it if he likes.'

'How strong is your current collection?' Freddy asked her. Kitty shrugged. Of course she wouldn't tell him. He was her fiancé but he was also a competitor of sorts.

And anyway, there was a problem – a *huge* problem. Insurmountable. A labour that even Hercules would have balked at. There *was* no finished collection so far. Things had sort of naturally ground to a halt after Gabriel's murder. They had been tied up with mourning. Burgess was too busy selling the whole package. Chloe was solid with PR, milking every opportunity to turn negative press into positive publicity. Hester was in another world of her own creation. Perhaps Raphael, Gabriel's designer, had been getting on with the job. Who knew? The reins lay slack on the ground right then. Gabriel had always taken care of business. What nobody had realized was that he'd trained no one to run it properly when he was gone.

Kitty felt sick and cold. Too many chiefs, all of a sudden. Her head was too focused on the horror of her father's death to bother. Every day brought something more. New little details, leaking like a rusty tub. Murder. Mutilation. Suicide? Revenge killing. Her mind was still on that pavement, alongside her father's corpse. Who could do such a thing? How much more was there to emerge about the death?

Freddy kissed her hot forehead. Kitty realized that now she had his attention she could no more confide in him than slice off her own hand. Her thoughts were too dark and obsessional. She wished he could kiss them away altogether, like a mother can kiss pain away when her child has a small graze. Perspectives had changed. Her whole life was out of kilter. There was nothing that was right or normal now – not one single solitary thing.

Until Gabriel's death Kitty had had roles. She had been a bride-to-be. She had been hands-on in the business, taking over the bits of real work that Burgess rarely saw and Chloe tried to ignore. Helping her father. Not figures on a screen or cuttings in a book, but manufacture. Chloe thought work ended once the collections were over. She hated the factory and the outworkers. Kitty loved them. It was the part of the business she would miss the most once she and Freddy got married.

She rubbed her temples. 'The collection is great,' she said. Why was Freddy so interested, all of a sudden? Did he have some sort of hidden agenda behind all of this? Did he have some part in her father's death? And since when did crappy, paranoid thoughts like that start filling her scrambled-egg-for-brains head?

Up until Gabriel's death there had been so many of them – family and friends, a thick, suffocating duck-down quilt-load of relatives and people. Now she felt isolated and lonely. Distrust was completely alienating. Who had killed Gabriel? She would be alone forever if she did not find out. Even her father would not turn to face her. When she tried to picture him now he was further away than before, his back totally hunched over his work. It was him she needed to confide in, not Freddy. Yet the conversations with Gabriel were strictly one-way.

'Who, Kitty? *Who*?'

Later, in her uncannily quiet apartment, with only herself for company – and in this little relief, for her head-full of dark nonsense could not be left outside the door like the rubbish – Kitty lay alone in the shadowy silence, sifting through her thoughts, tidying them into piles. Things to do. Things to think about. Things that can wait. Things that can't. Things too goddamn awful to think about until your brain heals a little.

She phoned Nula.

'Nule?' Her sister sounded tired and sleep-sodden.

'Are you okay?' Gabriel would have looked after Nula. He would have looked after Kitty, too. The tears began again, tears of loneliness and self-pity, not worthy emotions at all. The pecking order had changed now. The top name in the whole flaming set-up was struck off the list. Kitty searched in her own mind for the next in line, the family member who would stand up to be counted now that the big cheese was gone. The one to do a little looking-after of the others. A rock strong enough to shoulder the business as well as the sorry mess of a family. Unfortunately no name came to mind.

Who was looking after Hester? Would China bother? A large felt-tip had just been applied to the list of those above her in the natural, hierarchical line of succession of authority and responsibility. Suddenly there was no one there to look after *her* – Kitty – yet there were many other things and people in urgent need of her care and attention *themselves*.

'Are you okay, Nules?' she asked her sister again. There was a series of grunts and then a yawn.

'I was asleep, Kit.' Not complaining, just telling. Nula had never been a complainer or a whiner. Nula was quiet. She just got on with life.

'How's Mother?'

Another yawn. 'Okay, I guess. She's sort of out of it too. She has a jab of something. She doesn't come up again until noon.'

'What kind of jab?'

'A doctor-sort-of-jab, Kit. It's okay. He doesn't want to leave her tablets, in case . . . you know, in case she gets greedy, or anything. He calls at night like Doctor Death with his leetle syringe . . .' Her voice broke suddenly. 'Kit, you know what she's done? Did you see the piano? Can you come and live here, Kit? Can I come and stay over with you? Burgess got a nurse in but it's gone like a fucking mausoleum here, and now China's threatening to stay, too.'

'China?' This was new.

'She's pregnant, Kit, did you know?' There was a pause. Both started to laugh, despite their misery. *Because* of their misery. The sort of incredibly against-the-odds, unbidden, hysterically huge type of laughter that only occurs when it really shouldn't. When tears get diverted and come bubbling up through your nose instead of your eyes, making you whoop and choke.

Stephano *avec bébé*. Stephano in Mothercare. Stephano at antenatal classes . . .

But Nula's laugh went on just too long. 'Nule?'

Eventually the girl stopped abruptly, as though she had been garotted. 'I'll phone you when China gets here,' she told Kitty. 'Maybe I can come and stay then, eh?' And then she was gone.

Suddenly the loneliness became unbearable. Kitty pulled on an old, fleece-lined tracksuit and woolly hat, with which to fool the doorstepping press, and took a cab for a second trip to the studio.

It was the nearest she could get to Gabriel, standing in his deserted office. Being in there after his death was not the same as being in there while he was alive. He was a formal man. She was there again without permission. She clutched the edge of the massive desk with her palms as a wave of vertigo ran over her. When had she last eaten? Hester would have nagged her endlessly. But it didn't matter. She could buy a sandwich from the all-nighter on the way home.

Moving carefully, almost like a burglar, she began to open drawers and cupboards. She didn't know what she was looking for, but felt there would be answers there for her somewhere.

'Who, Kitty? *Why?*' The question had changed recently. Why was he murdered? What was the reason for her father's death? She loved him so much she could have forgiven him anything, but her view was biased. She'd spent hours trying to think herself outside that love – to see Gabriel as others would have seen him. To examine his faults. To view his imperfections.

Vain? He was a meticulous man, a perfectionist – in his own image as well as that of his business. But then Gabriel *was* the business.

Ruthless? He could never suffer fools gladly. If something or someone didn't work he would dismiss it without hesitation. What was wrong was wrong. But surely that was admirable?

Arrogant? But he had been at the top of his profession for too long to be anything else. The business thrived on arrogance. Any designer who was not also a dictator was a failure. Hesitancy and indecision were anathema to the craft. People had to be *told* what they wanted to wear, not *asked*.

A family man? Gabriel's values were as firm at home as they were at work. He set the example and the rest of them were expected to follow. He was an adoring husband and father and expected the same in return.

Kitty was the only child he ever indulged. Burgess had suffered the most. It was easy to find favour with Gabriel – all you had to do was copy him. Anyone failing to do so would meet terrible tempers or absolute coldness. It was this coldness that had destroyed Burgess, but then it had been his own fault.

She pulled out business diaries and notebooks. Many of them contained entries in her own hand. There was one cupboard with more personal effects: some cloth from his first sold design; a couple of precious press cuttings; a designer of the year award that was faultlessly polished but never displayed; a child's shoe – a baby shoe, hand crafted in pale lemon kid.

Kitty pulled it from the cupboard and examined it. She hoped it was her own – she so wanted it to be hers. *Her* baby shoe, not one of the others'. Selfish, selfish girl, wanting to be the favourite, even after all this time. Even after his death. She turned the small memento over. There was a tiny initial embroidered on the bottom: 'B'. Not her shoe, then. Burgess's shoe. Her eyes stung with childish disappointment. Like a stupid, jealous child. Why her brother's, though? Why, when they had such a difficult relationship? Why not hers? She put the shoe carefully back into its place.

Apart from that the cupboard was disappointingly empty. Kitty sighed and looked around the office. Then she stopped. Next to the Krupts coffee machine that she had bought Gabriel for his last birthday lay what looked like a small pile of picture frames. Had they been there before? She had no memory of seeing them there the last time she had paid a visit. And she was sure she had made herself a coffee then, to take some of the sting out of the brandy. But she had been misty-eyed with grief. Perhaps the police had just moved them. She walked across to examine the pile.

Some of the frames were large and quite heavy. They were stacked in careful order, not a speck of dust on them. Gabriel had planned to have the office re-decorated after this next collection and the pictures all had notes stuck to them, telling exactly where they should be hung.

The top frame held a portrait photograph of Hester, taken recently, as Kitty remembered, by Terry O'Neill. It

144

was flattering enough to embarrass her mother, but Gabriel had loved it, for it was how he saw his wife. Then there was a shot of her father himself, accepting an award from a smiling Princess Diana. One more portrait of them all as children – a telling shot in retrospect. It showed China in the days before she had no identity, smiling at the camera while keeping a watchful hand on Chloe's shoulder; Burgess, grinning playfully in the days before drugs took the playfulness away; Nula trying to totter out of shot while Kitty held her back lovingly – had they all looked so much alike in those days? They could have been in training to become one of those ghastly all–American family pop groups, with their cute bobbed hair and their matching white-toothed grins.

There was a much older picture beneath that one, a black-and-white shot of a Victorian workshop, with all the staff scrubbed up and posed for the camera. Kitty pulled it closer to the desk-lamp. Had she seen it before? She had no memory of it, though it could have hung on a wall in the studio for years beneath patterns and swatches.

The original must have been sepia. Gabriel must have had it re-shot and re-framed. Kitty peered closer and smiled. The age of the picture meant the people in it were posed rigidly and self-consciously, but it was still possible to spot an expression or two of utter amusement. Kitty felt the assembled staff would have all collapsed with laughter once the shot was taken. There were three women seated in the foreground, all in aprons and caps, and six men lined up behind them, all with their arms folded and beards down to their chests. Behind the men stood two young boys, both also aproned and with caps on their heads. In

145

the distance Kitty could make out the workroom itself, with the blocks and steam irons.

'Who, Kitty? And why?'

She put the picture carefully to one side and looked at the last one in the pile. It was as old as the previous one – maybe older. A formal studio shot. A wedding photograph, the bride seated, clutching a huge bouquet that covered her legs and the groom standing warily behind her.

'Who?'

Smiling, Kitty turned the shot over to see how it was labelled. To her intense disappointment there was no information on the back, apart from the photographer's mark: 'Max Warkofski, Society Photographer' it read, and there was an address underneath.

Kitty turned the shot right-side up again. She looked hopefully at the groom's outfit, but her stomach dropped with disappointment when she saw he was not wearing the wedding suit that Hester had given her. So who were these two?

The bride was beautiful, and apparently quite comfortable in front of the camera, to judge by her tilted head and smile. Even her pose was quite artful, with her back held straight but her shoulders turned slightly away to flatter the neckline of the dress.

The groom appeared far more fazed. His pose was wooden and his expression nothing more than a blank stare. Even so, it was easy to see that he must have been a good-looking man.

'Who, Kitty, who?'

'Look at your birthright, dearest. Discover your past.'

Kitty shuddered suddenly. The room felt cold. She hadn't noticed before. She considered taking the pictures but felt she would be grave-robbing. If her father had put them there then that was where he must have wanted them. Placing them carefully back onto the table she pulled her coat about her shoulders and picked up the phone to call for a taxi.

CHAPTER FOURTEEN

ZG

LONDON 1889

BROADCLOTH
The original broadcloth was a fine woollen fabric, cut
wider than most other cloths so that it could be used
for the voluminous shirts that were once the fashion.
It is also the name of close-weave woollen suiting,
which has a smooth, lustrous nap.

Kitty,

The old lady at the hostel is Mrs Sourdean, known as
'Queer Tess' because of the severe squint she has in one
eye. She is the cleaner of this shelter where I am arrived,
though she takes me through to the superintendent with
an air that would imply she is the owner of the place.

I am told I can stay here fourteen days, though most
residents will leave before that time. They will help trace
relatives, though when I tell them I am bound for America
they say they cannot search outside the capital unless I
have an address, which of course I do not. I am informed
I should leave my money with the superintendent and when
I say I have none a nought is penned into a large ledger
and I am led away to a bath, instead.

'You should give him your dosh,' Queer Tess tells me.

'It could be stolen otherwise. You can trust the staff here, you know.' Her speech is an odd mixture of English and Yiddish.

My clothes are taken away to be disinfected and I am left with just my case, which I will not allow out of my sight. When my garments are returned their smell makes me cough and my skin begins to itch. By the time I am led down into the dining hall I am all but famished, though cough and retch too much to eat all but a few meagre mouthfuls. We sit in rows at long tables and there is much talking and laughter, which surprises me, for I had thought all the women would be wretched and miserable creatures like myself.

My bed is on the top floor of the ancient building, in a dormitory so overcrowded that it has hammocks slung between the rows of small metal beds. I take off my clothes, folding them into a pile and buckling my belt around them to keep them together in one package with my case. I then sleep in my underwear and boots, tying the end of the belt to my wrist and pulling the scratchy grey blanket provided above my head to drown out the noise, for the women are still talking. I hear them laughing at my security arrangements.

Someone lays a hand on my shoulder and says, quite kindly, '*Schwer und bitter ist das Leben.*' Hard and bitter is life. My mother's lament, and that of many Jewish women before her. I remain beneath my little blanket for I do not want the shame of being caught crying. The room becomes quieter. Then one of the women begins to sing. Her voice is unexpectedly beautiful, and all the more so in contrast to the ugliness of our surroundings. It flies and soars around the room like a trapped bird. The song she sings is an old one from my home town. How I miss Papa and the clean whiteness of the snow and the warmth of Bubba's old room when all the family were there!

I have been in this country for several hours now but I still do not have a plan formed in my mind! How to get to America when I have neither money nor friends? How will I live once fourteen days have passed in this place? I try to think but once again my wits let me down and I am soon asleep.

I wake before dawn, my stomach groaning with hunger. Few of the women are stirring and some still snore. I dress in the dark, nose running and arms and legs shivering with the cold, and tip-toe downstairs to the communal privy in the yard. Queer Tess is about and rattling her buckets loud enough to raise the dead.

'Up to take a stroll in the morning air?' she asks. I believe she thinks I am a little too grand for my situation.

'You're early, too,' I tell her.

'We're toshers,' she says. 'Toshers always rise before everyone else. That way we don't have to see the looks on their faces when we set about our work.'

'Toshers?' I ask.

She places her hands on her enormous hips and I believe she stares at me, though her squint is so severe it is difficult to tell the precise direction of her gaze. I notice that she has only one tooth in her head. She is not altogether a pleasant sight.

'Toshers are professional men,' she smiles proudly. 'You want to see a tosher going about his business? Run for your coat then, angel, you're about to get your first sight of a London tradesman going about his honest day's trade.'

Despite her size, Tess can move at quite a rate and I am forced into a trot to keep up with her, which is difficult on an empty stomach. Fortunately we are only round a couple of corners before she stops, panting.

'Caught them,' she says with some relief, 'I thought we might be too late.'

In front of us, down the narrow alley and pitched into strange silhouette by the first glint of the sun, are a thin, ragged-looking man and four young boys – very similar in height and shape to the boys who stoned me in the street. I can make out little of their appearance as they are mere shapes in the gloom, but assume from Tess's tone that this is her husband and sons.

It seems the mother is sole treasurer of the Sourdean family blubber, for her sons are as lean as Tess is fat. In the guttering light the boys appear as sticks clad in rags, though I am impressed at the relative speed and grace of their movements as they teem about a spot on the gleaming cobbles. When they sense our presence they spring up like hares, looking as alarmed at my appearance as I do at theirs.

'Don't worry,' Tess tells me, 'they're toshers. They don't know how to speak to decent folk.'

She waves to her husband and the man nods back. Even from this distance I am assailed by a stench so potent that it makes my poor stomach contract again with nausea. I pinch my nose with my fingers and Tess laughs.

'Sweet, isn't it?' she asks.

Her clan re-groups around the spot in the road. The smell intensifies, and becomes so unbearable that I heave and retch like a spewing cat. There is a scraping of metal and suddenly the boys vanish into the ground, one at a time.

Tess laughs at the astonishment on my face. 'They work down the sewers,' she says. 'They go down at dawn and come up after dusk. We make our living off things people lose down there – buttons, rags, the odd piece of jewellery if you're lucky.'

The smell is so foul that, now I have the cause of it in my mind too, I have to walk away. This seems to amuse Queer Tess for some reason.

'Do they make much money?' I ask through my hands, when I have voice to speak again, and this convulses her. Her laughter echoes horribly as we make our way up the narrow alleys that lead back to the shelter.

'Tess,' I say, once she is quieter, 'it's money that I need if I am to get out of this place. How can I make some? Where can I earn the fare to get to America?'

'You're plain, but not ugly,' she tells me. 'You could earn quite a bit as a bride.' She is walking slowly now, having used up all her breath on her laughing.

'A bride?' I say. 'But I already have a fiancé waiting for me in America.'

Tess is chuckling again. 'Oh, I don't think the sailors will mind that much, angel,' she says, 'most brides are long married. The punters aren't that fussy, you know.'

I would ask her what she means, for either her Yiddish is poorer than I thought or she has ceased talking sense. Then I begin to wonder if she is a little deranged, as her laughter has an hysterical ring to it, and I decide merely to smile and nod agreement politely.

That evening I approach a group of rather more kindly-looking women in the shelter and ask them how one can become wealthy in this city. Like Queer Tess they appear amused by my question. Eventually one woman – a tall, bony-looking peasant from the east of my country – tells me that the most money to be made locally is from one of the three Jewish trades: shoe-making, cabinet-making or tailoring.

One of the wealthiest men around is Israel Bloom, she tells me. This gentleman has a business in the Commercial Road and a sweatshop employing sixty souls in Fieldgate Street, off Whitechapel. Bloom's is known best for its coat manufacture.

'It sells to large retail outlets in the West End,' one woman tells me. Her uncle is an employee of Israel Bloom and she will be working for him herself once her family come for her.

I am both excited and peeved by this information. Excited, because this is the very business I carry some skill in, and peeved because I remember Baile telling me her relations in London were engaged in the same occupation.

The women seem pleasant enough and the conversation continues.

'What is a greener?' I ask them, remembering my conversations with Queer Tess.

'It's the name they give immigrants when we first arrive,' one woman explains. She pulls a face, as though the word is an insult.

'And how may I earn money as a bride?' I ask. This time

all their expressions change at once. They rise together, clutching their knitting to their chests, and I find myself abandoned yet again.

'And we thought you were a good girl, from a nice Russian family,' one of them whispers as she takes her leave.

It is Friday evening – tomorrow will be Sabbath. I walk a little way from the shelter, hoping to chance upon Fieldgate Street and see Israel Bloom's vast empire for myself. I have it into my head that I too can make money in this trade.

I remember how we used to live in Russia before we were banished to The Pale of Settlement. We too were wealthy. Papa and Rintzi lived well – Rintzi reminded me of this many times.

'We dressed you in finest furs, little Rosa,' she would say. 'Other wives and mothers would stop to stare in the street when we walked by. You looked so enchanting, you were spoilt by everyone.' The fur must have covered my rabbit's ears for anyone with half a wit to be so impressed by my poor face.

My ramble takes me up Angel Alley and along Fashion Street to a wider road, called Brick Lane. The small strip of sky overhead turns indigo at dusk but there are people everywhere, so I have no need to feel afraid. I scurry past houses so grey with crumbling filth that they could barely be described as shelter, yet outside each one of these dwellings is placed a chair made of rusted iron or splintered wood, and upon each chair sits a character so advanced in years you would think them already dead and awaiting removal by the funeral cart.

These folk have the look of farmers or peasants from

my childhood. Amid the clatter of Yiddish I hear Russian and Polish words used. I see chickens peck around their feet and peas and beans growing from boxes on their windowsills.

My legs begin to ache. The whole world appears to be covered with a layer of grime, yet everywhere there are yellow candles flickering in parlour windows to see in the Sabbath. I smell butter and honeycakes above the bitter aromas of soot and burning coal, and my stomach growls when it thinks of the *challah* bread that will be eaten during the sacred meal that night.

Somehow I reach Fieldgate Street and wander the length of it, looking for signs of great wealth and hope. Eventually, when I have all but given up my search, I notice a gloomy doorway and a faded, painted sign outside that reads: 'I. BLOOM. OUTERWEAR MANUFACTURER.'

This is no empire, though. The building I stand in front of is large but not huge. Its black bricks look as sturdy as cake-crumbs. The only windows are small, high and barred, and as impenetrable with filth as the walls themselves. The place is still there today if you look, Kitty. Is this how wealth appears in this country? I think of the vast ivory mansions and palaces of my birthplace and the sugary stucco townhouse we inhabited before we left for the *shtetle*. How clean things were there!

Hunched with depression I stare shrewdly at the place. The doors part and a group of whey-faced workers spew out, smelling sour as vinegar from the oil they use on their machines. I place myself in their path.

'Are there jobs in this place?' I ask. One of the men looks at me and spits onto the ground.

'Greener,' he says, speaking in English.

I try my Yiddish on the others, but none of them appears to understand. Alarmed by their aggressive expressions, though, I walk away at speed.

The streets are becoming quieter and I yearn for the protection of the shelter. Attempting to retrace my steps I become momentarily lost in a maze of streets and, by the time I reach Leman Street I am in a welter of terror and sick with relief.

A small band of well-dressed women waits outside the hostel. Nearly fainting with exhaustion, I take the gloved hand one of them offers me and she holds my arm to steady me while the others all smile and click their tongues.

'Are you hungry, my dear?' one of them asks in faltering Yiddish.

I nod and she hands me some bread.

'Do you need money?' asks another. I wonder if I am dreaming, or whether these women are angels, come to escort me to Papa.

Nodding again, I hold out my hand, but it appears that no coins are forthcoming.

'You will receive both money and succour as soon as you convert,' the eldest woman tells me. She has such a pleasant face and her coat, though ill-fitting, has been well crafted from emerald velvet.

'Money to get me to America?' I ask. They look at one another before resuming their smiles.

'You are in England now, my dear,' the first one tells me, 'all we ask is that you become Anglicized.'

I smile politely enough, though I have no idea what it is they are talking about.

'You will find us in Bethnal Green,' the older woman says, handing me a pamphlet. 'If you want good kosher food and money for yourself then come for conversion and let us save your soul.'

At that moment two of the women from my dormitory walk past us on their way into the shelter. Seeing me caught in conversation they push me – rather rudely, I consider – in through the doorway before I can even take my leave.

'Taking the penny for conversion now, are you?' one of them asks me when we are inside. I now conclude I am more unpopular than before with my fellow inmates, and not through any doing of my own.

Regardless of this, on the Sabbath I fall in with the other women from the shelter and we walk in a large noisy group to Brick Lane, to the Great Synagogue. The building is packed with worshippers. To my enormous humiliation and to the deep embarrassment of the other women I find myself shaking throughout the entire service.

On the way back to the hostel the women walk quickly and in silence, afraid, it seems, of the very shadows themselves. As the street widens I look up and the grey smog parts a little and all at once I see the stars – the same stars that twinkled overhead when I walked in the snow in Russia. I am still Rosa, then, and must be like those stars – unchangeable. My courage returning, I walk to the front of the timid little group and march ahead, quoting an old Jewish prayer. This brings gasps from the women and some would try to keep me quiet, though a strange-looking girl I have heard is called Hannah comes up to join me both in step and in prayer, and I am pleased to

157

hear her voice is more pleasant than my own, which sounds like a saw against tree-bark.

We are no further than maybe a hundred paces before a stone hits the side of my face and I know from Hannah's scream that she has been struck too. I turn, expecting the same ragged group that greeted me on my arrival to this country, but instead find a crowd of women, each one with a face more ghastly than the next. To my horror one of the ugliest walks straight up to poor little Hannah and butts her square in the head.

'Jew!' the woman screeches at me. I find myself laughing into her face. We stare full-on and I see a pink circle on her forehead where she butted Hannah like a goat.

'Tosher!' I shout to her in English, and I pinch my nose with my fingers as though I can smell the sewer about her. Who would have imagined that one of my first words in the new language would be such a fine insult to hold me in such stead?

There is an expression of eruption behind the woman's eyes and her cheeks begin to wobble.

'Tosher,' I repeat, making as if to retch. This is splendid. For a moment I feel more like my old self again. I laugh delightedly as the woman backs away in shock and shame. Clearly no whey-faced Jew has dared to stand her ground before.

Helping Hannah to her feet, I pull my group on and we join hands, and this time they all walk together.

What a line we make as we march back to the shelter! At last I am Rosa the heroine, rather than Rosa the tearful cry-baby. All will be well now, I know it.

When I lie in my bed one of the women places a second

blanket over me, patting the edges in like a mother would do to a small child. This brings the hated tears back into my eyes, but I manage to squeeze them back in, which makes me very proud.

CHAPTER FIFTEEN

ZG

BUSK

In the late-nineteenth century, long, knife-shaped strips of whalebone or shell were inserted into corsets or stays to give women the S-bend silhouette shape that was popular at the time. In 1881 the Rational Dress Society was founded, in a bid to resist these fashions which restricted or deformed the body. Via its mouthpiece, the Gazette, *the RDS advocated boneless stays and the wearing of no more than seven pounds of underwear, and made a stand against the fashion for high heels.*

Kitty,

My life has much improved. I have now left the shelter for another establishment in the Mile End Road called the Young Jewish Girls' Association. I must say that this place is still not the sort of home Papa would have wished to see me inhabiting, but it is eminently more suitable than Leman Street, and the twenty or so inmates much younger and less likely to be caught dribbling over their broth-bowls at night. I am told this place is for friendless but respectable foreign girls. The building leaves much to be desired but in two weeks we will be re-housed in new premises in

Tenter Street, Aldgate, which sounds prettier to my ears than Mile End.

The regime here is strict, and the place run by a matron who has more pairs of eyes in her head than a floor-bug, but I am not in the least sorry to have left the shelter. I had thought Queer Tess befriended me out of pity, but was told by a fellow inmate of the establishment that the old witch had found me, 'a strange sort, and a great deal too full of myself, too'. She had been using the story of my visit to her verminous family to amuse the other women of an evening.

At the Girls' Association we are kept clean and taught to speak in English. I am given a navy pinafore to wear, made of simple serge that holds its dye so poorly that a single boil reduces it to a fade. I notice this immediately and send mine to be washed, which at least reduces the smell and stiffness of the fabric. When the others undress at night I notice the dye has left dark stains on their underclothes.

I have decided I must track down Baile. She told me she had an uncle who owned a high-class dressmaker's, and much as it galls me to beg from her I feel I must find a job if I am to save up the fare for New York. Besides, she owes me this at least, as it is her brother whom I have to thank for my current predicament.

I remember how much Baile spoke about the wealth and class of her English relatives. They own vast factories that would make Bloom's sweatshop look like a cottage by comparison. If Baile is already married there may be no need for me to see her at all. Perhaps I could beg a job or some money from her family and be on my way before she pays a visit. Maybe they will be so full of shame when I relate how much was stolen from me by Baile's precious brother they will reimburse me immediately. I am so full of hope at this thought that my hands shake. In a few weeks I could be away from this grey place and on a boat bound for America.

I take to roaming the streets in search of the Kluchersky name above a manufacturer's doorway. The weather is improved now, although the sun does little to penetrate the gloom of the streets. I am so determined to be of an optimistic nature, though, that the minute it appears I run to where I can feel its pale heat upon my cheek. There are small patches of clear ground in this city, surrounded by metal railings and laid to unhealthy, patchy grass. I spend some time in one of these areas, along with many other local residents. We sit on painted wooden benches and turn our grateful faces to the sun.

Eventually, after several exhausting days' search, I am forced to lie to the benefactors of the home and claim Baile as a long-lost relative, in the hope that they will discover her for me.

There is no news for several days. Then the matron presents me with an envelope containing a list of families with the name 'Kluchersky' and their addresses. I devour the list greedily, though there appears to be no way of telling if any have a young greener called Baile, just arrived in this country.

None of the addresses is commercial and only three of them are in London. With closed eyes I place a pin in the page and allow it to pick out the right address for me. This was Rintzi's way of bringing luck wherever a choice was to be involved.

My mother's luck has followed me. The house, when I find it, is home to Baile's uncle and his family. Far from being the mansion I had imagined, though, the place is a small room in a tenement block near the Mile End Road. Any joy I might have felt at discovering the very place I have searched for so close to my own doorstep evaporates at the sight of it.

I am viewed warily and not invited to cross the threshold, though behind Baile's aunt's skirts I espy a dull-looking room that I could hardly describe as clean. When I ask about her niece's whereabouts I am directed to a factory less than a mile from the tenements.

The walk is easy enough, for I have a good memory for streets and am beginning to know the area well. When I reach the factory, though, the shock I feel on viewing it leaves me weak and exhausted.

The place is an eighth of the size of Bloom's – a tiny sweatshop on the fifth floor of a grimy warehouse near the docks. Can it really be owned by relatives of the wondrous Baile? If so she will never have graced the premises with her presence for fear of grubbying her expensive kid gloves.

When I push through the painted double doors I am immediately assailed by nostalgic smells – so much so that I am forced to steady myself on the wall and close my eyes to recover. The heat in the room is unbearable, and so is the smell of labouring flesh. To most visitors the stench would be overpowering, but my nose has been trained to seek out sweeter scents. There is cheap, rough fabric here, but quality cloths, too.

The room is less than twelve paces in length and six in

width. Its walls are barely visible, hung as they are with brown paper patterns of all shapes and fit, strung on large metal hooks of the type used by butchers to hang a carcass. What wall can be seen consists of fetid and stained plaster, crumbling with damp and filth and covered in parts with peeling, dark-green paint.

In the centre of this room are six seamstresses, two working on sewing machines that create so much noise as to render any attempt at speech worthless, and the other four working by hand, their backs bent so low that their faces are hidden.

A tailor in a dark jacket and skull-cap sits cross-legged on a high stool, sewing buttons with a long thread, and beside him the finisher and steamers with their press irons are lost in a haze of scorching steam.

Behind this cloud I catch glimpses of a small and very elderly cutter unrolling a bale of dull-looking fabric on a long wooden table. There are blocks and dummies behind him and behind them a small mountain of cloth waste and off-cuts.

There is no floor in this place, just a carpet of fluff and dust. The only light comes from hissing gas mantles on the walls as the only window is too covered with grime to allow natural light to penetrate. At a desk near the door sits a young Jewish boy, smoking a pipe that adds to the fetid air and scratching into a ledger with a quill pen.

Beneath his desk I spot pelts of finer quality flannel, some light China silk linings and some woollen broadcloth dyed for gentlemen's suits. Above him hangs strips and rolls of Petersham ribbon and Russian braid for trimmings. Near my elbow as I turn is a rickety table upon which lie a sleeve-board and a tailor's ham for pressing darts. My father had these things in his own workroom. His were clean but these are so shabby the fabric is worn right through. Nevertheless, I remove my glove and reach to touch them, for they remind me so of home.

My movement disturbs the boy, who looks up at me through the thickest spectacles I have ever seen.

'My name is Bertha Cecilia Zigofsky,' I tell him. 'I am the daughter of Zigofsky the Master Tailor from Moscow. I am an acquaintance of Baile Kluchersky, whose family own this business. I have come here for a job. I need temporary employment.'

The boy's laughter rings cruelly in my ears. I consider shouting at him for his rudeness, but then notice that he is pointing down the workroom. I look in the direction of his finger and see one of the pressers peering in our direction.

'Israel!' the boy calls with some mirth. 'Israel Kluchersky! You forgot to tell us this is your business, you old rogue! Why did you keep us in the dark all this time? Eh? Did you think we'd be after your money if you admitted to such wealth? Eh? Now we have another greener here from the old country, keen to cash in on the Kluchersky fortune. What did you say your name was, miss?'

'Bertha,' I tell him, confused, 'Bertha Zigofsky.'

'Miss Zigofsky is here for an appointment, sir,' the boy yells across to the old presser. 'Shall I tell her to wait?'

The old man waves his hands about in agitation and shakes his head many times in apparent confusion.

'He works here too?' I ask, equally confused.

'Oh yes,' the boy says, exploding into laughter again.

'Oh you could say Israel's job is his life. He even sleeps right here in the workroom, along with his employees, did you know that?'

'Stop it!' I hear a woman's voice shout above the racket of the machines. One of the sewers is standing up.

'Baile?' I cannot believe it is the same girl I left at the docks. Baile is either heavier or her posture is no longer upright enough to give shape to her figure. Her hair is concealed beneath a scarf and her face looks grimy.

'Baile?' I repeat. 'You work here in the family sweat-shop?' I had no idea she could even thread a needle. When I look down at her hands she is quick to conceal them behind her back, but not before I notice that they are stained with dye and dotted with pin-pricks.

Suddenly I feel sorry for the girl. She arrived in London to stay with wealthy relatives, only to discover Israel Kluch-ersky is mean enough to sleep on his own workroom floor. No wonder she has been enlisted to graft here, too. What a shock it must have been! I almost join in with the boy's unsuppressed laughter.

Baile hurries down past the sewing machines, tucking stray hair into her scarf as she does so. 'What are you doing here, Rosa?' she asks, angrily.

'Baile,' I begin, 'I am stranded here in London. Your brother took my money and then bought the wrong ticket. I need a job to earn money to get to America. It is the least your family can do for me.'

'Menachem is dead,' Baile said, her face pinched into a frown. 'The guards killed him. That is why he never got on the ship. You shouldn't speak so of him any more, Rosa. You have no right.'

'I have a right to my money,' I tell her, for I doubt Menachem is anywhere other than a smart town in Russia, with a decent house to live in and a full belly. 'But I'll earn it, Baile. Tell your family to give me a job. Please. I'm desperate.'

Baile's face puckers further.

'You're standing here on paid time, Miss Kluchersky,' the boy tells her, 'there will be no breaks for the privy this afternoon now.'

I see fear cross Baile's face and it is then that the true extent of my own stupidity begins to occur to me.

'This place isn't owned by your family, is it?' I ask her. Her head drops. I would have paid to see such shame on her face while we were travelling together, but in my present predicament it brings me dread, rather than pleasure.

'My uncle Israel works here, Rabbit,' she tells me, 'we don't own it. I didn't think you'd find out. I'm working here until I am married, then it will all be over. This is just temporary, just to pay my uncle back for my keep.'

'But you sleep on the floor!' I tell her.

She shakes her head. 'No, Rabbit, we sleep on benches. It's not so bad.' But there are tears in her eyes, nevertheless.

I look about, feeling sick. 'I still need a job,' I tell the boy. Baile's head pops up again in surprise.

'No more greeners,' the boy replies, grinning. 'Jobs are to go to locals or those who have lived here one generation or more. Didn't you hear about the *Judenhetz*? The natives are getting upset, Miss Zigofsky. Do you want pogroms here too, eh?'

I match his gaze. 'I need a job,' I say.

He looks across at Baile. She tosses her head and I see

something of the old haughtiness there. I also see that the boy has an eye for her.

'Can you sew?' he asks me.

'Better than her,' I answer. 'Didn't you hear? My father was a master tailor. He taught me all he knew. Tell him, Baile.'

Baile nods, quickly.

'Can you operate a Singer?' the boy asks.

'Of course,' I lie. What can be so difficult about a machine like that?

'We can only take you on as a general hand,' he says. I know enough from listening to other girls in my hostel to know what this means. 'That's the lowest grade,' I tell him, 'I'm skilled.'

He laughs again. 'Israel has slept on these floors for twenty-two years and has only achieved middle grade,' he says. 'Look at him work – do you think you could do better?' Israel's hands move so quickly across the cloth they are almost rendered invisible. Even my father could not work with such speed. I shake my head reluctantly.

The boy slaps the top of his ledger. 'Agreed, then,' he says. 'You work from five in the morning until midnight for six days a week. Sabbath is, of course, your day off. You will be paid fourteen shillings and sixpence a week plus tea. There will be one break per day for use of the latrine – any others will be deducted from your wages. You may sleep on the floor of the workroom at night if you wish and if you want to purloin a bench for sleeping on you must negotiate with the other workers. I must warn you there are vermin on the floor at night though, Miss Zigofsky.'

168

I do not give him the satisfaction of watching my expression change as he gives me this news.

'Agreed?' he asks.

'Agreed,' I say, 'but I have no need of lodgings, tempting though they may sound.'

I estimate that it will take me three years to save the money for my journey to America. This is sad news, for I doubt Aaron will wait that long for me. I will need to be resourceful. On the way back to the hostel I take myself off to the Christian Society in Bethnal Green. Here I give a false name and tell the smiling woman at the entrance that I wish to convert to the Evangelical faith. The woman, a buxom grandmother who should know better, falls to her knees in front of me, raising her eyes heavenward and clasping her plump hands in prayer.

I am given a plate of kosher food for my pains, which is good enough to be sold to some of the fatter girls back at the hostel. After joining in prayers that I do not understand I am asked if I will agree to be baptised. When I inform them it is my dearest wish I am presented with a few coins, which I quickly secrete into my hankie with much relief.

As I leave the establishment I ask the woman if she works on conversions every evening. To my delight she says she does not. With any luck there will be a different grandmother there every night, and all with the same problems of deafness and short sight. My baptism could take a long time at such a rate, while my purse will become fuller.

CHAPTER SIXTEEN

ZG

THE SWEATS

*In 1888 there were one thousand and fifteen tailoring
workshops in Whitechapel alone. Many immigrants
who could not get work in the sweatshops became
costers, getting stalls and selling whatever they could.
'Greeners' found it hard to get work from the
Gentiles, who often had a 'Britons first' policy to
employment, while the long-settled Jews in the area
could also be harsh in their criticism of the new-
comers. Wages in tailoring, which had held at around
two pounds a week, began to fall to one pound and
lower as the steady influx increased.*

Kitty,

I ache from the effort of so much work, and my only
pleasure is in seeing precious Baile toiling just as hard,
even though she is less suited, having had no experience
of labour in Russia. I write to Aaron each night, then send
all the notes once a week, for that is all the postage I can
afford. As I have no address for him in America I am forced
to send my packages via his mother, in the hope that she
will pass them on for me. I must let Aaron know he should
wait for me. If he believes me to be lost he could marry
another. I have written some of my letters to him in English,

to show how well I will do when I am finally in America.

I have also been in regular contact with my mother, but as yet have received no reply, either. Papa would have written. Papa would have been direct on the boat to collect me and save me from my predicament. Rintzi has neither the wit nor the money. I pray that both she and my darling brother Gregory are safe and not killed as Papa was. I force myself to cease these thoughts. Self-pity is difficult enough, but if I begin to worry for my family too I shall be mad within the month.

I tell myself all is well. Rintzi is not a natural at putting pen to paper. If anything were wrong I would know. Comforted by these and many such ideas I am left free to worry about no one save myself.

In the meantime I have fallen into a passion, though I would not admit it if my eyes were gouged out and my tongue split in two. Richard Galliard is part-owner of the business that now employs me, and the handsomest man I have seen in my entire life. Is that a wicked thing to say, when I am promised to Aaron? I think not, for I am sure Richard would be admired by any woman, whether married, betrothed or a lonely old maid.

He visits the premises once a week and the day has become the highlight of my time here. His manners are those of a gentleman and his clothes are the finest I have seen in this country. I have noticed him in three different suits so far, and each has surpassed the last in cut and finish, though all were subtle enough to imply no hint of vanity in their design.

He is tall – though not too tall – with fine auburn hair and moustache. It is his eyes, though, that I believe to be his finest feature. In a country where I have seen only need, greed, or blankness in people's eyes, Richard's hold an expression of intelligence and pride.

I have seen Baile blush when he arrives in the workroom, so suppose that she, too, is fascinated by this man. When he arrives we are all to work as though our lives depended upon it, which is what we do anyway, though to keep the bosses happy we make a special show. It is difficult to watch Richard Galliard with my head bent so low over my work, so I have borrowed a small vanity mirror from one of the girls at the hostel and keep this beneath the garments on my bench, just in case. Through this I can watch him without appearing to stop work. Baile sees what I am about and seethes with jealousy at my cleverness.

I wonder he can bear to stand in this workroom at all, for the place is so fetid and airless, yet he gazes about politely, for all the world as though he were breathing the country air. There is something about him that reminds me of Gregory and I see for a moment how my brother might have looked had he kept all his wits and become a man.

I know there is no sense to be made of these emotions that I suffer, for I am to marry Aaron. However, there are moments now when I am reminded that Baile and I are little more than children ourselves, so what is in some harmless fun?

A hair fell from Richard Galliard's head as he passed my table and I have it kept in my purse. This annoys Baile so intensely that it gives me enormous pleasure to wave it in front of her nose. However much she

172

tosses her head, I know she would kill to own that hair herself.

Through constant persistence Baile and I have forced Uncle Israel to tell us some of Richard's history. Born to a French father and German mother, both of whom began life wealthy but died half-starved and persecuted somewhere in Europe, Richard spent some time in the army before arriving in London, disembarking at the very same docks that Baile and I passed through. It was there that Richard encountered Turgis Fasukinos, the Lithuanian Jew who shares this business with him. Richard was keen to invest in a concern and saw in Turgis the skill and knowledge he himself lacked.

Richard had money, smuggled from his homeland by his father. Turgis had many years' experience in the clothing trade in Lithuania and was delighted to have bumped into the very man to back his ideas for a venture in England. In ten years they have built up a going concern, with three workshops in the East End and a high-quality salon in a better part of London.

While Turgis cracks the whip in the sweatshops Richard uses his charm and manners to woo high-class clients in the West End. While Turgis has spent his ten years in this country expanding his family along with his business, Richard is yet unmarried.

Baile and I listen to all this like children hearing a fairy story. There is meat on the bare bones now. Baile hates me for my interest in the man she considers her own infatuation, I can see this in her eyes. To enrage her further I tell little lies, informing her I met him on the steps on the way into the factory one morning and that he tipped his hat

173

and smiled. Or that the boy on the desk has told me that Richard asked him for my name. I know Baile doubts these stories, but they make her pink with rage nevertheless.

The new hostel is colder than the old but smarter too, and I am sad to know that my time here is limited, for there are many other girls in search of accommodation in much worse plights than my own. Matron knows I have employment and the offer of a place to sleep. I wonder how long it will be before I am asked to leave.

There is a great commotion one morning at the hostel. Matron comes running to me after much loud conversation in the doorway and informs me that I have a visitor. I can tell from her expression and the way she waits with folded arms that my visitor is a man.

'He says he is your cousin,' she tells me. I read doubt in her eyes and she must read doubt in my own, for I have no cousin in London.

It is Max Warkofski, the know-all young man from the boat, who waits in the porch of the building, with his hat in his hand and a look of perfect innocence on his face.

'Cousin Rosa!' he cries when I approach, and I can tell this is for the benefit of the matron who stands less than four paces behind us.

In my surprise I am rendered speechless for once.

As Max moves closer to grasp my hand he whispers, 'Tell me the address of the place where you work.' I shake his hand solemnly and mouth the address back to him, though I don't know why, for I have no great desire to see him again, as his arrogance annoys me. He has come looking for Baile, I am sure of it.

We hold a stilted conversation, during which he informs me for the matron's benefit that my aunt has been searching for me some ten weeks and will be delighted that I have now been traced.

I leave for work earlier than normal and find Max waiting, as expected, in the dark outside the factory, his hands stuffed into his pockets and looking for all the world like the rogue that he is. We walk around the corner to a crowded immigrant tea stall in Garden Street and he treats me to the best brew I have tasted since leaving home.

'So!' he says. 'Little Rosa!' His clothes are clean and smart but less expensive than those I saw on the boat. He may have lost a little weight, too, though the expression of constant amusement still burns bright in his eyes. I believe he thinks of me as sport. Perhaps he is bored in London and found himself in need of someone to tease. At any rate, I am full of suspicion that his circumstances may be no better than my own, despite his devil-may-care air. His shoes alone give hint to that, with their scuffed uppers and worn heels.

'You may have talked me out of my place at the hostel, Max,' I tell him, which only makes his smile widen.

'Excellent!' he replies. 'That flea-home is for the poor.'

'Which is exactly what I have now become!' I inform him. His smile still holds in place. Is there nothing that will remove this grin?

'And is that factory the place where you poor folk scratch a living?' he asks.

'It is certainly where we scratch for fleas!' I say, for his good humour is unfortunately infectious and I have started to laugh.

175

Perhaps there is a limit to the amount of misery a young girl can carry on her shoulders. I know I am tired of my own grief. Laughter feels good on my cheeks and in my belly. I laugh some more and Max roars with me. It feels good to be silly and girlish again.

'It's the way you view the world, young Rosa,' Max tells me, tapping me with his finger to make his point. 'Anyone can be happy if they set their mind to it. It's the way you perceive your own circumstances that counts.'

'I'd like to see you be happily employed as a pure-finder!' I tell him. These poor souls spend their time collecting dog-dirt from the London streets, for use in shoe polish. I could not imagine employment worse than that of Queer Tess's brood until I watched these unfortunates at work.

'Oh, I don't know, Rosa,' Max tells me, 'the hours aren't bad and you're in the open air. I daresay you'd like a view of the sky now and again. And maybe you could become something of an expert on the product and grow to enjoy the job . . .'

I stop him before I begin to feel ill.

When our laughter ends Max asks me the question I know he has been saving. 'Do you see anything of Baile at all?'

So that was his purpose in tracking me down. I shrug. 'I suppose I see as much as I need, as she sits at my elbow most of the day, feeding fabric into my machine.'

Max looks surprised. 'Then you'll give her my regards?' he asks.

I nod and finish my tea. 'I have to be at work,' I say. I have had enough of acting as his matchmaker.

Max grabs my arm to halt me. 'You haven't heard my offer yet, Rosa,' he says.

'Offer?'

'I can't bear to see you living off charity,' he says. 'I thought you were set for America. I was surprised to find your name listed at the Temporary Shelter. I went there looking for a young nephew who never arrived and saw your name as I went through the records.'

I turn away a bit at this. 'Baile's brother sold me the wrong ticket,' I say in a low voice, 'I'm reliant on charity only until I can afford my fare to America.'

Max taps me on the head with his glove. 'I have my own business now, Rosa,' he says. 'I've set up as a society photographer with prospects. My place is in Brick Lane, but not the mean end, you know. I find I have room to spare there. How would you like to rent space so that you can live within independent means again and maybe turn your luck with your employment? What about being your own boss, Rosa? You must be tired of slaving under this roof for your penny.'

I am caught by the brilliance of his eyes. Max is a great magician with his words – all sounds easy when uttered by him. He has me in his thrall and for a moment I feel my heart take a squeeze of excitement. So he is successful after all. I was wrong in my rather hasty assessment of him. I blush with guilt.

'How should I afford rent?' I ask him, with a deliberately bashful expression. 'All my money saved is for my fare.'

Max strokes his chin and I can see he is fooling with me again.

'Suppose we set rent so low even your little purse could accommodate the cost, and then chalk up the rest to be paid back when you're rich and famous, as I know you shall be one day?' he says.

'And why should I ever be wealthy?' I ask. I am thinking of my father's words – 'Never be poor, Rosa, and never grow old.' How quickly did I let him down!

Max looks into my eyes. 'Because you have a good brain and you have chutzpah, Rosa,' he says, 'and I've yet to meet the man or woman with both intelligence and boldness whom God did not eventually reward.'

He smiles. 'Will you think about my offer?' he asks.

In an impulse I nod before taking my leave and rushing off to my meagre employment. Thank God I am to be saved from this life at last! Max is my rescuer and in my eyes that makes him above reproach. In an instant I forget his arrogance and idiotic attempts at what he must consider a 'lady-killing' smile, and concentrate instead on his generosity and his business acumen. I write to Rintzi that night to inform her how my luck has changed, and that I am going up in the world at last.

CHAPTER SEVENTEEN

ZG

1998

BAGHEERA
*This uncut pile velvet was once popular for evening
gowns. A fine-textured fabric, it became less fashionable in the later part of the twentieth century,
although imitation bagheera is now made from
rayon crepe.*

The wedding suit lay untouched beneath Kitty's bed, which
was where Freddy first found it.

Freddy's upbringing may have stinted a little on taste, but
could never be found wanting when it came to manners. He
neither touched the case nor asked directly about it.

'You know you have what appears to be an extremely
aged box beneath your bed and that it is shedding rust
onto the floor-tiles?' was all he said. Kitty changed from
being semi-slack and calm to defensive and emotional in
an instant. So quickly, in fact, that Freddy would have
liked to have *seen* the transition as well as *heard* it. If he
had watched Lon Chaney morph into the wolf-man on
video and then run the whole event on fast-forward it
would have had a similar effect.

Unfortunately he had been hanging upside-down over the rim of the mattress, searching for his glasses at the time, so he saw the case but not Kitty's expression when he raised the subject. By the time he had righted himself she was almost cross-eyed with stress.

'What? What's up?' he asked.

'Nothing.' But she could control neither her tone nor her eyes.

'Hey, hey hey!' Freddy said. He was both young and old: twenty-four going on six when there was a stupid joke around, and fifty when it came down to observing mood fluctuations, which was very unnerving.

'Hey what?' Kitty reached for the TV remote control.

'This isn't you, Kit,' he said, 'not you at all. "Nothing." That obviously means, "Yes, something." And something quite major, at that. Isn't that classed as sulking? You never sulked before. You were never evasive before.'

Kitty sighed. A pretty sigh, not a middle-aged exhalation of hopelessness. 'It's a suit,' she said. She had spots on her face for the first time in her life. Grief spots, maybe.

'Something of an heirloom, evidently,' she added. 'You're supposed –' she checked herself, suddenly.

'I'm supposed what?' Freddy asked. When she looked up he was glancing at his watch. Ordinarily that would have annoyed her – angered her, even – but today it was okay because it meant his mind was more on a meeting than her half-hidden suit.

When he was gone she pulled it from its case. She was careful because she had been taught respect for all good garments. When she laid it out across the white bedspread it looked very much as though it was waiting to be worn. Or as though someone who was wearing it and lying sprawled had just de-materialized inside it.

She picked up the waistcoat and held it to the light. Then she pulled on her glasses and looked again. The stitches were so small and perfect she could barely believe a human hand had done them. She peered some more. Some were slightly different, small, but a little larger and less deft than the others. Not clumsy – certainly not clumsy. Still much tinier than most human fingers could execute. But different, all the same. So two people had stitched this.

She stopped. Looked away. There were words stitched in there, too. Kitty inhaled softly and bent her head again. It took a while to re-focus. It was small print, almost lost in the intricate design, in hebrew letters.

Why had she been so defensive and secretive when she saw Freddy find it? She started to chew her nails. He was supposed to wear it at their wedding. She stared at the garment. She hadn't even tried to see if the waistcoat would fit him. She lifted it carefully and held it to her own chest, then padded across to the mirror to have a look.

What wedding to Freddy?

Had she really thought that?

Of course they would be married – she just needed a little more time, that was all.

She touched the stitching. How much love had gone into that garment? Could what she and Freddy had ever match it?

The suit was like a reproach, reminding her of her history

181

and her culture but most of all setting a yardstick against which her own emotions should be measured.

She felt the dumb tears start to well again. Her father had worn the waistcoat at his own wedding, proud in the knowledge that he was carrying on the family history until he died. And now it was to stop. The business would be sold.

Kitty phoned Hester. Her mother sounded remarkably alert, almost as though she had been expecting the call. Maybe the jabs had worn off. Some of the madness had gone out of her tone.

'Is China there?' she asked. She knew already, though. She could hear kitchen noises in the background. China was as quiet as the dead in the rest of a home, but in the kitchen she became a demon, banging and crashing and whirling and washing.

'Nula says she will stay with you for a while, Kitty,' Hester told her. 'Is this a good idea?'

'I don't know, Mother,' Kitty replied. The thought of China's activity was making her feel tired. 'Look,' she said, raising her voice so Hester could hear clearly, 'about the suit, the old one you gave me . . .'

'The wedding suit,' Hester corrected her. 'You want to know what the words mean?'

Kitty paused. Was there something life had not yet told her? Was her own mother psychic?'

'It says: "Rosa, the daughter I love".' Hester hadn't waited for her reply. 'It was made by Dovid Zigofsky in Russia. He died making it, Kitty. Has Freddy seen it yet?'

'No,' Kitty told her quietly, 'he hasn't.'

* * *

182

The daughter I love. Had Dovid Zigofsky handed on his business to his daughter, too, along with his love and the wedding suit?

And had his daughter shuddered with fear at the prospect – the way Kitty was doing now?

CHAPTER EIGHTEEN

ZG

CALICO
*One of the most ancient of fabrics, calico takes its
name from Calicut, in Madras, where it was first
made. A coarse, cotton cloth, it is often used in the
trade to make up a fitting shell for a garment before
cutting the more expensive fabric.*

Kitty,

How easily am I fooled! Like Baile, Max promised a palace and yet here I am in lodgings that make the hostel look like a place of wondrous comfort!

Imagine the sinking of my heart as I stood outside the Brick Lane premises of Maxwell Warkofski, Society Photographer! Count the amount of times I read the brass wall-plate announcing this legend, all the while wondering whether I have still possibly made a mistake in my translation! Follow me into the soot-darkened doorway, through which even I am forced to stoop, and up the bare wooden banisterless stairs to the attic!

Listen to the *schlemozzle* of wailing, prayers and crying that emerges from each of the floors! It sounds as though all the Jews in the world are packed into this one small house! I smell *borscht* and *lockshen* and burning firewood, and when I touch the walls the paint feels coated in grease from all the cooking.

'Rosa!' Max has the door open before I can knock and I marvel at the fact that the shape and height of this gangling tall young man can fit into a room so small. Max *is* the room – he fills it almost entirely. I am shocked at the size of him there, suddenly, so much so that I take a step backwards before his white teeth devour me.

'Come in,' he insists, waving his arm with a flourish. It is only as he moves to one side that I see the scene in the room behind him. There is a white sheet hung from low ceiling to unclean floor and perched in the middle is a waxen-faced female clad only in a length of draped cloth.

'Miss Zigofsky,' says Max, 'meet Miss Molly d'Arboire.'

The girl rises to meet me, extending one hand while holding onto the fabric with the other.

'My name's Molly Nodd and I work as a nippy at the tearooms round the corner,' she tells me with a dimpled smile, 'but I pose for Max on me day off. He calls me d'Arboire because he says French sounds a little more classy. I don't know, though. I think he's pulling me leg. He's always pulling people's legs, did you know that, miss?'

Classy? To imagine how a man like Max would know anything about class! Richard Galliard is the one to tell you about class, breeding and business success, not Max Warkofski the conman!

Max begins to translate Molly's English, but I have understood enough to smile weakly in agreement. I look across at Max and he looks at the bags I am carrying and grins.

'So you decided to move in,' he says. I search my brains for a way out of this predicament but I have now quit the hostel and know I will be destitute if I leave this place.

Max doesn't wait for my answer in any event, but instead picks up my bag, though I am quicker than him and have hold of the case with the wedding suit before he can take it.

'Where is my room?' I ask, looking round. I hope it is not on the floor below because I heard barking dogs down there and wonder if there would be any sleep to be had.

'Here,' Max tells me, and Molly lets out a little spurting laugh.

Max moves to the end of the small room, which takes all of one pace, and tugs on a curtain that falls away from the wall. 'We use this to partition the place for now,' he says, 'then I will build us something more solid as soon as my last client pays me.'

I stare at him as though he is gone mad. 'I can't share this with you!' I say. 'I'm a respectable girl!'

Max smiles. 'And I'm a respectable man, Rosa,' he says, 'there's no need to fret. I use the place as a studio most of the day, which is while you'll be working, and you'll find I'm out most nights, so you'll have nothing to share. We'll barely meet to exchange greetings, let alone anything else.'

I sit on my case in the corner, thoroughly miserable at my plight, while Max finishes taking his photographs of Molly. Even in the depths of my sulk I notice how much the girl comes to life in front of the camera and how her ordinary features become almost beautiful as she changes her expression. Max, too, is a different character while he works. His long back is almost bent double over the camera and his features become serious for the first time. I feign indifference but in reality find myself totally absorbed by the strange scene in front of me. When Max straightens

186

and announces he is finished for the night I look more disappointed than Molly.

I inform Baile of my change of address but tell her nothing of my new circumstances. The slack season in the rag trade is coming up, and we all work as hard as wasps in case we are selected for laying-off. Baile and I are already cut to a four-day week, which means I have nothing left to save. Max leaves food for me, which is all I have to exist on as I cannot afford to buy more. Sometimes he will leave a coin on the table and I will walk around to Bloomberg's on the corner of Old Montague Street to buy cheap off-cuts of delicious-tasting salami for our tea.

Max has partitioned the room more soundly and I sleep better at night behind my own little wooden-planked wall. Now that we have more than just curtain there, Max will often return home before I am asleep.

I am acutely embarrassed to be so close to a strange man. I find the smell of him in the room overpowering. He is clean enough for anyone's taste, but still I have discovered that men have a vastly different scent from women. It is an intimate smell, brashly animal and rather earthy. When I hear Max come home at night I stuff my blanket into my ears so that I will not hear him. He is a noisy sleeper. I pray I make no sound myself and take great pains to move as little as possible when I am in bed, so that my body is sore and aching in the morning from being coiled up and still all night.

Apart from the evenings, then, I find myself almost happy in the routine at Brick Lane, and the shorter week may be painful for my purse but it has greatly improved my health.

This is a ghetto where I live, but it is a friendly enough place nevertheless. Everyone is industrious and most people work to improve their lot and get out of the area, which is exactly what I am doing myself.

Their optimism is contagious. I am invited to visit neighbours – large families in cramped rooms where there is not one item of beauty and the beds stand with their legs in dishes of paraffin to keep bed bugs away – yet they all seem happy and proud enough and all are waiting until their business buys them places in Golders Green, where their wealthier relatives are already housed.

On the Sabbath, the Sabbath goys arrive to light up and although I have no coins for them there is one who does the job anyway, for nothing. His face was instantly recognizable to me, but it was some weeks before I identified him as one of Queer Tess's brood.

'So you have bettered yourself then?' I asked him, smiling. He looked surprised. 'You're no tosher, then?' I said. He blushed at this. 'I know your mother,' I added. 'Queer Tess works at the shelter where I first arrived. She showed me her family at work. When I saw you last you were about to go down a sewer.'

I saw by his face that I had embarrassed him. 'My name is Stanley and I am no tosher, not now,' he said, red-faced. 'My mother, who you call Queer Tess, died two weeks past of tuberculosis.'

I watched his back as he reached up to the gas mantle. I had forgotten that Tess's nickname was given by the women in the shelter.

'I'm sorry, Stanley,' I told him. He is barely a year older than myself. I asked what else he did during the week and he told me he delivered for the kosher poulterer in Wentworth Street, and that he and his friends will push a brazier around the streets on a barrow at Pesach, crying, '*Choomez, choomez*', when the Jewish folk will bring out their bread and pay the boys to take it away.

Stanley is committed to teaching me one word of proper London English a week. My first word is 'Asshole', which is a religious observance day in the English calendar, like our Sabbath. When I mentioned this day to the Evangelists they ushered me out of the building without my conversion coin.

Stanley has asked me to an evening at the Yiddish Theatre in Spitalfields. When I tell Max he looks annoyed. 'You should go if you wish, Rosa,' he says.

'I need a chaperon,' I tell him. He looks surprised.

'Why?' he asks.

'Because I am a young girl from a good family,' I say. It is the first time I have seen such an expression of seriousness on Max's face. 'My father may be dead,' I assure him, 'but there is no reason for me to become loose.'

Max is studying his large hands that are twice the size of my own. His head is dropped. Even uncombed, his hair gleams like pale seal-skin. His face, which is hidden, looks like that of an Italian nobleman, with a straight long nose and dark thick brows.

'Rosa,' he says sadly, 'all this stuff about being a well-brought up girl from a good family. You have no need to lie to me.'

I am confused.

'I am your friend, Rosa,' he says, raising his head, 'and friends are not judgmental. Whatever you have done is done. I would just ask you not to lie to me, that's all.'

'Lie?' I ask him. I feel angry at his accusation, but his tone has started me off crying.

'I know about the baby,' he says, gravely, 'I heard the talk on the ship. I'm sorry.'

I let out a wail.

'Rosa,' he says, clutching my hands, 'it doesn't matter – at least not to me. It only matters when you pretend to me to be something you're not.'

So he thinks I am a whore. I can barely draw breath for the shame that overwhelms me.

I stand up, choking.

'Rosa!' Max tries to take me in his arms and for a moment succeeds, so that I am pressed against his chest and surrounded by his smell and the soft fabric of his shirt.

'I see you now, Max!' I shout, pulling away. 'You think I am easy because of my dead child. You're wrong, you know. You understand nothing about what happened.'

I hate him for his concern and I hate him for knowing my secret. Does Baile know, too? No – she could not have kept information like that hugged to her chest for more than a moment.

As Max stands before me I see the expression in his eyes change. He is still mocking me but there is more there, too. He tries to take my hands but I am too fast for him and pull away. I dread his touch.

'Rosa,' he whispers, 'I just want to help.'

God save me from his help and his pity! My circumstances mean I am trapped like a fly in a web but I will not be grateful to Max Warkofski, photographer of half-dressed women! He might think of me as a damned and

190

lost woman, but I know the truth of my circumstances. I may be fallen lower than others of my sex, according to my religion, for what happened in the snow in my homeland, but I know I fought harder than I would for my life. Max has chosen his circumstances. Surely that must be worse?

How ugly my face must be right now, with its angry little expression!

I see the smile start to build across Max's handsome chops but I am there first with a sneer of my own.

'Rosa,' he says, 'why do you think I want to help you?'

'Oh, that is easy to answer,' I tell him. 'You wish I would tell the beautiful Baile what a gentleman you are so that she will take an interest. I am smarter than you think, Max. Did you believe I didn't know what you were about?'

Max sits down cockily on a chair and sets about lighting a cigarette. This proves to be quite a business as his matches appear to be damp.

'So why should I make a pass at you just now?' he asks once the smoke is rising.

I shrug. Who knows why men do what they do, as far as women are concerned. Menachem, Max, the man with the birthmark who raped me in the woods – can women ever understand such animal instincts?

'Could it be that it is little rabbit-faced Rosa that I love, I wonder?' Max asks. And then he laughs. He crosses his legs. His feet are big and his shoes are in need of repair. I wonder whether he knows this and I hope that it rains next time he leaves the house.

'You love Baile,' I tell him.

Max has a wonderful habit of which I am madly jealous

– namely, he can raise one eyebrow without disturbing the other. I have noticed this trick on many occasions and have always thought it the cleverest thing. It makes him appear reckless and sophisticated and I have tried to copy him for many hours while in my bed at night, but always fail. He does it now, and I feel the bile rise in the back of my throat.

'Tell me you don't, Max, and I'll call you a liar,' I say. To my shame I attempt the eyebrow stunt but only succeed in a bad imitation of Queer Tess's squint.

'Rosa,' Max says, his mouth chewing a laugh, 'at the risk of being called the greatest liar in the country I will state now that it is you I have feelings for. Maybe I should keep quiet and play the game for longer in the hope that you will come to your senses and realize this fact for yourself, but I'm not a patient man and – who knows, we could both be dead of the fever this time next week.

'I have never mentioned the child to you before because it matters not one wit to me how you came to bear it. I can only assume it was Aaron's and that this was why you were so relentless in your pursuit of him after he had fled to America.'

He pauses to inhale more of the odious smoke and I feel tears build in my eyes at the injustice of what he has just said.

'Rosa,' he is whispering now, but his voice is deep and it still fills the small room, 'it's you I have feelings for. I'm not a particularly religious man and I'm not a traditionalist. What's done is done. Did you imagine all men seek only beauty? I love your wit and your humour, though most of it is unintentional, and most of all I admire you for your spirit.

'We're very similar, you and I. We both want much out of life and we'll both fight to get it. You believe you want a marriage to Aaron, but I know you need more than that. Save the money for your journey if you must, but I'll stake my life you never spend it on the ticket.'

He is so smug, I could kick him.

'Once I have the money I will go,' I say.

To my intense irritation I watch his smile widen. He stands suddenly and is across the room in a leap to fetch something from a cupboard beneath the sink.

'Look,' he says, throwing a bag across at me, 'open it up.'

There is money inside the bag – enough for my trip from Liverpool and more besides.

'There it is, then,' he tells me, 'it's all yours, Rosa. You can be with your Aaron within the month. I would ask to take your wedding photographs but I'm afraid there's only enough in there for one fare.'

I stare at the notes and I look up at Max, wishing I were old enough and smart enough to play him at his own game. He has me now, though. He knows what I know. He knows America is just my dream. He knows I will never take the trip. Aaron didn't want me. I am not a fool. I know this much. If he did, he would never tolerate me after the shocking event in the snow. No good Jewish man would marry me now. I am worth less than nothing. Aaron has been my dream. He left Russia to escape me. Max has spoilt my game by calling my bluff. I hate him for this. Without our dreams and self-delusions we cease to exist. I push the money slowly back across the floor.

'Little Rosa.' He is out of the chair again and moving towards me. I see droplets of sweat on his brow and realize I have been fooled. He would never have allowed me to take it.

'Where did you get the money, Max?' I ask. He is silent for a change.

'Is it even yours?' I can't believe his cheek. He is shaking his head and smiling.

'No, Rosa, I'm looking after it for a friend.'

'So what if I had taken it?' I ask.

'I knew you wouldn't.'

'You cheat!' I cry.

'I needed to be sure,' Max tells me. 'Now I know you're staying for good.'

He believes I turned the money down for him. He thinks I have chosen him over Aaron. But it would choke me to tell him that Aaron doesn't want me.

'I am staying because I have fallen in love, Max,' I tell him, and the hope in his eyes is well worth the lie. 'I have feelings for the young man who owns the factory I work in,' I continue, 'his name is Richard Arthur Galliard and he is a gentleman with a proper business. I have written to Aaron's mother to break the news and she tells me Aaron is distraught. But who can decide whom to love? That's why I'm staying, Max. For Richard.'

I turn my back so that Max cannot see my face, which is full of the look of my own lies. He goes to move but then I hear him pause. I have ended his fun, then. He won't mock me any more, pretending to love me.

'Does this gentleman know about your child?' he asks. His voice has changed. It is so low I can barely hear it.

A baby cries from the floor below and I shudder at the coincidence.

'Of course,' I lie.

Another silence. I should feel victorious, but I don't, I feel ugly and hateful. Max just wanted to tease me. I should have laughed when he told me he loved me.

'I look forward to hearing of your betrothal, then,' Max says. He is taking the joke too far now. When I turn to face him his expression is stricken. I had no idea he was such a talented actor.

I join the game, smiling. 'Maybe you will get to take my wedding photographs after all, Max,' I tell him.

A darkness comes across his face without settling. Then it is gone and his smile is back, though there is something like anger still in his eyes. 'It would be my pleasure,' he replies.

'Rosa,' he adds, as he turns to leave the room, 'you could achieve many things if you would just be truthful to yourself.'

He is right, of course. I must forget Aaron and set myself towards other goals. Perhaps I am not so crazy in my new dreams about Richard Galliard. As Max said, not all men seek beauty in a woman, and I think he was honest enough about this, even if he lied about everything else.

Richard is wealthy and charming. Aaron did not want me and Max could not provide a good home for a goat. Would Rintzi and Gregory mind so much if I came home married to a different man, as long as he is capable of looking after us all? Perhaps I could keep my history to myself. Max has done me a good turn after all, with his teasing. I will marry Richard. I am sure of that now.

CHAPTER NINETEEN

ZG

KIPPERS
Girls who worked in the gentlemen's tailor shops of
Savile Row were never allowed to work on their own,
for decency's sake. So they earned the nickname
'kippers', because they always went around in pairs.

Ever since I can remember I have been terrified of thunder-storms. Now I lie curled in my little bed one night and my stomach is sick with fear at the sight of the lightning from my window.

There is more to fear. Max is murdering Molly on the other side of the partition. I can hear her screams and am too much of a coward to move. First there was a wailing, with much shushing from Max. Then the wails rose to cries before I heard the sound suffocated, as though Max had his hand over the woman's mouth. Next he will be cutting her throat, I am sure of it.

Could our argument have prompted such murderous anger? My hands are over my mouth, stifling my own cries of fear. Could Max be the Ripper? I think back. He arrived in England the same time as us, not long after the Ripper had started his work. But was this Max's first visit? Could I have been living with a butcher for so long and not have known?

The cries are quiet now but this only makes me shake more, for I fear it means the job has been done and the woman is dead.

Somehow I fall into a sleep and when I wake it is to the smell of cigar smoke and frying eggs. I hear Max quit the room and make the long walk down to the water-closet in the yard and I creep around the partition, in mortal terror for what my eyes may find waiting.

The bed is empty and so is the room. I search everywhere but there is no body and no blood. Only eggs burning over an oil lamp.

Max returns, whistling and stamping his frozen feet.

'Rosa!' He is all smiles and his hair is uncombed. I look away quickly, for he is still in his nightshirt. 'Do you want some eggs?' he asks.

'There was a woman here,' I say, my voice trembling.

'A woman?' He is teasing me again. I wonder if he would murder me too.

'I can smell her perfume,' I tell him. He sniffs noisily and laughs.

'Are you jealous then, little rabbit?' he asks.

'Jealous?' My voice emerges as little more than a whisper. Who can be jealous of a corpse?

The following night it is much the same thing. I ask about the Ripper at work and someone gives me an old newspaper to read with much of the story inside it. My English is good enough now to make out the gist of what is written and I am sick at what I read. Could Max be this evil? I work late at the factory that night, rather than sleep in my own bed. When I do return to the house, almost fainting from tiredness, I hear a woman's shrieks as I climb the final flight of stairs.

Terrified, I almost fall down the steps in my hurry to find help. I thump on the door of the downstairs room and shout until I hear the children cry and the face of old mother Grosselli, the children's grandmother, appears in the small gap between door and frame.

'There are murders upstairs!' I cry. 'I can hear Max Warkofski killing again!'

The old woman pulls a shawl off a peg behind the door and wraps it around herself before pushing past me and tramping upstairs. She is half my height but I am too nervous to walk anywhere but behind her.

Her legs are so thin and bandy I can see the bottom of our door through them as she bangs upon it with her wizened fist.

'Mr Warkofski! Mr Warkofski! What are you up to in there?' she shouts in Yiddish.

The door is pulled open and I stifle a scream. Max is there, stark naked and huge in the doorway. I look away quickly but not before I catch a glimpse of the room behind him. Molly is in his bed, smoking one of his cigars.

'You should be ashamed of yourself, Mr Warkofski!' I hear the old grandmother trill. Then there is Max's voice, amused and polite, apologizing for the noise and promising it will not happen again.

He has even charmed Mrs Grosselli, for it is me she is angry at now. 'You should learn to grow up, girl,' she says as she waddles off to her bed, 'you could have scared me to death with your shouting!'

How much of a child can I still be? How much can I

hate myself for my stupidity? The screams were a result of passion, and I thought they were cries of agony. Can this be what love is like between two people? I thought what I suffered in the snow in the forest was different from that which occurs between husband and wife, but it seems I was wrong. Do women suffer pain each and every time they are with their men?

It is at moments like this that I am at my worst, Kitty. All my courage goes and I wish to howl and be comforted. How much I miss Papa and Rintzi! To feel either of their arms about me and hear them shush me and kiss the top of my head would be worth more to me right now than my life itself.

Why does my mother not write to me? Has she heard of my current circumstances somehow? Is she shocked that her daughter has fallen so far? I think of our life in Moscow, of the days when we lived like royalty, when Papa was a master tailor and people came from miles to be fitted for his suits. The smell of the food in the house. The warm fires with the curling smoke.

Never be poor, Rosa.

'Never, Papa,' I promise out loud, 'I will never be poor again in my life.' If I am granted a way out of these circumstances I will be as wealthy as we were then, Kitty – wealthier, even.

Max appears to think this last embarrassment is all one huge joke and has not stopped laughing for over a week. He has no shame in his body, yet the neighbours still greet him warmly enough, while I am lucky for a nod.

*   *   *

My mood was raised a little at the workshop this week. The place is nearly empty now, as the slack season is upon us, and I had been sitting alone sewing French lace onto the collar of a frock when Richard Galliard walked into the room, accompanied by another man.

One of the machines had broken at the start of the week and it seemed Richard was about to attempt to mend it himself. From my position crouched over the work-table I watched as he removed his jacket and hung it over the back of a chair before rolling his sleeves up to reveal pale bare forearms that gleamed with downy fair hairs.

I could smell him, Kitty; not a stench of cheap soap and coal-smoke, which is how Max and I smell these days, but a scent of linen and fresh cloth and perfumed hair oil and lime cologne.

I cannot describe how this scent affected me, Kitty. It was as though part of my old life, my childhood, had walked into that grimy room to take me back to happier days. It was the smell of leisure and honour and fine values and refined pleasures. It was the smell of a man who takes time about his toilette, not a poor hungry wretch who barely splashes cold water about his person before rubbing himself with orange to mask the stench.

When Richard bent over the machine I was bold enough to raise my head. I could not have done otherwise, Kitty, even though I risked the sack. His hair fell across his brow, which was furrowed with concentration. I blushed to think that I had imagined him as my husband. What would he have ever noticed in me? And yet pride will allow its own delusions.

All at once he let out a cry and straightened, holding his index finger, which was covered with blood. My mouth dropped open but I was forced to double-back over my work, for fear of a reprimand.

Suddenly my name was called: 'Miss Zigofsky?' I looked up. Richard was staring at me. 'I wonder,' he asked, 'do you have any skill in first aid?' He was smiling, despite the blood. At that moment I believed I had never seen a man quite as brave.

I was off my stool and at his side in an instant, my face burning with delight at hearing my name from his lips. Not 'Rosa', or 'Rabbit', either, but 'Miss Zigofsky'.

Kitty, I cannot emphasize enough the thrill I felt at being appealed to in this way. Since leaving my homeland I had become a nobody to the outside world – my worth had diminished to the point where I could have been snuffed out like a candle and few would have noticed. The sound of status and respect made me fit to weep; that is the pitiable state I have come to, dearest. Max with his jokes and his sarcasm; the wariness of the other Jews in our ghetto, who now give me a wide berth on account of my strange circumstances; the contempt of the other bosses and employers; Kitty, it is all I can do not to agree with their assessment of me.

And yet here was the highest of them all, and he spoke to me as though I were a lady. His tone was soft and gentle. He smiled as he looked at me, but the smile was *for* me, Kitty, not caused by me. My spine straightened with pride at the sound of it.

'Miss Zigofsky.' The way Richard Galliard said those two words made me feel like the person I should have been, had Papa not been forced to move us all to The Pale of Settlement.

Richard held out his wounded hand. 'I hope the sight of blood does not make you feel faint, Miss Zigofsky,' he said.

I shook my head, blushing. If only we had met in another place at another time in a different situation. If only I had been well-dressed and my cheeks had been rouged with cosmetic, rather than mortification. If my poor, pin-marked hands could have been gloved. If I had smelt of anything other than machine-grease and coal tar.

How long did I stand there, Kitty, staring at Richard's proffered hand and not daring to step forward to touch it? Can you imagine the first contact of flesh with a man from whom you had previously been banned from raising your eyes?

You are of a good family, Rosa, I told myself over and over, calm yourself or he will think you are simple in the brain.

Two drops of ruby blood fell to the floor between us, shocking me into action. I know you will think me soft, Kitty, but I feared he might bleed to death before my eyes and that it would be no one's fault but my own.

How did his flesh feel as I was bold enough to touch it? Like any other skin, but softer and warmer. It was the colour of camel-hair fabric next to my own pallid fist. Even Papa did not have hands like that, for he had always worked physically and it appeared to my eyes that Richard never had.

All I felt from this man as I examined his wound was kindness and politeness. His concern for my own well-being seemed to far outweigh any for himself. As our heights were so disparate he sat on the tailor's stool and nimbly lit a cigarette with his free hand.

We were so close, Kitty. And do you know what my thoughts were of? Of how I would crow to Baile about the whole thing. Even while my heart lay in the back of my throat, flapping like a landed fish, my main thought was of how jealous that girl would be.

My English became confused, yet I was able to tell Richard with some authority that the cut was not a deep one, but that it should be washed and bandaged.

'Well, let us do that very thing, then,' he said. I looked up into his eyes, which were directly upon me. I wanted more than anything in the whole world to return his smile and I think I did, though I cannot be sure. Perhaps I just kept the surly little rabbit face I normally wear these days. In any event, his own expression did not falter.

We walked to the sink and I turned the tap, taking care not to splash us, while he held his finger beneath it and all the while I could smell the many scents from the fabrics that he wore.

He watched me as I bandaged, not my handiwork. Looking at his wound and feeling his eyes upon me I thought all at once of Gregory and his poor fingers in the snow. I felt a rush of tender affection that was as much for my beautiful brother as for this auburn-haired man beside me, though the affection overwhelmed me, nevertheless.

'Where are you from?' he asked. I did not dare look up now, for my eyes had tears of remembrance in them, but told him in a strong enough voice that I had family in Russia but that I lived in Brick Lane.

'In a nice warm family house?' he asked. I paused and then nodded. What else could I say? If I told him the circumstances of my life he would have thought less of me than he already did, as a mere employee.

When I had finished tying the bandage he held the finger up for examination. 'A splendid job!' he announced, which set me off blushing again. 'If only you had not used our most expensive lace to do it,' he added. I looked up with shame. In my hurry I had pulled out the nearest cloth that had come to hand.

'Never mind, we can take it from your wages, I expect,' he said. Then he saw my expression. 'Or maybe not – look, there was a lot of blood. Have some of this, won't you? I believe we've earned it for our bravery.' He took a silver flask from his pocket and poured some liquid from it into a small cup that formed the lid, offering it to me first before downing the lot in one when I refused. Some colour returned to his face when the alcohol had taken effect.

'Thank you,' he said, smiling. I tried to hold that expression in my mind like a photograph, to cheer me through, like soup on a cold day. If only Baile had been there to see us my pleasure would have been complete.

I awake to the sound of whispering from the next room. My body is bent and my leg, which is underneath, is dead.

'Keep yourself quiet,' I hear, 'for I don't want to wake Rosa again.'

There is a woman's laugh. 'I believe there is something between you two, the way you talk of her.'

'Unfortunately not. She won't have me.'

'She?' More laughter, but suppressed. 'Max, you are joking.'

'No, but – like yourself – she is convinced that I am.'

I hear the woman's laugh turn to something else between a snort and a groan. There is silence save the movement of sheets, then I hear Max moan, low and quiet. I can stand it no more. I am shameless but I no longer have control over my actions. My room is dark but a candle flickers on the other side of the partition.

Sliding out of my low bed I tiptoe the two steps to the dividing wall. The wood feels cool as I place my face against it. I pause for a second before turning to look. The wood is old and cracked into slits. I press my whole face against the largest crack, which I can peer through into Max's half of the room.

The light is yellow and dim. There is Max's small bed, as narrow and low as my own, and on top of it the model, her face turned to the ceiling and her plump legs bent and parted. There is a blue bruise on her fat knee and another smaller one at the top of her thigh. Her eyes are closed to slits and her mouth is held open in a half-smile. It is an expression of happy reminiscence. 'Ah yes, now I remember that!' is what her face says. She gasps a small gasp and I have to turn away from the intimacy of the scene.

My body throbs in warning. I fear I will be ill from shock yet still I turn back for more. I know something of what is what – I am a child who has lived in the country and who has watched animals at work on one another in the fields. I have had the same treatment myself, though I can see nothing of my own suffering reflected on this girl's face.

Max is a fine beast. How could he behave in such a way? His body is huge and rippling in the candle-light. If the partner beneath him had been a horse I could understand the pleasure his heavy thrusts might cause, but she is a frail girl like myself, despite her chubby legs, and I cannot see how she can survive such an onslaught, let alone savour it. I want to cry out to stop them, for she reminds me so much of my own self, when I was taken in the snow. Max is little better than the creature with the mark on his forehead.

The whole of his body is tensed with concentration and effort, as the father's had been when he took me. He is between her legs and his torso lays where her body is most vulnerable. Without clothes to cover him his body is golden and damp.

How can they be so unashamed? There is no sheet to hide them and yet they go about their business with happy concentration. The girl begins to moan and Max bends his head to kiss her quiet. Such a kiss! His mouth is full open and devouring! Her arms fall to her sides and coins tumble out of her hand and roll onto the floor as her fingers unclasp and straighten.

She could be in a swoon now, except that her back is arched and the soft moans spill endlessly from her lips. The throbbing is worse in my body. Why do I watch when my pain almost matches the agony of my memories? Can spying be such a sin that it brings its own punishment in the form of disease? I feel my whole body burning and press it against the cold wood to cool. My breathing is so loud from fear that I am terrified they might hear me and know that I have been watching.

The veins on Max's body stand out in dark relief. His face holds an expression of such agony I am forced to wonder if the effort is worth it. His buttocks curl in and his body contorts as though a current has run through it. He pulls away from the girl suddenly and violently, throwing himself back onto the mattress with a cry of pure agony, his penis a swollen, dark wet thing that spurts fluid in an arc with each and every convulsion of his body.

I feel waves of sickness and horror coursing through my body with each and every spurt from his own. I turn away quickly, disgusted and ashamed and ill. My legs are too weak to carry my own weight and I slide to the floor, shivering.

This is no good, this is bad. I am a girl from a good Moscow family and this is the most wicked thing I have ever done or seen. What happened in the woods was not of my choosing, but this I have stood and watched like a common whore. I retch silently, trying to banish the taste of my own spit from my mouth. My stomach is in spasm from the wretchedness of it all. I must move away from this place where wickedness happens. I belong in a world like Richard's. It is my birthright. It is what Papa would have wanted for me.

When I wake in the morning I have a fever and am unable to raise my head from the pillow. Max discovers me and brings the doctor, even though I tell him I am unable to pay the fee.

'Is it the tuberculosis?' I ask when the doctor has gone. There are two sick of the same thing in our workroom and I know the disease is rife in the garment trade all over London.

'No, Rabbit,' Max tells me, smiling, 'you have a slight fever, that's all. A couple of days in bed and you should be back at your beloved machine again.'

He strokes my hair gently and I am too weak to complain. I am disgusted, repulsed and at once fascinated by him. I would never marry such an animal. A gentleman would never treat his wife in such a way. I would rather die than submit myself to such a trial.

My fever is worse than Max supposed. I drift from sleep to half-sleep and he always seems to be there.

'Tell me a story,' I ask one night, for I have become a child again in my dreams and Max is my papa, stroking my hair from my hot wet face while he waits for the fever to break.

'I won't tell you a story, little Rosa, I'll tell you a truth,' I hear Max whisper into my ear. His voice sounds kind and gentle enough. This is Max my friend again – the animal has gone.

His story is of himself when he was a small child in Russia. His parents were farmers and he was the youngest of six boys, all of whom were old enough and big enough to help their father in the field all day.

It was Max's greatest dream at the age of six to be man enough to help his papa too. There was a small stream dividing the house from the fields, though. The ditch was the symbol of manhood in the family, because only when a boy was big enough and strong enough to jump the stream could he join the others on their walk to the fields.

Each day Max would join the line of men and boys as they walked to the fields with their plough tools over their shoulders and each day he would find himself left behind as the others leapt the stream while he was left scrambling about on the bank. He would be at least twelve years before his legs were long enough, his father told him.

Max was six years and three months before he had his great idea. He disappeared from the house at night and in the morning when his father and brothers walked to the fields they found Max had toiled for hours, digging earth into the ditch to narrow it to the point where he could just about hop across on his little plump legs. He joined his brothers in the fields that day, even though his arms were too short to handle most of the adult tools.

'So you see, little Rosa,' Max whispered into my ear, 'you can achieve anything if you will only be honest about your goals and determined enough to be clever.'

At least I believe that is what he tells me, though my brain is too addled with the fever to know whether I am dreaming or not.

CHAPTER TWENTY

ƵG

HAUTE COUTURE
*Exclusivity was once essential to the fashion business.
In 1868, the* Syndicale de la Couture Parisienne *was
established, becoming the* Chambre Syndicale *in 1911.
Designs lodged with the* Chambre *were protected by a
strict copyright. Today, couture is seen more as a lost
leader, with just two to three thousand clients
worldwide.*

If Kitty needed reminding about the history of her family's
business, she had only to look in the newspapers. As the
story of their tragedy rolled on, so the size and scope of
articles on the subject increased.

There were double-page spreads in the more up-market
tabloids now. Many found poetic comparisons between
Gabriel's murder and the predicted, some said, inevitable
death of the British rag trade. The *Telegraph* contained a
grisly-looking shot of the whole family arriving at the
inquest: Burgess princely and contained, his hands stuffed
into jacket pockets and eyes fixed firmly on distant hori-
zons; Hester arm-in-arm with China, both clad in understated dark sheaths and wide-brimmed hats; Chloe out
front in a navy crepe trouser suit she had purloined from
the current collection and festooned with black pearls;

Nula lagging behind away from the rest, head down and face hidden behind fly-faced shades; and then Kitty, of course. How did she look? Determined? Confused? It is difficult to read your own face. Young? Old? She looked shocked. Stricken. They all did.

And there, behind them all, strode Nicky Kofteros. Only his expression was clearly defined – one of respect, solicitude. Greed? Glee? Kitty peered more closely but the picture dispersed into impressionistic newsprint dots.

So Nicky had even wormed his way into the family group, now.

Kitty tilted back her head as a nuclear cloud of anger grew inside her. How could this happen? Gabriel would have . . . but she switched that thought off quickly. Enough people had been misquoting her father already – 'Gabriel would have wished this,' 'It's what your father would have wanted.' It didn't need one more voice interpreting his thoughts for him.

Yet she was unable to stop herself. Gabriel would have been incandescent with rage at the sight of that man walking with the family group in such a complacent manner. And at such an intimate time. He would never have allowed it. It was the type of disrespect he had died trying to prevent.

Another paper had the same photo, but with the copy reading more as a fashion spread, each outfit dissected in minute detail. What was this, funeral fashions? How much could Kitty do to avenge her father? Should more lives be ruined, for the sake of . . . what? What would she be fighting for? Her head filled with thoughts that spilt from her eyes in the shape of yet more salty tears.

She pulled off her glasses. Only they weren't *her* glasses.

They were her father's, the pair he wore for designing. She had picked them up in the studio and then pretended to herself she'd put them on by mistake, thinking they were her own. They were too big but not unwearable. They smelt of him. They made her look more like him. When she concentrated on the newspaper she even pulled the same face. The focus wasn't bad.

The phone rang.

'Kitty, my dear, I believe you should be informed of a certain unpleasant development.' It was the showroom manager. 'I tried to contact your brother Burgess, but he is evidently in meetings all day. At any rate, you should know too. You spent more time with us while your father was alive. Prepare yourself. Raphael has left. Walked out on us. Gone. What a bastard, eh?'

'Oh.' It was all she could say. The manager ranted for a few minutes more before Kitty placed the receiver in its cradle without further comment and stared off into space.

Her father's precious designer, Raphael, whose destiny it was to save the house single-handedly, according to Gabriel. His protégé. The first rat to leave the submerging tub. The first one to choose to avoid going down with the rest of them. Kitty wished she could be more surprised at the news. Who could blame him?

There was worse, though. Something her feigned indifference couldn't quite cope with. An unexpected low punch while her attention was momentarily diverted. Something the showroom manager had said that was taking longer to sink in than the rest.

It was Freddy's father who had poached Raphael. Of course. It was the sweetest pain, almost unbearable in its intensity which – thank God – was relatively short-lived. Kitty squeezed her eyes shut as she waited for the worst of it to pass. She heard the rational voice, the 'Kitty' voice, like soothing ointment in her mind: He had to go before we closed ... we offered him nothing ... he worked for our father, not us ... why shouldn't Freddy's father take him? ... isn't all fair in business? But the *new* voice, the voice of the anger cloud, rose up and roared louder: Raphael deserves to be trodden on, squashed, like a worm. Freddy's father warrants worse. It was disrespectful. They were taking the piss. Dancing on her father's grave.

It should never be allowed. Never.

'Fight them, Kitty. Do not allow this to happen.'

Who had said that? The woman's voice, heavily accented.

Kitty's head snapped up, her eyes wide open. Who had she heard? She looked around but the room she stood in was empty.

Fight them?

And get killed as well?

Who had said such a dangerous thing?

The phone rang again.

'Did you see the photographs I left for you, Kitty?' It was as though the receiver had become red hot in her hand. She threw it onto the floor before scrabbling to get it back onto the cradle.

Voices, so many voices. And now the murderer – phoning her to gloat. The photographs. The wedding shots. Had he been in her father's office? Did he have keys? He knew her address and her phone number. The voice had sounded sleepy and distorted. Did she know it? The phone rang again, making her jump.

'No!'

She let it ring. When the noise became unbearable she curled into the foetal position and closed her eyes. The clues were all there. The voices were driving her mad. She had to think. She needed time.

'Kitty, dearest?'

'Keep quiet.'

It had to be said.

CHAPTER TWENTY-ONE

ZG

LANDSLEIT

In September 1888 the Jewish Chronicle *reported the death of a four-month-old child, found '. . . suffocated in bed, probably by overlaying.' It was discovered that the child's parents lived together with their seven children in a room in Spitalfields that was only twelve foot square, and for which they were paying four shillings and sixpence per week.*

Should I tell you more about my work, Kitty? First I must say that it is something I am good at. When I watch Baile, who was first to the job before myself, I am amazed at her comparative lack of talent. While she is still classed as 'General Hand', which is the lowest grade of worker, I have been promoted to operating one of the Singer machines, which is an easier life indeed.

I arrive in the dark and I leave the same way. When my feet make their way up the narrow brick stairs – rushing, for I am usually close to being late, thanks to Max's nocturnal activities, which are difficult to sleep through – I smell hot oil from the finisher's lamps which must burn the whole day through as the old man's eyes are growing weak with age.

There is a general movement from among the piles of

old rags on the floor, which means the rest of the poor folk employed there are stirring from their sleep. The smell is none too pleasant, as you may guess, and there is a rush for the latrines as any further acts of defecation during the day will mean pay being docked in lieu of time off.

We have one worker off with tuberculosis and two stricken with the cough, which is audible above the clatter of the machines and which makes my stomach heave. During the lean season we are no more than four in the whole room, but in busier times we may number as many as twelve. There is a great amount of chattering, hawking and general groaning, but all this noise ends abruptly the minute the shift starts.

We are all made aware of this magical moment because young Mr Yanzdoff, the boy who sits at the desk by the door and who takes it upon himself to act as our overseer, will clamber onto his desk and stand to attention for a full minute, staring at his pocket watch, his arm raised in the air. When the hour strikes he will fling his arm down to his side in the most dramatic fashion, which would make us all laugh were it not for the fact that we have to commence work at that point, and quickly, too – or else!

My machine is off like a rocket, whether or not there is fabric on board.

From that moment on there is nothing but work, and the only voice heard all day is that of the new under-presser, who is ancient enough to be so close to death as makes no difference and therefore deaf as a post and unable to hear his own Yiddish mumbling.

Our main product is men's wear, and cheap and terrible

stuff it is, too. The fabric is mostly the coarsest serge, which is so thick in texture that it will buckle anything other than the largest and most cumbersome of needles, this being a fact that failed to be pointed out to me when I commenced my job, along with the rule that those needles that I did manage to bend in my labours would be replaced with money from my own pocket. The quality of this cloth is so poor and its nap so cruel that I wonder at the fate of the skin of the people who wear it, for my hands are chaffed raw as I sew it.

The colours are drab, Kitty, and the dye holds badly enough to stain our fingers. I am mainly engaged in sewing trouser-seams, and there is a gentleman tailor given the task of working on the gusset-seams, as it is considered indecorous for a young unmarried lady to be handling such areas.

On the whole I find this work hard and unfulfilling and tend to allow quality to be sacrificed to quantity. Occasionally, though, there will be garments sent in from the couture side of the business, when a rush job is needed, and then the story is different.

It was Mr Galliard who first involved me with this, careering through the factory red-faced and carrying armfuls of exquisite fabric.

'Where is our little miracle-worker?' he asked. My head rose slowly but my heart leapt when I discovered him looking in my direction. 'Yanzdoff tells me you can do skilled work,' he said. Yanzdoff – not master or mister! I could not resist the urge to peep at the overseer's face, which was the colour of the flesh of the ripe watermelons that are sold in the park!

'I can, sir!' I cried. And I heard Baile snort with laughter at the desperate, willing tone in my voice.

But Richard was smiling with relief. 'Can you do anything with this?' he asked, throwing the fabric down on top of my machine.

I fell silent at the first touch of the fabric. Suddenly I was back in Moscow again and my father was teaching me all about cloth and sewing. The scent of the stuff overwhelmed me and I discovered in an instant that fabric will smell as good anywhere in the world. I wished to press my face into it all and suffocate in the beauty of it. I have no memory of colour, only texture and scent. I was home again. My eyes filled with tears. It was as though Richard were bringing me my own past, piece by piece.

I pulled the garment away from my machine, for fear the oil might stain it, and shook it so that it fell the length of my lap. It was a morning-dress, partly finished, but with the bodice and sleeves unattached and much of the fine stitching and embroidery still to be done.

'We lost the tailor to TB last night,' Richard whispered, 'and the dress must be finished by tomorrow. Can you manage? There are no other workers to spare right now.' He spoke politely as always, but almost as though we were friends.

Max says the feelings I have for my boss are no more than a girlish passion, but there is more to it than that, I know it. His was the only free and untroubled soul that I had seen since Papa had died. He was there to remind me that another world existed outside my own miserable circle. He provided hope of a better life. His smile was so easy and his brow so clear. He was clean, Kitty, clean and

218

well-mannered. I would have clung to him if I could, for he was the only hope I saw of improving my lot.

I thought for an instant of the poor wretch of a tailor who had died like my father with his work unfinished. Then I nodded. After all, none of us has a lot that is easy to bear, exactly.

'Good.' Richard looked around, relieved. 'Good!' He stopped short. I followed his gaze. To my amazement Baile had risen to her feet with an expression approaching anger on her pretty, pale-pink-pig face.

The whole room stopped work to look at her. Her hands were clenched into fists and her arms shook. The pinkness drained slowly from her face, along with the prettiness.

'I could do that work.' Her voice came out as little more than a whisper, but she could have shrieked the words for the impact they had.

Richard smiled politely enough and began to turn away.

'I said I could do that work,' Baile repeated, louder this time. I would have gasped at her daring had I had the guts in my belly to do so.

Richard turned back to face her. 'Well, the job is Miss Zigofsky's now,' he said, still with more manners in his tone than Baile deserved.

'Richard!' The word came out of Baile's mouth in a wail. I watched the boss's face redden as the smile fixed upon his mouth appeared to tighten, then he turned again and was gone.

My own jaw was hanging open like a gaping idiot's and would not close. 'Richard!' The word hung in the air as embarrassing and distasteful as a fart. I believe we all expected a combustion at that moment, the room was so heavy with expectation at Baile's show of disrespect. In the end it was I who signalled the silence to stop, by spurring my machine into action, which broke the spell and sent us all back about our business.

When some sanity had returned to the room I paused in my sewing to study the dress on my lap. It was pale, silvergrey wool – the colour of the moon as seen through the grime of the small window in my bedroom. The fabric had the appearance of a *piqué* – firmly woven but soft as suede to handle, and lined with a cream sateen.

I supposed the garment to have been near completion at some stage, but then pulled apart following a fitting. At the waist hung a line of small pale yellow silk pockets, all weighted to keep the bodice in place against the corset. I ran my fingertips across the feather stitching that held the darts in position. The tailor had a good eye, but not as good as my father's. The skirt was simply cut – straight at the front but fuller at the back and hemmed in stitching that matched the tiny gold glass beads that decorated it.

I did not dare use the heavy pins I employed for the serge, so stole some finer ones from one of our tailors who was still, happily, in shock from Baile's outburst.

The skirt was so heavy it took all my efforts to stop it falling onto the floor. I needed a dummy to work on, to take the weight, yet there was only one in the building and that the size of a portly old man.

I was so excited by my task by now that thoughts of Baile and the scene she had caused merely flitted through my mind. What was she about? I caught her eyeing me more than once, but decided to pretend not to have noticed the glares that she threw me.

It was not yet dawn when Richard returned and I, to my shame, was sound asleep over my machine.

'Miss Zigofsky?' His whispered voice in my ears had me awake in an instant. His dear face was the first thing I saw as I opened my eyes. He too appeared to have slept badly. His hair was uncombed and there was a sour smell, like alcohol, on his breath.

'It's finished!' I said, watching the knot of worry in his expression unravel with relief. I held the dress up for his inspection.

'Try the thing on for me, it's no good throwing it about, and we have no stand in this place,' Richard said. I stared at him.

'Try it on?' I asked. I looked around at the live-in workers but they were mostly sound asleep and snoring. I held the garment at arm's length, thanking God I was a regular with the soap and hot water, and so would not soil the thing by putting it onto my body.

I felt this was my God-given moment come at last. In the wonderful dress Richard would see me as the well-bred girl I once was, instead of the poor, unfortunate wretch who currently graced his stinking workroom. He would be overwhelmed by the sight of Rosa Zigofsky, the master tailor's daughter from Moscow, and wonder why he had never noticed me in such a way before. I could make him love me, I was sure of that, if I could only once get him to see me in my proper position in life.

I was sent outside to the rag-room, where the air hung heavy with the stench of mildew. I had no great love of this room and avoided it when possible. Stacked high with mouldering bolts of cloth and paper awaiting collection from the rag man, it was home to many large brown rats. Clearing a space with my toe in the middle of the floor, I tore off my own shabby outer-dress and pulled the pale grey *piqué* over my head.

I should have guessed. The dress fitted me no better than a potato flour sack. It hung about my scrawny neck and my mean undergarments, which were grey with age, showed front and back of the generous bodice. Mortified, I emerged slowly from the rotting room and stood stock still as Richard struggled to prevent the pity from showing on his face.

'It is, of course, fashioned for a much larger client,' he said, kindly. I looked down at my arms and realized they were about an exact match to the colour of the fabric itself. Only my bosom appeared keen enough to be on nodding terms with the dress – the rest of my torso shunned all contact whatsoever.

I silently vowed to eat any and all food I could lay my hands upon in future so that I should never be shamed in this way again. The sight came into my mind of Max's model, Molly Nodd, laying stretched out like a cat across his bed. Her legs were as fat as little sausages and her knees had dimples. How would my legs look under such circumstances?

Suddenly, in my exhausted state, I saw myself pinned to Max's mattress like a pile of grey kindling while his entire body heaved on top of me. I heard his cries as my skinny legs rose into the air, like flagpoles, at the passion of it all . . .

'Miss Zigofsky?' Richard was looking at me. 'Are you well?' I heard him ask. 'Your face is flushed.'

My hand flew to my throat. Max Warkofski was the devil, I decided. Look what he was doing to my thoughts!

Perhaps the most galling thing of all was that, while I grew thinner, so Baile grew plumper by the day. Her uncle's family must be feeding her up for the wedding, I decided, though no mention of that event had been made for many months now and I began to suspect that it may have been consigned to the same fate as my own glorious marriage to Aaron.

I decided her delayed marriage to be the cause of her outburst in the workroom. She ignored me for days afterwards, and when she did relent and speak to me at last I was surprised at her tone, which was unexpectedly bitter for such a doll-faced girl.

'You do know how stupid you are, Bertha Zigofsky?' she asked me one morning as we passed in the street outside the sweat. 'Do you think Richard Galliard would look twice at a rabbit-faced girl like yourself? You may think you know everything, but allow me to inform you there are many things of which you are entirely ignorant – many things.'

'Ignore her, Rosa,' said the voice in my head, so I applied what I took to be a superior expression and planted it upon my face. If Baile Kluchersky was idiot enough to imagine Richard would as much as look at her twice after her show in the workroom, then she was an even greater fool than she looked.

223

CHAPTER TWENTY-TWO

Z_G

COSTING
Costing a garment can be an elaborate business.
Besides the cost of the fabric and trimmings, the price
must include the amount of labour involved at every
stage of the outfit's evolution. A couture dress may
take as long as a month to be made up.

A fashion house showroom at season time should be a place of rabid mania. When Kitty walked into Zigo, though, the only noise to court her ears was an eerie hush. Chloe had draped the windows in acres of dramatic black tulle as a gesture of mourning. The place looked and sounded like a chapel of rest. There was more racket from the paparazzi stomping about on the pavements outside than there was from staff in the workrooms.

One or two of the finishers sat stitching in a rather aimless fashion – though more from habit than anything else – their glasses resting on the ends of their noses. Otherwise, Kitty found herself stared at in silence.

She walked to the end of the workroom, to the board where the sketches of the new range were pinned: eighty colour crayon drawings, mostly in Raphael's hand. Maybe a dozen or more were in her father's smudgy style, too. There were always eighty garments in Gabriel's off-the-peg

224

collections – no more and no less. The first season Raphael had worked for them he had sketched eighty-two. Gabriel had lit up a cigarette and told the designer he would have to scrap two of them. They had argued for over an hour. Raphael had roared and thrown things. But at the end there had been only eighty – there always were.

'Are we finished?' asked Georgina, Gabriel's PA. Impossibly posh but grimly loyal, Georgina had once been Gabriel's house model and only moved backstage when a car accident had left her with an arthritic knee.

Kitty had always been rather in awe of Georgina. At only twenty-seven she had the air and carriage of a *grande dame* and the laugh and language of a navvy. Her face was long and pointy and her red hair cut into a sharp, earlobe-length Louise Brooks bob.

'You do know Raphael's pissed off?' she asked. Kitty nodded.

'How many of these are finished?' Her mouth pursed in concentration as she gestured towards the sketches. Georgina whistled through the characteristic gap between her front teeth. 'You know the marking system, Kitty,' she said, 'gold stars for finished, mauve dots for those done in the workroom, green for the outworkers, that's . . .' she squinted her eyes, 'fifty-five finished and costed, ten at final fitting stage, three lurking somewhere in your sister's wardrobe, two out being shot by *Vogue* for an exclusive preview deal rigged up by the PR, eight still being seamed and two at pattern stage,' she said.

Kitty frowned. 'Can they be finished in time?' she asked. Three in Chloe's wardrobe. Two being ruined on location. The anger cloud was trying to form in her head again.

The PA raised her eyebrows and shrugged. 'I think we all thought this season was dead in the water by now. When Raphael walked, we –'

'We have three days,' Kitty interrupted her. 'Can the range be ready for the show?'

'Oh Jesus, Kitty, without a designer?' Georgina's alarming laugh transmuted into a cough.

'Where's Alain?' Kitty asked.

A lanky, dark-haired young guy in black jeans and a baggy white shirt ambled across on cue. He said a couple of words in French to Georgina and then half-smiled at Kitty.

Alain was Mr shit-hot-graduate from St Martin's. Gabriel had snatched him from the previous year's shows at the Business Design Centre in Islington to be Raphael's workroom manager and assistant. As a manager he was crap – which was why another, more experienced man had been brought in for the job – but his talent as a designer had impressed Kitty's father immensely.

'Can you get this lot finished?' Kitty asked him. His laugh was spasmodic, like Georgina's.

There was a mania buzzing round in Kitty's head like a lazy fly, waiting to settle. Where was Burgess? Why wasn't he doing this? What about Chloe? Why was she home playing dressing dolls when she should be there kicking ass by the knicker-load?

Alain saw Kitty's expression and his laugh downgraded to a shadowy grin. 'In three days?' he asked, rubbing his chin. 'Without sleep,' he shrugged, 'maybe.' He was cropped-haired, unshaven. His eyes looked as though he had missed a few nights of slumber already. His deep voice made him sound older than his twenty-three years. He smelt of French cigarettes and a surprisingly nifty lemon cologne.

Kitty led him into the machine-room. The place was noisier, friendlier. A radio was blaring pop music. Women chatted above the insistent rattle as they worked. There were boxes everywhere, all overflowing with a jumble of hats and accessories for the coming show. A girl sat beside a pile of thirty-nine pairs of shoes, taping the bottom of the soles so that the models could turn smoothly on the catwalk. In the larger studio the finished samples hung bagged and with last-minute instructions in Gabriel's hand pinned to the front of each one.

This was the first season Kitty had not been involved in since the age of ten. This was the year she was supposed to get married, not immersed in the usual chaos of missed deadlines and screaming schedules.

She fingered a couple of the outfits. There was a lull, an unseen intake of air – a pre-tempest vacuum about the place. Something vital had been sucked out of the room.

'If we go ahead with this show and it is anything less than a total financial success, we get eaten alive by the men-in-suits,' she told Georgina and Alain.

'And if it works?' Georgina asked.

'Then we probably sell to them anyway.'

'I see.'

'And are all these suit-men like the one that is sitting scratching his balls in your father's office right now?' Alain asked.

Kitty looked at him. 'Who?'

Georgina almost blushed. 'Nicholas Kofteros,' she said, looking down. 'He's been here for over an hour. He said he was waiting for you.'

Kofteros had his back to the door when Kitty entered – and for a frozen-in-aspic, show-stopping moment she thought it was Gabriel waiting there for her, for both men had the same broad shoulders and thick, greying hair. Therefore her anger had time to dissipate, first into hope and then into fresh-laundered grief, before he turned.

'I'm sorry,' he said politely, 'I was told I could wait for you in here. I'm afraid I became fascinated by these photographs behind your father's desk . . .'

They were the shots she had found the other evening. She stared at Kofteros's smile and a terrible suspicion started to form in her head. Could it have been his voice on the phone? Had *he* sent her the picture and left the others piled up for her to see? Was it Kofteros who had had her father killed, and who was now trying to scare her out of the business?

'I hope you know you are just exactly like a vulture, Mr Kofteros,' Kitty told him, 'circling in the skies on behalf of the Waika Group . . .'

'My actual job description is European Marketing Director for Waika,' Kofteros replied, his expression unchanging, 'and I came here to tell you some good news, not to hover.'

He paused. There *was* no good news he could tell her, Kitty thought, unless he was about to combust spontaneously and die in agony right there on the carpet.

'They have arrested your father's murderer,' Kofteros

said soberly, offering her her own father's chair to sit down on as the news sank in.

Kitty stood. 'How could they?' she asked. 'You're still here.'

She hated Kofteros and she loathed his arrogant manner. She wanted it to be him who had planned the execution. He was someone she could almost enjoy hating. She'd wanted to shock him – she'd hoped to wipe the expression of mock-concern off his face with her words. To her amazement she discovered she was no longer scared for herself, only determined that this man would never succeed in taking over the business.

'I wish you could understand whose side I am on, Kitty,' Kofteros said. 'I am here to help you and your family's business.' He moved towards her. His hands were even stretched out to take her by the arms. He was going to pretend he was worried for her now. Kitty stepped out of his reach. Carefully, but not nervously. Something flickered across Kofteros's face at last. Had he really looked hurt? His hands dropped to his sides.

'The man who is being questioned about killing your father was one of his outworkers. Ricky Khan,' he said quietly. 'As you undoubtedly know, Gabriel laid off his entire factory last season. Zigo was evidently their main source of regular income, and the business was due to close as a result of the lost revenue. The murder was done professionally – a revenge killing. Mr Khan must have paid a great deal of money . . .'

'Ricky Khan was one of my father's oldest friends,' Kitty interrupted him. 'He is also like an uncle to me. When Ricky first arrived in this country it was my father who

229

gave him a job and enabled him to bring the rest of his family over. He understood my father's decision was a business one, and inevitable. He would never have had my father killed.'

Kofteros shrugged. 'I understand your doubts,' he said, 'but stress can do strange things to a man's mind. Evidently Khan's business was his whole life – something I'm sure you can sympathize with. Perhaps the loss of it drove him a little crazy . . .' he looked into her eyes with an expression of apology for the news he had brought. 'I just wanted to tell you before you heard it from the press,' he said. 'I'm sorry. It must be hard to take in. I'm sure you would have preferred it to have been me.'

'You're sleeping with my sister,' Kitty said, suddenly. The idea had appeared in her head without warning, yet she knew as soon as she thought it that it had to be the truth. Where else would Chloe be getting all the New-Age jargon if not from the Waika offices? Who else would have told Kofteros all these things about Ricky Khan?

He didn't miss a beat. 'I'm sorry if you disapprove,' he said, without a trace of sarcasm.

Kitty smiled. 'You're already screwing the rest of my family,' she said, evenly, 'why shouldn't Chloe have a little fun, too?'

Kofteros stared at the floor for a second. 'Kitty, if my company does take over your business, I would like to imagine we can work together,' he said. 'It will still have the feel of a family concern and we will retain all of you in your current positions. Nobody will suffer and nobody will be out of pocket. You will be an extremely wealthy woman in your own right, without that wealth being tied up in the business, as it is now.' He moved one step closer again. 'I'm not a fool, Kitty,' he said, 'I know your passion for this business is almost as great as your father's, but believe me, you personally have nothing to lose from this take-over. If we pull out, the receivers will be at the doors within approximately two weeks.' Kitty grinned at the news as though she didn't care and Kofteros sighed.

'I believe your father left you all a stake,' he said, 'and we intend to honour his wishes once – *if* – we take controlling ownership.'

'You'll close down the couture side of the business and milk the ready-to-wear dry. You and your company haven't got the slightest interest in fashion, Mr Kofteros,' Kitty told him, 'because the product is of no importance to you at all. We could manufacture computer parts for all you care. Generations of work and pride and craftsmanship will get crushed as soon as you have what you want. You see us solely as a means to an end – just like my brother Burgess. Figures on a sheet of paper –'

Kofteros leant across the desk suddenly, cutting her off mid-sentence. His eyes were softly dark. For a moment neither spoke, they both just stared – Kitty in anger and Nicky in something that could for all the world have looked like intelligent, sincere, knowing sympathy. Kitty was the first to break the gaze. What was he trying to do now – hypnotize her? For a moment there she'd almost felt he was being kind.

'I have more interest in the fashion business than you think, Miss Zigofsky,' he said in a deep voice, 'and maybe my knowledge of your history and lineage is even greater than your own.' He paused again, looking as though he

231

had intended to say more but then changed his mind. He smiled politely and the old, smarmy Nicky Kofteros was back again. 'I was told you were very much like your father,' he said, 'but I supposed you were a little too young to despise commercialism quite as vehemently as he did.'

'. . . and then you will get rid of us,' Kitty went on, undeterred, 'each and every member of the family, one by one. Burgess first, probably, because he understands most what you are doing and – despite the fact that he is probably wholly in your camp by now – may cause the most problems by wanting to interfere and have a voice.

'My mother will just be forgotten, along with Nula. China will go once you have paid off Stephano. Then me, because you know I won't be bought and you need to suck the last few details about the running of the business from my head.

'Chloe will last longer because her profile is the highest. The fact that you are sleeping with her will not give her the protection she hopes it will. You need a family face for the name of the business, though. She'll be eased out so gradually that she'll barely notice there are board meetings going on without her presence. You'll keep her so busy doing PR she may never realize she is nothing but a name . . .'

'If that is what you like to think,' Kofteros began, shaking his head, 'but I can assure you that you are wrong.'

'Of course she's right,' said a man's voice behind Kitty, 'it happened to most of the big fashion houses in Paris. There's no single reason to believe that it will not happen here, too.'

Kofteros's expression gelled with suppressed anger and

arrogance at this new challenge. Kitty turned to see Alain leaning behind her in the doorway, looking wonderfully sleazy and unkempt.

The two men gazed at one another for less than a second, but Kitty got the impression that a lot had been decided between them in that brief space of time. It was Kofteros who moved first, pulling his coat from the chair and extending his hand to Kitty as he murmured excuses and left.

Once he had gone, Kitty felt a desperate need to recover lost ground in the room. She spun her father's huge leather chair around and sank down into it, staring at Alain across Gabriel's desk.

'You know it rather suits you?' the designer said, throwing himself into the chair opposite.

'And you know you probably just talked your way out of a job,' Kitty told him. Alain shrugged. What were his circumstances? Kitty tried to recall her father's file on him, but she'd only glanced at it once before deciding he was an unlikely suspect. Was he from a good family? Did he need an income to survive? She didn't want him involved in her battles, especially as she knew she had every chance of losing.

There was a moment of uneasy silence. Kitty sat, lost deep in thought as Alain rocked gently backward and forward in his chair. He was a man who was comfortable in silences, she had noticed that before. It was a talent she wished she possessed. Gaps in conversations made her twitchy. Her mother had taught all her daughters that social silences were like the kiss of death. It was an inheritance Kitty still had to fight bravely to overcome.

'Do you think the new range is strong enough?' she asked at last.

'It's not bad,' Alain told her.

'Do you want to show it?' She watched his face closely.

'Why not? I didn't have much planned socially for the next few days.'

'And do you ever show more enthusiasm than you are displaying right now?'

Alain looked at her. 'No. Absolutely not. Under no circumstances. It is very un-cool.'

Kitty smiled and he responded with a grin. 'Good,' she said, 'then we'd better start work.'

It was after two o'clock by the time Kitty got back to her apartment. The bulb in the hall had blown and she searched for her keys on the stairs. As she approached her doorway something moved in the darkness. Something large, down on the floor.

'Shit!' Kitty jumped back like a scalded cat. Her brain did a quick mental inspection of the contents of her bag. Nothing, she concluded, not one solitary item that could be used as a weapon. Unless she hacked away with a credit card. Instead she raised the bag in a wild gesture of self-defence.

'Kit?' It was Nula, huddled and miserable, camped out on her doorstep.

'Oh-God-Nule-don't-speak-give-me-a-minute-fuck-fuck-fuck ... do I need a heart attack right now? Oh Lord!' Panting with shock, Kitty leant against the wall until her heartbeat straightened. Then, when she could breathe again: 'What the hell are you doing here?'

Nula scrambled to her feet. Her hair had gone wrong and her eyes glowed with tears. 'You said I could stay,' she told Kitty. Her voice told of utter misery that was as yet unemployed.

Kitty ran a hand over her hair. 'I know, I know, I just didn't expect ... God, you gave me such a fright! I thought ...' Kitty stopped herself in time. She'd thought they'd come to kill her like they killed her father. Unspeakable fear. Unutterable, unfathomable dread. How courageous had she felt in facing out Kofteros, and how stupidly, idiotically, cowardly did she look right now. Was this what bravery was like? Did it flow and ebb in waves? Somehow she'd expected it to be a more constant attribute. '... I thought you'd come over during the day, that's all,' she finished. She pulled her sister to her and hugged her. 'You shouldn't go camping on doorsteps, Nule,' she said, 'it's not safe.' Her sister smelt spicy and fresh, like a bun. She unlocked the door and pulled Nula inside. All she'd brought with her was a small rucksack.

'I thought you'd want to stay at the house,' Kitty said. With our mother, was what she meant. Nula adored Hester. Hester cherished little Nula. For the pair of them to be apart was remarkable.

'Can I stay here?' Nula asked her. 'Will Freddy mind?'

Freddy. Kitty had forgotten all about her fiancé.

'He's busy,' she told her sister, 'it's season time, remember? I'll be tied up enough myself. You can help, if you like.'

'Help?' Nula sounded weak and confused. Was she on drugs? Kitty made a mental note to check for signs. She heard Nula's face turn up towards her own and felt, rather than saw, the smile that tried to spread across it in the dark.

It wasn't until Kitty turned the lights on in the hallway and caught sight of them both in the mirror that she realized they had both become nervous wrecks. Nula looked ill, but so, too, did she. She took a deep breath. She needed to be strong. She had her sister and her mother to look after. She had a murder to solve. She had a business to run.

Nula stood with her elfin face sandwiched between her hands. Her nails looked chomped. 'I couldn't stand it, Kit,' she said. Her voice had changed since their father's death. Kitty wondered whether her own had, too. 'It was that picture, the one on the piano. I couldn't live with it.' Her eyes looked wild and haunted. Her hands were shaking.

'Okay,' Kitty soothed, 'okay, okay, okay. Do you like the taste of brandy?' She led her sister into the kitchen and poured them both a shot of cognac. Nula took a sip and started to cough, but the colour came back into her cheeks and she almost managed a smile.

'We'll start at the studio tomorrow,' Kitty said, throwing her brandy back in one. The effect nearly choked her but she managed not to gasp. Start as you mean to go on, she told herself.

When she dreamt of Gabriel that night she could not be sure, but she thought that maybe his back wasn't turned quite so squarely away from her as before.

CHAPTER TWENTY-THREE

ZG

1892

VOILE

*A fine, sheer fabric traditionally made from cotton,
silk or wool. Simple fabrics like cotton voile and
chiffon received a fashion revival amongst wealthy
women at the end of the nineteenth century. Much of
this was due to the growing popularity of the sewing
machine, which made elaborately trimmed dresses
available to the lower classes for the first time. In a
move of inverted snobbery, the upper classes switched
to having layers of delicate fabrics, which required
massive amounts of laundering and pressing to keep
them looking good. The wearing of these simple
garments made a subtle statement about the numbers
of staff employed by the household.*

Dearest Kitty,

I have been in this country three years now and speak
the language every bit as well as the others in the area. Yet
for all that I still feel very much the outsider and alone.
Most, if not all of the folk here, arrived in families. It is
the men who come first and then send for their wives when

they are settled. I, of course, have no family here and am finding it hard saving money for fares home as well as sending odd pieces of cash back to Russia when I can.

People here live very much as they did in the villages at home and a young girl alone as I am, sharing quarters as I do with a young man like Max and with no parental chaperon or guidance, is looked at very much from the corners of folks' eyes. Of course I have had offers of help and food – many from those with little enough to spare, too, I can tell you. My shame at what happened at home and the subsequent birth of my child that died has forced me to keep very much to myself though, Kitty.

Shame such as I carry will be with me all my life and I shall have to learn to bear it or collapse beneath its weight. I know now that I could never have brought such disgrace to Aaron's marriage bed. Yet I still have a dignity, Kitty, and that dignity is best left to itself. I am a young woman who was brought up well, by a good family. My father was well-respected and my mother one of the bravest women I will ever hope to know. I must carry some of this with me despite my fall. I am eighteen years old now and quite able to speak my own name with the self-esteem it deserves.

Max is so puffed up with his own conceit that he is quite unbearable. His photographic business has provided him with enough cash to expand a little and so he has placed an advertisement in the local newspaper, and the sight of his own name in print tickles him very much.

He is so full of himself now that I wonder he doesn't advertise his wonderful services in a society periodical – and tell him so to his face just to bring him down a peg or two. Imagine my expression, then, when he turns to me in all seriousness and informs me that is exactly what he has in mind, but only once he is in better premises that a lady would want to visit. I could poke his eye out for this last comment.

'So what about the lady who already lives here?' I ask him, at which he places his hand to his eyebrows and looks around the room as though hunting for the woman I refer to.

Molly Nodd, the model, is back in Max's room again tonight. I lay in silence in the darkness and my bed feels hot enough to toast me. How long can we live like this? The girl's moans slither with dull regularity from whispered pianissimo to broad fortissimo, and are full of tragic pleading, too. I wonder Max can be so cruel in ignoring her cries, but then realize she is begging for him to continue his ghastly behaviour, rather than stop.

There is a horrible contagion to the whole ritual. My own body, which I normally ignore, save to throw clothes over it in the morning and douse with soap and water after work at night, discovers demands of its own as I am forced to listen. My legs have taken on flesh around the bones at last and now my toes stretch out like a cat in the sun. My hands are balled into fists of anger that I cannot unclench. My breathing has become prominent enough to deafen me with its noise.

This is shameful! Like a ghost I am drawn from my mattress and my face is pressed again to the crack in the wall. Oh dear God, this time it is the girl who rides and Max who suffers beneath her! I stare at his face and see Richard there instead, and all at once I am so lonely there

239

in my poor excuse of a room that I could howl out loud, were it not for the fact that Max would know I had listened and watched.

I turn into my darkened chamber. It must be possible to not listen. I force my brain to seek other stimulus. Something dull. Something perfectly mundane. Baile's wedding is very much the thing at last, and a long time it has been coming, too. Baile loses much of her prettiness by the day and if she is not soon married then I fear no one will have her.

I find the diversion I have been seeking, then. Baile the bride. I am finally able to sleep and, when I rise, I take the thought of Baile's nuptials into the factory with me. Then I have a shock. I have been trying to find a mirror to see what has become of my looks since I arrived in this country. In the end I am bold enough to climb up a step and peep into the one the tailors use when they are grooming their beards in the morning.

The face I see rise up before me like a little sun, with curiosity written all over its expression, is not my face. Instead it is Rintzi who I see there, staring into the glass. I gasp and nearly fall from my step with surprise. Have I become my mother then? I stretch up to the mirror once again, cautiously, but her face still waits there.

It is four years since I left home. Is that all it has taken for me to become my mother's doppelgänger? A fear grips me that I may inherit her madness, too. Bubba's body and Rintzi's face. I feel my features with my fingers. Is that so bad? I am a little taller than I was, that much I can tell from the way my skirts hang short to my ankles. My hair I suppose to be much the same, though I keep it plaited and pinned tight to my head all the time. I run my fingers roughly over my features, trying to recall the face I had when I left my home.

When I turn at last I find that Baile has been watching me. She never once spoke about her famous outburst over the couture garment that I stitched, though one of the girls told me she believed Richard Galliard had kissed Baile one night, after the others had gone, and that it was this shocking act that had boldened my friend into believing she could speak to him in such a disrespectful manner.

I believe this to be nothing more than a lie, of course. Baile was a victim of her own jealous temper, nothing more. She is lucky still to have employment and I will tell her this if she ever steps out of line again.

I now take regular work from the company's better garment range, which ensures my enduring unpopularity with the other workers. Sometimes I am invited to visit Baile's family at their home, but these trips are generally not pleasurable. Baile has become very quiet since her scene at the sweatshop and, if I was not so sure that her head is empty of a brain I might almost describe her as reflective in mood. When Richard arrives at the factory she stares at him hollow-eyed. Perhaps it was *she* who kissed *him*. She is vain enough to try, I know that much.

Letters from home come occasionally, but they reach me less frequently now – though they were never more than three times a year once they started. I was in great despair over the fate of my family once I understood Aaron was lost to me forever. How would they manage without my protection, or that of my husband? Would Rintzi become quite mad and relieve Gregory of the rest of his fingers?

The times when Max did not treat me to a night-time concerto I would spend tossing over these thoughts in my mind.

Then one day one of Baile's many aunts happened to mention that my mother had bettered her lot and I found myself shocked, rather than delighted at the news.

'Rintzi?' I asked her. This particular aunt of Baile's is a very old woman with little concentration for anything other than food. When she is not cooking she is to be found consuming the fruits of her labours, which has made her as fat as an ox – too large for one chair, she rests her bulk across two planks supported by chairs either end, though she complains the wood causes her sores on the backs of her legs. I wonder with some pleasure whether Baile will look like this once she is older. 'My mother is happy?'

'She's been left money from a relative and moved to a better house, according to what I hear,' the aunt said.

My letter is off to Rintzi that very night and this time her reply is quite prompt. Yes, she has come into some money and spent it all on better lodgings for Gregory and herself. Am I happy for her? Happy? How could I be anything but choked with delight! What worry I have had for her, yet all the time she was safe in a new home! Kitty, you know me well enough by now to understand that I was beside myself with rage. My whole concern has been to provide for her and my brother, and yet there she is, a well-off woman and without once thinking it worth the effort to inform me. Could some of that money not have been used to bring her daughter home?

I consider a return to Russia. Perhaps I could write begging Rintzi to fund me. My heart suffers much pain at the thought of the place, yet I know now that what I miss most is no longer there. Russia is still full of danger for Jews – greeners arrive every month with tales to make our hair stand on end. My mind finds more work for it here in London, for I realize that it is here where my dreams lie now.

This news of Rintzi's has set me thinking. I no longer need worry about returning home with a husband. I now have no responsibilities in life, save myself. This is a curious idea that will take time to come to terms with. Max, of course, has his own philosophies about my situation.

'Just think, Rosa,' he tells me, 'you are free to pursue your own destiny.'

This is the sort of talk that makes my poor brain spin and I wish he would not continue with it, but Max is like a dog with a bone when he has an idea.

'Rosa, you have great potential,' he tells me, all flushed from his latest triumphs in the local rag. 'You must make a success of your life. You're as driven as I am, if you can only see it.'

His flattery embarrasses me and I look for the ulterior motive; I know he must be mocking me, as always.

'You mean I have potential as the new flattening-iron for your bedsheets, Max,' I say. His head goes up.

'Rosa, you know how much I want you, I've told you often enough,' he says, 'but I want success for you, too. You have talent and courage. Look how you've survived. I know you only see grime and muck in this country, yet there's great wealth here too, believe me. For people like us the possibilities are endless. Don't you fancy the life of a Mayfair lady, Rosa? Look, come with me. Do you have an hour? Yes? Allow me to teach you a few truths.'

Before I can speak he has my hat upon my head, albeit back to front, and we are out in the streets and he is whistling for a cab.

Once I am bundled inside Max grabs me by the arm. 'For one time in your short life, Rosa, be quiet and listen,' he says.

I sit back with my lips pursed. I will not allow Max to get the better of me – ever – but I am curious enough to do what he says.

The cab rolls down Brick Lane, past the mean lodgings, where buxom Jewish matrons sit on doorsteps alongside young Jewish men smoking their pipes, and via the Great Synagogue with an enormous clatter upon the cobbles, pulling round Sclater Street and up Curtain Road to Old Street, where the queues for the chief rabbi's soup kitchen wait with some dignity for their salt and bread and their turn at the six huge steam-jacketed pans.

The tenements are brave new buildings looming over the older, three-storey lodgings of the sort that Max and I inhabit. These are called model dwellings and three rooms plus other conveniences can be had for four shillings and sixpence per week. Needless to say they are full to bursting with immigrants of every kind, but I would like to fancy that I may be able to save enough to move into one myself before long.

I am lost beyond Old Street. For me the world ends at City Road so I stir with undisguised interest when the cab continues its journey down Bunhill Row and on to St Paul's.

'Did you ever visit the better parts of London, Rosa?' Max asks me. There is something rather intimate about the cramped cab and we are constantly thrown together as the wheels churn on the corners. I cling to the side of the window with all my strength, which makes Max laugh.

'Am I so repellent to you?' he asks, smiling. If he showed one ounce of self-doubt I might find it easier to like him, but here is a man who is completely aware of his good looks and engaging manners. He is staring at me with those eyes that miss nothing and I watch his hand reach for mine.

'What about your young lady?' I ask. Max laughs and shakes his head.

'Oh, I should say that ours was more of a financial arrangement, Rosa,' he tells me. 'I supposed you realized that by now.'

'You pay her to do those things?' I ask.

'No, she pays me.' He is laughing out loud at me now. 'Yes, of course I pay her, what did you think, Rosa? I pay her to do what we would do, if you would only see sense and marry me. Anyway,' his eyes are back to my face, 'how did you know what we do?'

I curl up back into my seat. 'I would have to be deaf and blind not to,' I tell him in a whisper, though I am too shocked and embarrassed by this conversation to wish it to continue.

We travel in silence, punctuated only by Max's occasional head-shaking snorts of laughter. The roads are broader now and better paved, so that the cab has stopped its tooth-loosening rattle.

I will not tell Max, but I am impressed by the view – so much so that I am rendered quite dumb. We drive for many more minutes and the view improves with each street we turn into.

'This is Mayfair,' Max tells me with a flourish of his hand, 'what do you think?'

It is every bit as beautiful as Moscow. There are people everywhere on the pavements, and all dressed in the most remarkable clothes. Here are colours that I have not seen for many years: golden-sand silk crepes, Delft-blue taffeta, rose-pink linen for the women's dresses, and greenish-brown alpaca or fine midnight or slate-grey wool for the gentlemen's suits.

'Take in the buildings too, Rosa,' Max whispers at me, pleased by my expression of childish awe, but I cannot for I am too busy memorizing each stitch and tuck of the clothes.

We take tea in Regent Street and I try to ignore the waiters' faces when they spy the sad little rabbit that Max has brought with him.

'I have never known you so quiet,' Max says to me, 'and you have barely touched your cake.'

'I'm not hungry,' I tell him. In truth, I am sick with longing.

'Would you like to live like this, Rosa?' His voice is a seduction in my ear. His hand is upon my arm, but I no longer feel the urge to complain. 'One day you will walk in here again, Rosa,' Max continues, 'only you will be dressed in clothes more exquisite than any other woman in this room. You will be seated at the best table by waiters who trip over their own boots in their rush to pander to your every whim. The tip you leave for the waiter who charms you the most will exceed one week's money from the sweatshop. You will leave food on your plate – not because you are sick from the excitement of it all, but because fine food bores you and if you are confronted by one more sliver of Scotch smoked salmon or another silver spoon laden with prime caviare you will scream from *ennui*. Now, how does that sound?'

I am sitting up like a little dog, mesmerized. 'I will have all that when I marry,' I say. My mouth is dry.

'What if every woman in this room were wearing an outfit created by you?' Max asks.

'By me?' I have no notion whether he is mocking me or not. With a touch of his fingers he turns my face towards his own, so that all I see is the texture and landscape of his fine features. I have been wrong about Max, perhaps. His eyes now hold the most infinite kindness and sympathy. I stare at them. His lashes are long, dark and thick. Max's eyes are perhaps the most expressive I have ever seen, which is why I always avoid their gaze when I can. There is longing there, along with the pride and the humour. Two orbs of soft chocolate silk on a bed of dove-white satin, topped with a fringe of frayed black crepe. Hair as thick as astrakhan. There is a small crumb of teacake beside his mouth and I yearn to brush it away.

'Rosa?' his voice is soft enough to be nearly inaudible.

'Max, you are not a gentleman,' I whisper. 'You behave like an animal half the time and the rest of the time you find sport in mocking me. I may not be a beauty but I will wait for more than you can offer.' I believe this with all my heart. Max may be a good and generous enough man at times, but somehow I feel he is little better than the beasts that raped me in the snow. Perhaps it is not his fault, but it is a quality that terrifies me all the same. He is not a gentleman and never will be – no matter how well his business does. A man like Richard has been bred to treat women like ladies. He would never act as Max does in his bed at night.

Max reaches for his teacup and I notice with some surprise that his hands are shaking. Could my words have made him so angry? He looks about the room.

'I may not be a gentleman, Rosa, but I would die for you, you know. What more is there that you could want?'

This is said so quietly and evenly that I stare at him, wondering if I have misheard. Then his face changes, the neediness vanishing to be replaced by all the old arrogance.

'So, now you've seen what London has to offer, Rosa,' he says in a changed tone, 'let me tell you the bad news. The cab and this tea used up all my money. I'm afraid we're walking back. Wrap your teacake in that napkin and conceal it in a pocket – we'll need it for the journey home.'

CHAPTER TWENTY-FOUR

ZG

TROTTEUR
French for 'walking suit', the trotteur *was one of the most popular outfits of the 1890s. It consisted of a men's-style buttoned jacket trimmed with braid and a skirt that was flared at the back for easy walking.*

There are curious events at the sweatshop, Kitty. First we are informed by young Mr Yanzdoff that Richard Galliard's partner, Turgis Fasukinos, has died. At first we fear this means the business will close, but then the rumour is that Richard had borrowed sufficient money to buy the place from Turgis's family. As you may imagine, Kitty, this news alone has been enough to keep us all simmering like kettles with speculations that we whisper around the room when Yanzdoff's back is turned.

Then more intrigue. A fellow machinist who we all know as Red Aggie on account of her hair, which has the colour of the ochre dye used for hat trimmings, is seen to be unwell, though she declines any offers of help. Baile has been eyeing her strangely for some months now and I see them whispering together often, which is an offence that could relieve them of their jobs, if they are not more careful.

I have met Baile's prospective bridegroom now, Kitty, and can only say that I hope he has a good fortune, for his face is not the sort to win prizes and his body I can only describe as showing signs of malnourishment. I told Max about the impending nuptials as soon as I knew, watching his face carefully for signs of regret, for I still believe he carries a torch for Baile, despite all his protestations.

To his credit, though, he managed a smile of the usual gleaming variety, accompanied by a shrug and a, 'Good luck to the groom.'

Baile plans to leave the sweatshop once she is married and good luck to her too for that, though I have to admit I will miss her despite everything, as she is the nearest thing to a friend that I have in this country, for all her annoying ways.

Last night I unpacked the wedding suit from its case. This is the first time I have given it an airing since I arrived in England and the reason for that is because I fear the pain of the loss of my father will be doubled at the sight of it.

Max, needless to say, arrived in the room the minute I had the garment out of its tissue and he was full of questions that I had no desire to answer.

'Whose is the suit, Rosa?' He pushed his hands into his pockets and leant against a wall, regarding the garment with a tilt from his head. He lit a cigar, which angered me for I did not want the smoke to dirty the precious fabric.

'Mine,' I told him, sounding annoyed.

'A *gentleman's* suit, Rosa?' he asked. 'Are you tired of your own sex already and keen to change? Although you were dressed as a boy when we first met, as I recall.' He was joking again.

'Max, this is my husband's suit,' I told him. Already the scent of the fabric was filling me with nostalgia. I watched Max tap his foot thoughtfully.

'I wasn't aware you had a husband,' he said.

I stood up to face him. 'This is a wedding suit, Max,' I said, 'my father made it to be worn by the man that I marry on our wedding day.'

Max fingered the fabric. 'It's very fine,' he said, 'though a little small in size.'

And before I could stop him he was holding the jacket to his chest and checking the length of the sleeve.

'For you?' I asked, incredulous.

'Can it be altered, Rosa?' he says.

I snatched it away so quickly the fabric almost tore. 'Oh it will fit very well, thank you, Max,' I told him. Richard is much leaner than Max and I knew he would fit the suit perfectly.

'Oh, you still have your gentleman in mind, do you?' he asked, and there was something especially nasty about the way he pronounced the word 'gentleman'.

'Of course,' I said.

'And do you believe your prospects are any more real with this suitor than they were with Aaron?' Max asked. His tone was not unkindly, but I became angry at his words.

'You seem to think I am not good enough to make a quality marriage!' I shouted.

Max was across the room in an instant and had me by the arm. 'No, Rosa,' he told me, 'I believe you are *too* good for these men!' he said, equally annoyed. 'Aaron must have been an idiotic fool and your precious boss is no

251

better! If you think you've found a gentleman in him, perhaps you'd better speak to your friend Baile before it's too late!'

'Baile?' I asked him, but he would say no more, no matter how much I questioned him. In fact I believe he thought he had said too much, for once.

'How did *you* come to speak to Baile, Max?' I asked him after a pause.

He smiled at that because I understood he believed me to be jealous.

'I went to congratulate her on her forthcoming wedding,' he said, 'and to see if I might have the honour of taking the photographs.' He threw a card onto the table in front of me. *Max Warkofski* it said in gold leaf, *Leading Society Photographer, catering for weddings, balls and formal portraits.* 'I have new premises, Rosa,' he said, 'I'm on my way, just wait.'

I have since quizzed Baile many times about Max's comments, for I am not so stupid as to allow pride to stand in the way of curiosity. This morning she told me that Richard is, '. . . not as much of a gentleman as you would think, Rosa.' And then later informed me that he has '. . . trouble with the drink.'

Of course, Baile would have had no experience of real gentlemen in her life, growing up as she did with that prize fool Menachem presiding over the household, but I must tell you, Kitty, that I have been somewhat concerned over Richard's consumption of alcohol myself, as he frequently has the smell of it about him when he pays his visits to our poor sweatshop.

The Jewish community in the East End is on the whole

well-behaved with good moral standards, despite the poverty of its ghettos. The sense of family here is even stronger than at home, and whole areas are populated by *landsleit*, which are families that come from the same town or *shtetle* back in Russia. These people form their own communities, Kitty, with *steibels* and home-stores providing the gathering-places that ensure the rabbi's sermons on the evils of bad behaviour will be heard and discussed at length. The main vice of the men is gambling, and many have regular dealings with the local bookie, a fat man in a loud suit, who works his pitch outside the corner shop by the butcher's.

I have no idea, Kitty, how morals work in other, more affluent communities, and expect alcohol consumption to be a recognized sport among them, and so therefore not the great sin it is seen to be with us. Richard Galliard *is* a gentleman, Kitty. If you could only see him you would know at once that I am right.

CHAPTER TWENTY-FIVE

ZG

BARATHEA
Made of wool or silk, and with a light, pebbly
pattern, barathea is mainly used for suits.

Five months have passed, Kitty, and it is obvious – to myself at least – what the problem is with young Aggie. Her corsets are laced as tight as possible around her waist, but I notice them straining more each day and see the way her back pains her when she is bent over her machine.

I take her aside, Kitty, for I have suffered the same fate myself and remember the fear and pain that it caused me, though I suspect Aggie is not quite the innocent victim that I was when I left my home.

'Are you with child, Aggie?' I ask her. She is a pretty enough girl but her face twists with emotion at my words.

'How did you know, Rabbit?' she asks, pulling a hankie from her purse and snuffling into it.

'From your belly,' I tell her. I know I can provide her with some comfort and pity and wish I had had a similar friend myself under the same circumstances. 'Aggie,' I go on, 'you will need comradeship at this time. Will you not allow me to help you? Can I speak to the father on your behalf and tell him how alone you are?'

I look at her again and discover not tears on her face, as I had supposed, but laughter.

'You?' she starts to scream. '*You* help? What would you do, you pious little cow? Yes, you can go and tell the father what he's done, though I doubt it would do me much good if you did. But then you are Mr Galliard's favourite, and we all know you have a lust for him yourself, so maybe he will listen, after all.

'Next time he gives you some of that fine stuff to sew tell him he's to be a papa, will you? That should put a finish to your career – and mine, too, I should think!'

I look at her stomach, blushing. 'You're lying, Aggie,' I tell her politely, 'Richard Galliard is not the child's father.'

'No?' she asks, and a look at my solemn face sends her into such convulsions of laughter that I fear she might be sick.

I stare at her. 'Then you must have seduced him.'

She is clutching her sides in her mirth. 'Yes?' she asks me. 'Well, he was blind drunk at the time, I'll give you that. I doubt he'll remember his little adventure, but I believe he was a reasonably willing party to the deed.' She pushes her face into my own. 'Now why don't you fuck off, Rabbit, there's a good girl,' she says.

I leave her, as she wishes, but I will try again, Kitty, for I know she will be keen enough for my help in a few weeks' time.

Baile's wedding is a huge event, though I see no sign of the wealth that she insists is to be part of her life as a wife. In a fit of something approaching almost sisterly affection, I choose to fashion her dress, and she is well pleased with

255

the result – and surprised at the fine work too, to judge from the look on her face.

'Rosa, this is beautiful!' she tells me when I take the box to her house. I have stitched it by hand at night, for I did not dare to smuggle it into the workshop to make use of the machine. The fabric is not quality, for she had only a few shillings to spend on it, but I used broken or spent beads from some of my couture samples and worked enough of them into the design to have it looking like a dress worth ten times the price.

I am happy to see the pleasure in Baile's face, for she has softened a great deal in the final days before her marriage, and it is almost possible to like her when this less abrasive mood is upon her.

I ask her if she is to give up her job at the workroom and she says she will with time – which also makes me wonder about her new husband's finances.

Needless to say, Max is there at the wedding too, looking smart, though a little too dapper, in the new suit he has acquired for the occasion. He is now renting a shop off the Mile End Road and the idea is this: he attends the wedding to take shots of the bride and her family, then he is off in a cab back to the shop so that he can greet the new husband and wife and take their portraits in the studio there. There is usually much kerfuffle outside the shop when word gets around that a bride is about to arrive, and the pavements are often full of onlookers, which pleases Max no end, as he says crowds are good for business.

I must admit, Kitty, that at Baile's wedding I am hoping to hear some stray compliments about her dress as she walks smiling into the shop. Imagine my annoyance, then, when I discovered that she has thrown a coat about her shoulders, 'in case of draughts'. I make sure her coat is missing when she steps outside to leave again, and my face glows to see the smiles of admiration that the dress evokes among the still-waiting crowd.

Max – who as you know by now misses nothing – catches the look of pride in my eyes and returns it with a wink and a grin. Once the photographs are printed he hands one to me, too. 'A memento of your dearest friend,' he says. When I open the folder I see Baile's head has all but been cut off at the top of the shot and my handiwork on the dress is lit to full glory. I shall not, however, give Max the satisfaction of seeing that I am pleased.

All seemed quiet after Baile's wedding. Like dust tossed into the air, the atmosphere in the workroom soon settled and all was much the same as before, except that Baile returned much sobered and not, I thought, as happy as you might expect a new bride to be. But then perhaps this is the reality of marriage, Kitty. Pick your own husband with care, dear. Avoid being a bride with the same look in your eyes as that I perceive in Baile's.

A month later and it was a day like any other in the workroom, Kitty – only this day was to change my life forever.

Red Aggie, I noticed, had been pale all morning, rubbing her back and groaning when she moved. No one else seemed perturbed by this. Her story is that she is grown fatter because her uncle has taken a job in a bakery, and that the free bread he brings home at night has been enough to account for the widening of her waist. She wears a coat all through the day now, too, despite the heat of the room. This makes it hard to see exactly where the new pounds have been added.

By midday Aggie was white enough to use for notepaper and I saw her rise from her stool and walk unsteadily off towards the outside latrines.

Her return was so tardy I noticed Yanzdoff studying his pocket watch on at least three occasions. When she was finally back his voice broke the silence: 'One and a half hours docked for latrine time, Miss North.' I glanced up at her but she was back at work and the cheeks that had been paper-white now sported two bright and feverish spots of pink.

'Aggie?' I said as we were leaving at the end of the day, but she pushed right past me and I wondered if she were drunk. 'Sod off,' I believe she said, but her voice was so slurred I could not be sure.

When everyone was gone from the place, apart from the workers who slept on the floor, I walked through the rag-room and out towards the privy. The place was deserted. I lifted the lid and peered down into the pan and hunted behind the seat and down around the darkest corners of the floor. There was a stain that I believed could have been blood, but apart from that, nothing.

I went back through the rag-room and then I stopped. There were more spots of blood on the stones of the floor – a tiny, splattering trail that led off to one side. I looked in that direction. Before me lay the largest and most stinking pile of rags in the room. There was little light there, save that reflected from the workroom, and I dared not open the door wider for fear someone might come and ask what I was doing.

Taking my courage into both hands I slipped into the workroom and stole one of the passer's small paraffin lamps from the shelf. My hands shook too hard to light the matches and I must have wasted over a dozen before I could get the thing alight.

There was an acrid smell from the burning wick and suddenly the dark mouldering corner was suffused with an eerie, ochre light. I believe I preferred the dark, for the sight of the rotting stuff was a horror to me and I fell to imagining sightings of all the vermin that must have considered the heap as their home address.

To my terrified eyes, the ghastly pile appeared to writhe in the dull, flickering light. My task was a grim one, yet I was determined to complete it. Have you guessed what I sought, Kitty? I was looking for Red Aggie's child, for I was sure she had given birth out there that very afternoon. As you know the fate of my own poor child you may understand my obsession for ensuring this one at least had a decent burial.

Climbing a couple of feet up the pile, I began to pull away with my bare hands, at first with my eyes closed for fear I might see a rat, but then with them open – for it occurred to me that my fate might be better if I spotted the rat before it saw me.

I started to cry softly then, for the memory of my own awful plight on the ship brought me to tears of self-pity. I had tried to imagine that the whole episode was a dream, but the mind will always know the truth and will make you believe your own history eventually, no matter how hard you attempt to push it away.

Some of the rags were wedged into sodden blocks, but one pile came out easily when I touched it and I stood on tiptoe to peer into the gap that was left. It was as dark as pitch. I lifted the lamp to my face, fearing all the while that I could be in danger of starting a fire like the one in Koenigsberger's the furriers in Commercial Street – when five floors went up while all one hundred hands were working. This was before I arrived in London, but the story is still told as a warning to all of us in employment. The light did little to penetrate the gloom and I knew there was nothing for it but to push my bare arm into the space.

How great was the yell I had to smother when my hand encountered dampness! I fell backwards, biting my lip in my attempt to keep silent, and the lamp fell from my grasp as I hit the floor, which sent me scuttling to retrieve it even though my head had been banged on the stones and all I could see was a whirling roundabout of stars and flashing lights.

For a moment I believed my leg was broken, too, for I had fallen with it beneath me and heard a crack, which I thought must be the bone. Holding the newly retrieved lamp above my skirts I felt the length of the limb, discovering to my relief that it was whole and hearty and that the only breakage was the lamp-chimney – which would take some explaining when I finally returned it.

Sore and sick with shock I looked again at the hole in the rag-pile, knowing in my heart that I must return to it, even though my urge was to run to my home and shelter in the safety of my small bed.

Rolling my sleeve back further I regained my foothold in the rag-mountain and plunged my shaking arm back into the gap. What if it was a rat I had discovered, bleeding and trapped in its own lair? It would have my fingers off in an instant, I was sure of that. Yet the damp thing did not move when my hand encountered it this time.

Clutching at some fabric that appeared to cover it, I began to pull it forward and received no resistance. A knot of crumpled cloth slowly appeared, followed by a large bundle wrapped tightly in the same stuff. The wetness was blood and some other stain and it was then that a sadness overcame me and I started to weep silently.

This was a dead child, I was sure of it. Aggie had given birth in the privy and abandoned her infant in the rag-pile, to let it rot or be consumed by the rats. I pulled back the cloth that swaddled it carefully, whispering to it all the while, though I knew it could hear nothing on this earth, for it was so still I was certain it had to be dead. By now I had it in my muddled crazy head that this was my own child come back to me, to give its poor ignorant mother a second chance.

A small foot fell out of the bundle, no larger than that of a doll; it was blue, which made me sob more tears. The creature was tiny but perfect, and cold as the grave to touch. It was a boy. In my madness and grief I studied its forehead. There was no mark there, Kitty. Yet still I persevered in the idea that the small pathetic thing I held belonged to me.

Removing the soiled cloth that enveloped it, I wrapped it in some clean white woollen stuff that had been thrown out that morning, with its dear face left bare, just as though it were alive. Then I clutched it to my chest and sang quietly to it, Kitty, rocking it in my arms and reciting an old Yiddish song that Rintzi had sung to me many years before.

It was at that moment that all the unfairness of life suddenly occurred to me at last, Kitty. When poverty is your lot you can be so busy working at your own survival that the great injustice of your situation passes you by. As I held that child I saw the whole perspective of our situation, and a sorry sight it was, too.

If that infant had been born to wealth it would have lived and prospered as you do, Kitty. Instead it was spawned in the immigrant ghetto and so was destined to draw less than a few breaths of rancid air before it died. Why should we be forced to live like that? My father was a good man and a skilled worker, yet he is dead and his daughter no more than a skivvy in a foreign land, along with many thousands of others consigned to the same fate. Why? Kitty, I am too stupid to provide an answer to that question.

'Never be poor and never grow old, Rosa.' That was my papa's liturgy to me and it is the message I pass on to you now, Kitty. Remember the fate of all who went before you. Seize the chance when you can and never allow the blood and sweat that was spilt to have been given in vain.

CHAPTER TWENTY-SIX

ZG

TAFFETA
*One of the finest fabrics made, taffeta must be
handled as little as possible and stitched only once, as
holes will remain after the stitches are removed.*

I took the child home, Kitty, carrying it beneath my coat.
I had no plans for it but knew the pathetic thing deserved
more dignity in death than my own child was afforded.
Tears coursed down my face and for once I was glad of
the cover of darkness.

Once in my room I washed the small scrap as carefully
as if it had drawn breath, cooing to it all the while, and
dried it and bound it in clean fabric. Its face was beautiful,
Kitty, not ill-looking or scrawny, but as round and clear-
expressioned as a cherub's, its eyes closed as if in sleep and
its small round mouth curved into what I fancied to be the
hint of a blissful smile.

To my relief Max was out at the theatre and not due to
return for several hours. Exhausted and still sore and
aching from the bruises of my tumble, I fell back onto my
bed and slept for several hours.

It was dark when I woke, but I knew it was morning
for I heard movements in the house below me and smelt

the first scents of cooking from the stoves as the women prepared breakfasts for their husbands.

The bundle still lay crooked in my arm. A feeling of dread overwhelmed me. What had I done? Was this a sin? I had become sadly out of touch with my own religion since my arrival in London, and even though I racked my brains I could remember nothing in the rabbi's sermons that dealt with the removal of dead children.

My head ached from the battering it had received against the floor the day before, and when I opened my heavy lids I found I could barely focus my eyes. When I stared at the baby beside me I saw two pink faces peering from the blanket. There was a sound somewhere, a thin wail that I took to be issuing from my own mouth or from the kettle that Max used to heat his water for washing.

'Rosa?' I heard Max's voice, but my head still would not clear. My name bounced and echoed loudly inside my skull and the wailing danced with it. 'Rosa? Rosa!' Max's voice could have been next to my ear. Then I felt him shaking me and the fog lifted a little.

'Rosa?' Max sounded concerned and also angry. 'What have you done?'

I closed my eyes and opened them again. The room had stopped moving. 'Are you drunk?' Max's voice sounded normal. 'Rosa? What's this you have?' The wail had suddenly ceased.

I looked down at the small open mouth by my side. Instead of the blueness and white stillness I expected I saw pinks, creams and the mallow tones of warm, breathing flesh, plus wild, pearl-grey and moonstone eyes that took in too much at once. The child was alive. A miracle had occurred.

'It's a baby,' I told Max. 'My baby.'

I would go down to the synagogue within the hour and pray thanks for this until my body dropped from exhaustion. I peered at the child. Its face looked angry at its fate, but it appeared well enough and its skin felt warm when I touched it.

'Max, it's a miracle,' I said, 'this child was dead last night.'

For once Max was lost for words. He sat down on the bed beside me, which caused the springs to squeal mercy, and he stared at me with what I can only describe as tempered fear in his eyes.

'You think I am mad,' I told him. I was too happy to be concerned about his opinion, but I told him my story anyway, for I needed to share it with someone and knew I could hide little from Max, owing to our living circumstances.

'You cannot keep the child,' he said when I was finished.

'Why?' I asked. 'What else should I do? Return it to its mother? Take it to the poor home? Red Aggie abandoned this child – she could have tried to kill it, for all I know. It has fallen on me to protect it, Max. Would you want to see it left to the mercy of the paupers' house?'

Max shook his head and sighed. 'What makes you think you can provide better for it, Rosa?' he asked. 'You are impoverished enough yourself.'

I smiled at Max. 'You said I could become wealthy if I wanted,' I told him, 'you always thought I had talent and prospects.'

He shook his head again. 'Rosa, this is madness,' he said.

'No, Max,' I told him, 'this is right. I *know* it is right. This child has been given a chance. I have to respect that. I can care for it and I can find it a future. In the poor house its only fate would be to live all its life in the ghetto at the mercy of others. I will find something better for it.'

I didn't tell him the absolute truth though, Kitty, that while I feigned sanity, in my thoughts this was still the soul of my own child – come back to me. I hid my euphoria beneath a cloak of rationale for Max's benefit.

Max leant across and stuck his finger in the baby's hand. 'How can you build empires now, Rosa?' he asked, but I heard in his voice a respect that was new to my ears. Although he thought my decision was wrong, I believe he was impressed by it, nevertheless.

'I'll do it, Max,' I told him. There was, of course, another piece of the story that I had not told him, and that was that the child might be Richard's.

The next day the factory was closed for the Lean Season. We had no idea until we arrived. Baile was there weeping on the pavement outside, along with the other workers, who had also lost their homes. They all looked stunned at their loss. There was a letter pinned to the door telling us to turn up again in a month's time. Aggie was there too, Kitty, though looking as close to death as her child had the previous night. I could have felt pity for her but when I smiled she simply swore at me and hurried on her way. We never saw her again.

Someone said later that she had returned to her parents

and died of tuberculosis the following spring. There was another, more awful rumour that she had either jumped from a bridge or drunk herself to death. The tales sent shivers through my entire body.

I walked back to the house quickly, as I had promised the old woman downstairs a few pennies for looking after the baby while I was at work and I wanted to get the child back before enough time had expired for her to demand payment.

I had told her the child was my sister's, Kitty, and that she had died in childbirth, leaving me to care for the infant. The old woman had looked at me oddly, for she knew most of the comings and goings of the house, and I had never had a sister visit me there. I believe she suspected the child was my own, and a result of some illicit goings-on between myself and Max. Who knows who was carrying a child with the shawls we women wore wrapped about us throughout the year, on account of the damp and the cold that persists here – even in summer, it seems. I stuck to my tale, though. This was the story I had planned to tell everyone. So here I am, dear, without a job or friend in the world and with this small baby to whom I have promised so much.

Is this Richard's child? I look at its face to see how the features resemble him. I must name the child, too. I call him David, Kitty, after my father Dovid. I heat milk for him on Max's small stove, but the old woman downstairs says I should find a wet-nurse – though that will cost money that I do not have at present.

Max tells me he has a surprise. When I get back to the

267

rooms from taking David for a walk in the park, there is a sewing machine and a tailor's dummy beside it.

'What's this?' I ask.

'It's your own business, Rosa,' Max tells me. 'It's what you will need to start building your empire.'

I turn to look at him. 'Why should you do this for me?' I ask.

'Friendship,' Max says.

I look back at the machine. 'This must have cost good money, Max,' I tell him, 'what will you expect from me in return?'

He roars with laughter at this, which sets the baby off crying and angers me very much.

'Very well, Rosa,' he says, sitting down, 'you want a good business footing for this thing. Then I will tell you my plan, shall I? I sell your wedding dresses to the brides as they book my services. In return for that you pay me a commission on every dress you make. Now how does that sound?'

I stroke my chin thoughtfully. 'How much?' I ask.

Max whistles through his teeth. 'Ten per cent of the retail price?' he asks.

'Seven,' I reply, 'and I will pay off the money for this machine in regular payments as soon as I am in profit. Agreed?'

Max sucks his teeth. 'You drive a hard bargain, Rosa,' he says. Then he puts out his hand and we shake. I smile up at him.

'Do you know, I believe that's the first time you've smiled at me?' Max says.

'One more thing, Max?' I say, still smiling.

'Anything,' he tells me.

'I need a pressing block and a steam iron,' I say.

Now we are both laughing, and it may be my imagination but I believe even baby David looks amused.

Sometimes when I look at Max, when his smile is open and genuine and without the mockery or sarcasm that so often accompanies it, I could wish that he were less of an immoral rogue so that I could perhaps be open with him and trust him and maybe even love him. But only as a brother, of course, Kitty, for my true heart is given to Richard and that will never change.

Kitty, it is now some months since I discovered David. Already he seems to have doubled in size and, despite my reduced circumstances, he seems healthy enough. Each night I lay awake in terror that he may be taken from me again, and every morning my relief at seeing his gummy smile is almost equal to how I felt when I first discovered he was alive. Sometimes in the silent darkness I will press my ear to his tiny chest, just to hear that he breathes. The responsibility fills me with dread and yet there is a growing confidence there, too. David is my gift, and a sign that I will succeed. I know that he would never have been given to me if I was destined for failure. We will not starve, I am sure of that. The apathy I felt when I was alone has gone now. Survival is crucial, for there is more than myself dependent upon it. My mind is freed for the first time in my life, and it is now that I have my other great idea.

I call on Max at his studio. He has two women there – both properly dressed, I may add, and high-class, to judge by their clothes. I have had six commissions for wedding gowns since Max made the suggestion and he says there will be more once spring begins to show.

I wait until the women are photographed and gone in a cloud of expensive scents and raucous chatter. The studio is small, but Max has done much to make it look good, hanging drapes from the ceiling and adding a vast plaster urn on a pillar and filling it with lilies, which he says gives a bright feel to the place. Hung around the walls are portraits of women, mostly flattered to such a degree as to make them unrecognizable by anyone but their closest relatives.

There are at least three faces here that I see in passing every day, yet I would not have known them had it not been for their names inscribed in gold leaf along the corner of each shot.

I begin to laugh. 'Max, you are a magician, not a photographer!' I say when he emerges from his room. 'How did you make the old French polisher's wife look twenty years younger? And what about this bride over here?' I asked, pointing. 'I could swear she has a squint in real life, yet here her eyes are as straight as my own! And where are the warts in this picture?' I peer more closely as though expecting the woman's imperfections to reappear. 'Max, I swear you could even make me look beautiful!' I chuckle.

When I turn around he is watching me from the doorway with an impenetrable look upon his face. 'Do you know, Rosa,' he says, 'for a moment there I found myself imagining how it would feel if you were my wife come to visit me at work with our own child bundled in her arms.'

I wish he would not talk in this way, Kitty. I know he

270

is laughing at me but it makes me uncomfortable never-theless.

'What are you here for?' he asks when I am silent.

'I've come for a picture, Max,' I tell him. I am all serious-ness now.

'A baby portrait?' he asks, plucking David from my arms and bouncing him about in a way that he has.

'Mother and baby, Max,' I whisper. 'I want you to do a photograph that will look like a naming portrait.'

'But you're not his mother, Rosa,' Max tells me, his face gone cold.

'I am as good as,' I tell him. 'Maybe I will want to pass him off as my own child at some time.' I am careful in what I say. To me David *is* my child already, but if I tell Max I believe him to be the baby returned to me from its grave in the sea I know I will never hear the end of it.

Max pulls me back roughly onto the small *chaise-longue* and places David back into my arms.

'Tell me,' he says with anger in his voice, 'why might you want to pass him off as your own? Who is the child's father?' His face comes close to my own. 'Who, Rosa?' he asks.

I look into those eyes that I sometimes feel know me better than myself. It is Max who knows the worst side of me, Kitty. It is Max who I fear has always understood the truth.

'David is Richard Galliard's son,' I tell him quietly, 'sired when my boss was too drunk to know what he was doing. Aggie seduced him, she told me as much. If I tell him that David is my own son instead, then I may get Richard to marry me.'

I look down at the baby. 'I am not a fool, Max,' I say, 'I know a man like Richard will never want a girl like me. I am plain enough to be close to ugly and I have no money of my own. I could never charm him with my looks. But I love him and am determined to make him love me as much, and I know he will, if he will only see me in a more serious light.'

I have daring, Kitty, and I have had to learn cunning to survive. Richard may not know for sure who seduced him on that night, but he is an honourable man and I believe in my dreams that he will do the right thing by me. This plan of mine may sound insane, Kitty, but there is little deception in it. I love Richard and I love David. Does it matter so much who the real mother is?

Kitty, I could never describe the look on Max's face at these words. I had not expected him to encourage me, of course, but the violence in his eyes makes me blanche.

'You are mad, Rosa,' he tells me. He looks as though he loathes me.

'Why?' I ask, as David begins to emit a thin wail. 'Why is my plan so insane? It is founded on true feelings. Without me David would have had no future, yet through him I may be able to bargain the best prospects for all of us! Is that so lunatic, Max? Is it any worse than your dreams of a wealthy life as a society photographer?'

Max stares at me. 'You are using this child as your bait,' he says, quietly.

'No!' I cry. 'I love this child as my own and I would love him whoever his father. He *is* my child, Max! He was given to me!'

'If you want what is best for the boy, why not give him

272

straight to his father?' Max asks. 'Why allow him to grow up in poverty when he could have a good life?'

I cannot answer that question, Kitty. How could I? The impact of the guilt that accompanies it is enough to buckle my legs. Said in that manner, I must appear very evil indeed to keep David from his birthright. How can I explain my feelings? All I can say is that I feel him to be mine, and could no more give him away now than cut off my own right hand. Is this selfish, Kitty? Perhaps I am mad. Perhaps I am become like Rintzi.

'I could never part with him, Max,' I say, hugging the small babe to my chest and weeping with confusion.

And that is how we spend the night back in the house, I with my child clutched to my chest for fear he will be taken from me, while Max sets about exorcizing his own demons in the only way he knows how – by long and noisy shenanigans with his dimple-kneed model.

CHAPTER TWENTY-SEVEN

ZG

BLOCKS

*Every fashion house has its own blocks, and it is
these blocks that create the house style. A block consists of the pieces of brown paper pattern that act as a
blueprint for every outfit made by that house. The fit
of the shoulder, width of sleeve and shoulder-line are
all saved on the blocks, along with the other descrip-
tions of cut and fit that form the shape and look a
designer becomes known for.*

Alain sat astride a wheel-bottomed stool, frowning at the
sample worn by the house model who stood swaying
slightly in front of him.

'It's okay,' Kitty said. Georgina nodded.

'No,' Alain told them, 'the hem is wrong. I swear I saw
puckering.'

'It's the lights in here.'

'The lights are good. The hem is wrong. Turn. Turn
again. Turn slowly. Wait. Who the fuck did this stitching?'

Four other models stood banked up behind the first:
tangerine cellophane velvet with the transparent pile; Ulster
calandered linen in over-cast grey; cinnabar nubuck leather
with sherbet faux-fur trim; laminated tweed in flame
orange and tonal grey; lichen tencel with almond-green

jersey. Kitty knew them all by description now. Each new design had been costed for wholesale and sketched for the press. Now Alain was about to unpick them, and yet they looked okay to her and to everyone else.

There had been a moment soon after midnight when someone should have cried out or wailed or sobbed, and maybe they would have stopped after all – just ground to a senseless halt. But the moment had passed unrecorded, and so Alain merely picked up his huge tailor's scissors and set about defiling the dress.

There was a vapour-cloud smell of tea and pizza in the air overhead. The workforce of twenty – ten machinists, five juniors, four pattern cutters and one presser – had been almost doubled by the arrival of agency workers, called in when things got desperate. This meant the normal hum of friendly chatter had ceased, to be replaced by an uneasy and rueful stinking silence between regular and agency staff.

The PR plunged about regardless in a puddle of undiluted optimism, splashing the air with Calvin Klein One to mask the brewing sweat-cloud, auditioning replacement models for the show, cooing to the models' agents over the mobile, booking cabs, phoning the press to assure them that, yes, the collection was still happening, despite rumours that it would be cancelled, and running off to the toilet in terror every time she got trodden underfoot when Alain went on the prowl.

Chloe arrived at dawn. 'We need to talk, Kitten,' she whispered into her sister's ear.

'I'm too fucking busy,' Kitty told her, her mouth full of pins and her brain full of crushed and smouldering resentment.

'He's okay, you know,' Chloe continued. That was the way she always spoke. As though Kitty had said nothing. 'Too fucking busy,' and yet she still chattered on.

Nicky Kofteros was okay. Good. Hoo-fucking-ray.

'He really is on our side, Kitten. He knows you don't like him and he respects that. He understands it. All he wants to do is see that the whole thing goes through smoothly and fairly. Nobody will get ripped off. The company is honourable. Talk to him, Kitten. Hear what he has to say.'

Kitty ignored her sister. Alain frowned across at her before glancing quickly back at his work. Then his focus settled upon the scent-filled gap where Chloe had just been standing. He stared so long Kitty had to turn around, too.

There was a young woman standing there. Chloe was looking shocked beside her. Kitty stood up. Pins tumbled from her mouth onto her chest, where they stuck, Gulliver-like, into her shirt. The visitor was about twenty years old, attractive in an unfashionable type of way: long black hair that had been badly permed and then grown out again, a pink suit that was a little too tight, a confident, chin-up posture but hands that worked nervously at the handle of her bag.

It was Ricky Khan's daughter.

'What the hell . . . ?' Chloe began. The girl ignored her. Kitty inwardly admired her chutzpah.

'I was hoping you might find time for us to speak,' she said to Kitty. Her voice sounded polite and cultured. 'I need to tell you a few things about your father's death. It's time you were told the truth.'

CHAPTER TWENTY-EIGHT

ZG

BUCKRAM
A light cloth, rather like cheesecloth in quality,
buckram is usually used with a glued finish for
hat-shaping, belt-stiffening and interfacing.

There is much knocking on the door of our old house the following day, Kitty, which is a strange thing to hear, for everyone in the ghetto knows that doors are rarely locked in this area and ours is bound to be open.

I hear voices calling out to the visitor, but the knocking does not cease. In the end I hear a man from two floors below make the slow path across his bare wood floor and out into the narrow hallway. Then it is my name I hear called: 'Miss Zigofsky! There is a gentleman here at the door for you!', in Yiddish.

It is Richard Galliard, and I am barely got together for it is still early. I smooth my hair behind my ears and then pull it out again, for I do not want to make too much of my ugliest feature.

'Miss Zigofsky?' His manners are impeccable, even in this terrible place. Then I know at once why he is there. Max has written to him about the child and he is come to reclaim it. I hold the door half-closed in readiness.

277

'I'm sorry,' Richard says, 'I must have startled you, but this is an urgent matter. Could you bear to take on some work for us, Miss Zigofsky? We have laid off most of our workers as you know, and need seamstresses of your calibre rather suddenly.'

'At the sweatshop?' I ask, confused. I am both terrified witless, embarrassed and also excited by the sight of him in my doorway.

Richard smiles. 'No, not there. In the couture house, Miss Zigofsky. Do you think you could manage it?'

'When?' I ask, reddening.

'Now,' is his reply.

Kitty, I am dressed in my shabbiest gear and my hair is doused in soot from the fireplace, and badly in need of a brush. While my face and hands are clean I was still awaiting Max's departure for the studio before I could see about the toilet of both David and myself! I believe Richard spots my plight, though.

'Er, I have a little business to attend to nearby,' he says, smiling. 'Perhaps half an hour?' I simper with relief.

In a flurry of excitement I have David placed with the woman downstairs, who says she will be hard-pressed to notice one squalling head more among her own vast brood, and have changed so quickly that Richard discovers me waiting in the hall on his return. I watch his smile fade as he approaches. In an effort to smell clean I have poured some of Max's cologne inside my corsets. To my shame the stench is overwhelming. I must reek like a streetwalker.

We take the carriage to the West End and I feel my poor dress turn shabbier with each rotation of the cab's wheels.

Richard is polite but the smell of the scent is so overpowering he has a handkerchief held to his nose before we are out of the East End.

The salon is in Berkeley Square and an extremely grand place it is too, with black-and-white marble on the floors and crystal lights all the way up the curving staircase. I step along the wood on the treads in case my boots soil the fine carpets.

The name above the door is perhaps the most impressive sight of all: 'Galliard Couture and Co. Court Dressmaker and Ladies' Tailor'.

I wonder that I am not shoved into the tradesman's entrance, and the expressions on the faces of some of the other staff when they see me make me wish that I had been. But Richard is all beams and smiles and introduces me as though we were guests at a society ball.

The salon is like a palace, Kitty. Everywhere are lights, and each light is reflected a thousand times in crystals or mirrors. The daylight throws rainbows around like confetti, dotting the floor and dancing on the walls. This is the prettiest place I have ever seen, Kitty.

They leave me in the salon and for one glorious moment I am alone there to take it all in. I am careful, though, checking my boots for mud before walking on tiptoe across the floor to stand directly beneath the central chandelier and looking up at it. Then I begin to rotate myself slowly so that I see the sparkle from each crystal in turn. In my excitement I start to spin and Bubba's coat flaps out like the wings of a rook.

Suddenly I stop and look straight ahead in the grand, gilded mirrors. Do you know what I see, Kitty? I see a small, pitch-haired girl with a face so white and so comically melancholy she could do the music halls without so much as a lick of greasepaint. She has thick, beetle-black brows that curve in permanent surprise, eyes like two chips of coal and a mean little mouth that looks as though it is spoiling for a fight.

Did you ever see those tiny dogs, Kitty? I forget their name but you will know them from my description: thin bent legs constantly splayed, barrel-bodied and round of head, they are the size of a cat yet feel themselves to be as good a fighter as the nearest mastiff. Their eyes see everything and they would challenge anything, so strong is their conviction that they would be the victor.

This is the look of the girl I see, Kitty; arrogant and cocky despite her size. Her chin juts and her head is high. I laugh at her and she laughs back and her smile splits her face and her teeth are white and her tongue pink. Her feet beneath the great coat are clown's feet – flat and long, and the ankles are thin as sticks.

I am reminded, Kitty, of the droll comedian at the variety halls, and quite tickled by all this until I realize that the woman I am looking at is myself. I try to make amends then, reaching up to smooth my hair or make good my outfit – but what is to be done? The face I see may not be much but it is my face, Kitty, so I cannot hate it. It is neither ugly nor handsome but lies somewhere between the two, which is to say it is neither as repulsive as Queer Tess's, nor as vacuous as Baile's. I like the spirit of its expression, and also its eyes, which show defiance and intelligence when they stop looking startled. Rintzi is there, but then so is Papa.

People think buildings are haunted, Kitty, but I believe it applies to faces, too, for it is there that one can see the ghosts of those who have died. When I hold my head so, I can see Bubba. When I smile Papa re-appears. Look in the mirror, dearest. Do you find my own face there anywhere? Search among your own handsome features some time – is there not a hint of arrogance in the tilt of the jaw? Or a trace of the same daring in your eyes? Those looks were mine, Kitty, and my mama's, papa's and Bubba's before me.

It is not Richard, thank God, who finds me in this day-dream, but another pinch-faced machinist come to collect me and take me off to the workrooms. I am full of questions as we walk. I know that I should be silent but cannot help myself, Kitty.

'Does this whole place belong to Richard Galliard?'

'*Mr* Galliard, yes.'

I am enchanted.

'To do with as he wants?'

The girl looks at me queerly. 'I suppose so, yes.'

I know I sound stupid, Kitty, but I must discover answers to the questions that are buzzing about my head.

'If Mr Galliard were to have a wife and child I suppose the place would be theirs as well, then?' I ask.

The girl stops and stares at me with her head on the tilt. 'Are you simple, or something?' she asks.

'No.'

'Then what of interest is it to the likes of you?'

I raise my nose as high as her own, proving I am just as able to put on airs when required. 'I'm just asking,' I tell her, 'would she or wouldn't she?'

'Maybe,' is all the girl will allow, but that is enough for me.

We pass through a design-room first, Kitty, a long space lined with rolls of the finest fabrics I have seen and hanging with toile, calico and paper patterns that I would give several years of my life to be allowed to look through.

There is a horsehair dummy in the midst of all this, and on it is pinned a half-made dress of peacock blue shantung. A woman as young as myself is on her knees killing the hem with stabs from a mouthful of pins, and another tacks the back with mother-of-pearl buttons so small they will need a hook to fasten them.

I am led carefully around this area by the gentleman machinist, a man large enough to make two of me, but who nevertheless proves light on his feet when we tiptoe around cloth and papers on the design-room floor. I am close enough to touch the dress and would do so too, as my fingers itch for the feel of good fabrics again, but one look from the seamstress is enough to inform me I am not good enough to be sharing the same air as the garment, let alone herself.

We dart up some narrow backstairs, which are bare of carpet, and arrive in a small room that is every bit as cramped as the sweatshop in the East End. There is natural light in this room, though, from a large skylight in the slanting roof, the effect of which is to lend an eerie, greenish glow to everything as the glass is thick enough to take on a tint.

Around the four walls are tables laden with cloths of all types and in the middle sit the rows of tables that hold the machines. At one end is a small paraffin stove and three well-dressed, long-stemmed women sit around it dipping finger biscuits into bone china cups filled with pale, aromatic tea. One of them is smoking and I am full of admiration for the way she points her rouge-painted mouth to the ceiling to emit perfect rings of billowing white smoke.

The machinist has returned to his seat. Everyone ignores me, which is of little matter, for it means I am free to stare where I will.

There must be as few as five garments being produced in here. At the sweatshop in the high season we would have more than that many on the go a-piece. The floor around the machines is covered with sheets of muslin to keep the garments free of dirt and I notice the workers wear slippers made of the same stuff over their boots.

The smell in this room is of camomile and lavender – one from the blend of tea and the other to repel the moths. To my left are wooden boxes filled with all sorts of delights – beads of every colour and size, small swatches of braid and embroidery silks and a tray of silver needles so fine and small you would need an eye like a bird even to thread them.

'Have you come as a replacement?' one of the biscuit women asks me. Her hair is pinned so tight upon her head that the skin of her face is as taut as that on a drum. I nod at her, the sudden movement of which sets Max's cologne off again, so that I am sadly aware of the stench myself.

'What grade are you?' she asks.

'Skilled,' I tell her – which is a lie in name but not deed. 'My father was a master tailor.'

She musters what might pass for a smile. 'So your father will be here to do your work for you, will he?' she says.

'No, my father is dead,' I say. She is all in black herself,

283

which makes me suspect that someone from her family must be recently deceased.

'Then we shall keep you to sewing on buttons for the time being, shall we?' she asks, re-aligning her padded buttocks on the small gilt chair.

And so this is where you discover me now, Kitty, perched on a stool so high my feet barely touch the ground when I point my toes, still in Bubba's coat for I am so ashamed of the dress I wear beneath it, sweating in the heat from the paraffin fire, holding threads between my teeth so tight my jaw aches, and furiously sewing on buttons so tiny they could be strung and used for pearls. There is a young girl beside me and, as chit-chat appears to be allowed here I attempt to strike up a conversation.

'Is her bereavement recent?' I enquire, nodding towards the woman in black. In reply I hear a muffled snorting noise and the girl presses her round, flat-featured face into some calico she is sewing.

'*Madame* Corby is attired in *noir* because she is a *vendeuse*,' she tells me, claret-faced with her mirth. 'All the *vendeuses* wear *noir*. So does the salon *première*. A *vendeuse* has a small white apron that she wears in the salon, but the *première* is all *noir*. Like a crow. I will be a *vendeuse* when I am old enough.'

I study the woman in black. 'I should imagine you will need to wait until you are at least ninety years if that woman is anything to go by,' I say, 'she looks as ancient as a tortoise.'

'She is my mother,' the girl says, and that is all the conversation I have from her for the rest of the afternoon.

*   *   *

284

Kitty, we are so busy in the salon, yet the work never exhausts me for I have such a passion for the garments that I am employed upon. Each seam and dart hold an eternal fascination for me and there is so much to learn here that I fear my head will not hold it all.

Each day I am endless with my questions until someone tires of me and I am told to keep my silence. And because we have daylight, I can see the sky. When the heat becomes unbearable a *vendeuse* will pull a green-dyed rope that hangs from the skylight and, *voilà*! From my little stool I have an adequate view of the clouds, as well as the occasional draught of fresh air, so my surroundings have improved immensely. I am also able to learn a few words of the language of fashion, which is *Français*.

There are some twenty staff employed here in all, which means it was more than three weeks before I had caught sight of them all. There is a strict order of superiority though, Kitty, and this is how it works: the salon is run by the manager, a silver-haired gentleman with a face like a cheese, named just 'Monsieur M'. Flapping at his flanks in adoration are the five *vendeuses*, all known as 'Madame', and all clad in dyed, bat-black challis from top to toe. Their hair, Kitty, is a marvel of construction and under-pinning. Each has a centre parting as straight as a rule from which the hair is combed back so severely that their scalps resemble little less than arrows. At the back are plaits so long they wrap three times around and all this is greased with pomander until it appears lacquered.

During the season there will be a dozen more *vendeuses* arriving, so I am told, and I wait to see if they all look alike.

Do you know, Kitty, there are no less than four women employed to clean the salon? Two work at night, polishing brass and crystal until the place gleams, and two arrive by day to ensure crumbs are swept away the minute they drop from the clients' plates.

Upstairs are the two designers, a pretty-looking couple of mice who spend their days pinning and snipping, and with them work a cutter and sewer who are both in suits as they work in full view of the clients when they arrive for their fittings.

Then there is the attic where we work, Kitty. We are governed by the *première* who is well above God in rank. When this woman arrives in the morning it is the job of the *petites mains* to take her hat and coat, polish any street mud from her boots and furnish her with a *demie-tasse* of sugared French *café*.

I am now a *seconde main*, Kitty, which means I am officially allowed to operate a machine. No fewer than two other *seconde mains* were set to watch over me when I was first set to work in such a way, no matter that I have worked machines in the sweatshop for more than a couple of years. My hands were inspected for grime before I was allowed to touch the fine fabrics and they are inspected in the same way each morning, before I start work.

Directly below our attic room I have discovered the most wonderful place, Kitty. In a long chamber without windows stand line upon line of horsehair dummies, all made to the size of the most regular and important clients.

Hannah, Madame Corby's daughter, has been involved with the making of these dummies and a fascinating story she tells, too. She was given the task of holding the pins when a certain English aristocrat came for her fitting. The woman was dressed in the *toile de corps*, which is a tight-fitting vest that moulds to the figure. The *toile* was then stuffed with horsehair to match the woman's shape exactly from neck to thigh.

Do you know, Kitty, these dummies are never seen by the women they were made for? Can you imagine why? Because most are too vain to view their true shape in the flesh! If a client is thin and straight then a more shapely dummy is shown but, if the woman is too well-rounded for her own tastes then a narrower one will be produced. All is done to keep the client happy, according to Hannah, and a more difficult job I could barely imagine, if their vanity is so great!

CHAPTER TWENTY-NINE

ZG

CHALLIS
*A light, plain weave of wool that is used mainly for
summer-weight dresses.*

The season has begun, Kitty, and a kind of madness settles
over all. From my stool in the attic I can just see the street
and so watch the fine carriages as they pull up around the
square. The women that arrive at our door are all kinds
of ages and sizes, but each one, without doubt, is very
wealthy.

Each client has her own *vendeuse*, who is at *madame*'s
beck and call, and who will show her all the latest styles
that she knows will be suitable to her customer. Each *vendeuse* has her own list of clients that she alone will serve,
and there is much hissing and spitting over any new customers that are introduced. All the saleswomen have their
lists etched into small black leather-bound ledgers which
are attached to their aprons by small silver chains. These
clients are their life, Kitty, and anyone attempting to peep
into those pages could well find themselves hacked to death
by a set of well-honed talons.

I spoke of vanity before, Kitty. Let me tell you now that
I have spent the past month attempting to part my own

288

hair straight in the middle, though without much success, for my own mane is as thick and springy as the horsehair used to stuff the dummies.

Max, of course, has caught me at these endeavours and much sport he found from it, too.

'What are you about, Rosa?' he asked. I tried shushing him, Kitty, for my darling David was sound asleep in a basket at my feet, but this only drove him to come nearer and investigate more closely.

'You are trying to slice your head in two like an apple?' he asked, watching me raking my scalp with my comb.

'I am changing the style of my hair,' I told him. To my intense aggravation he squatted down on my bed to watch. I cannot bear people watching me at careful work, Kitty. My patience was all but worn out as it was, and now I found myself more than usually clumsy, thanks to Max's curiosity.

'Why?' he asked, bending over the basket to offer David a Havana cigar before lighting up himself – a joke that appears to have endless potential as far as Max is concerned, though I miss the humour of it myself.

'Because the new style is *très à la mode*,' I explained. This, of course, proceeded to tickle Max more than the cigar routine.

'And on whose authority do we receive this missive?' he asked.

'It is the style sported by the *vendeuses* at the salon,' I told him. He nodded sagely.

'Then perhaps I should be adopting it myself if it is so *à la mode*,' he said, fingering his own hair. I turned to him at that.

289

'I wish for once you would take me seriously, Max,' I said, 'you are nothing but jokes and satires. If I had fewer wits about me I would be all in knots and possibly in tears, too. Is there nothing you can say that does not have some other meaning? Why must your comments be so full of sarcasm?'

Max stood up slowly, shaking his head. He is so huge in my small partitioned room, Kitty. When he stands there he makes David and me look like dolls in a dolls' house.

'When I am serious you never believe me, Rosa,' he said, 'so why should I bother? Eh?'

I turned back to my mirror. My face looked pale with the hair pulled back so hard and my eyes appeared huge, like a child's. 'I cannot remember ever hearing you try,' I whispered.

At this he had his hands on my shoulders and had turned me about so quickly that my heel caught in my skirts and David started to awaken.

Max's face was so close to my own that I stared deep into his eyes and beyond. Did you ever stand in a high place, Kitty, and look far down to the ground? Then you will know of the pull I felt as I stared. What a horrible thing! For a moment I felt a magnetism that could have had me falling into his arms! Is this the trick that men use to charm women into submission?

There was much talk in London last year of a hypnotist who was working the music halls, mesmerizing members of the audience into doing acts of great stupidity against their will. While others, including Max himself, appeared to find these antics roaringly amusing, I always thought them a little sinister.

It has now occurred to me, Kitty, that Max may have been doing more than laughing at the act. What if he was also studying the techniques used? I believe the stage hypnotist employed a large pocket watch to put his patients under, while I have no memory of Max retrieving his from his pocket before I felt the magnetic pull. This is of no use as a guide, though, Kitty, for if he is so adept at the art he may also have been able to make me forget the sight of the watch altogether!

I *wanted* Max to hold me at that moment, Kitty. I would almost say I *yearned* for him to touch me more. The breath became short in my lungs and my thin legs lost their strength. Now what else could have caused that to happen if it were not some wicked skill or trick on Max's behalf?

Next time I see him reach for his watch, Kitty, I will remove myself from his presence with great speed, you may be sure of that!

My new hairstyle is not a great success in the salon as it appears many of the *vendeuses* believe a mere *seconde main* like myself should know her place and not attempt to ape her superiors. Nevertheless I shall continue with it, for I feel it gives me some style which my poor clothing, alas, sorely lacks.

Kitty, I have omitted to make much mention of David, but not because he is forgotten – rather that all those I work with inform me that I speak of very little else. He is the most marvellous child and very beautiful, too.

I stare at him for hours when he is asleep and when he wakes I feel a new joy that I cannot describe. When I hold him and feel his little skull cupped into the palm of my hand and watch his tiny fingers clenching around my own pin-scratched mitt I know that I have done the right thing in caring for him.

In the morning I carry him in my arms to the woman downstairs and I know he is happy there until I return to collect him at night. He is growing plump and healthy as I did as a babe, Kitty. When I sing to him he smiles and I still feel him to be my own infant, returned to me whole from the depths of the ocean. I am not mad, Kitty. My mind knows full well that he is not some wraith come back to haunt me, and yet my heart tells me another story at the same time. I know the child is not mine in body, but there is nevertheless an instinct in me telling me strongly that discovering him was more fate than coincidence. I believe he was intended for me, dearest. Perhaps there is some of the soul in him of the child that I lost.

Spiritualism is very much the vogue in London right now and seances take place in all the best parlours on a regular basis. The other day there was thick fog upon us and Max remarked drolly from the window that it was maybe all the left-over ectoplasm that the mediums had left leaking about the atmosphere. If so many educated people may believe in such things, though, then it is my belief that I should be allowed to as well. Bubba always told us folk tales of lost spirits and ghosts, and although they terrified poor Gregory witless I was always fascinated by them, no matter how many times they were repeated.

I have persuaded Max to take the photograph that I wanted, even though I had to trick him a little and pretend it was merely a portrait. I made David a little white robe from some lace off-cuts I saved from one of the bridal gowns, and I put on my best frock and borrowed a decent hat from Baile.

Max posed us against his best backdrop, which is a rather fanciful arrangement of draped fabric and waxed fruit in front of a painting of cobalt sky and overblown clouds.

Max is very much the professional in his studio, Kitty, and it would make you laugh to watch him about his business. There is a jacket he wears for the job that I feel makes him look ridiculously pompous, though he informs me that all photographers of note wear them. The thing is made of dark crimson velvet with lapels of blood-red satin. Do you know, he even has a small matching pill-box hat with a gold braid tassel that he would place upon his head? I was forced to beg him to forget this particular item of photographer's costume, for I would have barely been able to hold my pose for laughing.

Max appeared deeply offended at this, flinging the offending item across the studio and working in studied silence for a full hour following – though I caught him putting the hat onto David's head and laughing later, when he thought I was not looking, so the thing cannot be quite so serious after all, now, can it?

The photograph is wonderful, Kitty. Max has quite captured David's expression when he is at his most cherubic and I do not look so bad, either, despite the fact that Baile's hat is a size too large and had to be stuffed with tissue to prevent it slipping around my ears. I believe Max to be quite proud of his work, too, for he has made a copy for himself that he has stuck in a little frame and placed beside his bed.

'I wonder my face does not keep you awake with the nightmares,' I said once, attempting a little joke of my own.

'It does keep me from sleeping, Rosa, but not in the way you think,' he told me, which made me blush. Sometimes I find his manner of turning an innocent comment around quite exhausting.

The season has passed now at the salon and we are a little quieter, even though there are still the fittings and makings to be done. I am worried now about my future, for I fear the same laying-off of hands that we had at the factory. I have two to feed now and worry that David may suffer if my work falls off.

In preparation for this I am hard at work getting commissions for more wedding gowns. Max has offered to keep a portfolio of photographs of the few I have already made in the studio so that the new brides can see them and judge the quality of my work. I tell him this idea has its limits, for how many brides will want to order a design that another has already worn?

Max informs me that since my designs are all copies anyway he fails to see the problem. This is of course true, but I do not like him any the more for saying it. My wedding dresses to date have all been taken from photographs Max has shown me of other brides' gowns, even though I will alter a neckline here or add some little frill or other there.

'I'm a sewer, Max,' I tell him, 'how can I be expected to design something new as well?'

Max shrugs. 'You see enough clothes, Rosa,' he tells me, 'surely you will have learnt a few tricks by now?'

'And you spend most of your evenings at the music halls watching the comics, Max,' I tell him indignantly, 'so I suppose by the same token you will be able to form your own routine by now.'

This is, of course, a mistake, as Max sees it as his cue to leap to his feet and begin rattling off jokes with Baile's hat pulled onto his head and a stupid expression on his face.

I would rather chew off my own nose than let Max see that any of this amuses me, and so cover my face with my hands, though David begins to crow with delight at all the racket, until I am forced to lift him from his basket and show him the whole wretched performance.

As Max comes to the end, I begin to feel a little dizzy and suddenly I am on the floor and David is crying while Max is calling my name and unbuttoning my bodice at the neck. I am about to reprimand him for this but find myself too weary to raise my head. Max is all concern now. I feel him lift me into his arms just as though I weighed as little as a rag doll, and I am placed gently upon his bed.

'When did you last eat?' he asks me.

I try to think, but I cannot remember clearly.

'Rosa!' Max is sounding serious now. I open my eyes and stare up into his face. If he pulls the pocket watch from his waistcoat I shall be crawling back into my own room despite my fatigue.

'David?' I ask. I can still hear him crying somewhere.

'The baby is fine,' Max tells me. 'I have given him your hat to play with.'

'The hat is Baile's!' I struggle to get up but Max holds me pinned to the bed.

295

'Rosa,' he repeats, though more gently this time, 'you are feeding the baby at the expense of yourself. Now you faint from lack of nutrition. Am I supposed to watch you starve yourself, Rosa?'

I turn my head to the pillow. Max watches me a while and then I hear him go out. His bed is softer than my own and I can do nothing but fall into a deep sleep. When I wake up Max has returned and has made tea for me to drink.

'Strudels and honeycakes,' he says. There is a platter of treats in front of me and, after breaking some off for David I am ashamed to say I eat the lot. Max sits watching me and sipping at his own cup of tea.

'Rosa,' he says quietly after a while, 'am I right in assuming you will not marry me?'

I am feeling stronger now after my feast and I snort a little and laugh, for I know he is back to his jokes again.

'Then you must make some plans,' he says, 'or you will either have to take charity or starve. The salon must fall quiet soon. Do you have work at the factory if it does?'

I shake my head. All fashion work is seasonal and all seasons are the same.

'Then what are your alternatives?' he asks.

'To make up models for some more brides,' I tell him, 'perhaps take in some private alterations and repairs.'

'Weddings are very much seasonal too, Rosa,' Max tells me. 'Didn't you know most brides like to be married in the spring? And repairs will hardly keep you in bread for a week.'

I lay back onto the pillows. 'Is all this said just to depress me, Max?' I ask. 'I know my plight. I'm not a fool.'

Max stares at me. 'You should tell your boss that you have his child here,' he says.

I have a sudden vision of Richard in my mind. I have seen him less at the salon than I did at the workshop as we are mainly segregated there and Richard does not appear much above the first floor.

'No,' I say, 'not yet.'

Max still stares. 'Then come and work for me,' he says, 'I am in need of a lady receptionist.'

I smile because of his cakes and because of his offer, which is, I believe, genuine. 'My skill is in the garment trade, Max,' I tell him. 'If I am to make my fortune then I believe it will be in that business.' I also have no wish to leave Richard's employ.

Max sighs. 'Then you will take a cut in your rent,' he tells me.

'No, Max.' I need to thank him for enough already. If he takes less rent he might be asking for favours in kind.

Did he read this in my eyes? I see a change in his own, a look of disbelief. 'You wouldn't take help from a friend?' he asks. 'Not even on behalf of the child?'

'David will never go hungry,' I tell him.

'No – not as long as you are prepared to starve on his behalf,' is Max's reply.

I sit in the design-room holding pins for the seamstress who is doing a fitting on a large matron with corsets like the sails of a ship. I am neither to stare nor to move any more than is necessary. This is difficult because the fabric of the suit we are altering has a nap that flies up like fur when it is cut and my nose itches and my eyes sting.

When the client is gone I am either allowed tea with the *vendeuses*, or they do not notice me there with them, which is the more likely option.

There are wafer biscuits on a dish that they share and my stomach groans, but I would not dare to lean and take one. I am squeezed between two of the part-time *vendeuses*, both remarkably elderly ladies with a strong scent about them of eau de cologne and mothballs. Part of their conversation is spoken in a very strangely accented French, and part of it in Yiddish, but the story I hear from them is that the older lady is about to retire.

Unfortunately both are deaf, so the conversation is of limited pleasure, but it seems that the retiring lady, known as Madame Gisele, is becoming too hard of hearing to serve the clients, and even her oldest and most loyal customers – though how many can be left alive by now I am led to ponder – have become agitated at the way orders will go astray or be completely misheard.

I gather that one elderly duchess, in particular, has been vociferous in her complaints after a brown satin tea-dress she ordered became somehow translated into a broadsilk tweed vest on the garment list. There is much rustling and twittering among the other *vendeuses* at the news of this woman's retirement, for whoever bids the most will be able to buy her client list from her when she goes.

This evening I am told I will not be needed at the salon again, though I may be called back when the next season starts. Kitty, I am sickened by this news, even though it was expected. What am I to do? I see myself a pathetic figure now – eighteen years old and soon to be queuing at the Jewish poor house for bread and hot tea. All the way home I tell myself that I have a brain in my head and that I can live on my wits, though my stomach rumbles hard enough to assure me I need bread as well.

The woman downstairs gives me a look as she returns David to me. 'There is a letter come for you,' she says. I can see she is all ears as to the contents so I deny myself the urge to rip it open there and then, stuffing it instead into the pocket of my apron as though receiving letters were an everyday occurrence.

Once in my room I place David on the floor to play while I rip open the envelope and read the letter inside.

It is from the Temporary Shelter. They have been trying to trace me for many weeks to tell me an immigrant has arrived in the country naming me as a relative they might find shelter with. I am to call at Leman Street within a day of the letter's arrival to take part in the longed-for reunion. The name that has been given is in print: ZIGOFSKY – nothing more. I wonder if one of my uncles has come from America having fallen on hard times. How pleased he will be then to see the succour that his clever little niece can provide for him!

I tell Max of this news and he is all finger-wagging and dire warnings. 'Don't take in any more strays off the street, Rosa!' he says.

I look at David and then across at Max, my eyes wide with anger. 'Strays?' I ask.

'Of course,' Max replies, walking over to the baby and lifting him shoulder high. 'You have no objection to being called a stray, do you, young man?' he asks David. He then throws his voice into the baby's mouth, saying, 'No!' in a child's tone, which is his latest trick stolen from some stage ventriloquist he has seen at the halls. He would take this joke further, but I pull David from his hands while he is still laughing at the cleverness of it all.

The fog is thick and I have no pennies for a cab and so must walk to Leman Street to meet my lost relative. I leave the house dressed in good order, for I would not want an uncle to see my true situation, but by the time I am two streets away the fog has made a huge damp halo of my hair and the mud from the carts is splashed all over the hem of my skirts.

I never relish walking about the East End after dark. I remember the tales of the Ripper that haunted me when I was a greener. The murders may have stopped but the monster was never discovered, and in my imagination he is waiting around each and every dark corner to claim me as his next victim.

A greater dread comes upon me as I approach the shelter, though. This is the place I first stayed when I arrived full of hope for my marriage to Aaron. What a child I was then! The smells here are still familiar to me. In those days I supposed I would be rid of this East End grime by now and married and living far away in Russia again, with my husband, taking care of my family. To think I came here as a saviour of them all and instead my mother is well and I am the one in need of help.

For the first time the idea occurs to me that I should save up for a ticket back to my homeland and search for my mother. But I know I can never do that now. My duty is to my own child and my dream is to marry his papa. Russia is still a cruel land for Jews and David could be slaughtered as the son of one just as easily as my own papa.

I am cold. The light is there in the doorway of the shelter and, although I am repulsed by the too-familiar smells of the place, I force myself to walk inside.

The warden, who greets me, is a decent sort who appears genuinely pleased that I have come to search for my relative. I had almost been expecting to see Queer Tess squatting there, before reminding myself of her death. I sign my name to some paper and am kept waiting some fifteen minutes while the warden goes off on a search. I hear two sets of footsteps returning but only the warden's voice, chatting encouragement.

'Come along, son, she's here to fetch you. Did you eat your supper? Good. Bring your coat from the peg for it's a cold enough night and you don't want a chill.'

Is this a child he has fetched for me, Kitty? I peer around the door but the corridor curves too acutely for me to see. Then I have them in my view, the warden, small and bearded, clutching a light in one hand and a coat in the other. And beside him – Gregory! Grown so much I would barely know him in the street, but my Gregory, nevertheless.

He is taller than I remembered and his face is bigger, though still quite beautiful. Like myself when I arrived he has an expression of bewilderment in his eyes. There is a sad, hand-knitted cap upon his head and his hair beneath it appears in need of a cut.

'Gregory?' I take a step further towards him. Then he raises a hand in welcome and I know it could be no one but my brother, for there are no fingers on that hand, they are buried in the woods in Russia.

'Gregory!' I am more fearful than pleased to see him.

How has he got here? Why has he come? He is smiling openly now at the sight of me. He breaks into a shambling run and then he has his arms about me and I feel my own tears pressed into the shoulder of his jacket, though I had no idea before then that I was crying.

Gregory rocks back and forth as he clings to me. 'Rintzi, Rintzi,' he cries. He is cold, very cold – shivering beneath his clothes. I take his coat from the warden and place it about his shoulders. I begin to speak to him in English, which is now my tongue, but realizing the confusion in his eyes switch quickly to the language of my childhood.

'How did you come here? Are you alone? What has happened? How did you arrive?'

But all he does is smile at me as fat tears snake down his face.

The warden is back with a small sack in his hands. 'Here,' he says, giving it to me. Inside are all Gregory's possessions – a comb, some soap wrapped in paper, a handful of bone collar-stiffeners and the equivalent to approximately three pounds in roubles. 'Good luck to you, son,' the warden says, raising a hand.

'What do you mean?' I ask. 'Where is he going?'

The old man smiles. 'To live with his sister,' he says.

'I have no room.' I can barely hear my own voice. 'I thought he could stay here a little while longer. I have nowhere for him to go. What shall I do?'

'The boy is fed and has enough money for lodgings,' the warden tells me. 'When the money runs out you can take him to the poor house. You know his time here is limited.'

I lead Gregory out into the street. The cold is now acute and the fog has thickened. As I take his hand I feel his shivers have increased until his entire body seems almost to be held in a fit. For want of anything other to do we begin to walk in the direction of Brick Lane. Gregory holds my hand so tight he almost breaks the bones, though I dare not prise him off for fear I might lose him in the fog. Carriages roll close to us, making us both jump. All noises seem magnified in the gloom, even the sound of our own feet.

'Are you well, Gregory?' I ask as we rush on our way, and he nods once. 'Are you hungry?' He shakes his head, 'No.' I suspect that he is lying – Rintzi always taught us to ask for nothing when we visit another's home – but I am relieved, as there is little food in the house.

When we reach my place I usher Gregory up the stairs like a reluctant dog, and into my room. I can see from his face and the way that he pauses in the doorway that he was expecting more. I see the room with new eyes at that moment. It is a pauper's place, clean but impoverished. There are not even chairs enough for us both to sit down.

'Were you expecting a palace, dear?' I ask my brother. He shakes his head silently, rubbing his hands back and forth on his cheeks to thaw them. Suddenly he looks at me and smiles and it is as if my heart has opened up and been torn from my chest.

He is the same boy that I knew and loved. Gregory, my dear brother, here in my room in London. The same pale-skinned face. The same calm beauty – though now tempered with age. How old must he be? Twenty-three? A man. Yet he smiles like a boy and his crooked teeth are the same. His brown hair has been combed flat to his head and ironed there by the cap. I watch as he suddenly throws himself down onto the bed, exhausted. When I return from downstairs with David in my arms I find Gregory sound asleep already and bend quietly to prise the boots off his feet.

Soon he is snoring loudly. I crouch down on the floor by his feet and sit there in silence, rocking David in my arms in the dark room.

'Two children now, David,' I whisper, 'two helpless and trusting babies to care for and nourish. What is to become of us, eh? What are we to do?'

CHAPTER THIRTY

LONDON 1997

BRICK LANE
*Of all the buildings in the East End, the Great
Synagogue in Brick Lane must most represent the changing
face of the immigrants in that area. Starting life as a
French chapel, while the Huguenots wove their silk in
the neighbouring attic rooms, it was a Wesleyan
chapel before becoming a synagogue. Following that it
became a mosque.*

It was raining as they left the studio. Alain came after her.
'Take this,' he said. He eyed Khan's daughter as he handed
Kitty her mobile.

'What, do you think I will try to murder her?' the girl
asked him. The word 'murder' hung in the air menacingly.

'We have garments to price,' Alain said to Kitty, ignoring
everything else. 'Thirty minutes max, okay?'

The two women climbed into a cab. Sitting together
provided a kind of intimacy that made both uncomfortable.
Riva smelt of scent and lunch. For want of something to
do Kitty rolled her sleeves as though she were hot. The
silence between them was unbearable. In another minute

she knew she would have cracked and made some facile comment about the weather or the cost of muslin that season.

In the event it was Riva who tossed a fistful of words into the vacuum. 'Thirty minutes to prove my father did not kill yours.' She pulled the scarf off her head and shook it.

Kitty had grown up knowing the girl, but they had never been friends. Riva had always seemed fascinatingly remote. She was older, too; nearer Chloe's age. The cab smelt stale, like a damp dog. They sat side by side but both staring ahead.

Kitty was cross-eyed tired. The cab was warm and dank. Riva pulled a small perfume spray out of her purse and puffed it about fussily.

'You believe Ricky Khan killed Gabriel Zigofsky?' she asked quietly. It was as though she spoke about two strangers, just commenting on something she'd read in the press. So what is your opinion? As though it barely mattered.

'I only just heard,' Kitty said. 'I didn't believe he'd been arrested. Has he been charged?'

When Riva turned to face her she could see the calmness was all an act. Her features looked smeared in the street-lights. Kitty knew the look and she knew the feeling. Nothing worked properly any more. Eyes, nose, mouth – they all took on new functions with the shock and the grief, most of them to do with snot and tears. There was liquid bubbling up and down the back of her own nose. Ears, nose, throat – who realized their similar liquid functions until grief placed that knowledge in your path?

306

'He didn't do it,' Riva whispered. 'How could you think he did?'

Kitty stared out at the snakes of rain dripping down the glass. 'I think everyone did it right now, Riva,' she said. 'I'm so crazy with it all there's not one person I don't suspect – Kofteros, Burgess, Hester, even you, Riva, and even me. Especially me, as a matter of fact. Perhaps he was protecting the business for my sake. Christ knows the number of well-meaning people who have bothered to tell me my father intended passing everything on to me after he died. That it was me he saw as his true heir apparent. What if he got in the way of progress for *my* sake? Those are the sorts of thoughts that are currently keeping me awake at night, Riva.' She sighed. 'Did you ever have a head so full of sadness and garbage that you'd like to empty it of everything? And none of those thoughts are going anywhere, either. They just roll round and round; suspicions, technicoloured guilt-trips, giant snow-storms of grief, loneliness . . .' she turned suddenly. 'Sorry, sorry,' she mumbled. 'I'm tired. You don't want to hear all this crap.' She pushed her hair back off her face and breathed deep lungfulls of stale, nicotine-scented air.

'The cigarettes are winning again.' She laughed, nervously. Riva's hand plunged into her bag and for a moment Kitty thought the perfume spray was coming out again. Instead it was a tissue – white, with a floral border, like kitchen-towel – which Riva handed across with a small sniff of her own to accompany the gesture.

They drove to a street in East London that Kitty had never seen before – and why should she have? There was nothing there to visit; it was a middle-of-nowhere place.

307

The sort of street you only go down to get to somewhere else, and then probably only if you're lost. The only noise in the road was of things happening elsewhere. There were two derelict buildings; a flat-fronted cement block that looked as though it had been concocted in the fifties; some hoardings bearing layers of fucked-up posters, ragweed growing out between them.

'There,' Riva pointed, 'that was where he was found.'

A great gust of horror blew over Kitty. She stared at Riva as though she were a magician. Empty street one minute, graveyard the next. 'This is where your father died.' As easy as that. And Kitty had had no sensory warning of what was about to occur. Her own father. Her nerves should have been alive with foreboding. Some unknown perceptions should have signalled an alert. Nothing.

There was still tape. Kitty stared at the ground. Of course she had been told. But she had had no curiosity. This was not on her list of places to visit. She hadn't even looked it up on the map.

There was wet pavement and there was rubbish. She thought maybe someone should have swept it tidy, shown some respect. Golden Wonder packets and Kit-Kat wrappers hung around the spot like rubber-neckers. Someone several streets away was singing: 'I plucked a violet from my mother's grave . . .'

Kitty stared.

'Kiss me, honey, honey, kiss me . . . Thrill me honey, honey, thrill me . . .'

Her eyes were soldered to the pavement now; welded to the seal-like wetness. Every crack, bump and sweet-wrapper was being methodically consigned to that part of the brain that will never forget, no matter how hard you try. The bit that hangs on to insults like they were precious jewels. The section that has total recall over every argument you have ever had in your life. The one that can summon up all the ugly, sickening visuals of your life like an over-zealous picture library. And now a new scene had been filed away: the place where my father was killed, as seen at night, in the rain. It was an image Kitty would have preferred to forget, but now it would be with her always.

'Don't care even if I blow my top, but honey, honey . . . don't stop!' A drunk sang on, *sotto voce*.

'Kitty?'

There were objects there that she couldn't identify in the dark. Rusted bits. Lumps of dirt. Rubble. A bus ticket? Cellophane.

'Kitty?'

'Why did you bring me here?' she heard herself ask.

'Kitty, it's that guy from your showroom. He wants you to tell him you're still alive.' Riva pressed the mobile against her ear. She could just about hear Alain above the roar of the sewing machines. She badly wanted to be there, warm and normal in the workroom, not here.

'I'm just in the street,' she told him, 'I'll be back soon.' Her eyes had still not left the spot.

'You were always your daddy's little girl, Kitty,' Riva said with a sigh. 'I hated you. He spoilt you, remember? You used to sit up on the piles of cloth where he had lifted you like a little Buddha. A pretty little doll. I was working.'

'Ricky is like an uncle to me,' Kitty whispered, 'my father loved him . . . they were friends, old friends.'

'My father hated Gabriel when he took his business

309

away,' Riva said. 'It destroyed him. But he didn't kill any-one. He died inside. He didn't ask for revenge.'

'I have to get back,' Kitty said. There was no real world available to her now, but the salon was as close as she could get.

'First come with me,' Riva told her. They walked further along the street, past The Spot. Then round a corner, to a pub – or what used to be a pub. It was boarded and black. But there was noise, all the same.

'It's a club,' Riva told Kitty, 'a private club. Dangerous. A sex club.'

Kitty looked at Riva.

'Tell me one other reason why your father would be in an area like this,' the girl said, evenly. There was a white fleck of dried toothpaste in the corner of her mouth. Kitty heard the words in her ears, but it was minutes before they burrowed through to her conscious mind.

'He was visiting the club, Kitty,' Riva said. 'He must have had another life, you know – one you were not aware of. We all have hidden sides of ourselves, Kitty,' she added, 'no one is perfect, you see – not even your father.'

CHAPTER THIRTY-ONE

ZG

PRESSERS
*Garment pressing was often done by men. They had
to be strong, because an iron for top pressing could
weigh as much as fourteen pounds.*

Kitty, I am of the belief that life consists of many levels and we have settled at a lower one than before, and that is the truth of our situation. Gregory has grown very feeble-minded so that however much I love him the notion is forced upon my poor brain that he is a burden to us all.

How can I describe my brother? His face is grown less pretty but I feel this is more down to an habitual expression, which is one of bewilderment and lazy dependency, than a change in its features. He is big now – bigger than me – and will sit and watch me for many hours on end unless I find him some task to do.

I try constantly to lure tales of the *shtetle* from his mouth, but he is not eager to communicate and often the only reply I will receive to my endless questioning is a nod and a smile.

I have become crafty out of desperation, Kitty. Gregory's appetite for food is voracious, yet his manners are good. When we sit down to eat I will place the steaming dinner

311

out of his reach and lean across to hold his hand and get him talking about home. His eyes fix onto the food like a dog's yet he dare not reach for it. While he is thus distracted it is easier to talk.

'How did you get here, Gregory?'

'By boat.'

'Did the family see you off?'

A shrug.

'Was it your idea to come to England?'

'Of course.'

'You were not sent, then?'

'No, Rosa. I am a man now, I think for myself.'

'Then you must have earned wages to pay for the trip?'

'No.'

The questions go in circles, Kitty, without sense or answer. It is important I employ all my patience, though. I believe in time I will discover the whole story. At the moment I keep pieces of it in my head, like a jigsaw, waiting for other bits to fit so that I can have the whole picture at last.

'How is Rintzi, Gregory?' This always evokes some strange look in his eyes before his head goes down.

'Did she receive my letters?'

'Yes.'

'Why didn't she reply? I wrote my address at the top. Did she tell you, Gregory? Did she say she would write to me or was she so terribly angry that I did not marry Aaron? Does she speak of me much, Gregory? Did you fight? Is that why you came here?'

Kitty, I received the most terrible answer to my questions last night.

'She is dead,' Gregory said, and his whole face seemed to burst from the effort of the words, so that mucus and tears spilled out in a torrent.

'Rintzi?'

Not happy, then. Dead.

Gregory was lost to me, though. His crying became heavier until David could stand the noise no longer and was forced to join the chorus.

'Rintzi is dead?'

'Killed,' was what I heard.

Kitty, I have more pieces for my puzzle now and spend much time sitting on my bed in the attic moving them all around in my mind in an attempt to make them fit.

Rintzi is dead, I believe this much to be true, and it seems fire was the cause – though brought about by whom I have yet to discover. At first Gregory told me she had killed herself, and this I could have believed, for my mother's mind was always unsettled, as I have mentioned before.

There were many more tears and sighs, Kitty, before I could get the idea from my brother that she had been burnt to death in a pogrom, along with many others.

This image haunted my mind for several nights and in my imagination it was the same youths who had seen my father off in the barrel. Max is away at present, sleeping at the studio so that Gregory has a bed to use. I must admit I have missed Max's common sense right now and his way of making light of things, though even he would be hard pressed to find humour in my current problems.

Much of the time I am at the machine, doing repairs that I have taken in to keep us in food while the slack

313

season is upon us. My work is good but if I sewed day and night without stopping I would not earn enough to feed us well. Max has not asked for rent for many weeks and I am in no position to remind him. I should tell my poor brother to find employment somewhere, but I have not got the heart to ask him and am too busy discovering the truth from him to want to insist.

When Max returns I inform him there are only a few more weeks of this and then I will be back in the salon, which is true. His photographic business flourishes, thank God, and he has recently employed a sensible young girl called Isabelle to work as receptionist. She is quite smart, with an accent that implies her background must be wealthy. Max is delighted with her and says her voice alone will double trade.

This has made me think of my own voice. How do I sound to Richard? If I spoke like Isabelle perhaps he would love me. My passion for him is not subdued, Kitty. I miss him badly and each time there is a hammering on the front door of the house I imagine it is him come to fetch me back to the salon again.

If it were not for David I believe I would never leave my little attic at all, but children need fresh air and so I am methodical in our daily trips to the park.

David is not a strong child, Kitty, but I refuse to believe that he could receive better care and treatment than that which I lavish upon him. His chest is rather weak, which is a common complaint of children around here, though I cannot do more than my best when it comes to the freshest air I can find for him. When the sun comes out again to warm us he will be better, Kitty, I am sure of it.

Do you know, dearest, I am so set in my own current plight that it was many weeks before I realized that the whole ghetto suffers in a similar way? For we are all in the main tailors, pressers and sewers here, save the cabinet-makers and cobblers. Either that or our trade depends upon those who are. So we all eat together and we all starve together, depending upon the season.

Despite the poverty, though, what dignity there is here! To watch these stricken people go about their business you would think they had all the riches on earth! There is a constancy to their lives, Kitty, that leaves me feeling humbled. They talk, gather, observe the rituals and attend the synagogue through lean seasons and busy periods and if anyone mentions the harshness of it all they will raise their hands into the air as if to say, 'So?' They are the chorus of idealists, Kitty, the congregation of their suffering voices becomes a soundless echo as it travels across time.

Help is offered to me from many sources, and all from people who have little more than myself. I am proud, though, Kitty, too proud for my own good. I see myself as the provider for both David and Gregory. I am young and able-bodied and will die before either of these two goes hungry for as much as a minute.

I feel the sins of my life preclude me from joining this generally honourable society too, Kitty. Who am I to sit in their rooms and pray in their synagogues? I have had a child outside marriage and currently care for one that is, by law, not my own. If I befriended others of my community then I would fear every day that the truth of my situation would emerge and David would be taken from me and placed in the poor house. Save Gregory and Max

I am a loner, Kitty. Even Baile is something of a stranger to me since her marriage. This is how it must be, though. I have no wish for it to be otherwise, for who else can you trust in life other than yourself, Kitty?

And still I question my brother. Gregory and I are become like two old boxers, punch-drunk and weary from our nightly battle of wits yet neither able to give in.

'Who killed Rintzi, Gregory?' The food before him is not much but I can hear his stomach growl at the sight of it.

'Men,' he says. I have heard this reply for five nights running.

'What men?'

He shrugs. His face is pale but the tears have not come yet, which gives me hope.

'Were you there, Gregory?' I ask, stroking his good hand.

'No!' His tone is angry and defensive. He pushes his chair back and begins to rise. 'No!' He is shaking his head so violently his hair whips about. I pull him back down into his seat.

'Max says you should have a job, Gregory. Would you like that?' His anguish has forced me to change the subject.

'I wasn't there, Rosa.'

'Leave him, Rosa – can't you see how affected he is?' I am surprised to hear Max's voice. He is standing in the open doorway, watching in silence, smoking a cigarette.

I turn to him in exasperation. 'I *have* to find out what happened to my mother, Max, don't you see?'

Max is serious for once. He walks across to Gregory and places a hand on his shoulder. 'He's frightened,' he tells me.

I look at my brother. I love him but I must know. I push the bowl of food across towards him and he starts to eat noisily.

'You shouldn't force him,' Max tells me. Gregory has learnt no English so we are free to talk.

'I have to know if my mother is dead,' I say. I sound stubborn and girlish, which is not my intention.

Max takes another mouthful of smoke. 'She is,' he tells me. He pulls a small metal flask from his pocket and pours alcohol from it before handing it to me. I sniff at the drink. It is brandy – I know the smell. It reminds me of Richard.

'How do you know?' I ask.

'Your brother told me,' Max nods at Gregory.

I purse my lips to look shrewish because what I want to do is cry. Of course Gregory has told Max. Why would he not? I have used time and patience and many bowls of food to discover what Max has found out during a brief chat.

'He talks to me a lot while you are out in the park with the baby.' Of course. 'He is frightened of you, Rosa. He loves you but you scare him.'

'He told you that?' Max nods. Gregory still eats.

'Why should I scare him? I am just his little sister.' And for the first time since I have met him, Max looks uncomfortable.

'Rosa, perhaps it would be better if you left him alone,' he says. 'He is confused. Let me get him a job. If he has a salary of sorts he can rent his own room nearby. There are a lot of things he needs to forget, but that is impossible with you quizzing him each night. Pay your attentions to David instead, Rosa. His cough is getting worse, I believe.'

Max says all this in a kindly voice but I am tired and becoming angry.

'David has nothing more than a little cold,' I tell him, 'how can you imply I ignore him to deal with my brother? No one could care for a child more, Max!'

He knows this to be true enough, I can see from the way his eyes fall to the floor and the apology he is immediately forced to make.

We move around in upset silence for a bit, but in the end I have to ask, 'Why is my brother frightened of me, Max?'

Max stubs out his cigarette, unable to look me in the eye. 'He says he killed your mother,' he says in a low voice, 'he says when the men came and burnt her house he locked the door and watched her die.' He rubs his hands across his face wearily. 'He says other things at other times, Rosa. Sometimes the house burnt while he was away and he came back to find her dead. Another time he told me he started the fire himself.' Max sighs. 'He believes many things, Rosa, and all of them contradictory. Leave him. He doesn't know what he is saying. He came here for sanctuary and you must give him some peace.'

This is a very wordy speech from Max. I pick David up and clutch him to my bosom despite the fact that he, like his uncle, is happily at his food. I find it hard to sketch my emotions as I stare at the back of Gregory's head. Three images run through my mind: Rintzi dead and Gregory returning to discover the tragedy, just as I did with Papa; Rintzi leaning screaming from the window while Gregory weeps and holds the door firmly shut; Gregory throwing straw about and lighting it while Rintzi sleeps. Which one do I believe? All of them, Kitty. Could my brother have murdered my mother? What a thing to have to decide! What a choice Gregory has presented me with.

But at the same time I feel that Gregory is still my darling brother and know he would never bring harm to any living thing.

'Are you all right?' Max asks. I kiss David's head. He has downy hair now. His flesh smells sweet. He is innocent and beautiful, as Gregory must have been as a baby.

'Be careful,' says Max, enigmatically.

I don't question Gregory much after that. Sometimes the truth can be unbearable. Sometimes it is better swept beneath the corner of the rug, along with the dust.

SIZING

*Until the 1930s women's clothes were sized as
'maid's' or 'matron's', then later as SW, W and WX.
It was the influx of Berlin and Viennese tailors that
led to the sizing revolution, creating a size ten to sixteen standard, and allowing women to buy a good fit
off-the-peg.*

We live in mists and fogs here, Kitty, locked safe inside
our own little dramas by the shroud the elements throw
about us. I have a candle in the window and it burns deep
yellow, like the yolk of an egg. Our house is like a doll's
house as there is no outside to be seen. I feel as though
there is no time and sometimes I feel as though I have seen
too much time and am old.

David is four years. Gregory has employment, found for
him by Max. By day he stacks fruit and by night he eats.
Max has taught him to smoke, which is something I regret.
My work at the salon has kept us going but only just. This
year the weather has been bad enough to affect trade. In
Russia we worked through as much snow as nature could
provide, but here the ladies will not come out from their
homes if there is as much as a spit of rain or – as now –
fog.

There is a smell of sulphur about the place. The fog is jonquil yellow and impenetrable. It induces a dream-like state about the place and we all move more slowly about our business, as though nothing mattered without the visual stimulus of other buildings and other people. At night I become frightened and once I woke believing the rest of the world had truly disappeared.

And who do I feel the most need of at these times? Max, that is who, for in our doll's house it is Max who is reality and Richard who barely exists. Max is solid against the mist. He is large and full of laughter and it is he who we must depend upon for our very livelihood and sanity.

Let me tell you what our day is like. I wake to the sound of Gregory banging about on the other side of the partition. He lights a candle and then he is dressing. His next thought will be of breakfast and so will David's, for already Gregory's racket has woken him and he is calling out my name.

His hair is grown longer and has started to curl a little. He wears clothes I sew for him and Papa would be proud for he is so well-dressed that people in the street must wonder how his mama comes to be so out of fashion with her own clothes.

He is a happy child when his health is good, and much in love with Max, who spoils him. I am forced to keep an eye on the pair of them constantly, for I swear Max would have him smoking and drinking already if I were not so vigilant, even though Max would tell me it is all a joke.

Gregory is strangely anxious and agitated most of the time, though I never know what about. He takes his job seriously and presents me with the money he earns at the end of every week. He watches David a lot but appears incapable of playing with the boy, even though I feel he loves him. He has never asked about David's father but calls me the child's mama nevertheless. Is it a sin for me to be grateful for his simple mind at times like these? For how would an older brother act otherwise if he arrived from the old country to discover his unmarried sister with a child?

Isabelle, Max's receptionist, adores David and Max allows her to care for him while I am at my work. We walk to the studio together and the girl will be there waiting for us with a hot barley drink ready for David, which he loves.

She is a friendly, open creature, just five years older than myself. I envy her roundness and her hair, which is ginger and curled into ringlets that hang down from the pins. I know they would laugh at her lack of fashion in the salon but her clean round face is like a breath of pure air in the midst of the choking fog.

She demands no payment for minding David as she works, but I pay her in dresses, which Max says is a fair enough bargain.

If I have work at the salon I arrive early in my best outfit. My hair is now smart enough to keep in the same style as the *vendeuses* and I have made myself a grey crepe day-dress that is passable enough.

Heavier fabrics are less popular for women's fashions now Kitty, despite the weather, and we have less stiff satin and plush at the salon than before, the newer look being for chiffons and lace, which is all very pretty.

The designer is very set on producing a new look for

spring and has settled upon something we all rate as rather daring, which consists of a high-waisted bolero bodice attached to a corselet skirt which falls almost untrimmed to the feet.

Max has a magazine called *The Lady* on a small gilt-painted table in his reception, for the women to thumb through while they wait for their portraits to be taken. I notice a lot of second-hand mantle sales in here and the prices are interesting, being as much as fifty shillings for a good quality walking-dress that sounded way past the latest mode, or seven shillings for a plain cloth skirt. I told Isabelle I could make my fortune if I only had the fabric, which I could see set her to thinking, for she is a very clever girl, I believe.

If there is no salon work I will walk Gregory to his job and then spend the morning on repairs or alterations, with maybe the odd bridal gown thrown in for good measure. I have to charge in advance for these gowns or I would not have the money for the lace, let alone the yards of satin needed. Isabelle says I could do the same with other orders but I would find it hard to take money without any proof that I could do the job.

In the afternoon I will collect David and walk him around the park. Do you know there are live cows there with women selling their milk? I buy some for David as often as I am able, for I have watched many other mothers doing the same in the hope that it will make their babies grow healthily.

David will sit and play happily in the afternoon while I work at my machine again and then I will read to him from books Max brings until Gregory is home for his supper.

Does all this sound idyllic, Kitty? With money it might be, but I am so wretchedly poor that I barely see the good moments in my life for all the worry that must accompany them. At night I am so tired I have often slept in my clothes, being too exhausted to remove them.

This night I am awoken from my sleep, though, with the fog inside the room and choking me in my throat. I cough and rub my eyes in an attempt to see clearly. Gregory must have opened a window, which is fatal in this weather, as the mists thicken inside the house so readily that you would be unable to see your own walls before five minutes have passed.

'Gregory?' I am angry with my brother for causing this inconvenience. Blinded, I stagger to the small window that we share and attempt to pull it shut, only to find it is not, as I had supposed, open.

'Gregory?' I am further awake now, though my brain is still reluctant to form proper thought. I turn but there is little to be seen around me.

'David?' In my confusion my only thought is for my child. I am still in my work clothes, which I discover as I attempt to walk quickly across the room and trip over my hem. Landing on the floor I discover the fog is less dense there and that I am able to see. Eyes still streaming, I crawl around on my knees like an animal.

'David!' I am full of dread now. There are loud cracking sounds from Gregory's room and I find I am unable to breathe. I try to stand but my legs are not strong enough and at least on the ground I can see.

I crawl along the walls until my hand touches air and I

know I am at the doorway. It is then that I realize this is no fog in my room but a fire.

'Daaaavid!'

A hand has my own hand held so firmly I jump with fear.

'Max?' I would cling to him like a limpet but my child is in the room behind me somewhere and also my brother, as far as I know.

Max lifts me into the arms of another man just as easily as if I were a child myself, and the man begins to carry me down the narrow stairs. This is not an easy task for him because I fight like a vixen to get free.

'My baby!' I scream. 'My child is inside!'

I look back and Max is staring at me. A fearfully long time seems to transpire as our eyes lock – mine round with horror and his near-concealed beneath a frown of concern. His face is white and smeared with soot. Behind him I can see the first dull red shadow of the flames that threaten to take my boy. There is much said between Max and me during that last stare, though all of it in silence.

'No jokes this time, Max,' I tell him, 'this time it is serious. If my son dies I will want to die too, it is as simple as that.' I am blindly selfish in my terror. David and Gregory. Max must save them, for without them I will perish too.

Does Max look for his own status in this equation? Do you die also if *I* die, Rosa? Would life be worth nothing for you too if I perish in these flames behind me? But his answer is obvious. Without expression he turns and is gone into the black smoke, a tall figure as dark as Beelzebub.

Kitty, I cannot tell you how long and unendurable the wait is as I stand shivering on the pavement outside my home, watching the smoke pour from my little window above. How many times am I caught as I try to run into the building and how many arms and faces do I punch as they try to prevent me?

I see the small body being tipped into the waves and hear the quiet splash that is gone so quick with the cries of the gulls.

'David.' Was he ever there to be mine at all? Or did I dream his life in some bout of madness that followed the death of my own child? Was that just a corpse I plucked from the mountain of mouldering rags in the factory? How could life have been breathed into it as it lay in my bed the long night? I howl out like a hound, Kitty, frightening all about me until I am left to stand alone as they back away in terror.

Then at last Max appears in the charred doorway, black and exhausted with smoke rising from his hair and his coat. I am upon him at once, pulling at his sleeves in desperation as neighbours do the right thing, which is banging him with their hands and swatting him with cloths and rugs before he combusts in front of us.

We are pushed from the hallway as other friends run up the stairs carrying buckets of water to deal with the flames. But the whole street could burn down for all I care. I have my hands upon Max's cheeks, pulling at his ears, his hair, screaming at him.

'David? My baby? My child, Max – is he dead? Did you leave him to perish?' I am about to unleash a stream of abuse and curses but suddenly I stop just as though struck by lightning. A scream? Was it mine?

Then I hear another scream. David. Coughing and wheezing for air Max pulls his coat open and there is my precious child, wrapped inside. He is pure pink to Max's blackness and grime. So the fire never reached him. I laugh with hysterical delight and he laughs too, terrified though he is, and Max lifts him and he is upon me, clinging ferociously and being crushed by my hugs.

Forgive my hysterics, Kitty. It seems this was not a big fire, just some smouldering cloths. Nevertheless there was a vast quantity of smoke, on account of the fact that our linen and clothing is quite damp at present as we have no warm air in which to dry it, on account of the fog – and so to me the whole terrace of hovels that we live in was in danger of being consumed in the inferno, and my beloved child along with it.

Gregory was discovered cowering in an ancient cupboard in the hall and, again, there was much relief at the sight of his tragic face. We clung together for many minutes, Kitty, all counting our blessings and saying prayers of thanks while countless alternative and thoroughly shocking endings to the tale flashed through our minds.

David is now excited by the whole adventure and Max is firmly established as his hero, as if he was not before. The blackness of our rooms enchants him, which it does not me, for all I see is raw hands and sore knees from all the scrubbing I will have to do to restore it to its more usual state of squalor again.

Thank God my sewing machine was undamaged, and

that I had just delivered a stack of repairs to their owners, so nothing of value is in need of replacement.

Max is, of course, beside himself at his own bravery, especially since he is to be featured in the *Whitechapel Times* in his role as blaze hero, and sketched by their artist for an accompanying print this very evening. If he has studied his own reflection in my grimy mirror once, he has studied it a thousand times, Kitty. Not one angle or tilt of the head has gone untested and his best hats have been on and off his head so much they have caused a draught.

I would laugh along with the others at his antics, Kitty, for both David and Gregory find Max uncommonly amusing, but there is a terrible secret notion inside my head and the more it brews and stews the quieter I am forced to become.

When Gregory was led out from the cupboard he hid in during the fire I held him in my arms and he held me too – though I noticed only with his poor hand, the one without the fingers. Out of curiosity I looked down at his good hand and saw it was clutched so tight around an object that the knuckles were white.

When I gently prised his fingers apart, Kitty, what do you think I discovered? A packet of matches. When I looked up at his face I saw fear in my brother's eyes and it was then I saw Rintzi again, screaming from the little window of the house in the *shtetle*, while Gregory watched in silence from below.

What am I to do? My brother is unwell, I know that – his mind was damaged the day Rintzi took him into the woods. Only I have a child of my own to think about. With Gregory in the house I now know that David is in danger, yet my brother needs me every bit as much as David since he is incapable of caring for himself if I throw him out.

The neighbours claim the fire was the act of vandals and point to the word 'Jews' that someone has scrawled on the main door to the building. I pray this to be true, Kitty.

Max remarks constantly that David is in need of schooling. A child of Richard's should attend a good school where he will learn the correct way to talk and read the best books. I am afraid the boy speaks as I do, when he should speak English the way his father does. Should he be poor all his life? I fear for his future as well as his education. Yet I could never give him up, I am too selfish to do so. He is my everything, I love him and he loves me. He calls me Mother and cries when we are apart for too long. When I work in the room he will play happily at my feet for hours, content in the knowledge that I am near.

We are in the midst of a lean period of work. I am awake all night, listening to Gregory's snores, terrified that he will wake and repeat his dreadful act. Max tells me I look unwell. When he offers me money for food, as he does more times than I care to remember, I am forced to take it, for we are hungry.

Kitty, I am beside myself with anxiety. For several weeks now David has had a return of the cough that used to plague him as a baby. At first I put it down to the effects of the smoke, which hung around our room for many days after the fire. It was Max who pointed out what I had dreaded admitting – that the cough was getting no better, even after the smoke had gone.

So many children are ill in this area. It is the poverty that causes it. We live in houses that are damp, shivering in draughts that no fires will drive away. I chew my nails with worry, Kitty. Sometimes David is well enough for me to be cheered, but then we will have another night of coughs, followed by a pale face in the morning.

'The boy is sick, Rosa,' Max told me, as gently as possible – but there was no way to say those words without invoking my hysteria.

'He will be better,' I said, 'when summer comes he will be well again.'

Max paid for a doctor, but the medicine he brought did little save make the boy sick. One morning he was so pink-faced I began to be excited, thinking he was well at last, but when I felt his cheek with the back of my hand I discovered he was feverish and wrapped him in blankets and had him on my lap for two days.

Kitty, after much sad deliberation I have written a letter to Richard. I spent badly-needed pennies on the writing paper and yet how many sheets was I forced to tear up when the right words would not come?

I have told him I am the mother of a child – his child. I have explained that I kept the knowledge from him because I did not want to burden him, yet now we are nearly penniless I have no choice. I enclosed the photograph of David and me that Max took four years ago.

I am tired of being poor, Kitty. There is no end to this and I know Richard will want to care for us both now. Perhaps I am wicked to delude him and yet there is no delusion, for to me David is my son just as much as he is

Richard's. Yet I fear for our lives if I do not do this thing. David is ill and my own health has become frail. If I do not work we will all starve.

Last night I took the wedding suit from its case and pressed it carefully before hanging it behind the door. The case lid is so snug it does not even smell of the smoke from the fire. Touching it is a bitter pleasure, Kitty. The silks are as vivid in colour as the day Papa sewed it and the fabric is as soft as the moment it came off the roll.

'Will it fit?' Max asked, seeing it hanging there that night.

I stared at him. 'I have written to David's father,' I said. 'Now all we must do is wait.'

Max looked across at Gregory but my brother was happy watching David at play. 'You believe he will marry you then?' he asked. His jaw looked set with anger though I could hear him controlling his voice carefully.

'He is a gentleman,' I replied. 'What else would he do?'

Max paced the room a bit before throwing himself down into a kneeling position in front of me.

'Don't you think this trick is a little wicked, Rosa?' he asked. 'Can't you see your idea is terribly wrong?'

I stared at the floor. 'You'll knee your trousers if you're not more careful, Max,' I said.

'Don't you mind that he'll never love you?' Max asked.

I looked him in the eye at that. 'I can make him care for me,' I said, 'I only need a chance to show what I am like. I know I'm not pretty but I share his love for the business and I'm lively enough to keep him on his toes, which is more than just a beautiful wife might do.'

'And the lie?' Max asked. 'What about the fact that you are not the boy's mother?'

I looked across at David. 'I feel that I am, Max,' I whispered. 'I don't know how anyone could be more of a mother to the child. There's no lie there, that I see. If Richard was too drunk to know who took advantage of his situation he won't know if it was me or not. The real mother gave birth without anyone knowing for sure, apart from me, and now she is dead.

'Most of the time we're only seen behind the machines by the other workers, so who can tell if we're a bit fatter than usual sometimes? Even proper ladies often corset themselves so tight you'd never guess – I've seen them at the salon, going all white and blue in the face as they struggle to keep the laces done up.

'Max, there's nothing evil here,' I added, 'I was given David and now I'm to find him a father and myself a husband. You know our situation. What else should I do?'

Many other things, to judge by Max's expression, but he said nothing. After a while he rose and stood by the door, staring at the suit.

'Will you walk with me, Rosa?' he asked quietly.

'It's dark,' I said.

He looked out of the window. 'But it's a beautiful night,' he told me, 'the fog has cleared and the air smells of spring at last. You can leave David downstairs for an hour. Come and allow the breeze to put the roses back into your cheeks.'

I did as he said. We walked down along Brick Lane and through Fournier Street to the market in Spitalfields, which had the smell of rotting vegetables about it at that time of the evening.

Max is, of course, a well-known figure locally now, what

with the photographic business and the article in the *Whitechapel Times*, and I lost count of the amount of people who hailed him as we walked along in the moonshine.

'Would you like to take my arm?' he asked, but I was having no part of that.

'What would decent people think, seeing me clinging to you?' I asked.

'They would think I was lucky,' he told me, and I blushed, for I had intended to match his trick of sarcasm, not to go fishing for compliments.

We found a small bench in the grounds of Christ Church and settled there for a while among the ancient tombstones that lie in stacks against the walls.

'Rosa, why do you laugh when I tell you I would marry you?' Max began.

'Because I know you are making a joke, Max,' I told him. As though the graves were not making me feel uncomfortable enough Max had to add to my squirming.

'So you would rather marry a man you barely know?' he asked after a minute or two's thought. 'First you love Aaron, who you had met once or twice, and now you love Richard, who you have barely spoken to. Why don't you love me more, then? We have had so many conversations, you should be besotted.'

What was I to tell him? A thousand retorts flew through my brain. 'Max, you are a rogue,' I informed him as lightly as I could, 'and I intend to marry a gentleman.'

He could have no idea of the size of Richard's empire. Max's little business could be gone in an instant, but Richard's had true value and history.

Max tapped his finger against his lips. 'And what yard-stick do you use to judge a rogue?' he asked quietly.

'Someone who photographs barely-clothed ladies,' I said. 'Someone who has ... relations with them after-wards.'

Max nodded, and I could not see whether he was smiling. 'Someone you could not trust,' he said.

I looked at him by way of reply.

'Yet David's father must have had ... relations ... with at least one other woman,' he said.

I sat up straight at that. 'You don't know the woman involved,' I told him. 'Some of the girls at that factory are shameless. Aggie more or less admitted she seduced him while he was in no state to know better.'

'I see,' Max said. After a while he turned to me. 'And what if I were the victim of a shameless seductress, Rosa?' he asked. 'Would you forgive me and love me in the way you love your boss?'

'Don't confuse me, Max,' I said.

'You say you don't trust me,' he continued, 'yet you trusted me with the life of your child the other night.'

I felt his hand upon my face. 'Look at me, Rosa,' he said.

Next minute his lips were pressed against my own, only the night had become so dark and the flesh of his mouth was so soft I hardly knew they were there until I felt my own begin to part in a sigh.

What else could I do but kiss him then? He had reminded me how he had saved my beloved child's life. How could I argue that that was not worth a mere kiss?

334

'One day you will know that I love you,' Max said in a whisper.

Can words touch your body like fingers? It would be so easy to get lost in fine thoughts, Kitty, and forget your true destiny. I could have lost myself in Max and his words if I had had a mind to believe them, which I didn't. This is how more stupid girls are fooled by men, and there is a lesson for us all there. Max is a good man but not, I believe, constant in his affections. If this joke of his about loving me were to become reality, I fear he would be back to laughing and sarcasm the following day and that I could not bear.

Richard is a fine man and will make a good husband and father. He is serious and well-mannered and Max can be accused of neither quality. Max is erratic and mocking. Yet I returned his kiss for a full half-minute and of this I am much ashamed, for I will be married to Richard before long.

CHAPTER THIRTY-THREE

ZG

RAYON

*Launched as artificial silk at the Artificial Silk
Exhibition at Olympia in 1929, manufacturers used rayon
to keep up with the demand for the new mass market
in women's wear following the Great War.*

They were exhausted now, completely washed out. Totally
void. Alain still sat on his stool, but he hadn't touched the
garment in front of him for over ten minutes and was
staring, trance-like, at a photograph of Andy Warhol he
had pinned up over his desk. He was no longer capable of
judging whether the dress was finished or not. He couldn't
even tell if the hem was straight.

The outfit was on a stand – they'd had to let the house
model go four hours previously, after the third faint. Somewhere there were still machinists working and it was that
noise that prickled their guilt and kept them sitting securely
in their chairs.

Kitty had cleared weeping and hopelessness in a couple
of strides, sidestepped hysteria as it was too much of a
cliché, and fallen straight into the arms of empty, bottom-
less desolation. 'Why?' was the buzz word of the moment,
'Why? Why-in-God's-name? What-the-hell-is-this-all-for?'

People drifted in and out of the workroom, like Victorian

gentry visiting a madhouse. Chloe, China, the PR, a couple of models for the show, two very minor celebrities come to swig Chablis, and one huge star come to snort coke. Nula had arrived quietly, her little face pleading, can I help? A timid enquiry prior to settling in a pale and distant corner, gnawing at her nails and pulling at her hair in a demented manner.

Freddy had phoned but his dilemma was largely the same. What could you say? I'm exhausted? The whole of the rag trade was running on back-up batteries right then. Who had sympathy?

Years ago, Kitty had once asked her father whether the range could not be started a week earlier, so that it could be finished comfortably on time. They had all laughed at that, all the staff of the salon, everyone within earshot. Starting earlier was just not feasible. There were the fabric fairs to visit, the orders to chivvy, that was how the whole ball was set rolling. There was no scope for better planning – the whole thing was in the hands of the fabric manufacturers.

The garment in front of Alain was simple: a mud-brown coat-dress with a web of silver lamé hanging like a cloak about its shoulders.

'Shit!' he shook his head. 'It doesn't work and I don't know why.' He ripped it off the stand and threw it across at Kitty. 'Put it on,' he told her, 'I need to see if the fabric has stretched after being pressed.'

Kitty dragged the garment over her jeans and rose wearily to her feet to stand in front of the designer.

'Stop swaying,' he said, angrily, and then more politely, 'please.'

Kitty closed her eyes. The empty wet pavement her father had died on rolled instantly into view.

Alain smelt of smoke and soap. She listened to the noises he made as he worked, absorbing the sounds, like a child. His touch was light as he pinned and cut. Even when he ripped a seam from top to end she felt nothing.

Her father. Had he been at that club? Was Khan's daughter right? How many other dreadful things had she planted into Kitty's head?

Nula pressed an ice-cold can of diet cola into her hand and she held it first to her temples.

Gabriel was an honourable man. Faithful to his wife. Faithful to his business. Faithful to them all. He would never have been seen in such a seedy place as that boarded-up sex club.

Alarmed by her own thoughts, Kitty opened her eyes and Alain's face was her first focus – pale, tired, bristly and smudged from lack of sleep. In fact, looking very much as he usually did.

'You want this to work, don't you?' he asked her in a quiet, deep voice.

'Oh, very much,' Kitty told him, more into sleep than out of it.

'And your wedding?' Alain asked her. 'Your father spoke about it a lot. We used to say it was going to be bigger than a royal wedding. In fact, we were all pretty sick of it here, and it hadn't even started.' He laughed to show he was joking, then his face became serious again.

'Your father had begun designs for your dress, did you know that? He was compiling a portfolio of sketches to show you. It was a surprise. Raphael had worked on some

338

of them, and so had I. Your father did the most designing, though. Sometimes he spent the whole night here, sketching. He said your dress was going to have to be the most magnificent creation ever. This did not endear us to you, as you can imagine. His little princess, eh?'

Kitty smiled. 'Where is the folio?' she asked. 'Is it in his office?'

She pulled the coat-dress off and hung it back onto the stand. Alain took a swig of her cola and led her into her father's office, where he sat her down in the huge, padded chair before laying a large folio out in front of her.

'Oh.' It was all Kitty could say. The folder smelt of Gabriel. It didn't smell of the street, of dead crisp packets. It smelt of his cologne and his clean flesh.

'Do you want to be left alone?' Alain asked, watching her face with concern. Kitty shook her head. 'No. Stay. Keep the little princess company. Please.'

Alain grinned. 'Have some wine, then,' he said. 'A bride should always have some chilled wine when she picks her dress. Have a break. Get a little pissed.'

There was champagne in the fridge in the corner. He poured two glasses and sat down beside her, so close that their legs touched.

'Alain,' Kitty asked quietly, 'tell me, do you know what a "dark room" is?'

She watched his eyes disappear behind lashes and lids the colour of marble. She knew then that his first comment would be a lie.

'It's the place where photographers do their printing,' he said. Subject closed.

She leant forward. 'You missed my inflection,' she told

him carefully, 'I asked you what a *dark room* is – two words, not one.'

He looked up. Maple syrup eyes. 'It's what they call a room in a club,' he told her, 'a room where people go to have sex. Men, usually. Men with men. A private place where it's too dark to see who they're fucking. Why?'

Kitty looked back at the sketch in front of her. 'It's a term I heard,' she said. 'I just wondered, is all.' It was where Riva Khan had said her father went. 'The dark room,' she'd told Kitty, 'I know about this. My uncle told me.'

In her mind Kitty's eyes scanned every inch of Riva's face. She had held her head high as she spoke to Kitty, as though two generations of prejudice and oppression had endowed her with an expression of one who hears nails scratching a chalkboard. Her contempt had been obvious.

'The dark room.' How romantic it sounded. A place for forbidden sex. Anonymous. Her father would never have contemplated such a place. He could have given Riva herself lessons in pride and fastidiousness. Gabriel was a strong, honourable man.

Kitty forced herself to refocus her attention on his drawings. He had been designing his daughter's wedding dress when he died. A tear splashed onto the page and Kitty blotted it up quickly with her sleeve. Alain said nothing. She thought he would be embarrassed. It was awkward now, the silence between them.

Gabriel's writing was spidery on the page. His drawings were substantial but his words and instructions surrounded them like fine, faded gauze. *Extended shoulder with pleats sitting in pads*, she read . . . *cinched waist with full taffeta*

340

bow, . . . white silk embroidered crepe lisse flouncing and white India silk . . .

Rosa, the daughter I love. It was as though the words of two fathers' voices echoed in her head.

CHAPTER THIRTY-FOUR

ZG

NUN'S VEILING
*A lightweight wool fabric made with a very plain
weave in plain colours, similar in appearance to a
wool batiste.*

There is no reply to my letter to Richard, Kitty, and I am distraught. I felt patience to be one of my virtues, yet I am pacing the room like a tethered beast.

CHAPTER THIRTY-FIVE

ZG

STAYS
For much of the nineteenth century tight-lacing was the fashion, with women striving to have a waist no wider than twenty inches. Many of these stays were made of silk coutil *and trimmed with lace and came with 'bust-improvers'.*

A response from Richard at last. A note arrived this morning and, though not exactly wordy, it is polite enough and – once I had read it for a fifth time – I considered it to sound almost friendly and warm in tone. It read:

Dear Miss Zigofsky,
   I have studied your letter with interest. If suitable to yourself I shall send my carriage to collect you and the child on Sunday at two.
       Yours faithfully,
       R Galliard Esq.

My hands shake as I hold it. Max says I am being quixotic and this makes me angry despite the fact that I have no idea on earth what the word means.

CHAPTER THIRTY-SIX

ZG

CENDRE DE ROSE

Grey with a pink tone, cendre de rose *was one of
many colour names that became obsolete after the
nineteenth century. Others include:* esterhazy — *a
silver-grey*, fly's wing — *graphite*, terre d'Egypt — *a rust*,
dust of Paris — *ecru, and* bouffon — *a shade darker
than* eau de nil.

Kitty, Richard has taken my child. How stupid I have been,
how naïve. It has been five weeks since I took David to his
father's house and he is still there.

What hopes I had as we climbed into Richard's carriage
to make the arranged appointment. We were dressed and
ready before dawn, so acute was my excitement. David's
hair was combed flat and wetted to make it lie straight and
his little face polished by my hankie until his cheeks
gleamed like a new, shining apple. He appeared healthy
enough, Kitty, his cough had all but cleared. I had no idea
of the horrors that were to come.

The house was less grand than I had expected, but smart
enough for all that. David had caught my excitement by
the time we arrived, even though he was unaware why we
paid the visit, and his legs had him up to the door before
it was opened.

I'd expected to see Richard there waiting to greet us, but then I know nothing of these matters and it was some servant who peered out with a face like old boiled mutton.

We were shown inside the hall, with me grabbing David by the hand before he got up to some mischief with all the porcelain that was displayed in there – for although he is a good child for the most part he was rather over-excited, as I have said.

The servant showed me to a chair and, while I was being asked if I would care for refreshment, David was taken from me and led into another room without so much as a backward glance. I saw only a glimpse of the room he was taken to. There was a log fire burning well in the grate, and a tall, elderly man in a suit standing alongside a woman dressed in an outfit that I took to be a nanny's.

I waited a full two hours in that hallway and neither tea nor David were brought to me. I became frightened then, and believe I made a fool of myself, for I banged on the door that David had been led through and called out for my son.

It was Richard himself who emerged, taking my hand and leading me back to my seat with many polite apologies, which made me quiet again. His face looked concerned and rather pale, but beside that he appeared well enough.

'Well, Miss Zigofsky,' he said, 'you have given me something to think about here.'

I stared at his face.

'When was the boy born?' he asked, and I told him.

He nodded. 'Forgive me if I am rather crude at this point, Miss Zigofsky,' he said, 'but I have no memory of your being ... unwell ... around that time. I know a few years have passed but surely ...'

I had my answer ready for this. 'Nobody noticed,' I said. 'I was rather thin at the time and – if you remember – there was a fashion that season for the empire line so I, like a lot of the girls, had my waists hitched and tied with ribbon. You may have forgotten another important occasion because I'm afraid you were drunk when the child was conceived.'

I said this deliberately to embarrass him, for I knew it would make him uncomfortable about questioning me further. I was right. He was gentleman enough to look away.

'May I ask why you have taken until now to show the child to me?' he said.

'I explained in my letter, I had no intention of being a burden,' I replied, simply.

He turned to look at me again. There was no denying he was the boy's father, their faces were as alike as peas in a pod. When I looked at David I looked at Richard, and vice versa. His son's face must have been a shock to him.

'Miss Zigofsky ...' he began.

'Under the circumstances I believe it would be appropriate for you to call me Rosa,' I said.

'Rosa.' The word seemed alien to him. 'We are in a very difficult situation,' he said. 'You are an honest woman, I know that much from employing you. I feel a great amount of pity for your plight. Your life with David must have been ... difficult ... and you have behaved well in bringing him up in these circumstances.' His eyes looked friendly and polite. 'I hope you can see the difficulty of my situation too, though, Rosa,' he went on. 'I find I have a son about whom I knew nothing, and here he is and here you are . . . look, I must be blunt with you. You cannot expect decisions at once but at the same time you must understand I am keen to spend some time with the boy and get to know him a little. He seems to be a splendid chap and quite comfortable with me already. What say he stays here for a few days while we both have time to think?'

I rose from my seat at that, for the thought of leaving David was too much to contemplate.

'Take me to him,' I said. 'We must leave now, thank you.' But Richard held me by the arm in a gentlemanly fashion and for a moment we were close enough for me to feel his breath upon my cheek.

'You can't take him, Rosa,' he said in a gentle voice. 'If he is my son – and I have no reason to doubt your honesty – I must insist he stays here with me, for the time being at least. You have had him for four years now. I am probably asking for as many days. You know he will be safe and I will send him home to you directly there is any sign that he is unhappy.'

'No!' This time the hysteria must have been apparent in my voice, for Richard released my arm in shock. I ran towards the door that I had seen David led through, calling out his name as I ran.

'David! Come to me, darling!' I pulled the door wide open, no longer aware of my manners, but the room was empty, apart from the tall suited man, who stood warming his hands by the fire.

He turned in surprise as he saw me enter. 'My dear, calm yourself,' he said in a kind voice.

'Rosa,' I heard Richard say behind me, 'this is Dr McDermot, one of the noted paediatricians in London. I invited him here to examine David when he arrived.'

The doctor took my hands in his own and held them cupped there. 'I'm afraid the child is unwell, madam,' he told me.

I felt my legs begin to crumple beneath me and both he and Richard had to help me into a chair.

The doctor looked concerned. 'He may have tuberculosis, I am afraid,' he told me.

Kitty, can you imagine my distress? At this moment David came out of the room behind him, led by the servant and with as happy an expression as I had ever seen on his little face. In his hand was some toy; I do not remember what, exactly, but it was large and expensive and much more than he had ever been given in his life before.

I was out of my seat in an instant and clutching him so hard in my arms I heard him cry out.

'He is well!' I said, releasing him and looking at his face. 'Look – he is smiling, aren't you, David? He had a little cough, didn't you, dearest? But that is gone now. I will take him home right now and tuck him into his bed. He has had nothing worse than a cold. When the summer is here we will be out in the park again – I take him every day, don't I, dearest?' My tears began to fall onto the child's poor head.

When I looked up I saw that the woman, whose uniform I now recognized as that of a nurse, was standing with her hand on David's shoulder. My child was prised gently but firmly from my arms and it was all I could do to stop myself from screaming.

The doctor led me aside, away from David's earshot. 'If the boy does not receive the best of care I fear he will not see another summer, madam,' he said, gravely. 'Mr Galliard has told me your circumstances are . . . reduced. The boy will require more than you can provide for him, I'm afraid. The houses in the ghettos are damp enough to kill a healthy adult. The air is unclean. Allow the boy to be removed to better conditions, I beg you.'

My face was distorted with anguish and indecision. 'Please, Rosa,' Richard begged behind me.

What was I to do, Kitty? Tear my child from that house and take him home with me to die? Yet how could I bear to be parted from him? My dilemma was unimaginable. I had thought we would be well provided for and that Richard would take us both under his wing.

'I must be allowed to see him every day for as long as I like,' I begged, the tears a veritable downpour now.

The doctor stroked his chin. 'Perhaps after a while,' he said. 'At the moment there is a risk of extra infection. You look unwell yourself, madam. If you were to bring extra germs into his surroundings . . .' He patted my arm. 'Might I suggest you make an appointment with your own doctor?' he asked. 'He can tell if you have any contagion, and also may reassure you about your child's best interests.'

Richard's eyes were full of silent begging. I could tell he loved David already, and that I had no choice but to leave the boy as the doctor had requested.

'May I hold him one last time?' I pleaded. Kitty, his little head smelt so sweet beneath my nose. 'I will see you very soon, darling,' I whispered, without knowing for one moment whether or not that promise was true.

Max was there when I got home, but I would not tell him what had happened. Gregory was silent and would not eat his food. I wept all night, and then again in the morning when I woke and discovered David's little cot was empty beside me.

I have been summoned to a meeting with Richard, this time at the sweatshop. I tell Max I believe he is about to do the honourable thing, but Max replies that, if he were about to propose, it would not be in that Godforsaken den but somewhere with a sweeter perfume. He also adds his many-times repeated theory that I am being dishonourable in passing myself off as the boy's mother and am therefore no straighter than the bookie in the checked suit outside the greengrocer of a Sabbath.

I am about to tell him again that I am David's mama in the eyes of anyone with an ounce of decent sympathy in their veins, but discover I do not have sufficient energy, even to rise to Max's bait.

His behaviour is almost hostile these days, just when I am most in need of commiseration. Kitty, I am the loneliest soul in the world right now. Is Max right? Am I a cheat? Is it so wicked to dream of life in the room that I glimpsed in Richard's house, playing with my son in front of a warm hearth?

'That is not the way for you, Rosa,' Max says. 'You have too much going for you to want to be housemaid to a cold fish like that.'

'I plan to be Richard's wife, not his flunkey!' I shout.

Max shrugs. 'In their world it amounts to the same thing,' he says. 'Why not make your own money, Rosa?

350

Then you will be able to live as you choose, without saying thank you to anyone.'

There is a silence. I am panting with anger. 'Love is more to me than money,' I say.

Max smiles. 'Tell me that again when Richard has paid you off,' he says.

Kitty, I hit out at that, striking Max across his face with the back of my hand. He neither flinches nor ducks and his eyes never leave my face. I fully expect him to slap me back and hold myself full height to prove that I am every inch as brave as himself.

'Is that how you think you will carry on when you live in Mayfair?' he asks quietly.

'I will be without these aggravations then,' I tell him. I am so sorry for having hit him that I am almost in tears.

Max is so very good to me in many ways and I know I could well be starved in some alley without his help, Kitty. Perhaps it is this very dependence that makes me spit like a cat when I am around him. If only he could stop mocking me for one moment I could be as fond of him as I am of my own brother, but he just will not allow it, he is always baiting my bad humour with his jokes and so I suppose we will always fight.

My desperation is so acute I am early for my meeting with Richard and the sweatshop is locked when I arrive. There is snow beginning to fall and I am quite white with it by the time his carriage pulls up.

I have never seen the place empty before. Richard keeps the shutters closed and lights a candle instead, which fills the place with wisps of black smoke as it burns.

'How is my son?' I ask straightaway, wringing my hands

like one possessed. 'Is he well? Is he happy?' I cannot survive without him and feel he must be the same without me.

Richard smiles and pats my hands. 'Don't worry,' he says, 'you know he is safe. His health is quite improved already. The doctor is happy with his progress.'

I watch him light a cigarette from the match he has used for the lamp. The flame burns down so low he drops it quickly and laughs.

'I'm very proud of you, Rosa,' he says. 'You've done well with the boy. The illness was not your fault.'

'Thank you.' I smile back at him, hoping my hair still covers my ears, which must be blue with cold as well as rabbit-like in appearance.

'I would like to pay you for the cost of all your care,' he says.

I remember Max's words and my face falls. 'Then pay your son for the pleasure he has given me,' I tell him. He is at my side in a minute.

'Rosa, I have offended you!' he says. 'Please excuse me, I am nervous and clumsy. You must think I am a fool. Would you forgive me? The last thing I want to do is upset you.'

He runs his hands through his hair and lets out a nervous laugh, suddenly looking very young and very much like my child. 'Do you believe it? I already love the boy,' he tells me, and his eyes are suddenly sad and serious.

'You're asking his mother,' I say, proudly. 'I could not imagine anyone not loving him.'

The nervous laugh again. He begins to pace the small space on the floor. 'No, I mean I love him like a father,

Rosa,' he says. 'Isn't that incredible? Do you know for years I have been under incredible pressure from my family to marry and have children, but – to be honest with you – the idea never really appealed to me. I had no time for children or for home life. Then suddenly I am presented with a son and immediately I find he has become the focus of my universe.

'He's changed my life already, Rosa – can you believe that?' I watch the excitement on Richard's face as he speaks. This is, of course, what I wanted and yet I find myself filled with inexplicable dread at his words. 'Of course,' he goes on, 'there will be difficulties explaining his appearance, but I'm not really worried by that, to tell the truth. Scandals are quite the thing these days, especially in the fashion world.'

His enthusiasm is contagious, despite my fears, and I find myself smiling with him. This is *more* than I had hoped for, Kitty. I thought there would be many difficulties before Richard accepted David as his own. My relief at hearing David is well has made me giddy. I feel myself falling and Richard is there to catch me, leading me to a stool and watching my face with concern.

Suddenly he places his hands on mine and kisses me on both cheeks. 'You must be so proud of him,' he whispers. His face is in front of mine, close to mine. He smiles. 'Do you remember that time you bandaged my finger?' he asks. 'I never forgot that moment, Rosa. I believe I knew you were something special right then. What did you think of me? Did you imagine I was like some foolish small boy who has injured himself? Was I important to you then? Do you remember?'

How can I describe my feelings on that day? All I do is nod feebly.

He kisses me then, Kitty – so suddenly that I jump. His lips are warm upon my own cold pair. I would close my eyes, but I want to see everything and remember all.

'Rosa,' he whispers, and the pleasure I feel at hearing him say my name like that is beyond all measure.

I relax a little now, knowing that much of my struggle is over. My shivering has stopped and the warmth of Richard's body has heated my own. My eyes close. His lips are upon me again. This will stop, it has to stop, but for the moment I will allow it because my happiness is in sight at last.

'What's wrong?' Richard asks, seeing my expression. 'Did you mind the kiss?' He looks surprised, as well he might – for he has been told by me that we have been as intimate as possible on one other occasion.

I put my fingers to my lips, trying to hold Richard's kiss there, watching him walk away and light another cigarette.

'I should go,' he says, smiling. 'I need to organize the books at the salon or you'll have no job to go back to.' Another small laugh.

'Will you take me to collect David?' I ask.

'Rosa,' he begins.

'What is it?' I ask, quickly. 'You said he was well. Were you lying? Is he close to death?'

He pulls my arms back reassuringly. 'Look, Rosa, this is very difficult for me. David is not seriously ill but the doctor has told me that, apart from the illness he is a little underweight for his age and there are signs that his lungs may be permanently damaged, even once he is recovered.'

I clutch my hands to my chest. Richard pulls them away.

'Please, Rosa, you have become so pale. David is well. He is just a little malnourished, that's all. But there is so much lung disease around we will need to be careful. A few weeks on good food have made a remarkable difference in him already.'

'I feed him well and keep him out of the cold at all times . . .' I begin.

'I know you do.' The nervous laugh again. 'It's just that – as the doctor told you – there is a lot of damp in the old ghetto houses. It's not your fault, you have done your best for the boy, anyone can see that. I'm just glad you brought him to me when you did.'

'You mean to keep him,' I say in a whisper. My ears are buzzing and there are voices in my head. Why can I not understand what Richard is saying?

'Rosa, he needs the best and I can afford to give it to him,' Richard says. This is true and it is why I took my son to him. I believed he would want his child's mother too, though.

'Can he stay a little longer?' Richard asks. 'Just until he is back to strength?'

What am I to do?

'I must see him,' I say.

We drive to Richard's house and I am shaking with anguish the entire journey. When I see myself through Richard's eyes I realize how ridiculous I have been with my dreams. I am shabby and plain. Yet I thought him decent enough to marry me in spite of that. I am a poor woman he has employed and who, he believes, he was drunk enough to be seduced by several years before. I have taken his child and nearly killed it for him. I must be a nightmare to him.

I am taken to an upstairs room where a warm fire burns, and discover David there, tucked sleeping in a cosy little bed with blankets up to his chin, while the kindly-faced nurse watches. David's night-clothes are so pretty; I see a little lace-trimmed silk sleeve where his arm has emerged from the side of the quilts. Does he think of his poor mother when he dreams, I wonder?

All around the bed are the most beautiful toys, Kitty.

I look at Richard. There are tears in his eyes, too.

'Can he stay?' he asks.

I nod. I have no voice to speak. I know by his tone and his expression that he means longer than a few days – that he is talking of keeping David for the rest of his life.

'Until he is properly well,' I tell him. He nods, relieved. He has already told me David's lungs may never be strong. How can I ever take him back with me to the cold grimy house I live in at present? I would be murdering my own child. I could never do that, and Richard knows this as well as I do.

We stand together in the hallway.

'I would still like to reimburse you for all the care you have given him,' Richard says.

I look him straight in the eye. 'One hundred pounds,' I say. There is a flicker of surprise across his face. He thought I would leave empty-handed. He thought I would go away and never come back. I repeat my offer.

'One hundred pounds.' My voice holds strong. He has lost the look of pity now. I have shocked him. He thinks he has judged me wrongly.

356

'That's rather a large amount,' he says. Even the nervous laugh has abandoned him now. So his child's mother is a hard-faced rogue, after all. I no longer care. I hold my gaze and say nothing.

'Very well. Of course. It . . . it must have been difficult for you . . .'

He is gone for several minutes but returns with a package in his hand.

'Thank you, sir,' I say. Then I walk out of his house with my back and head as straight as I can hold them.

CHAPTER THIRTY-SEVEN

ZG

ARMURE
*A rich blend of wool and silk with a barely-visible
triangle, chain or twill design on the surface.*

Do you think me very hard and terrible, Kitty? Do you
believe I have sold my child? Well, allow me to tell you,
dearest, that in that moment standing in Richard's hall I
realized a truth that I had missed so far in my short life:
I understood that Max has been right all along, and that
it is everyone for themselves, and that anyone who thinks
otherwise is a fool. It is a lesson I would wish you to learn
too, Kitty, before you find out too late, at terrible cost, as
I almost did.

If I want my son back and a gentleman for a husband I
shall have to earn them, and not through mere wanting,
either. Richard has bought my boy from me and I shall
buy him back again. We will have all we need, David and
I, and without another to provide it for us. Max has been
too kind already and Richard too tolerant. I have no further
need of their pity but a craving bordering on mania to see
respect in their eyes instead.

I walk for many hours, but without becoming tired. My
energy is ceaseless and my feet fairly fly along the cobbles.
How clear things seem to me now, suddenly. I feel like a

fish that has been swimming round and round in a grime-filled pond and is suddenly placed in a sparkling clear lake. I knock on doors until I discover what I need to know. Then I am off running down street after street until I reach a road called Eagle Street, in Holborn. It is a distance of some miles yet I have energy to spare and feel that I could run forever. Time is something I have little to spare now, Kitty; the longer my plan takes, the longer David will be apart from me.

A small and very smart French woman answers the door to number eighty-three – a tiny red-bricked dwelling which leans onto the side of The Eagle public house for support.

I introduce myself, trying to look pleasant enough, though my head is bursting with all that has happened and more, and she takes me through into the tiny parlour to meet her mother. The old lady does not recognize me at first and, even in my current state, I cannot help but be tickled by the fact that she does not have her teeth in at present.

'Rosa,' I say, 'Rosa Zigofsky. I work upstairs at the salon in Mayfair. I am one of the casuals – a sewer. Sometimes I come down to help with the fittings.'

When she recognizes me at last I see her back stiffen. A sewer! In her house! And she a *vendeuse*! She looks across at her daughter.

'What do you want?' she asks.

'I heard you say you are retiring,' I tell her. This is not time for polite chatter. 'I wish to purchase your client list.'

There is a sound from her mouth that could be laughter or scorn.

'How much do you want?' I ask. She tilts her small

scrawny head and looks up at me from the side of her eyes, like a bird.

I pull the envelope out of my vest. 'I won't argue with you,' I say, 'fifty pounds should be enough. Most of your clients are as near to death as makes no matter. This is no investment and you know it.'

She looks at me with the same scorn in her eye but then she looks at the money I hold. 'They would never allow you near the clients,' she says in French.

'They will,' I say.

There is a pause. I glance across at the daughter and catch the look of longing in her eyes as she, too, looks at the pound notes I have laid on the table. Then I look about the room. There are one or two good shawls and cloths draped about, but the furniture they cover is as rotten as my own few sticks.

'Very well,' says the mother, and I hear a sigh of relief from her daughter. I hold my hand out and she places her own claw in it reluctantly.

'*Salut*.'

'*Salut*.'

I am a *vendeuse*.

CHAPTER THIRTY-EIGHT

ZG

CHICOREE
Material cut with its edge left unhemmed.

Well, Kitty, as I look back I can find many things that have amused me in my new life in the salon, despite my constant distress and grief at being parted from my child. I have found it possible to laugh again, but my laughter sounds bitter and there is a new look of hard hostility in my eyes.

Imagining me as you heard me before, can you picture me now, one of the most sought-after *vendeuses* in the salon? Two years have passed since that terrible day when I gave my child to the care of his father. I am now very much the smart Frenchwoman, with long dark hair which is plaited so tight it looks varnished, and dressed in a chic black dress that flatters my pale skin.

I have tried hard to lose my accent as well as to learn the French that all the other *vendeuses* talk in. I wave my arms about less as I speak, and my walk has been copied from the deportment of all the *grandes dames* who grace our establishment in Berkeley Square.

I visit David once a week, and I cannot tell you, Kitty, how precious and yet sweetly painful these visits are. I take him to the park or the shops and I flatter myself that I am no shame to him now as we walk along together, for even though I am still living within modest means I no longer have to wear Bubba's coat or shabby, paper-lined boots.

David loves me, that much is obvious to all, but he is happy with his father. He is a beautiful boy and very bright, too – but then I am his mother and so maybe not totally impartial.

There was so much fuss the day I walked into the salon and announced I had bought the old *vendeuse*'s list you would think war had broken out. First they tried to shoo me upstairs, but I would not budge. Then they called the chief and then I was laughed at and finally they screamed at me. Then Richard arrived and the shock on his face when he saw me standing there beneath the chandelier was a picture I will never forget.

'Miss Zigofsky!' he said smiling. 'What is the problem?' The other staff agitated around behind him, flapping their skirts and pulling faces as though I were a flea-raddled cat that had somehow wandered into the room by mistake.

'There is no problem,' I said, clearly, 'I am here to start work. I have bought *Madame*'s list of clients and I will need training if I am to serve them in the correct manner.'

Richard stared at me in silence, and I could see the confusion in his eyes. I had shocked him and I was proud of that.

His laugh surprised the other staff. 'Good,' he replied after a while. He ran a hand through his hair. 'Good.' His voice had no enthusiasm, only a rasher of politeness above the more solid flesh of embarrassment.

I walked towards the back of the room, cutting a swathe through the open-mouthed staff as I went. You see, Kitty,

Richard was in a situation very like my own at last; he had no choice really, and he knew it.

He caught up with me as I was lighting the kettle for tea. 'This is a surprise, Miss Zigofsky,' he said, still smiling. 'I had no idea you had such plans for yourself.'

A decent man, fallen from grace. What fools men are, to allow alcohol to stigmatize their lives in this way. My own shame stemmed from violence beyond my control. It would never have happened any other way. Yet men like Max and Richard chart their own downfall through unnecessary and voluntary weaknesses. This was never my father's way, Kitty. We were both brought up to warm ourselves in the rays of correct behaviour, and I thank God for that, too.

And yet I still love Richard, Kitty, and perhaps it is a love that has matured with age from a childish passion to a more enduring affection.

'And neither did I, until yesterday,' I told him in reply. He coughed and looked about the room. We were alone.

'I had no intention of hurting you, you know,' he said, in a whisper. 'I only want what is the best for the boy.'

I said nothing.

'Do you intend telling anyone . . .' his voice trailed.

'That your new son is my child?' I asked. 'No.'

His shoulders slumped a little from relief and he closed his eyes. 'Perhaps it might ease your difficult situation if I found you a better job in another salon,' he said.

'Please don't bother,' I told him, 'I prefer working for you.'

He stood for a while, taking it all in, then started to

walk out, turning once he reached the drapes which were used instead of a door.

He appeared agitated and bemused. 'Did you buy that dress for the job?' he asked.

I nodded. I had bought it from a small private seamstress I knew, whose door I had nearly broken open with my knocking the night before, on the way back from Holborn. It was plain jet-black crepe with a large collar that tied into a bow and simple frills down either sleeve. The seamstress had insisted it was all the mode, and that it had been made for a fashion lady for the funeral of her sick husband, who had since recovered.

'Perhaps you would allow me to have one made here for you,' Richard said, and in that one moment I saw the dress for what it was – showy and dreadful and totally lacking in style.

I turned slowly to look in the mirror. What had looked smart and elegant last night now appeared comical in situ. My hair, as well. I had taken the whole night preparing it while Gregory watched. It was piled as tall as I could manage, to give me more height. I looked like Bubba with a hat on.

Richard watched my face but he did not smile. 'I'll send Constance down,' he said.

The girl was a helper in the salon whom I had seen many times before but never spoken to, on account of my lowly position. To my blessed relief she had a new dress ordered for me within the hour and was snipping about the one I wore with the dressmaker's shears until it took on a semblance of style that I could not have imagined myself.

She also retied my hair in a simpler fashion that had me

looking almost as smart as the other women in the salon. All this was done in solemn silence, but once it was finished she made tea and chatted in a friendly enough way about the job I would be taking on. She was to train me and watch me, she said. When that was finished I would be placed with one of the older women. I could see she was as curious about my sudden elevation as the other women, but she kept her questioning in check. She was nice, Kitty. I felt a little better that night.

CHAPTER THIRTY-NINE

ZG

VELOURS DU NORD
*A luxurious fabric; black satin background shot with
a colour and covered with velvet flowers stamped in
relief.*

My work in the salon suits me very well, Kitty, and I am become a much better person because of it. There is not a friend in the place here, save Constance, but this does not trouble me much. Upstairs they think I have become above myself, while downstairs they treat me as if I were not worthy to spit on their boots.

The clients seem to like me, though, and this is what counts. They are all old enough to be counting their days and most are deaf, too. Their delight at being served by a younger voice and ears is obvious and prevents them minding the fact that I am new to the role.

I am treated as something of a pet, Kitty, on account of my age, and am often given sweets or little gifts as rewards for being polite and discreet. You would not believe how judicious I can be when I try, dearest! When the ladies arrive I am a model of politeness, so quiet and so quick to spot their needs before they have arisen that I could be a ghost. I have their names and titles off pat and only lift my eyes from the ground if I am spoken to directly. Nevertheless, I must have been noticed by many of them, for I have been given the name *Petite*, which they find easier, evidently, than learning my proper name.

Kitty, there is something else I must tell you, though I have been slow to notice it. My new hair and style of dress appears to have made me somehow more visible to men. I have been taking careful note of the younger clients who grace our salon and have fallen to copying many of their better ways. My carriage is straighter and my walk is much improved, after many nights of practice in my tiny room. I have spent precious money on a full-length mirror and, through watching my image, I have learnt how to place my hands, instead of allowing them to dangle by my sides or wave about as I speak. I have also discovered a knack of keeping my chin down but eyes up that I feel makes less of my rabbity ears and gives me a bit of a 'look'.

And now I notice the husbands of some of my clients are paying me attention. They are mostly more than nine-tenths of their way to their graves, Kitty, but it is amazing how much they pick up when I give them one of my newly-acquired 'looks'.

I even tried this glance out on Max to judge the effect, but he merely asked if I had been sitting in a draught and acquired a crick in my neck, which I suppose is one of his little jokes.

Even Richard seems rather taken with me now, when we are in the salon together. His stares are very hard to fathom but I feel he knows he has more to reckon with in me than before. He has tried to engage me in conversation several times now, even asking me what scent I wear one day when I have been bold enough to sample some *Muguet de Bois* that Constance's young man gave her as a gift. I am thrilled at this new development, but determined to keep my distance. I am pleasant enough, Kitty, but never anything more than polite. When I visit David, Richard is always absent from the house and this suits me.

I have plans now, Kitty – great plans. Learn from one who has been forced to become much wiser than you, dearest. Fight your own way in life and learn to depend on no one. How badly have I craved a family and friends about me! For these are the very bones of the society I live in – support from those dear ones during hardship and poverty. *My* only support has been from Max, and I know I will pay him back many times over once I have made my way. I mean to be rich, Kitty, for it is the only way to earn my place in the life that I want.

My work in the salon means I have access to some of the newest designs and styles. I study these fashions at great length when no one is looking, peering at stitching and seams until I have them memorized. Then I am able to sew cheaper copies at home, adapting the styles to suit more general tastes, and these I sell to any local women with more than a few pounds in their purses.

This home business of mine is proving surprisingly popular and far more lucrative than taking in repairs. I had no idea what great a part of a paltry income women will pay to be *à la mode*.

What happens is this: I have the newest style standing on a dummy but half-covered with a sheet in the corner of my little room when a customer calls to collect her repairs. While I am quietly busy making tea – taking more time than I need, I assure you – she will, of course, spot the garment and ask straightaway who it is for. I feign surprise, Kitty, rushing to cover the outfit properly with the cloth. I am shocked, I say. It should never have been seen.

After much persuading and begging from the customer I then tell her the name of a mutual acquaintance and settle to watch the many envious glances she pays to the frock as the tea is drunk. Eventually she will ask if a deposit has already been taken. I frown as though unwilling to be drawn on the matter but eventually tell her with even more reluctance that no money has changed hands so far.

'Has she seen the model?' I will be asked. When I say that she hasn't, the dress will be off the stand and over the client's head before the last sip of tea has been drained. Do you know they will often be pulling the bodice over their heads before their hats are off? I had one woman wedged tight in the neck-hole just the other evening!

Whereas Richard's dresses are modelled in places like Bond Street and the top Mayfair salons, mine receive their best airings on the hard benches of the Princes Street synagogue in Brick Lane.

My wedding frocks have received notice now, too. Just the other day the local rabbi was heard to complain about poor Jewish brides marrying on reduced fees who nevertheless managed to be conspicuous for the extravagance of their dresses, and this is, I feel, somewhat down to me.

The money I am taking has enabled me to pay a little investment into my own business. Just yesterday I took delivery of a new tailor's ham and a seam roll, for pressing, and I treated myself to a length of better quality Petersham for the waistbands, as some of the customers had complained that the cheaper version scratched at their skin.

If the orders become greater I will be forced to take on my first employee. I have already made enquiries at the People's Palace, where they train poor young Jewish girls in dressmaking. When I was shown their work I discovered more than one to be of a suitably high standard and was told the girls are keen to work for a very low wage. This would be suitable for me, or else I will take on a factory worker while they are laid off during the slack period.

CHAPTER FORTY

ZG

DRESSMAKERS
*Until 1854 high-class dressmakers supplied clothes for
the upper classes by sending sketches and fabric
swatches to individual clients. In this year, though,
Yorkshireman Charles Worth set up his design establishment in Paris, producing a collection of made
samples and holding the first known fashion shows to
display them.*

The staging of the Zigo fashion show was largely down to
Chloe, who in turn enlisted an army of producers, chor-
eographers, stylists and dressers to do the real work for
her, while she contented herself with handling the lion's
share of the appropriate ranting, wailing, hair-renting,
cursing and press calls.

It was a job Kitty neither coveted nor felt herself vaguely
equal to. In previous years Gabriel would have been a
calming influence; without him, Chloe was like a hyped-up
banshee. Yet the role was somehow made for her – or she
for the role. It was one she had been rehearsing every day
of her life since the age of five.

Not an ounce of her energy, not a grimace, smile or tear
was unsuitable or surplus to requirements. The thudding
of her feet as she tore down corridors and catwalks formed

a solid, constant, pulsating beat that gave rhythm and urgency to the others' meanderings. When she shrieked she was the factory siren that galvanized the softly dazed and unproductive into meaningful activity. It was a terrible noise but comforting, at the same time. It was almost like the old days. Like before Gabriel had been killed.

As Chloe ranted, so could she simper. The focus of her charm and adoration was Alain. While he largely ignored her, both backstage and in the workroom, she pulsated around him, issuing murmurs of affectionate encouragement.

Chloe was the devil incarnate because she blamed Kitty for the last-minute decision to show. They had their press already. The range was incomplete. Alain was a complete sweetie but he was hardly Raphael and he could *never* imitate Gabriel's brilliance. It was Kitty's fault that the model team was half-rehearsed and riddled rotten with last-minute substitutions. The whole event had been *cobbled*, she told Kitty repeatedly, pronouncing the word as though speaking to a foreigner.

'*Everyone* shows at the barracks, Kitty, which is total number one reason why *we* should not be showing here. Number two? Because the place cannot – repeat, *cannot* – handle the current levels of press attention we are having to cope with since the inquest. As you are aware, the whole sodding pack are due, including not just fashion but every sodding rag that is keen to drain more juice out of the murder. The foreign press is especially prolific and suddenly we are inundated with requests for tickets from every damn celebrity who wants to get an airing.

'Gabriel would have cancelled this, Kitty – you *know*

that, don't you? And sweet Jesus,' she suddenly honed in upon a new point of controversy, 'why are you dressed like that? What in God's name possessed you?'

Kitty stared at her sister. Chloe had never looked more stunning. She had always adored slagging Kitty off more than anything else on the face of the earth and looked her best when she was doing it. Her eyes shone and her hair glowed. She was painted and swathed in sepia from top to toe. In the midst of all the colour and gleam she stood out like a cut-out from an old photo. Her hair had been cropped and dyed, her face had a luminescent glow from hours of honest toil spent peeling and exfoliating, and her lips were frosted ochre. The fabric of her trouser-suit cost two hundred and twenty pounds a metre. Kitty remembered Gabriel laughing about it when he brought the swatch back from Interstoff. Yet it was wonderfully understated. A design that looked tattooed by pinpricks and a sheen only visible under certain lights.

Kitty was wearing a boy's white singlet a size too small and jeans two sizes too large. Someone had forgotten to do her laundry. What she wore was all she had clean. Chloe battled to pull her into a quilted jacket. Kitty tried just as hard to resist.

There was a sumptuous smell in the air – the scent of fabrics that had been heated and then cooled and thrown into the air as each of the waiting models had their first outfits pulled over their heads as the last-minute fittings began. There were fatty smells of make-up and the hard-to-inhale aromas of lit matches, foreign cigarettes, burnished hair and lacquer. Then the roasting smell of gels as the lighting men went through final trials, and too-loud bursts of music that the crowds would soak up with their bodies when the auditorium was full.

Kofteros sat alone in the third row of gilt chairs, staring thoughtfully at the empty stage. He was totally rapt, with a study of locked concentration, his fingers knitted and pinned to his top lip, his legs stretched beneath the seat in front, but not in a way that looked loutish or disrespectful of the pre-show, church-like atmosphere. He was irrelevant, in his four-button suit and satin tie. A buzzard again, waiting for them to fail. Waiting to pick their bones. He smiled at Kitty when he saw her. She looked away quickly, hoping he hadn't thought she was watching.

'He's an attractive man,' Chloe said. Kitty's mouth tightened. 'He's not as wicked as you think, Kit,' her sister told her, her tone suddenly mellowed. They both stared at him out of sight now, from behind a pvc-covered screen. 'You seem to have Nicky pegged as the villain of the piece. A rotter and a scoundrel, eh?' Chloe warmed to her theme. 'And just what exactly is your role in all this buy-out fore-play? Do you see yourself as some coy Victorian heroine? I really think you should talk to him properly, Kit, instead of all this snarling. Who knows, you might even like him.'

Kitty shook her head. 'He wants this to go down the tubes, Chloe,' she told her sister. 'If the season works out the banks might view us with more sympathy. If not, we fail and we fall into Kofteros's lap. You know it and I know it. And *he* knows it, of course. Look at him, Chloe. He can't wait for the whole thing to start so that he can be there at the downfall. He'll be drooling on the runway soon.'

An aria from *Don Giovanni* flooded the hall. Two carpenters scuttled across the catwalk on hands and knees, like beetles, hammering as they went. Kofteros closed his eyes, but whether to cut out the hammering or appreciate the opera, Kitty could not guess.

'We're shooting ourselves in the fucking foot, thanks to you,' Chloe said. 'If we'd cancelled the show there'd have been nothing for him to gloat over. You're the one that insisted we go down kicking and screaming for all the world to see. Where's the dignity in all this, Kitty? Do you think it's what Gabriel would have wanted? Then damn you for your fucking misplaced loyalty and schmaltz.'

Kitty looked at her sister. She was so close she could see the flecks of hazel in her irises. 'Did you really want to go down without a fight, Chloe?' she whispered. 'Is that really how you saw us? Does the money really mean that much to you? Burgess I anticipated, but I thought you might see the point in all this.' Her sister's face flushed suddenly and she looked away from Kitty's gaze. 'One last try, Chloe,' Kitty insisted, 'that's all.'

She moved even closer to say the unspeakable. 'What if it *was* them, Chloe?' Her sister's eyes came up again quickly, the pupils widened. She knew what Kitty was about to ask, it was obvious from her expression. 'What if they *did* kill our father? You must have thought about it, don't pretend you haven't. Perhaps it occurs to you now and again that you may be screwing the man who financed the assassination.'

Chloe went to walk away but Kitty pulled her back. It was the first time in their lives that she had had the courage to act in such a way with her bullying sister.

'What if it was, Chloe?' she insisted. 'What then? Roll

375

over and let them take the business as well? All those smiling faces on the screens? Grinning their little socks off at how easy it's all been? Is *that* what Gabriel would have wanted? You seem to be so tuned into his thoughts.'

Chloe pulled away. 'You're a fucking madwoman, Kit,' she said. 'You, Nula and Mother – all barking. Just excuse me if I sit this one out, will you? This is business, Kit – ask Nicky, ask Burgess. Ricky Khan murdered Gabriel. Ask the police.'

'His daughter says he didn't,' Kitty told her, receiving a look of such withering contempt in return that she wished she'd kept the last comment to herself. To change the subject she looked back at Kofteros. 'He even looks the part,' she said.

She meant that he looked like a killer. But then everyone she saw had murdered her father in her suspicious mind – even the ones who looked as though they hadn't. Kofteros looked very much as though he had.

'I don't know how you can, Chloe,' she murmured. She looked at her sister's face. Chloe was staring at Nicky and her expression looked unusually anxious.

A loud crackle of static rent the air like lightning, making both women jump and breaking the spell between them. Chloe straightened and snorted a laugh out through her nostrils, her old bravado restored. 'He is the *best* in bed, Kit,' she said, grinning. 'He does things with jelly cubes you could only guess at. If you promise to be polite to him he may even give little Freddy a few tips for free.'

Kitty looked at her sister. Was she joking? But she never knew. One thing Chloe was good at was giving nothing away. She felt a sudden rush of envy for her sister, for her shallowness, for her ability not to dwell and fester, like an open wound. Chloe was of the minute. Nothing existed for her beyond the present. Did it ever occur to her seriously for more than a fleeting millisecond that Kofteros could have arranged their father's murder?

The dark room. Kitty closed her eyes as the hammering grew nearer. Riva Khan's face hove into view. 'Your father must have been there before he died. Maybe someone he picked up in that room would have followed and killed him, think about that. Not my father, Kitty. Some pervert. A madman.'

Riva could have killed her father easily, the look on her face alone told Kitty that. If murdering Kitty would have saved her own father from prison she would have pulled a knife from her bag and gutted her on the spot, she could tell that. A proud woman. And vindictive.

Kitty shuddered, even in the heat of the spots. There was a small noise nearby. When she opened her eyes she saw Nula sitting heaped behind a rail of samples. Her hair looked wild and her large tragic eyes gleamed cyclamen as the gels were tested yet again.

'Okay?' Kitty asked her, tapping her knee with her toe. Nula nodded. The lustre in her eyes turned liquid.

'It's difficult,' Kitty said. Difficult without Gabriel. His size, his sweeping authority backstage. Difficult to forget he wouldn't appear on the catwalk at the end of the show. Chloe was happy snogging the press for now. A jittery Burgess had appeared to sit alongside Kofteros. China was home being pregnant and Hester was too sick to appear. She was holding together like Blu-tack but could become unstuck in the heat of the lights. Stephano stood at the back of the hall like a bouncer. The proud father-to-be. Kitty smiled.

And how was the chit-chat between the two suits? Burgess and Kofteros. Her uneasy-looking brother had sidled damply into the next seat and was whispering into Nicky's manicured ear. An odd couple, but at the same time well-matched; plucked from their nether world of virtual emotion to study the grubby fruits of their corporate existence.

Burgess wanted the take-over badly, Kitty knew that. She could almost smell his need from where she stood. It was Business he loved, not The Business. Like Kofteros, he could have been just as happy if they were manufacturing fitted kitchens.

The buy-out made logical, financial sense and Burgess was – above everything else – a logical man. But, like Chloe, maybe a slight malfunction in his programming had left a brain cell or two still pining for the glories of the Pyrrhic victory Kitty was attempting to pull off.

Burgess had never had a close relationship with Gabriel, who had seemed surprised and disturbed that such an odd, practical and unemotional character had apparently sprung from his loins. There had been no displays of affection between father and son. But Kitty had noticed Burgess studying them when she and Chloe had received praise and embraces as children, and felt both a dull sadness and hot-faced embarrassment that her brother had been side-lined.

There were figures on a screen and then there was real, messy life, Kitty thought. Nula unwound like a boa constrictor and rose up beside her.

'Do you want to help or watch, Nule?' Kitty asked her.

Nula thought for a minute. 'I'll help,' she said in a voice cracked with grief.

Kitty kissed her on the cheek. 'Stay together, Nules,' she whispered, 'don't fall apart on us now. We need you to be with us. Be strong. We need all the help we can get.'

CHAPTER FORTY-ONE

ZG

CARTES-DE-VISITE
*First introduced to Britain in 1857, the trend for
these small, visiting card-size photographic portraits
was slow to catch on, but by 1861 there were one
hundred and sixty-eight portrait studios in London,
most of them specializing in the* cartes-de-visite.
*Competition became rife, with backstreet photographers
offering a 'likeness and a cigar for sixpence.' The bad
quality of these shots meant they often faded in a few
days, but the better* cartes-de-visite *form a fascinating
record of the actual fashions of the last quarter of the
nineteenth century.*

Kitty, I am now set up with a new girl to take care of extra
orders, and still I find myself sewing through much of the
night as well. The girl is called Ruth Levi and she has a
mother involved in Slop Trade who will take on further
work for a few shillings, if I wish.

Gregory is much taken with young Ruth and the
improvement in his behaviour is remarkable. Knowing she
is to arrive each day he is up earlier than necessary and
about his toilet. When she is in the room he is far more
alert and charming and I feel relieved that there has been
good all round from her employment.

Ruth was born in this country of Lithuanian parents and

I believe she is almost as sharp as myself when it comes to spotting an opportunity for improvement. Just the other day I overheard her tell a customer that two of her relatives had already ordered for an up-coming *simcha* and within a week we had fittings under way for the entire party.

The family were so pleased with the result that Ruth and I were invited to the gathering and we laughed a lot to imagine how Richard would look if he could see some of his precious exclusive designs modelled by some of the fat old matrons we saw dancing to the twopenny fiddler's tunes.

It amazes me how rapidly news can spread throughout our *landsleight*, from *stieblech* to *schul*, via each Bar mitzvah, wedding and *simcha*. The women know I work in a top salon in Mayfair and each one who comes to me as a customer arrives in full possession of the knowledge that she has a right to the best looks a lady can wear, no matter how poor her circumstances.

There is a great pretence here, Kitty, and I am proud of it. The people are all poor but will not admit to such. Their poverty is something they hide inside their hovels. Courtesy makes them avert their gaze when they are forced to face the lowly circumstances of a neighbour. They live in rooms that are too small, they share their quarters with insects and vermin. Their beds stand in bowls of paraffin to rid them of bugs. And yet each day they live as though they were still in their fine homelands and dream of the time when they will be out of the ghetto and onwards to better things.

Did I tell you this place is like one huge collection area for immigrants? How we live in waiting? How the movement is upwards, no matter how remote the chance? Did I say that not once have I seen a face full of resignation? That even the old people plan for the day when their circumstances are improved?

So this is my life too now, Kitty. It is my lot to dress the optimism and pride of the oppressed and give it a face. With my twelve-shilling frocks they may sit in their badly-ventilated synagogues on the Sabbath, where the great wax candles eat up all of the air, chorusing their prayers until the windowpanes shake, and all in the knowledge that they are dressed every bit as well as the grand ladies in the tearooms up west. The fabrics may be of lowlier quality and the styles pinched and scrimped a little here and there to use up less *schmutter*, but the effect is the same – and good luck to them for that.

Schwer und bitter ist das Leben: hard and bitter is life, indeed, but at least we face it now clad in designs that could put Paris to shame!

CHAPTER FORTY-TWO

ZG

ZIBERLINE
*A thick, soft fabric of wool and mohair, with a
silky, lustrous nap.
By the 1850s, a desire to wear fashionable clothes
had affected every class in the social scale. This led to
a blurring of visual distinctions, especially as the
upper class habit of passing clothes down as soon as
they went out of fashion meant that even the quality
of fabrics worn could no longer be held as a reliable
clue to income.*

Ruth has been coaxing me to raise my prices a little. She
says our clientèle will feel more important if their purses
are squeezed. I tell her their purses are singing out with
the pain of the mashing they already suffer, but she claims
to know more – and so the prices are put up by a few
shillings, and I find that – as usual – she is right.

The Communists have already been round to enlist her,
but she is a good girl and says that they and the unions
will only have her asking for more wages and she knows
I pay her fairly already. She is a pretty girl and extremely
clever, taller than myself and with wild black hair that she
keeps tied beneath a scarf.

We are in the slack at the salon right now, so I take

Ruth down to Max's studio to see about the latest orders for brides. Max is more affluent these days and his shop is freshly painted. He wants two new outfits for his staff and he wants them identical, like uniforms. As I am taking measurements Ruth sits and sketches the designs I describe. She is only limited in her talents as an artist, though, and we all laugh when the sketches are finished.

'I'll make up a sample,' I tell Max. 'Ruth is much the same shape as your girls so I can pin it up on her and bring her round to show it.'

This causes much fuss, for the girls believe they are to have the style modelled as though they were in the salon with a mannequin parading for their benefit. Ruth's talents as a model, though, are as lacking as those of a sketcher.

'I could photograph her better,' Max says. And, Kitty, it is here that an idea occurs to me and I believe it to be such a good one that I start to sweat at my own cleverness.

'Could you photograph her in *all* my designs, Max?' I ask.

Max pulls a face, but I know he will agree. He is also rather charmed by Ruth and has been looking for an excuse to get her in front of his camera.

'How many?' he asks, rubbing his chin.

'Six, at present,' I tell him. 'And maybe the one wedding dress I have on the go.'

Before he can turn me down I am off along the street and back with armfuls of my best mantles. Ruth is pulled into each in turn and pinned to fit, while one of Max's girls has her hair combed and plaited into something half decent.

Poor Ruth! We have her holding boas and fruit, staring mournfully and smiling graciously, bending so that the more petite robes might appear long enough, and trussed into corsets two sizes too small so that she will appear slim enough for the more slender-sized orders.

Max is much impressed by the fun of all this and starts barking out orders like an army commander, which tickles all the girls but makes me blush.

Ruth begins the sitting posing shyly and nearly quivering with embarrassment, but after a few hours have passed she is posing like a dowager duchess and speaking in a voice to match, which has Max's girls in fits of hysterics.

I alone remain quiet and serious, plagued by doubts and excitements. I listen to Max playing to the girls and pray he is working professionally enough meantime. When the last one is finished he turns to me with a flourish.

'Madam,' he says. This is his new pet name for me, since my home business has shown signs of small successes. To him I am now a leading couturier, or at least that is his current tease.

Ruth comes up behind him, laughing. He turns, smiles, and places a kiss on her cheek. Kitty, there is a pang of jealousy which runs through me like a knife. What a good couple they make – she with her shining hair and quick, intelligent eyes, currently full of the admiration and longing I had been too blind to notice before, and Max with his handsome grin and huge body that dwarfs even tall Ruth. There is a moment, Kitty, more than a second but much much less than a minute, when we all wake to our own realizations. Ruth sees what appears to be prudish dis-approval written on my face while Max, who knows me best, spots it for the jealousy that it is and all at once sees his advantage.

'Rosa, you need some fun,' he says. He is still smiling. Ruth's eyes are full of what she feels to be shared sympathy.

'She works too hard,' she says, nodding.

'I need to,' I say, tersely. Max's arm is still about Ruth's waist.

'And you also need some wine,' Max says. 'I share a glass with most of my best clients so you should be no exception.' He looks at Ruth before releasing her. I know a man like Max could not fail to miss the girlish adoration in her eyes.

There is an awkward silence between Ruth and me as Max goes off to his tiny kitchen.

'Do you drink wine?' I ask Ruth while he is gone.

She stares at me. She is not stupid, she knows now how I feel. 'I have never tried it before,' she says. 'I have wanted to for a long time, though. Have you?' she asks.

'Only once,' I tell her, 'many years ago. I hated it.'

Max returns with three glasses and a bottle. 'This is burgundy,' he announces. It looks like blood. Ruth sips hers delicately and laughs. 'It's good,' she says, 'I think.'

I take my glass and drink it back in one, staring at Max as I do so. He is somewhat shocked and amused, yet rather pleased too, I think. Kitty, it is not only he who has learnt to read people's eyes over the years. I now have nearly as clear a view of Max Warkofski's thoughts as he has of my own.

He offers me a chair and then pulls one over for Ruth. 'So, what do you plan to do with your pictures, Rosa?' he asks. 'Will you have them framed and hanging on the wall of your salon?'

I ignore his sarcasm. I am holding on to my seat like grim death, for the floor is heaving and pitching like the sea. 'I plan to use them instead of samples,' I tell him. 'What Richard shows on models I can show in photographs. I can take them to my customers in a folder. They can make their selections in the privacy of their own homes.'

Max thinks a while before nodding. Ruth is clutching her glass with her eyes fired up and staring at me.

Do you know how I feel as I look at her, Kitty? I feel ugly and dull and I am so eaten with envy that I am incapable of hating her, for I am so busy hating myself. She is a nice girl. She is what I would want to be if I had the choice. That look in her eyes is the look I had when I bandaged Richard's cut hand in the sweatshop. The openness I see is the look I lost from my own eyes when I was raped in the snow in my *shtetle*. Ruth loves her mother and her father and is loved by them, while my parents are both dead. When she has a child it will be her own baby and no one will rob her of it. And she is a nice girl. And she loves Max.

'You're working outside your hours,' I tell her. And then hate myself for the blush I have put upon her face. She thought she was here as a friend and I have just reminded her she is an employee. She places her half-full glass on the table, stands to leave, lurches slightly, giggles.

Max is on his feet at once. 'I'll walk you back. Where do you live? You can't go like this. I should have mixed the wine with a little water. Excuse me, Ruth, that was my fault.'

There is none of the usual sarcasm or wit in his voice, only concern. Did he ever use such a tone with me? I try to remember but my head is too full of the burgundy. I am in a worse state than Ruth, but would never admit it.

It becomes dark while Max is gone, yet I do not rise to find matches for the lights. My seat is facing the empty sitter's chair. The only noise in the room is my own; heartbeat, breath, voices echoing in my empty skull.

There is a small Yiddish theatre just down the street. I hear a violin and then singing, some laughter, then a wave of hilarity. A comic song? I have no taste for such things. To my ears the song is sad. Too many melancholy notes, yet still the audience laughs.

I remember an act I caught some years before, a clown dressed as a comic bookmaker. He played the fiddle too, but the strings were joke strings that kept snapping and as they snapped he cried; great comic tears that rolled down his cheeks or squirted out into the front row. Everyone laughed, yet I cried with the clown, for I believed he truly wanted to finish the tune, and that the broken strings were preventing him.

I rise in the indigo darkness and walk silently across bare boards to the window. I can see the theatre from here. It is not much of a place, yet it appears quite grand when the lights are on.

'The Gypsy Princess.' The words are painted across boards at the front. I pull the window open to listen some more. Then I hear a cry, though I cannot hear the actual words that are screamed. There is no laughter now, just a roar, followed by more screams.

I watch the empty street curiously. A man in a dress-suit

emerges from the foyer backwards, his hands held to his face. A few people follow. Perhaps the performance is over. Or perhaps the performer has been injured on stage. People are spilling out everywhere now. The building looks like a colander with sand pouring through the holes.

I see Max cutting his way through the crowds that have now formed on the pavement. He has his hands in his pockets and his eyes fixed straight ahead. All around him is a crush of hysterical theatre-goers, yet he walks straight on like a blind man.

I return to my chair and it is there that Max finds me. Even in the darkness I can see the surprise register on his face.

'Rosa?' he says quietly. 'I thought you had gone.'

I sit very still, with my hands clasped in my lap. There is still noise from the street below; cries of anguish and laughter of relief.

Max pours himself more wine. He throws off his coat and unbuttons the neck of his shirt. 'So you mean to go into business proper?' he asks. He is massive in the room. I watch the swallow he takes go down his gullet to his chest. Has he kissed Ruth again? Yet why should he not? I am sulphurous in my bitterness. There is not a generous, well-meaning bone in my body.

I stand and the room is all whirling giddiness about me. Max is sprawled in his chair as though exhausted. Can photography be so tiring or has he become drained by his passion for Ruth?

I walk across towards him. He watches me approach and becomes eerily still. Even his breathing seems to have stopped as he watches and waits. There is no noise from either of us, save the leaf-like rustle of my skirts as I move. For a moment I stand watching him. And then I move closer still. There is a strange, dream-like weariness about me. As though I am standing on the banks of a river, contemplating throwing myself into the current and floating away until I drown.

There is nothing that matters any more, apart from this moment. I stare into the vibrant liquid blackness before me that is Max's two eyes and already I am engulfed by a carelessness I have never known before.

I stand between Max's flung-out legs – a tiny, neat and well-groomed figure before him, her hands clenched tidily and politely, small and dwarfed by the figure in the chair.

Max looks terribly puzzled. 'Rosa?'

I stretch out my arms like a somnambulist and place my hands calmly upon his shoulders. How do I look? Like an earnest child? He stays perfectly still. I am impressed by his patience.

There is laughter from the street, as high and as spiralled as the notes from the violin. Is that for me? Do I appear ridiculous, like the clown with the broken fiddle?

I bend then, to kiss Max on his broad forehead. My lips must barely touch him. I place them onto each brow, one at a time, and then the bridge of his nose. What do I want? I crave comfort, a secure shell that I can slither inside, slimy and snail-like.

I feel Max's hands about my waist. There is a cheer from the street. Do we have our own audience for this little tragedy? Yet we are in darkness and invisible to those outside.

'What is it you want, Rosa?' Max whispers into my ear.

Yet how can I tell him what I do not know for sure? How can a need so great it subjugates all sense of decency and virtue be described by someone with no experience?

I stroke his face silently. His eyes close.

'Rosa . . .'

A kiss could do no harm. I have survived a kiss from Max before, and to no ill-effect. I have hardly to bend as he is so tall, but I push my mouth against his.

Somehow this is not so easy when he is not taking the lead. I fumble on for a few seconds before raising my head.

'No, Rosa,' Max says. His voice sounds weak and I feel a sudden tremble of power. He clutches harder at my waist. 'No.'

'Max . . .' I will try again. It cannot be so hard.

Max pushes me away. 'Rosa,' he whispers, 'men are not built the same as women. There is a stage when we lose our senses and some of the power to control our own bodies. Especially when the present put before us is such a precious one. Don't offer what you mean to take away. Please.'

I have never heard him so indecisive. His words thrill me and I begin to kiss him again – only better, I feel, this time.

Our little battle of wills is over in an instant. Max pulls me in towards him, towards his body, pressing me there, holding me tight with his arms, his mouth and his legs. I throw my arms about his neck in response and we are lost, I know it.

I am laid upon a bed of lavender-sweet linen and my clothes are unpeeled, layer upon layer, until I am naked. Did you know snow can smell? It has a scent of its own and it is this perfume I inhale from the cool breath of Max's mouth. I have no fear and no sense of what is to happen, only a dull and frozen certainty.

Max can bring me to pleasure or pain if he wishes, I am as unprotected as a babe.

I see no other face while Max begins his work. He is neither Richard nor my rapist. When he touches me he is Max and what I desire to touch in its nakedness is Max as well. He uses my name many times in his whispers, so I am reminded of myself enough, too. Rosa and Max.

He shows me himself without inhibition. He knows me and I know him for this honesty. Only the darkness panders to my sense of modesty, yet I know Max would too, if I wanted.

I close my eyes and Max introduces my soul to a thousand blunt emotions. There are fingers in among my hair. My ears receive whispers and my throat is laid bare with the tip of a tongue.

I am lost now, completely. My mind drifts away. There is a gasp from the crowds in the street. And then another cry echoes in the night. What has happened down there? Is the theatre spilled out onto the pavements, with all its dramas and tragedies? Or do I imagine all the noise?

I float above the sounds. The snow is so deep that first my arms are lost and now my legs in its drifts. The cold is like fire, burning my fingers. I clutch out into the air, touching another waiting hand; with a cry I try to grasp it, but it falls apart at my touch. They are Gregory's dappled little fingers, lined up like sticks in the whiteness. There is a kiss flat upon my belly. The horse will be restless with the wait. What if he goes off and takes the cart along with him?

The wedding suit! I let out a gasp as my spine arches in spasm. I have it in my hand – I feel the soft leather of the strap that Rintzi has put around it so that I can take it on the train. I am spreadeagled now, breathing the flannel of my skirt, which they have pulled up around my head to smother my screams. And because I am so ugly.

I am in water now – great waves of spume-filled greyness. Fishes nibble at my face and ears and plant kisses upon my legs and chest. I am thrown from the ship into the waves. My small face is wrapped in cotton but I feel the icy grasp of the sea the minute my body is submerged. My arms are bound – I cannot swim. I would cry out, but there is no life in my body. When my small corpse floats to the surface the gulls will peck me for their lunch and I will be happy enough to serve them, in my own way.

Max is watching in the darkness, his gleaming face above mine, waiting his turn. I can hear the sharp rasp of his breath and see the thumb-print mark upon his head.

Another roar from the street and a cry for help. Max is upon me gently but urgently and spilling inside too. His carefulness is a torture I no longer want to endure. I wish to be driven so far into the snow that I will never claw my way out again. I pull and his weight is upon me. I hear his concern but how can he crush me when the snow provides such a mattress beneath us? I hear his soft whispers turn to cries of anguish and delight and wrap him into my body at the moment of mutual ecstasy.

Even now he will not release me. I am become a part

of his own soul. He clutches at me like a lost child. I stroke his thick hair and plant kisses upon his chilling forehead.

I fall from dreaming into sleeping and the strangest sleep it is too – the sort of drowse that children take, profound and ingenuous.

When I rouse myself at last it is not quite morning and there is a purple light in the room. Max still sleeps. I pull his arms from me and leave without waking him.

The air is as sweet as London air can be – which is to say it has the scent of coal-fires and cats and the musk of rotten fruits, but I drink it down keenly as I walk. I pass the small theatre and stop for a second. There is glass and debris on the pavement, which two young coster lads are busy sweeping up into sacks. I ask them what has occurred but receive nothing but abuse for my pains. There is a policeman present, but I have been humiliated enough and so continue with my walk.

I have no desire to return home, Kitty. Gregory may be there and I fear I will find it hard to face my own brother after what has happened this night. I take myself off to Petticoat Lane instead, to the Old Clothes Exchange, to watch the poor folk there with their sorry rails of mouldering garments.

From the moment I step into Rosemary Lane there is a stench of fried fish and frizzling cut meat and onions. Even at this hour the place is full of bustle and my mood is soon lifted by the noise and various stinks, which would only appeal to one who, like me, has dwelled in London for more than a couple of years.

This whole area, from the junction of Leman and Dock

Streets to Sparrow Corner, is concerned with the selling of second-hand clothing to the very poorest creatures in London. One side of the lane is formed by a mountain of old boots and shoes, while the other is mainly hats, edgings and cheap cotton prints.

I stop in front of a vast array of some of the cheapest garments imaginable: a sea of old flannel, moleskin, fustian and corduroy. Kitty, when I compare these things with the finery I am employed in making in Mayfair! And yet there is justice here, too. Many of these items will be sent to Ireland, I am told, and the unfortunates there will be pleased for them.

I am intrigued by the sight before me, as fascinated as a healthy person walking around a graveyard. Will any of my garments finish up here? The thought tickles me and I laugh out loud. The walk has done me good – it has pushed other thoughts out of my head. It is not until I reach Commercial Street that the worries of my life return inside my head.

Will Max be waiting in my room? I tiptoe up the stairs and am relieved to find the place empty. Gregory has left it in the usual disarray and I spend some time picking up pots and plates before placing them back in their original spots.

I know Max's feet on the stairs. My hands begin to shake and I smooth my hair along my temples.

'Rosa.' He is both smiling and looking concerned. In his hand there are flowers. Roses. Their scent fills the room already.

I have never seen Max look so awkward before. He paces the room with his hat in his hands. He wears the same shirt as he wore the day before. His hair is plastered flat to his head. He looks for a vase and, when he can find none, pushes the roses into Gregory's tea-mug instead.

'That will upset my brother for certain, Max.' I laugh.

He clears his throat many times but does not speak. When he turns again I see how young he still is. 'You . . . took off without waking me,' he says at last.

I nod.

He makes a move towards me. 'Rosa, darling . . .'

'Max . . .'

His hands are at my waist again. He would kiss me, but I turn my face away.

'Don't be ashamed, dearest,' he whispers.

I allow him to hold me.

'I love you.' He repeats this many times over, until there are tears in my eyes.

I wait for what seems to be many minutes and then, at last, I hear Max ask what I know he will ask. 'Rosa, we must be married now.'

Then I have to tell him what I know has to be my reply. 'No, Max.'

I feel these words run like a sudden current through his body and I pull away politely.

'Rosa?'

'Max,' I say, 'you have always known I will marry Richard.'

He stares at me as though I am gone mad.

'Still?' he asks. His eyes are changing. The youth is going. A hard, angry man is taking his place.

'That has always been my intention,' I say.

'You came to me last night,' Max says. 'It was you,

Rosa. I have waited. I have waited so long I thought I might die.'

'Richard is to be my husband, Max,' I tell him. 'No one else. He has my child.' Did he really think I would ever be stopped in my plan to get David back? My son is still my life. All I do and work at is for him. Even if I did not love Richard I would marry him just to have my boy returned to my arms.

Max stands full height and stares down at me. 'And you may carry *my* child, now,' he says, bitterly. 'Or did that not occur to you? *Your* baby, Rosa, not someone else's. Your own flesh – and mine. It could be forming right now, as we argue. What then? Will that make you love me as much?'

I have a moment of uneasiness for, to tell the truth, this idea has not occurred to me. I clutch at my belly in shock. What if it were possible? Richard would never look at me again if I carried a child. I let out a pitiful wail at the thought and take a seat before my legs crumple beneath me.

Max sees the change in my eyes and smiles horribly. 'Think, Rosa,' he says quietly. 'Think of that idea. Imagine a child of your own, fathered by a husband who loves you more than life itself. Then think of that cold fish you desire so much. Think of the lies and deceits your relationship is based upon, and the honesty of ours.

'I know you, Rosa – better than you know yourself. Richard would have to see your name written down before he even remembered it. He will not marry you, not in a million decades! Think!'

But I will not think, Kitty, I cannot, I refuse to. All I

know is that I will marry David's father and we will be a family. It is the only way I will have David back with me again. I can imagine nothing else.

Max taps my belly. '*My* child, Rosa – what about that? Was last night your attempt to get the thought of me out of your mind? Did you hope that by giving your body what it wanted you could push me away altogether?' He stares into my eyes. 'We'll see, shall we? We'll wait.'

I have never seen Max this way before. Am I the first woman to turn him down? Well, he has plenty more to choose from, so he shouldn't let himself worry. My hands still shake with shock and I push them under my skirts and out of his sight.

'By the way,' he says as he rises to leave, 'the theatre last night – the policeman told me the whole story as I passed him just now. Someone in the balcony seats called "fire" and there was a rush to escape. What we heard as we made love was the sound of seventeen poor souls being crushed to death in the panic. What a fitting tragedy, eh? How better could our timing have been?'

I shudder as he slams his way out of the door.

For three weeks the tension has been unbearable. Max is often here but he is always silent, just watching me and waiting. God knows why, but he seems so sure that what we have done will result in a child. His presence in our rooms is terrible and even Gregory has become distressed at the sight of his friend now.

My monthly bleeding has started, Kitty. Can you imagine how great my relief is? I send a note to Max, at his studio, for I cannot bear the look on his face when he is told.

When I return from work Max is sitting in the dark and there is a terrible enough tale in his posture alone. His back is to the door and he does not move when I walk in, even though he must have heard me arrive.

I see the case opened out on the bed and the torn tissue lying over the floor.

'Max?' My terror is complete now. There is a knife in his hand. I see its glint in the moonlight. 'Max!'

I struggle with the matches and three fall from shaking hands before I have the mantle lit. I am sobbing. 'The suit!'

He has the garment across his lap. From the smell of his breath I can tell he is drunk.

I throw myself onto my knees and take the suit from him, checking it over and over again for the cuts I am sure he has made in it. When I discover it is whole my relief emerges in hysterical tears. I press the waistcoat to my face and rock to and fro on my heels.

'Don't worry, Rosa,' Max says in a hoarse tone, allowing the knife to fall from his hand to the floor, 'even I couldn't commit such a crime. Your wedding suit is whole. It should fit Richard very well. As you know, it was always several sizes too small for me.' He laughs at that, Kitty.

Was this always a joke, then? I fold the suit more carefully than ever before, stuffing each piece of shredded tissue carefully back between each fold and layer.

'You should go now, Max,' I say. He rises unsteadily to his feet and grasps me by the arm.

'I wish you well, Rosa,' he says, smiling, 'you deserve all that you are working so hard to get. David is your whole life, I realized that as I sat here waiting for you.

I just hope Richard is clever enough to see what he is missing.'

He kisses me on the forehead as he always used to do. Perhaps we are friends again. As he leaves I am sitting on the bed, clutching the re-packed case to my chest.

CHAPTER FORTY-THREE

THE ALBUM

The celebrity cartes-de-visit *became popular in Victorian London and crowds would often form to view the latest photographs of political, sporting or theatrical figures in a studio window. Shots like these could be bought for one shilling and would often be given pride of place next to portraits in the family album, leading to confusion for later generations who were often left wondering whether they were in fact related to these famous or beautiful faces.*

Kitty, the idea of photographs is proving extremely useful. Each new design I produce is taken down to Max's studio, where he is good enough to make a picture of it for me and then either Ruth or I will take a folder of the best pieces around the neighbourhood door-to-door.

The concept is so novel that Ruth has been approaching women in rather more affluent areas and, to our delight, the reactions have been encouraging. There is no waiting for money now, either. Once a client has decided upon a model we can be bold enough to ask for a deposit up front, and this pays for the fabric, which means I have less risk to carry.

Tomorrow I will be interviewing girls to take on home

machine work, which means I can expand the business as I wish.

I have six ladies coming to see me at Max's studio today. Max has said he will be able to make extra folders of photographs and I have had the idea of sending well-spoken ladies out into places like Mayfair. It is remarkable how Max and I are able to continue with our business arrangement almost as though nothing has happened, but that is how it is. He has not mentioned the note I sent to him and, apart from a little polite coldness between us, which I believe Ruth would remark upon if she were not so tactful, things are much the same as before, apart from one terrible thing that I must live with. Since the night with Max I now see him linked in my mind with the man with the thumbnail scar between his eyebrows, and I am unable to separate what happened in his studio with what happened in the snow in Russia. I tell myself that Max is a good man at heart and remind myself of his gentleness, but the thought will not go, all the same. I concentrate my mind on business, for it is a terrible memory and one I would rather push away before I begin to doubt my sanity.

I know society women would only have their designs made couture, Kitty, at salons like Richard's, but I have noticed how each season we seem to lose a handful of clients there, and so feel that there must be many women no longer able to afford couture prices.

It is women like this I feel we must approach, who have expensive tastes but reduced incomes. If they can order my garments in the privacy of their own homes, who will know that they are not couture? There is a risk, of course, that they may turn up to Ascot or the opera and discover themselves sharing a box with a similar design, but I go to some trouble to ensure each outfit is different enough in the ways of trimming and cut to cause the minimum amount of embarrassment.

Kitty, I told you that Richard has taken to staring at me when I work in the salon. Well, now he has become quite talkative too, and just the other evening I made him laugh quite openly with a comment that I made about an elderly client of mine.

The seasons are becoming shorter at the salon and I have finished completely at the sweat, which leaves me more time to take care of my own business – though I have noticed the concern it is causing to Richard, so to hear him laugh so heartily was rewarding. He has laid off several members of staff recently, even outside the slack period – which was a surprise to us all.

Tonight, when the salon was closing, Richard asked if he might take me to supper. I have had barely enough time to run home and change, and what a decision that has been, too! I have a room full of suitable gowns to wear, but all are copies of the salon's top styles!

In the end Ruth has stayed back to help me take the bodice from one and fix it onto the skirt of another. With a silk shawl of Ruth's about my shoulders I believe Richard will never notice the similarities.

We dine at a restaurant in The Haymarket and I watch Richard relax until we are talking almost like friends.

'Do you know how much I have learnt to admire you this past year, Rosa?' he asks.

I look away, smiling modestly.

'When you took the job as *vendeuse* I must admit I believed you had bitten off more than you could chew. But you're popular with the clientele and that's not easy, for they're a difficult group of old baggages, as I'm sure you've discovered.'

He laughs at this and I am amazed, for I have never heard anyone at the salon speak of the clients with disrespect.

'Rosa,' he says, after a long pause, 'David is a fine boy. He is my life now, you know. The business is going through a bad patch as I'm sure you are aware. The economic climate is in decline and women are less able to afford our prices. Do you know I was advised by my bank manager to drop the costs of each garment a little to make them more affordable? Could you imagine anything worse? How can you explain to someone who is used to little more than figures on a page the value of the exclusive price tag?

'Do you think a man who has lived his life behind a desk wearing nothing better than second-rate worsted could ever grasp the concept of the heady excitement a middle-aged woman feels when she orders a model with a price-tag so high as to be well out of her husband's financial range?

'Would he know that trance-like state when a woman is presented with a bill that makes her suffer delicious waves of sickness as it is at least twice the amount she had hoped it would be? And then share the pride of modelling the dress that has been the cause of such suffering?

'If I drop my prices each frock will be less of a purchase. It is the price they are buying, Rosa, not the design.' He pauses to smile and sip his wine. 'You do understand?' he asks.

'I'm sure you're right,' I tell him. His passion for the business entrances me.

His hand is upon my own. 'Would you care to see David?' he asks. 'Right now?'

We take a carriage to his house and I am ushered quietly though excitedly into my son's bedroom. The smell and the sense of him overpowers me and I have to check myself not to fall sobbing at the foot of his bed.

David lies in the midst of a deep and simple sleep. His arm is thrown above his head and his face is turned upward. I hear him breathing. *This* is what I want and what I will fight for, I tell myself. With Max, there would be no David. How could he imagine I would ever have decided otherwise?

Richard taps me on the arm and I am led reluctantly into the front lounge.

'How well he looks now!' Richard says. He is nervous. Perhaps he feels guilty, after all.

'He has a good father,' I say, and Richard's smile is full of pride and relief.

'Do you know, Rosa, the change in you is remarkable too,' he begins. 'You look more . . .'

'I look more like a lady now, Richard,' I whisper, 'is that what you mean? Well I see enough now to model myself upon. When we first met I was a poor little greener. Now I know better. I'm pleased you noticed.'

I look up quickly and, do you know, Kitty, Richard is leaning to kiss me. I stand up suddenly. 'I must go,' I tell him, watching the surprise on his face. Did he really assume

I would be so easy to catch? I know he believes we have been intimate before, when he was too drunk to remember, but surely even he must have noticed the change in my confidence and stature since then?

I shake him by the hand, as a society lady would. 'Thank you for allowing me to see my son,' I say.

He blushes. 'A pleasure,' he tells me, backing off, 'any time. Of course.'

CHAPTER FORTY-FOUR

ZG

THE BUYERS
Retail organizations have different types of buying.
Multiples will tend to order centrally while many of
the stores can often operate on local systems. Local
buying will often guarantee more focus on the specific
customer base, while central buying has the advantage
of discounted bulk orders.

Kitty sat in her mother's lounge, a bone china cup of brand-ied coffee cooling in her hand. There was a smell of pot pourri, as though she were in the back of a minicab or the ladies' rest-room of a posh department store. Hester had taken to scenting all the rooms now.

Kitty was so barely out of childhood, and yet untold nostalgias pained her savagely, like nettle rash. Her whole life was in flashback: boarding school, synagogue, births, marriages, deaths, they all blurred into dream-like lagoons where little meringue islands, whipped up by anxiety and tension, floated by with a lazy regularity.

Hester sighed and patted her uncombed hair. She would never have worn capped sleeves while Gabriel was alive. Hester's upper arms were not her best feature. There was a hammock of spare flesh swinging beneath them, and the skin there was mottled mauve.

Maybe *she* did it, Kitty thought, maybe she killed him so that she could wear short sleeves.

'Never mind,' Hester sighed. 'You did your best. Your father would have been proud of you. He always said you were the only one with his eye for the business. 'Burgess is Mr Cashflow. Chloe is Miss Gossip Column. China is Stephano's wife, nothing more. You understood what was in the blood. You inherited a talent, Kitty. Never forget that. Don't lose sight of your father's dream – it was important to him.'

It was Kitty's turn to sigh and rub her hands across her face. She still hated all this 'in the blood' talk, how they owed it to the suffering and deprivation of their forebears to make a success of what they did today, take nothing for granted, work for their sake, if not for your own.

The fashion show had been a success – though not in the way she had wanted. With too many press packed into too small a space, the atmosphere had become claustrophobic and unbearable. The audience had not come to judge the clothes, they had come to judge the family: ghouls come to visit the madhouse and study the insane. An excuse, if any were needed, to re-run every detail of Gabriel's murder across the front and inside pages of all the daily rags.

The garments themselves had barely received mention. A couple of shots on the fashion pages – some half-hearted critique as an aperitif, and then back onto the main course of murder. Many had made mention of how obviously Gabriel's touch was missing. There were a couple of lukewarm plaudits for Alain – the sort of stuff you would hear for a last-minute understudy who has had to go on stage when the star of the show is sick. Kind enough, encouraging – patronizing, even. Lipservice, nothing more, nothing less.

They were finished, then. No contrived happy endings. Kitty wasn't surprised. She had known the range was nothing great. Good, maybe. Miraculous in its conception, given the odds, but still just good. It required Gabriel's presence for it to become a lifesaver of a range. Without his touch it could never have achieved as much as she had been hoping.

She had sat in an all-nighter somewhere, drinking lemon tea and fiddling with a toasted egg sandwich. The place had been totally apt for her mood – the sort of location a movie director would have chosen in a flash. Obscenely-bright strip lighting that bathed everything in a shadowless pistachio glow. Plastic ketchup bottles with shrimp-coloured dried drips running down the sides. Pyrex plates. Comfortless but comforting – the sort of place anyone would want to sit in while they waited for the next day's papers to arrive.

Freddy had been there too, looking healthy and clean-shaven, despite the ghastly lighting. He had been good-humoured and tolerant about the café, joining in the spirit of the place, nodding to cabbies and winking at the waitress and sifting streams of white sugar into his tea.

Kitty had wanted to view Freddy with affection, only she'd found that difficult since the Raphael thing. If the collection failed it would be easy to blame his father. Blame the father, blame the son. You couldn't segregate in the rag trade. The whole family in one blinding, molten lump.

It was the Jacobs's fault. It was the Jacobs family who stitched up the Zigofskys by stealing their designer a week

409

before the collections. No house could survive that, especially not one that had just been decapitated.

Maybe the Jacobs killed her father. So what about when she married Freddy, the much-adored and much-prized son of the clan? Would she create a new strain – the Zigofsky-Jacobs? Ripper-off and ripped-off in one? Killer and victim united?

She listed their possible reasons in her head:

1. Any Zigo success took business and money out of the Jaycee corporation. Not likely.

2. Murdering Gabriel gave them their best if not only method of headhunting Raphael. Again, not likely.

3. They wanted to stop the wedding. Inconceivable. It had been Frederick Jacobs Senior's idea in the first place, with a few encouraging hints in her direction from Gabriel.

So far the Jacobs were looking positively blemish-free compared to the Khans, Kofteros and the Zigofskys. Especially the Zigofskys. Her mind ran over familiar ground:

Motives:

>Hester – so she could wear odd stockings and short
>   sleeves for the first time in her life.
>China and Stephano – shortage of cash-flow, owing
>   to the inpending birth.
>Burgess – a clinical removal of impediments to sale
>   of business.

410

Chloe – a desire to step into the direct limelight and
    make herself fabulously wealthy into the bargain.
Kitty – a desire to take over the running of the
    business.
Nula – teenage angst.

Was it at that point that Freddy had pulled the egg
sandwich away from in front of her and replaced it with
the early editions? Kitty tried to remember, but the pot
pourri had infused her brain, robbing it of every coherent
memory, save one – The Show Was Not A Success. They
should batten down the hatches and prepare for alien
invasion.

CHAPTER FORTY-FIVE

ZG

BARÈGE DE PYRÉNÉES
*Barège is a fine, semi-transparent fabric made of silk
and wool. The silk is thrown up on the open mesh. A
cotton and jute blend was known as* barège grenadine,
*and one printed with foliage and brilliantly-coloured
flowers was named* barège de Pyrénées.

I have moved into better rooms in a house overlooking
Victoria Park in Hackney. Gregory was upset at leaving
Brick Lane, but now he has seen the place he is delighted.
We each have our own bedroom, with proper walls in
between instead of partitions, and there is a kitchen of our
own for the food and another room where I can work.

Even Max was impressed, although he said very little,
and I know Ruth is delighted as she says she can now
regard me as a proper boss, which made Gregory laugh.

My brother is much improved these past few months.
Max is now his friend again and it is good to see how
much Gregory learns from him that is good. He has more
friends in his job and, despite his shyness, is quite popular
with the elderly ladies around the park, who use him for
errands and spoil him like a child with cakes and sweets.

I have never mentioned the fire in Max's rooms, but
ensure all matches are kept locked away. Max's theory

was that it was the work of local boys, who are known to stick smouldering rags through Jewish letterboxes or beneath our doors. He thinks my brother was merely confused about Rintzi's death and I must say I now believe he is right about this, for Gregory is a gentle man, for all his simpleness.

I now employ fifteen women to act as agents for my models and very busy they are, too, as they work purely on a percentage of sales, which was an idea that Ruth suggested. It was not difficult to recruit locally – I have women calling all the time in the hope that I will take them on for selling, but will only employ those with a clean, smart image. Word of mouth was advertisement enough for the posts, though I also placed a carefully-worded, two-line advertisement in the newspaper, which has brought in some of the more genteel women.

The only exception to this plan of employing well-spoken women is old Mrs Ezra from Fournier Street. She is sixteen stone and hardly a model of elegance, but she is so ferocious she earns more than three of my better turned-out ladies put together, and mainly through what I can only describe as intimidation! There are women living around the Whitechapel area who would never have bought my gowns had it not been for Mrs Ezra's arriving unheralded in their parlours and drinking them out of tea and eating them out of honeycakes until they were forced to make a purchase to be rid of her.

Max has met the woman once when she called to collect her commission, and he said her stare was so fearsome he almost bought one of my mantles himself!

So this is my life now, Kitty – a flurry of manufacture

413

mixed with a few vital days at the salon to serve the paltry handful of clients I have left on my books, and to keep an eagle eye on designs I can copy.

Richard is always present now when I visit David and I am allowed into the house itself more as a guest than an employee. I see this as a great step forward and can tell he is more relaxed in my company.

And still there is Max. I feel we are friends again now, Kitty, for he acts as though nothing has happened, except there is a degree of coolness about him that was not there before. His time is as much taken with his business as my own. I have paid back much of what I owe him and feel proud of this fact. At night I think of him sometimes, and of what happened between us. But I know it will never happen again.

CHAPTER FORTY-SIX

ZG

EPANGELINE
*In the 1860s epangeline was the name given to a
rep-like material, made of wool. In the latter part of the
century it was used for a slightly corded, woollen
sateen.*

There has been much fuss in the salon. A client was contacted for the coming season and replied that she would never pay such great prices for frocks her staff might wear on their day off. Richard took a trip to see the woman himself and came back looking pallid with shock. We all sat in the salon in silence while he disappeared into a meeting with his director and designers. Over the next few days the whisper went round: the client had seen a copy of one of her mantles being worn by next-door's cook on her Sunday promenade. The woman had promptly fainted clean away, which meant a doctor was alerted and the story somehow reached the ears of the press.

Max is very delighted at this, for he found the story himself in his local rag. 'What now then?' he asked.

'What do you mean?' I answered him.

'Well,' he said, sitting down comfortably and folding his arms, 'how long do you think it will be before your fiancé discovers who is copying his designs?'

I ignored the sarcasm of his tone and carried on with my sewing. 'I'm only surprised he has not guessed before,' I told him.

He looked at me carefully. 'You don't mind?'

'No.'

I stitched while he considered this. 'You know you could bankrupt him,' he said at last. 'Either that, or find yourself standing in court.'

Now it was my turn to laugh.

'What about the boy?' Max went on. 'Surely it is his inheritance you are playing with? I thought you wanted a rich marriage.'

'And so I do,' I said, cutting a length of silk thread. Max is not the only one who can play games. I rose to make tea, leaving him sitting thoughtfully.

CHAPTER FORTY-SEVEN

ZG

THE EAST END

The West End may be tourist-raddled and full of
history, but it is in London's East End that the real
ghosts play. Permeated and blackened by ancient dust,
it owes its existence to endless echoes of the past.
There are no limits to history here; what began
centuries ago has never been finished. The scars of
poverty never healed; tenements are still tenements,
immigrants still arrive and work night and day to
better their lot. There are arranged marriages and
places of prayer, and only the religions have changed,
though the industries stay roughly the same.

Kitty took a cab to the East End. In her lap lay a Tupperware container full of home-baked cake that Hester had given her. Since when had her mother baked? She prised off the lid and a hot sweet smell leaked out, so she closed it again quickly before the whole cab stank. There was something in there covered in salmon-pink icing with sponge butterfly wings implanted in the buttercream. Was this how her mother filled her days now, she wondered? Was it some kind of therapy? Would *she* find herself turning to the oven when Freddy succumbed to the near-inevitable heart attack in old age?

She stopped off en route to check in at the wholesale showroom. The staff there tried to congratulate her on the show, but their eyes all said the same thing as her mother's mouth: 'Never mind.'

Harvey Nichols had cancelled an order because the buyer had decided on an American theme for the coming season: 'Never mind.'

She wandered out through the machine-rooms. Women were sitting drinking tea from plastic thermos cups. She realized she still held the Tupperware box so opened it and offered the contents around. They looked at her and smiled. Most of them took a cake but she guessed they were being polite and wouldn't eat it. They were older women, all about Hester's age, but unlike her mother they still had control of their figures.

Only Tilda, the house model, ate with any enthusiasm, sitting perched on a tailor's stool wearing only tights and a vest. A walking testament to the perils of anaemia, she rocked and smoked as she ate. When buttercream fell onto her front she tutted to herself before licking it off, like a cat.

They were taking short-order work to make up the figures. Gabriel would never contemplate the idea but Burgess had been insistent and so it came to pass. Betty, the sample machinist, sat lost behind a mountain of interlining, wadding, fusibles and pads. The others heard the zip of her machine and flicked their mugs in the sink before setting down to their own work. With their heads bent as though in prayer the message was the same; it rose from the tops of their scalps and permeated the air, along with the fabric fluff, steam and heat: 'Never mind.'

'Is my father's office unlocked?' Kitty asked the show-room manager.

The small room smelt stuffy. She walked around it, sniffing the air like a foxhound, opening drawers, picking things up. The manager watched from the doorway, his arms folded across his chest. He looked embarrassed. Had Burgess told him to watch out for her? That she might steal something?

She found two photographs; one was of Gabriel with his arm around another man, both smiling broadly. It was Riva's father. The shot was an old one, taken when both men had dark hair. The other photograph had been folded. Kitty straightened it out. Folding a photograph was like bending back the spine of a book – sacrilege. The boy in the shot had his back to the camera, but his turning pose meant that his face was visible. He looked like a professional model. Kitty looked closer. Raphael. Gabriel's designer. Frederick Jacobs Senior's designer now.

She flipped the shot over. There were four rings of dried yellow glue, one in each corner. Perhaps the shot had been stuck to a CV. Maybe it was sent when he applied for the job. Kitty put both pictures back in the drawer and closed it.

Think.

Why did photographs of the dead always appear to carry a message?

Think hard.

The dark room.

Kitty would have described her upbringing as open-minded but strangely moral. She had been having sex with

Freddy for two years, and yet knew very little about the darker side of the act. Nicky Kofteros could do things with jelly cubes. Kitty had no idea on earth what. Since her sister's boast she had imagined the little lumps of flavoured gelatine pushed into virtually every possible orifice, and yet none of the options seemed remotely erotic.

Was Freddy a stud? She thought not. Freddy was careful, patient, methodical. Or funny. He smelt clean and his skin tasted of the sun or of nice soap. It was Chloe who had told her Freddy was well-hung. She knew because she had once dated Freddy's brother and *he* had told her it was Freddy who had inherited all the size while he had inherited most of the intellect. Chloe had asked Kitty if she wanted to swap and Kitty had been embarrassed. Her sister always joked that that was why she was marrying Freddy. Their friends found this funny – even Freddy laughed – but Kitty couldn't share the joke, even though she knew this made Chloe worse.

'Why don't you laugh when she teases you?' China used to say when they were kids. 'She'll soon get bored. It's your little poker face that makes Chloe so wicked. Look at you.' She would hold the mirror of her powder compact up for Kitty to see.

China was always right. The face that stared back at Kitty was inevitably doleful and hapless. Yet she was an honest girl and couldn't bear to laugh when she didn't feel like it. Chloe could. Chloe could fake anything.

The dark room. Did Chloe know it? Did everyone go there?

Sex in the dark. Sex with a total stranger. Kitty became

420

absorbed by the notion. It stuck to her brain like stale gum to the bottom of a shoe. Smell and touch alone – did they ever speak to the people they fucked?

'Thank you – that was quite nice.'

'I hope my screaming didn't put you off.'

'Don't I know you? Don't I know that smell? Have we met before? Your hair and skin feel familiar. Isn't that the famous Jacobs schlong? I would have known it anywhere – you must be Freddy. It was your brother who inherited all the intellect in the family. Brain or brawn, eh?'

She had made love in the darkness but it had always been Freddy, no matter what. Freddy's chest. Freddy's stomach hairs, that rode in a thin and delicate line to his crotch. When she fingered those hairs gently his penis would rise like a drawbridge. When she touched the soft inside of his thighs his legs would part helplessly and he would give himself to her like a toy.

She could play with him for hours. Press this and this would happen. Touch that and that would occur. She liked it. She didn't want strangeness and jelly cubes. She liked the noise Freddy made when he came. Sometimes it would even make her come, too.

Kitty's taxi passed char-grilled-looking churches made of stones, speckled like acne from bomb-damage and pollution. There were brand new mosques surrounded by rows of housing so old and leaning they appeared to be tacked together by the flyposters' gum. Giant spray-blown swastikas and NF initials lay so faded on the brickwork that they appeared almost benign – as natural a part of the rotting landscape as the duckweed and billowing wisps of discarded wrappings.

There were structures tiled to waist-level in gleaming oak-brown and above in dingy cream, like decayed teeth. Cardboard boxes lay stacked and abandoned everywhere. Centuries-old signs bedecked buildings rendered unrecognizable by grime and bricked-up windows: BOYS' BATHS, RUBBER STAMP MERCHANTS, COFFEE AND CHOP HOUSE, THE EASTERN STAR, CHEVRAM SHASS SYNAGOGUE, SOUP KITCHEN FOR THE JEWISH POOR. The smell of ale and cigarettes welled out of the Jack the Ripper pub as a lunchtime drinker aired himself in the dim sunlight outside the main doors.

In the sidestreets of Brick Lane – Fournier Street, Wilkes Street, Princelet Street and Hanbury Street – the cab passed the traditional concentration of sweatshops, most of them Asian-owned. In the wider streets there were shopfronts with lengths of broad, spangled sari fabrics, swimwear and cheap children's wear on display. Outside one shop stood two life-size dummies, each dressed in sixties clothing and leering at all the passing traffic.

Riva Khan sat bent with concentration at her father's old desk. She wore a blend of traditional and modern – a khaki-green silk sari with a Conran jacket slung around her shoulders. Her feet tapped as she worked. One hand rubbed at her forehead as though trying to massage some sense out of what she was reading.

She looked up at the sound of Kitty's feet but her eyes remained dimly unfocused for a few seconds. A short guy in a raspberry pink suit came between them, pulling a rail full of polythene-clad dresses, and Kitty had to climb up the wall to get out of his way. She heard Riva start to speak but missed the first few words above the squeak of the metal castors and rustle of plastic.

'. . . is out of prison now?' Riva's eyes looked rattlesnake-lidded.

Kitty cupped her ear with her hand.

'I said, did you know my father has been released without charge?' she asked.

Kitty shook her head. 'No.'

Riva stared at her pencil. 'I'm trying to clear a few things up for him,' she said, 'he worries about the business. It was the only thing he asked about when they held him at the police station.

'We are all but closed down here now. He's too broken to come in. I told him I would help. Did you know I got my degree, Kitty? Did you know I passed all my accountancy exams? And yet he still wants to arrange my marriage for me. Much like your situation, eh? I heard you were engaged to Freddy Jacobs. Gabriel must have had a hard time pulling that one off. Keeping it in the family, eh? A business and political arrangement, just like my own wedding.'

Kitty cleared her throat. The walls to the workroom were bare tile, which gave her cough an echo. 'My father had no hand in my engagement,' she told Riva.

'Oh,' the girl said carefully, 'I see.' She smiled in the direction of the desk. 'So old Mr Jacobs won't be propping up the business for you, then?' she asked. 'That's very sad, Kitty, I heard your father had spent a lot of time over those negotiations. Your betrothal to Freddy was just the bait he needed.'

Kitty felt her face redden. Riva was fascinating to watch.

Her head barely moved, just her eyes. Her voice had a flat, nasal tone that was hypnotic.

'They could not find any evidence, you see,' she said, and Kitty's brain had to jump a step to keep up with the change of subject.

'Your father?' she asked.

Riva nodded. Suddenly she looked up and her expression changed. 'I'm sorry,' she said, smiling, 'I didn't even offer you tea. All that way from the glamorous side of London and I have not as much as offered you a tour of the place or refreshments. It's the grief that makes one forgetful, don't you find?'

She called for tea from a young boy who was passing. He looked surprised. Kitty caught Riva's quick frown of admonition before the polite smile returned. 'Do you think the place has changed much?' she asked, standing up and leading Kitty to the adjoining doorway. Kitty stepped through the doorless gap and looked around the workroom.

Khan had once owned two establishments, one of them a vast warehouse of a place in Old Street, with computer-programmed laser cutters and steam-injectors aiding the CMT process. When Gabriel had stopped employing him, though, he'd had to cut back to this, his older place – a ragged sweatshop with only six machines and an ancient Hoffman presser.

All the machinists were elderly women and all wore saris and tight grey buns. Soon even they would be out of a job if new orders didn't start coming in. Kitty glanced at a couple of the production panels.

'I've got them making up what you would call

424

schmutter,' Riva told her. 'Cheap crap for cheap prices. A far cry from the sort of stuff your father used to send us, but then who can afford to be picky when there are families to feed, eh?'

She walked around the workroom, stopping behind the chair of each machinist and telling Kitty exactly how many children and grandchildren each woman had. When her lecture was finished she stopped and smiled. 'But then I suppose a sophisticated westerner like yourself would wonder why they just didn't use a more effective birth control.' She laughed as though sharing the joke.

Kitty smiled to be polite. 'I need to ask you something,' she said when Riva was closer. The girl's eyebrows raised.

'The dark room,' Kitty whispered, 'what exactly did you mean when you told me my father must have been there?'

Riva put her head back and laughed again. 'I thought you said you didn't believe me,' she replied.

'I just need to know, Riva,' Kitty said.

The girl stared at her. 'I am a well brought-up woman, Kitty,' she said, 'exactly how much do you think I could know about a place such as that?'

'Please.' It took a lot for Kitty to say the word.

Riva's eyes gleamed like dark pebbles. 'Why don't you go and ask Raphael, Gabriel's ex-designer?' she said quietly. 'My father used to say it was one of *his* favourite haunts.' She paused. 'My father is a very moral man, Kitty. When he spoke of Raphael it was always with a tone of slight disgust. He could never work out what your father saw in the man. He adored Gabriel, but he always called Raphael his "blind spot".'

Kitty found herself politely manoeuvred to the main

door. 'I'm sorry,' Riva said, smiling, 'I have so much to catch up with. We may find the receivers knocking on our doors any day and I want to fend them off for as long as I can. You know how it is.'

She held out her hand. Kitty stared at it. 'What do you mean, "*see* in him"?' she asked.

Riva looked puzzled.

'You said your father could never work out what it was Gabriel *saw* in Raphael,' Kitty repeated.

Riva laughed a small, polite laugh. 'Oh,' she said, 'well, you must have known, Kitty. Raphael was your father's lover. His little toy. That was why he left after your father's death. He couldn't bear to work there anymore. He was as much in mourning as you are now.'

CHAPTER FORTY-EIGHT

ZG

LOVE
*A thin silk, striped with satin, that is used in the
making of ribbons.*

Dearest Kitty,

I am now well known in Mayfair as a copier of the
latest fashion for society ladies whose circumstances have
become reduced, but who still wish to retain an impression
of their original status and wealth.

My saleswomen pay a discreet visit to their houses with
their folios of photographs beneath their arms and, Kitty,
you would be shocked to hear some of the names of clients,
for it seems even the highest in the land have a nose for a
bargain, when it is presented in such a way.

As well as the outworkers I employ, I also make use of
a couple of sweats and at a very good rate too, for I give
them work during the slack period, so can negotiate the
lowest rates possible.

Of course there is some scrimping on designs, but on
the whole the fabrics I use look as good as the ones Richard
sells and, by using the workers during the slack and by
keeping the majority of the scrimping on the lower layers
and inner seams and tucks, I can turn out mantles that

look every bit as good as couture at less than a third of the price.

As I said, the exclusivity of each model is not assured, but we have taken to checking each client's social circle before they order and so can more or less assure none of the ladies will come face-to-face with a copy of their own style within the current season.

My only problem has been that of payment, for I find the higher the class of the client, the slower they will be at settling debts. Max tells me that this is only to be expected; that I should allow credit and not press for payment or I will lose customers. I have told him this is ridiculous. A debt is a debt, Kitty, and if my poorer souls can be prepared to scrimp their hard-earned money to ensure I am paid on time, then some of my wealthier clients can do the same with their shillings and pounds. They can pawn their jewels for all I care, Kitty. Allow one debt to go by and a hundred others will follow it.

As I said, the local souls are usually timely with their payments, for they have pride and honour and no wish to flaunt or even admit their poverty. Even so, I have been prompted to employ a group of local lads to pay visits – just as reminders. Two of these are Sabbath goys – boys who once earned their pennies lighting up on a Sabbath, and who find themselves in short demand now that the observance of kosher practices are rather in decline in the area. I have contacted Queer Tess's sons and they are more than delighted with the deal we have made. There is no menace in them at all, though I find women are pleased enough to pay up to get the scent they bring with them away from their doorsteps.

The same is true in Mayfair. I have taught the boys to be polite and respectful, but the sight of them alone is enough to get all bills paid promptly and I can reward the boys generously for their productive work.

Kitty, I feel at peace with myself for the first time since I left Russia. At last I am keeping Papa's warning: 'Never be poor and never grow old.' My income is flourishing and I am still young.

Gregory has shown some interest in the business and so I now employ him to manage the goys, which he thinks is splendid. Ruth is still with me, and in charge of the local outworkers, helped by her mother. I believe they rule with a rod of iron but this is all to the good, as our deliveries are known for their punctuality.

Max and I now meet as equals, as I have paid back all I owe. We talk business long into the night and I have even taken to smoking the odd cigar with him, which causes Gregory much amusement.

It is good to see respect in Max's eyes and he is much less amused by me now. I am surprised he has not wed Ruth, now that he knows there will never be anything between us. She is a very handsome girl and still much taken with him.

Gregory still moons around after her, but she treats him as a younger brother, to be indulged and made fun of.

Richard has discovered who has been cheating him at last. He came into the salon while I was serving a client and I saw him watching me with an expression of concern on his face.

'I will see you when you are finished,' he whispered

as I passed. I guessed immediately what the issue was.

'You want to speak to me?' I asked, smiling.

A muscle worked in his cheek. He stared at me for a second before nodding.

'Then you will make an appointment to come to my premises,' I said.

Kitty, you can have no idea how much this shocked him. His whole body appeared to absorb my words and his eyes widened in astonishment.

'*Your* premises?' he asked. In fact he almost spat the words out, Kitty. This was great sport – I wish you could have been there!

I had a printed card ready in my purse. 'Here,' I said, and went back to tend to my client.

Richard arrived the following day. I had the place ready for him. These are premises I have rented off Fournier Street, to house the dozen or so machines I have been forced to buy to accommodate the level of business. We are not yet to full capacity, although I intend to house some of my outworkers there, but I had Ruth's mother present sewing furiously at some good quality material, along with eleven of her colleagues.

Ruth herself was on a high stool, scratching away at an imposing-looking ledger, and I had several of my saleswomen taking tea in the corner, as well-dressed as any of Richard's *vendeuses*, and poring over their appointment books.

I led Richard to a room in the loft which I had furnished as an office, and offered him a seat on the other side of my desk.

He said nothing for a while.

'Would you have preferred coffee?' I asked.

'What?'

'Instead of the tea?'

He shook his head as though trying to clear it. 'What is all this?' he asked.

'I told you, Richard,' I said politely, 'this is my business, and very lucrative it is proving, too. I hope you'll be proud of me – most of it was founded on the money with which you bought my beloved son.'

He was watching my face now, and I saw him blush. 'Rosa . . .' he began, 'you must forgive me. I had no idea quite how much the child meant to you . . .'

I smiled. 'No, Richard,' I told him, 'you thought it was only the upper classes that have true feelings for their offspring. To the poor like myself they are nothing short of a nuisance. We're just like wretched animals, really – incapable of feeling anything more than the basest emotions.

'Did you really believe I would allow my only child to be bought from me in such a way? Did you think me some sort of a whore from whom everything can be bought for cash? I've used your money, Richard, and I've used it cleverly. Did you ever imagine how happily two people could feed off one business? *You* make exclusive designs for leading society figures and *I* copy them more cheaply for women with less money in their purses to spare. Doesn't that sound terribly fair and decent?'

His face had gone from raspberry to puce. 'You are bankrupting me, Rosa,' he said, quietly. 'Is that what you want for your son? For him to inherit nothing but a debt when I die? For him to lead a life of poverty when my business is closed?'

I smile at this. 'There is little need to worry,' I told him. 'I am his mother and *my* business is thriving. There will be plenty to go around when I am gone.'

'Rosa!' Richard was out of his chair.

'Don't worry, Richard,' I said, my expression serious now, 'I won't let your business fail.'

He was bordering on anger now. 'I could sue you,' he said.

'And I could tell everyone that David is my son,' I replied.

He fell back and sat staring at the floor for many moments. 'What do you want?' he asked, eventually.

I stood before him, my arms down by my sides. 'I want us to be married,' I said. 'I want David to have two parents.'

There was not a sound from him, Kitty. He could have been crafted from stone for all the movement he made.

'Think about it,' I told him finally, when the silence became too much for me to bear. 'You have five days, Richard. After that I believe the banks will be in touch with you again.'

CHAPTER FORTY-NINE

ZG

POLYESTER
*First produced by J. F. Winfield and J. T. Dickson
in 1941, and made mainly of ethylene glycol and
terephthalic acid, polyester fibres are now used in
the manufacture of many fashion garments. It is
crease-resistant, keeps its shape and dries quickly
when washed.*

Nicky Kofteros's car was waiting outside Khan's sweat-shop. Kitty tried to ignore it, to make out she hadn't seen it at all, and walked on by as though it was the sort of car you'd expect to see cruising a street like that.

He didn't slam his hand on the horn and he didn't wind down the window to call her, which was just as well – at least as far as his car was concerned, as she was ripe for a little violence and Kofteros's windscreen could have been a very tempting target.

What she really wanted to do, more than anything, was to run back into the office and slap Riva's face until the terrible words stopped coming out of it. She wanted to hit the girl until she confessed that she was lying. Kitty's father was an honest man and a loyal one. Every magazine article she had ever read about him quoted him as insisting that family came first at all times.

Instead of smashing and punching, though, she watched as Kofteros climbed out of the car and called her softly by name.

She turned. He wore a dazzling white shirt, which was open at the neck, and some casual but smartly pressed trousers. She was so mad with the girl that, for a split second, she was pleased to see him there. Then she remembered who he was and scowled.

'Your brother asked me to find you,' Kofteros said. 'There is a meeting at your offices. I believe it is urgent. May I take you?'

'Do I have any choice?' Kitty asked. To his credit he did not look exasperated or feign hurt pride. Instead he just waited.

Okay, Mr jelly-cube, Kitty thought. Then there was a noise to her left and as she watched him she saw his expression change. Suddenly, as she stared at Nicky's face with something like puzzlement, she collided with someone. Her focus shortened. There was a head in front of hers. In her peripheral vision she saw Nicky vault – not run around or crawl across, but *vault* – the bonnet of his car in his haste to get to her.

'Kitty! Are you here to see me? What a nightmare, eh? Did you speak with my daughter?' Ricky Khan's face was in front of her own, so puffed with grief it was almost unrecognizable.

He was a big man – taller than Gabriel and some two feet wider. So big he had to have his suits hand-made. He had always been smart, though – dapper, even. He favoured the old colonial look – pinstripe suits, overflowing silk handkerchief in the pocket, shoes you could see your

434

face in. Now, he could have passed for any of a hundred guys pulling dress-rails around in the street. His too-tight trousers were crumpled, he wore a white vest and the short-sleeved beige shirt he had on over it was minus a button.

'What a tragedy!' he was erupting with grief, it spilled out of every gap: tears, snot, shards of spittle, spreading sweat. His eyelashes were gummed up with crying. His hands fluttered about his head as though trying to pluck some rational thought out of the air.

It was Ricky's anguish that triggered Kitty's own out-pouring. How often had she seen this huge man socializing with her father? What a pair they had made, too – noisy, rumbustious, argumentative, proud and stubborn, but always good friends. Not friends, Kitty thought – allies. They were aware that they shared the same fate, those two. The circumstances of their heritage gave them a bond. When Gabriel watched Ricky set up his business he knew he was watching his own parents and grandparents at work.

Before she could speak, though, before she could hug the man or utter a cry of empathy she was grabbed by the arm and pulled backwards. Ricky's eyes changed from slits of undiluted misery to round 'o's of shock and alarm. His hands flew out towards her but as they moved she found herself going in the same direction, further away. Then there was an eclipse of the light and she found herself staring at Kofteros's wide back.

'Kitty!' Ricky was still trying to find her. Nicky was not unnecessarily violent or threatening, he just stayed where he was.

'You have to understand this is not a good idea,' he

told Ricky. 'Keeping a distance between Miss Zigofsky and yourself would be in both of your interests.'

Khan was still the taller man. 'A bodyguard, Kitty?' he asked, wringing his hands. 'Do you think that I did it, then? Do you think I would ever hurt you or your father? I loved him, Kitty, you know that!'

Kofteros pulled Kitty out of the way and pushed her through the open door of his car.

'What the hell are you playing at?' she asked when he was in the driver's seat. He looked at her. He was calm and not a hair had fallen out of place. He had not even worked up a sheen of sweat.

'That was the man they arrested for killing your father,' he said. It was just a statement – with no particular emphasis or implication. 'If he *did* kill Gabriel then he might want to harm you too. I know he is like an uncle to you, Kitty, but anyone can change. Besides, if he is innocent he should not be seen talking to you, it could harm his case. The lawyers could say he threatened you.' When he spoke a trace of an accent appeared, showing his concern.

He paused as the car turned into Commercial Road. 'I'm sorry if I startled you. You will want to yell at me now. Go ahead, I'm listening.'

'That poor man,' Kitty whispered, 'he's lost everything.'

Kofteros looked at her. 'And so will you,' he said. 'Is that what you want? Surely you have done the right thing by Gabriel now, Kitty. You pulled his final collection together and staged his show. You have been the daughter he wanted. Any man would have been proud to see what you did. You must have known it was just a gesture, though. Just as you are aware you must back down now.

'I'm afraid the bank will not support you on the strength of that collection. Your publicity was overshadowed by the circumstances of your father's death. Women don't like to buy clothes like that. They like to read about the murder, but it doesn't make them want to wear the clothes – not for a season or so, anyway. It would make them feel ghoulish. Next year we re-launch with a new designer and you and Chloe can afford to be seen smiling again.'

'You have it all planned out, don't you?' Kitty asked him.

He shrugged. 'It's my job to plan things,' he said. 'I can't help it. It's what I'm good at – working behind the scenes. Finding things out. Making sure things go as planned.'

'Ricky Khan is a good man,' Kitty told him. 'I believe you should understand that. Maybe there are no absolutes in your life, but there are certainly some in mine and that is one of them. He could not have murdered my father.'

As she spoke the hollowness of her own words made her feel hypocritical. What was still an absolute in her life? What did she now believe? The whole landscape shifted every day.

'So you still believe that I killed him, then?' Kofteros asked. 'Of course, I must fit the bill perfectly. A slithery foreigner trying to masquerade as a pukka English businessman. Smart enough, but a little too flash. Seducing your sister and taking over the whole show. Turning up where he is least wanted like the worst kind of animal. What else do you have me pegged as, Kitty?'

She looked out of the window. 'I have no interest in you,' she said.

Kofteros laughed. 'Oh, but you have,' he said. 'You find

437

me fascinating. I'm everything you have been told to keep away from. I'm the stranger you don't accept sweets or lifts from. I'm the one who will poison your entire family if you will only allow it.

'When you lay in bed at night next to your pretty little fiancé it's the thought of men like me that makes you hide away further under the duvet and thank God the windows are securely sealed and the garlic hanging above the bed, next to the crucifix, or whatever other symbol it is beautiful Jewish princesses like yourself use to ward off the evil ones.

'Look at yourself, Kitty,' he went on, 'you say you believe I am responsible for your father's murder, and yet here you are sitting beside me in my car. What does that tell us? That you enjoy taking risks? I don't think so. You are a careful and intelligent woman. Brave to a certain extent – the way you went ahead with the fashion show tells me that – but reckless and lacking in caution?'

He smiled. 'I think it tells us you don't really believe I am capable of murder, Kitty. I believe you suspect many people, but none of them seriously. I know you are frightened, deep down in your heart. You would rather I did it than someone closer to you. You want it to be me, Kitty. How much better me than a member of your own family.'

Kitty suddenly sat upright in her seat. 'I need to stop off in the West End,' she said.

To his credit yet again Kofteros didn't argue, even though she knew they were in a hurry. Instead he drove her straight to Freddy's London showroom without question, parking the car directly outside the door and slumping down in his seat, just like a professional chauffeur.

Freddy's father was inside, drinking tea with the Selfridges buyer. He half-rose from his seat as Kitty walked in, but she nodded and waved, 'okay'. Business was business, after all. She walked into the back and climbed the narrow flight of stairs to the design-room.

Freddy was there, working on some orders. He looked up, surprised and then pleased to see her. When he kissed her on the cheek she was drawn by his warmth and his familiar smell and his normality.

'Hey, Kitten,' he whispered, 'you should have phoned. We could have had lunch. Are you okay?'

'I'm fine,' Kitty lied. They both knew she didn't make impromptu visits to the showroom. The etiquette wasn't right, she was still competition, after all. Nothing would have been said, she would have been greeted warmly as a future member of the family, but it just wasn't done, especially during the Season.

Freddy put his hands on his hips. He was wearing a suit, which meant he was also selling. Kitty looked across and saw his German agent sitting by the pattern books, waiting.

'Don't let me interrupt, Fred,' she said quietly, smiling, mouthing, 'I'll see you later.' Bring jelly-cubes, she thought, only she didn't mouth that.

Raphael was at the far end of the room, staring at her obliquely. The window was behind him and she shielded her eyes from the glare.

'Hi,' she greeted him. He nodded in return. Freddy went back to the agent but Kitty guessed he was listening, along with all the other machine-room staff.

'I'm glad to see you got a new job,' Kitty told him.

Raphael straightened, wiping his hands on his jeans. He

pulled a couple of pins from his mouth. 'Kitty,' he said, softly, 'it's good to see you.' His tone didn't sound false, just as hers had no tone of vindictiveness.

Raphael looked just like his name sounded. He was strangely good-looking, although not instantly noticeable. His hair was a shade of brown that turned into black and his eyes were amazingly blue. His features were surprisingly irregular, though on the second glance they all worked. His appeal was subtle and serious.

Kitty had worked with him for years without really knowing him. He always seemed young, but remotely elegant and proudly sophisticated at the same time. But that was the way he was. That was Raphael.

'What did you want?' he asked. She was used to his directness. He had a busy job.

'I just wanted to see you . . .' Kitty said. So what? So now what? Did you sleep with my father? She could never have said the words. And so they just looked and whatever needed saying was said in silence. She wanted to touch him, to feel what her father had felt. She wanted to know if they had loved one another. But then she also wanted to know that her father could never have been unfaithful to Hester, too. That it was not in his nature. That Riva was a bitter, jealous liar.

'Did you find the wedding dress designs?' Raphael asked quietly.

Kitty nodded.

'Did you work on them together?' she asked. She looked at him then, and saw what she needed to see. Raphael's face was immobile but his eyes were milky with unshed tears.

'Your father did most of the work,' he said, his voice breaking, 'I only helped hunt for fabrics.'

There was something growing in Kitty's throat that threatened to choke her. 'Thank you,' she said, while the words would still come out. She held out her hand but Raphael didn't take it. The glance they exchanged was enough, though. Peace. They both loved Gabriel. What point in hatred when they both suffered from the same painful loss?

Freddy came across, curious to see what was going on. He kissed Kitty on the top of the head and his hands on her shoulders were steering her towards the door. He looked awkward. After all, his father had poached her designer.

'I think everyone imagines there might be a row brewing,' he said.

Kitty smiled. 'No, Freddy, no row.' She smiled her sweetest smile.

'Thank you,' he said. 'You would have been well within your rights.'

Kitty looked across at Freddy's father as she left. 'Never fight with pigs,' she said to herself, 'you get all dirty and they just enjoy it.' It was Frederick Jacobs Senior that she had her gripe with, not Raphael, and besides, she had worse villains than him to come to grips with.

CHAPTER FIFTY

ZG

PLISSE
*A plain-weave fabric, like crepe, which has been
specially treated to keep a wrinkled appearance.*

She dreamt of the club. Sometimes she would enter the dark room. She was searching for her father. The blackness was so profound she could see nothing – even her own body was invisible to her.

The silence was equally impenetrable, although – despite the quiet – she knew there would be others in there, waiting. The human body is never silent, it is a constant source of insect-like ambience. There is the hiss of breath, the whisper and bellows-sigh of the lungs, all the ferrying of mucus, the seeping of blood in the veins, the minute cracks and groans of movement – and yet she heard nothing.

But someone was waiting in there.

Who?

Raphael?

Freddy?

She took a step forward, reaching out blindly with her hands. It was like a children's party game – Blind Man's Buff. Laughing from fear. Playing, but hating it.

442

What if it was someone she did not know? But wasn't that the point? Anonymity. Sex with a stranger.

She lurched another step. Her blood picked up a faster rhythm. Her mouth had dried. Her tongue was like a piece of cured fruit. The darkness was threatening, but it was also like a blanket around her. The place smelt musky with the richly jewelled scent of sex.

She feared violence, but the hands that came out of the blackness to take her own were gentle enough. Dry, like a snake skin. Different flesh. Needy. Conclusive. Guiding her fingers to a face – broad features, clean-shaven, baked hot from the sun.

'It's okay, darling, you're safe.' The lips sighed the words when she touched them with her fingertips. It was a deep voice, marinating in the lower octaves. Full of the mulch created by tobacco and wine.

Gently he moved her hands further down, showing her himself by touch. Her fingers were greedy, though she feared recognition. The tips told the most – light feather-touch, to reveal texture, not shape.

Colour too, she discovered. Warm, skin-baked tan. A neck, weathered with age but not too old, supple enough, and then a bare chest, full of fine, well-sprung hairs. Older hairs – damp and springy, white or grey – she could feel the colour in their coarseness. Hairs that led a tangled route towards the groin.

'Kitty.' A younger, less crushed voice, but still tender. Another pair of hands pulled down the zipper of her dress. Her body shuddered at the cool on her back. Two more touches and she was naked. Invisible, though, safely invisible in the darkness. She felt lips pressed soft behind the soft indent of the backs of her knees, sending tingling sparks through her body like a spray of hot ash.

Then the lightest tip of a goldfish tongue, travelling slowly up the delicate belly-flesh of her inner thighs.

'Kitty.' It was the first man, the older man, who spoke this time, his voice full of urging. He directed her hands downward to his stomach and her palms touched against the rubbery tip of his penis. She felt the warm bulb of the end, wet with seeping juices.

'Kitty.' The word was lost in the warm rise of his voice, which became a whisper before evaporating, like steam, in the air above their heads.

There was a coldness, like an ice cube, upon her back. The tongue ran crazy crop circles between her thighs, making her legs uncontrollably bendy, like India rubber. Her stomach contracted in spasms of need and the flesh that was licked so greedily became the entire focus of her body. She was emptying of moisture, wet and damp in turns.

As her resistance oozed and leaked along with her bones and skin she fell into a childlike compliance: you have no choice. There is nothing you can do. Her will had been robbed by her flesh.

He turned her around easily, bending her forward like a rag doll, and she felt his penis pause politely before entering her. Her mouth was kissed by the mouth near the floor and so, too, were the insteps of her feet. So there were three of them, then. And yet all worked together like one.

They simmered and boiled together. When the delicious ache in her groin swelled and grew through her entire body so that she began to cry out it was the tender floor-mouth

444

that kissed her throughout. He held her as she climaxed and, when the shudders had quit her body he pushed her hair from her face and blew against her forehead to cool her.

His tenderness made her weep. It was what she wished to keep above all else – to plunder from her dream and take like a trophy into wakefulness.

A door somewhere opened. A thin streak of yellow light diluted the darkness. It was the face in front of her own, full of care and concern and, now, anger at being revealed.

Kofteros.

She tried to snap shut like a flower.

'Kitty.' His expression was anguished.

She struggled to get free, but he held her pinned by her arms.

'Kitty,' he was saying, 'don't look back. Keep looking at me, Kitty, whatever you do.'

She looked back, of course she looked back.

Gabriel stood behind her, his face whey-pale in death and coated with dew. She pulled away in horror, her arms circling in an attempt to escape more quickly than her legs could manage.

Her father. Naked. The dampness on his chest and groin not sweat and semen, as she had thought in the darkness, but wet, black blood.

There was a hole where his stomach should have been. What she had taken to be cries of passion had been his agonized death throes.

Gabriel. Her father.

She woke up screaming, still feeling for her own father's blood on her bare back.

CHAPTER FIFTY-ONE

ZG

ALBATROSS
*The name of a lightweight woollen fabric that is soft,
with a crepe-effect weave.*

'Why not give up and retire from business altogether?' Chloe asked. Her crossed leg ticked away impatiently. Wherever Chloe was she wanted to be somewhere else. She wore a rice-white pyjama suit with flat almond-green brogues. Her hair colour had been changed to parchment blonde, which made her skin look like toffee.

Kofteros sat beside her, reading. Next to him was Burgess, as immobile as garden statuary, apart from his right hand, which was doing some little tense picking thing with the arm of the chair.

'Retire?' Kitty asked. 'At nineteen? Jesus, Chloe!'

She yawned, just to annoy her sister further.

'You will have enough to live on from the deal that Burgess is setting up,' Chloe continued, her leg thrashing, 'and you are getting married, Kit. I'm sure Freddy will want to see you put out to pasture on the charity circuit – you know, organizing balls and suchlike.'

There were shards of glittering hatred exchanged between the two women.

'Is that what you plan to do, Chloe?' Kitty asked. 'Put yourself out to graze?'

Kofteros cleared his throat. 'I believe Kitty will be as much an integral part of Waika's future plans as you are, Chloe,' he said. Kitty tried not to look at him. The dream was still thick in her head.

Chloe sighed. 'I thought Nula was coming to this meeting,' she said, changing the subject.

Burgess studied the shine on his shoes. 'Nula doesn't have voting options any more,' he said.

They all looked at him now. Like a fly in aspic, he remained immobile beneath their stares. 'I bought her out,' he said, 'she had no interest in the business and she said she was in debt and needed the money urgently.'

'In debt?' Kitty echoed. 'For God's sake, Burgess, she's only fifteen! What could she need so much money for? Did you even ask?'

He shook his head and waved his hands. 'Maybe drugs?' he suggested.

'You gave her money for drugs?' This was Chloe.

'I was joking,' Burgess replied.

Kofteros rose to his feet. 'You selfish little bastard,' he told Burgess. Somehow he made the comment sound factual rather than spiteful. It was followed by a respectful silence. Burgess's face turned the colour of ecru. Kitty thought he looked scared.

'This is a family thing, Nicky,' he began. 'I would no more compromise my sister's safety than chew off my own arm. Of course she did not want the money for drugs. She explained her reasons for needing cash to me in some detail and there was nothing sinister there, I can assure you.

447

Perhaps you missed the note of irony in my voice. Perhaps you all did. I just don't feel it is appropriate to discuss family matters in public, that's all.'

Kofteros continued to stare. Kitty looked at him and was surprised by the level of anger he appeared to be concealing. 'And you could not possibly just loan her the money?' he asked.

Burgess's cheeks flushed blotting-paper pink. 'I told you,' he said, 'she has no real interest in the business.'

Kitty got up to walk out in disgust. To her surprise she saw Kofteros make a quick move to join her. Chloe noticed, too, and grabbed quickly at Kitty's arm.

'Kit, we need to come to some agreement,' she said, quietly. 'I know you want us to stay family-owned, but Dad is dead and things can never be as they were before.' Both Kitty and Kofteros gawped at Chloe in amazement, but she was shameless enough to continue.

'He would have been proud of you, Kitty,' she said. 'You pulled that show together and even I was surprised at your determination.' Kitty heard the 'but' coming from about ten miles off.

'But,' Chloe said, placing extra emphasis on the word for effect, 'it's over, Kitty, you have to see that. We owe too much. The banks won't bail us out. If we sign over to Waika at least we'll all have a job and enough money to play with. You did enough, Kit. Know when to stop.'

Kofteros still stood beside her. 'Perhaps you need more time,' he said. They all looked up in surprise at this.

'Waika need a decision now,' Burgess said in the background. 'Kitty, we all inherited equally but I could out-vote you now if I wanted. China's all for selling. Mother doesn't know what day of the week it is. But I want you to agree, Kit, don't you see?'

Kofteros was watching Kitty's face closely. 'Why don't we go for a drive?' he asked, quietly.

'Isn't that some sort of Mafia cliché?' Kitty asked him.

He grinned. 'You have my word in front of witnesses that I will bring you back in one piece,' he said.

They drove from Docklands to the West End. He bought her lunch at a deli in Soho and they ate it in his car. She was surprisingly hungry and ate quickly.

'Just mind the leather upholstery with the relish,' he told her. When she had finished she swabbed up with the paper napkins he passed to her one at a time.

'So now where?' she asked when she was finally ready.

Kofteros smiled. 'More clues, eh?' he said, almost to himself. 'Okay, Kitty, I think you need your photograph taking.'

He drove back out to the east, to an insignificant street near Khan's factory. When the car pulled up Kitty looked about. She had been to most of the area on business with her father but could see no sign of the rag trade in this particular part.

Kofteros stepped outside the car and opened her door, like a chauffeur. They were in front of a shop selling cameras and offering studio portraits. In the window were a dozen large colour shots of kids, dogs and graduating youngsters.

'Have you never been here before?' Kofteros asked.

Kitty shook her head. 'I believe most of our formal shots were done by Norman Parkinson,' she said in a snottier tone than she meant.

Nicky laughed. 'Then it's about time you gave someone a little more humble the chance to shoot your illustrious features,' he told her.

Kitty turned. 'Look, I don't really understand . . .' she began.

He was smiling. 'Do you trust me at all, Kitty?' he asked. 'One little bit?'

She thought about the question. 'No,' she told him.

His smile did not shrink. 'Okay,' he said, 'then I shall tell you nothing. Find things out for yourself. Just humour me, and get your portrait done. Okay?'

Kitty stared at him. 'My hair needs combing,' she said.

Grinning, he pulled a clean comb from his pocket and ran it carefully through her fringe. 'Perfect,' he told her. He chivvied her into the doorway of the place. Kitty looked inside. It was dark and old-fashioned. A joke. She turned around but Kofteros was driving off. Curiosity got the better of her. She walked inside.

There was an elderly woman sitting at a reception table, her grey hair dyed apricot and whipped into a meringue-shape upon her head. She stood up as Kitty walked in. Her sleeveless dress was made of lemon Crimplene and there were creases of white talcum powder around her bare armpits.

'May I help you, miss?' she asked, smiling.

Kitty felt awkward. 'I need a passport shot,' she said. The width of the woman's smile decreased by one centimetre.

'Passport?' She sat back down on her chair. 'Will you wait over there? The photographer has a sitting.'

Kitty lowered herself onto a padded bench which was covered with pleated turquoise satin. There were some

450

elderly magazines on the table beside her. She felt herself being scrutinized by the receptionist and so faced it out by pretending to inspect the framed photographs on the wall beside her.

Many were old – some were ancient. There were a few vaguely recognizable faces from the sixties and seventies – minor stars who had signed their names across their shots to register their thanks and eternal appreciation of the career boost the pictures had afforded them.

The photographer appeared in the doorway, making Kitty jump in her seat.

'Passport?' he asked. He was an old man, maybe the receptionist's husband, his suit well-worn but immaculately pressed, and the wine-stain-coloured knitted waistcoat he wore beneath it matched his bow-tie perfectly.

Kitty was shown upstairs, into a small studio where an Ikea pine stool sat in the middle of a paper backdrop that had been painted to look like the sky.

'There's a mirror over there,' the photographer told her. 'Take your time, miss, I will need to set up.'

Kitty pulled a curtain back and found a small chair in front of a wall-mirror. She studied her reflection. Her fringe had been flattened by Kofteros's comb. She looked ghastly. At least that made her smile.

There were more framed shots on the wall around the mirror. Some from the fifties, this time, and one or two many years older. Directly above the mirror, in what appeared to be the place of honour, hung an ancient wedding shot in an ornate Victorian frame. The glass was dusty – too dusty to see detail. Bored with the wait, Kitty wandered out into the studio. There were plenty more shots on the walls here – the place was like a gallery in a museum. Most were Victorian wedding photos, like the one in the changing area. Kitty browsed for a bit, barely interested.

The photographer popped his head round the curtain.

'Take your time,' he said, 'take a look. You don't see many of those around these days. Enjoy.'

'Thanks.' Kitty smiled politely.

'Great,' she whispered beneath her breath. What the hell was this? Had Kofteros dumped her here to keep her out of the way while they voted to sell or something? She looked around for the exit. As she picked up her bag, though, another shot caught her eye. It was a picture of a woman holding a baby, sepia-toned and faded with age as though it had been placed in the window at some time.

'*Kitty.*'

It was the only shot on the wall that hadn't been taken at a wedding. Yet the woman's face looked familiar – she'd seen it staring out from one of the other frames.

'*Kitty!*'

She backtracked slowly. Where was it again? And why was she even looking, when she ought to be gunning back to the city? Surely she hadn't started to trust Kofteros?

There it was – the same woman in her wedding shot. Kitty peered a little closer, smiling. The couple in the photograph looked rigid with fear – at least the man did. His bride was attempting a smile. There was a small boy in the shot, too. His face was beautiful but expressionless. Hadn't they placed children's heads in clamps, to keep them still for the long exposure?

'Hey, now, what's all this?' Kitty whispered. She looked back at the baby shot. The woman looked younger than

452

she did at her wedding. The child in the wedding shot would have been about the right age to be the baby in the first one. Naughty, naughty! Kitty thought, that must have got them swallowing their teeth, eh? Child first and marry later?

'*Kitty*!'

'Ready yet, miss?' the photographer called.

'No . . . I . . .' The glass of the frame was stained with nicotine. 'Wait,' she said, sounding rude but not caring, 'wait a moment.'

With shaking hands she grabbed her glasses from her bag and pulled them on.

The wedding suit. The guy was wearing *her* wedding suit.

Kitty wiped the glass with her sleeve to clean it. She saw the old photographer standing behind her in the reflection.

'Who is this?' she asked, pointing to the picture.

The old man shrugged. 'A wedding portrait,' he said. 'If you are really interested you could turn the frame around. The names will be written on the back. Most likely they didn't pay for their sitting and so the photographer kept it and hung it himself. It's not an especially good shot – the focus is a little questionable. I keep it for historical purposes more than anything. There are better ones in stock but that was there already and the frame is rather good.'

Kitty lifted the frame down carefully. She *was* right – the groom in the photograph was wearing the suit her mother had given her, the wedding suit. She might have mistaken the jacket and trousers, but the waistcoat was too unique to confuse. She turned the picture around. *Mr and Mrs Richard and Rosa Galliard*, she read. Galliard. The name meant nothing to her. She looked at the shot once more. Rosa. She stared at the woman's face. *To Rosa – the daughter I love –* the message on the waistcoat. So this was the woman for whom the suit had been made.

'So you found a man to fit it,' Kitty whispered, smiling.

How did this Rosa look? A small woman, dark, round, but with a small waist. Large ears. Big, expressive eyes. An elegant expression, her head held high with pride.

The old man reached across and took the picture from her carefully, protectively. 'I'd rather hang it back myself,' he said earnestly. 'If you must know it is something of a keepsake. It was taken by the founder of the business, Max Warkofski, a first-generation immigrant to this country. His wedding portraiture was legendary at one time, but he lived the life of Jack the Lad. A ladies' man was what my mother used to call him – handsome as the devil, too. Successful in business and successful in the boudoir, if you know what I mean.' He shook his head sorrowfully. 'This was said to be his last portrait, though. He killed himself the day after it was taken.'

He hung the portrait with a lot of puffing. 'So you see, the life of Riley couldn't have suited him as well as everyone thought now, could it?' he said. 'My wife has always considered there was a moral there somewhere – or so she keeps saying. "Mind you don't end up like Max," has been her line for the thirty years we've been married. He was her relative though, not mine. I always said the roving eye was more likely to be in *her* blood, you see.' He laughed without humour and Kitty smiled.

454

'Look,' she said, 'does it matter if I change my mind about the passport shot?'

The man looked at her.

'I'll still pay, of course,' she added, 'only . . .' she looked around for an excuse, 'only I think I have a cold sore coming and I'd rather look my best, you know?'

She was about to leave when an idea hit her. 'Did you see the guy who brought me here, by any chance?' she asked.

'Mr Kofteros?' the photographer asked.

'You know him?' Kitty sounded surprised.

'Of course,' the photographer said, 'his family come from around here. I watched him grow up, you know. I have shots of him as a baby, if you're interested?'

The idea was tempting but Kitty was in a hurry.

'He was always fascinated by the old photos,' the man said, 'even as a child. He would try to match face to face and then trace the families through each generation. Most of our sitters come back as regular clients, you know. Christenings, weddings, silver weddings, and then more births. There's a whole social document in these albums somewhere, you know.'

He looked at the shot he had just hung back on the wall. 'Many of these people did very well for themselves, I believe,' he said, screwing up his eyes to see better. 'Nicky said he'd probably end up working for one of these families one day. I used to tell him the only way he'd meet proper society figures would be if they fiddled their tax and ended up in the same cell as him in prison.' He laughed. 'He was always a little fanciful, though. You wouldn't believe it to look at him now, would you?'

Kitty took one last look at the wedding photo. 'Thank you,' she said.

The man smiled. 'It doesn't look all that bad to me,' he said.

'Bad?' Kitty asked.

He tapped his mouth. 'The cold sore,' he said.

Kitty was still blushing at her lie as she left the studio. She phoned Hester as soon as she got back to her apartment. 'Can I call round for tea?' she asked.

'I'll send out for cake,' her mother said. She sounded relieved – as though she'd been waiting for Kitty's call.

CHAPTER FIFTY-TWO

ZG

TIFFANY
A semi-transparent, silk-like gauze.

'You never told us much about the family,' Kitty said.

'Darling, you never asked,' Hester told her. 'You always hated it when we went on about the old days, remember? You used to laugh. "Roots", you called it, like the Arthur Hailey book. Passing the same dull old stories down along the line.'

Hester was dressed formally, as though expecting a visit from the queen. She wore an aubergine wool dress with matching tights and shoes. And a brooch. Kitty had never seen her mother wear a brooch before.

'Rosa,' Kitty prompted, 'who was the Rosa that the suit was made for? The suit you gave me for the wedding.'

Hester sighed. 'Rosa Zigofsky,' she said. 'You have been told about her many times, Kitty. How easily one's children can become deaf when they are bored by what they hear! She was a relative on your father's side. Nothing special, Kitty, why even ask? Eh? Only that it was she who founded the business. Only that it was to that woman that we owe all this.'

'Maybe you told Chloe, Mother,' Kitty said.

'No, Kitty, we told you all,' Hester insisted. 'Only your ears weren't open, as usual. Since when did children listen to their parents? One day you will know this for yourself.' She smiled. 'She was a clever woman, Kitty – just like yourself. Only maybe, unlike you, she must have listened to her parents' advice now and again.'

Hester took some cake from the tray in front of them and handed it to Kitty. Then she sat watching and waiting, her mouth firmly shut and her hands clasped tightly in her lap. There would be no more talk until it was done. These were Hester's terms and her daughter understood that.

Kitty took a bite of cake. Bribery. With a small smile of victory, Hester continued with the story.

'Rosa Zigofsky started up the first mail-order house in Britain. She had the idea of getting garments photographed and selling them to order in that way. And this was in the days before the credit card!'

'So she sold out when?' Kitty asked.

Hester shrugged. 'Your father would have known – it was *his* family, after all. I can only pass on what he has told me. Rosa sold the mail-order idea because her heart was in couture. She made her money selling to the masses so that she could move upmarket. Her husband had his own business and that was the one she had her eye on all along. It is what became the ZG label.'

'So she died wealthy?' Kitty asked.

'She died alone,' Hester told her. 'Your father remembered her funeral in the East End. Despite all her social climbing it was where she wanted to be buried.' Hester brushed a crumb from the side of her mouth. 'She became a real demon as she got older, Kitty. People were scared of her. You wouldn't want to be in her debt. As a consequence there was no one around to see her get ill. She had been dead several days before they found her body. I believe your father had many nightmares about this as a child.'

'So was she my great-grandmother?' Kitty asked.

Hester laughed. 'Rosa Zigofsky was nobody's mother,' she said. 'Her husband Richard had a boy – David Reuben, I believe – and they both doted on him. The child died, though, a year after they married. It was said to be a terrible tragedy for them both. The boy was what they used to call "sickly" in those days.

'Rosa never got over the loss, even though he was only her stepson. The rumour was that her husband was a cold man and that the marriage was never a happy one. Your father used to say his father told him it was never even consummated. The child's death must have affected them both very hard.' Hester looked up at the ceiling as though trying to prod a memory. 'I'm sure Gabriel said she was in love with someone else. I don't know who it was, though.'

She drifted off a little, obviously lost in thought.

'So how did Dad inherit?' Kitty prompted.

Her mother smiled. 'The business passed to Rosa's brother's children when she died,' she said. 'That's where your blood comes from, Kitty – Gregory Zigofsky. He was a handsome man, just look at his photograph! Look at that strong, intelligent face!'

Hester went off out of the room and returned clutching a framed picture. Kitty had seen the shot before, she realized, but she looked at it carefully now for the first time.

Gregory stood, tall and handsome, behind a beautiful woman who was seated.

'That was Ruth Levi – later to become Gregory's wife,' Hester told her, pointing. 'She used to work with Rosa Zigofsky and ran some of her businesses for her. She and Gregory had three children, and they all went into the business. That must have been a true love match – look what a handsome couple they made.'

The picture was the same as the one that Kitty had found in the stack in her father's office. She knew who had left it there for her now. The same person who had sent her her parents' wedding shot. The one who had phoned. Nicky Kofteros, local historian. The little boy who had spent so much time in the old photographer's studio, studying the shots and tracing the families. She wondered exactly how far he had traced her family down its tree.

'Maybe I know more about your history than yourself, Kitty.' He had said that. And he had been right. He'd known about Rosa and Ruth. He'd left clues all the time, like crumbs of bread for a bird. But she still didn't understand why. What was he trying to achieve? Did the crumbs lead into a trap? Was she acting like a mug? She rubbed at her temples. Think, Kitty, think. Why?

Why was she being so fucking thick? She looked across at her mother. 'So Rosa died alone,' Kitty said.

'She came over from Russia during the pogroms,' Hester told her, 'but I suppose you find that story boring, too.' She was smiling, though.

'Sorry,' Kitty said.

Her mother's smile widened. She pressed more cake onto Kitty's plate.

Kitty turned the shot around and studied the back. 'Max Warkofski, portrait photographer,' she read aloud. The date was exactly the same as Rosa's photograph in the studio. The shot must have been taken shortly after Rosa and Richard's wedding. Poor Max. Making clients smile for his pictures while planning his own death.

'Would you like to keep that one?' Hester asked her.

Kitty looked at it. Gregory and Ruth. With a slight shake of her head she placed the precious photograph back into her mother's waiting hands.

CHAPTER FIFTY-THREE

ZG

GENOA PLUSH
A plush with a short, velvet-like pile.

She was sailing through the darkness, clad in a gown of black Albert crape, beneath which she wore a plain nainsook camisole and long flannel drawers.

'Kitty.' He was there again, waiting for her. She could see nothing and when her hands reached out they touched only air.

'Kitty, my darling.'

But Gabriel was dead. She placed her hands over her face to hide her eyes. When she held her arms outstretched again it was younger flesh that they touched.

'Kitty.' His voice was hoarse with longing and the sound of it alone was enough to liquidize her flesh.

She touched his lips and then kissed them. His skin smelt of Oxo cubes. She waited for the touch of others, but this time they were alone.

Her man was already naked. He pressed against her long skirts and she folded him inside with her. They kissed full on the mouth and she felt she knew his body better than she knew her own. Her legs wound around his waist. He was tall and strong. He held her tight as they kissed, then lowered her softly to the ground without so much as a groan of effort.

His fingers worked quickly at her complicated clothes. Naked at last, apart from her stockings, she felt him lean over her and spread herself out to receive him.

He paused. 'Marry me, Kitty,' he said, 'marry me, or I shall have to die. I could never live without you, you know that.'

Kitty reached a hand up towards him, clasping his erect penis, guiding it gently down towards her, feeling it touch her body, her legs, then finally pushing softly inside her.

'I'm marrying Freddy,' she whispered as she felt his body eclipsing her own, 'I can't marry you, Nicky,' she whispered, 'you know how much I hate you.'

His lovemaking was impatient. She clung to him like a koala as he pushed inside her and cried out when he did – though he called her name with passion, while she just yelled. There was one more moment of closeness before they parted.

'That was your only time, Rosa,' he whispered into her ear, 'I wanted it to be good for you. Never forget me.'

His face pulled away. He was handsome, dark and young. He smiled at her but his eyes looked unimaginably sad. 'Max,' he said, introducing himself, touching his forehead. 'Max Warkofski.' His eyes were kind but mocking.

This time when she woke Freddy was not there beside her to comfort her as she cried. She had never felt so alone in her life. Nothing made sense. She was being told things but could understand none of it. Perhaps she was going mad.

'*Kitty.*'

'Kitty, please!'
She knew she couldn't stand much more of these voices
– not now that she knew who it was that spoke to her.

CHAPTER FIFTY-FOUR

ZG

LYCRA

*Known for its stretch and recovery qualities and
introduced by Du Pont in 1958, Lycra has recently
revolutionized the textile industry. Originally used in the
manufacture of girdles and roll-ons, in the seventies
it found use in tights and exercise wear and has
currently been incorporated into many more fabrics.*

She had never used the Underground before, she didn't
even know how to buy a ticket; another commuter had
had to show her how – a young black girl with a small
child in tow. The girl's patience was saint-like. She had
taken the coins and even added a few from her own bag
when the amount had not been enough. How would she
feel the next day, when she read what she'd done?

There had been a crush at the top of the escalator, which
was puzzling because she'd chosen a time she thought
would be quiet. The bottleneck cleared once they were on
the steps, though. She liked the posters on the way down.
Glossy and *Vogue*-style. A pin-thin model in calf-skin
boots. Two youths, intertwined in matching jeans. Boys or
girls? The ad was repeated a few yards down. A boy; and
a girl. Clever. Grainy. Her reflection stared back from
between their heads. She had the same vacant, bug-eyed

stare. A pretty face, really. Just unexpressive. Like most of the other travellers, she noticed.

The escalator journey seemed eternal, but that was fine, because she liked it; into the bowels of hell. There were articles of discarded rubbish along the gap between the banister and the wall where the adverts hung: crisp packets, cigarette cartons, orange peel. She thought she heard music. Perhaps you could live on these escalators – eat, sleep, listen to music, read adverts and fuck. She took the wet gum from her mouth and pressed it against the wall. A small piece of eternity, bought for the price of a tube ticket. The gum would dry like glue. Perhaps nobody would be able to get it off. When the stairs levelled out and chucked her off she rode up and then down again in the same spot. This time she pressed her little finger against the soft gum. A fingerprint – a source of individual identity. Hers and hers alone. Had they fingerprinted her father when they found his body? Was that how they'd known who he was? Would they have had his prints on record? A match, sergeant – it's that fucking designer chappie. Shall you tell his wife, or shall I? He had parking offences. Would they have had his prints from that? Computer matched – Burgess would have approved.

She tired of the escalator ride. After the fifth trip she imagined people had begun to watch. Or that there were security cameras trained upon her. She hobbled along down the lime-green-lit tunnels instead. There was a busker with a dog. The busker looked at her with indifference but she thought she caught a speck of pity in the dog's brown eyes.

There was a whip of wind and the tunnel seemed to

explode with noise, while the air in it imploded. Her clothes sucked this way and that. Terrified, she pushed her hands over her ears and squeezed her eyes shut.

Two foreigners pushed past her, laughing. A train. A train had arrived at the platform. She followed the tourists. The platform was a dazzle of raw light and noise. The train invited her on board, its doors wide open. The seats looked comfortable – she could have stretched out and slept on them. But she chose the platform instead. She had to wait.

When the train had gone she looked around the place. There were two platforms, joined by a tunnel: northbound and southbound. She didn't care which. The gap at the end of both was nice and black. She stood in the adjoining tunnel, right in the middle, just in case.

Right or left? She could have bet on which would arrive first. North. Or South? She placed her hands over her mouth and laughed now that the fear of the train noise had subsided. She thought of her mother and her sister. For some reason she thought of school when she was small, which was odd, because she'd never had a moment of happiness there.

Then the wind hit her once again and she knew her time had come. It tugged at her knees and tried to ruffle her hair. It lifted her like the hurricane lifted Dorothy in *The Wizard of Oz*, so that when she went to walk she was like a model in a pair of Vivienne Westwood platforms – plink, tip, tiptoe along. But the wind helped her keep her balance; in fact, it *assisted* her death, for by the time she had reached the platform she was no longer tripping and sashaying but stomping full-pelt in a troubled nothing-can-stop-me way, so that the only other person on the platform, an elderly man who had been through the war and so could have saved her had she been running in any other, less determined manner, stood back out of the way.

For this she smiled her thanks, for she had always been brought up to be polite, and then she was finished with the platform and onto air and space before falling into the darkness where the rats sleep and being pushed side-on by the force-field around the train, with the driver's face frozen: 'Oh!' and going down instead of up, because tube trains pull you under while cars will flick you over their shoulder like an enraged bull, and then – nothing.

CHAPTER FIFTY-FIVE

ZG

TULLE ARACHNE
A clear tulle embroidered in gold and silk.

It was the phone that had woken her from the dream. She sat up still for a moment, disoriented, before lifting the receiver and saying her name.

It was Burgess on the other end. His voice sounded so strange it was a moment or two before she could recognize it. Then she realized he was crying. 'It's Nula,' he said.

'Nula?' Kitty asked, rubbing her temples. 'She's here, Burgess, she's with me.'

'She's tried to kill herself, Kitty,' Burgess said.

'No,' Kitty told him, 'I told you, Burgess, she's been staying here since the collection. She's in bed, Burgess – she went off at about nine because she had homework and . . . and I took her a drink in myself around eleven and she was sound asleep. What is it? What's happened?'

'She tried to commit suicide, Kitty. Is Freddy with you? Jesus, I'm sorry. She threw herself under a tube train . . .' his voice broke up like a faulty mobile line. '. . . God, can you imagine? Why? We were all depressed by Dad's murder but nobody thought Nula was any worse than the rest . . .'

Kitty dropped the phone down and ran along the corridor to the guest bedroom. Her legs felt like lead. With every dull step she said to herself: she's in there asleep. I will open the door and wake her up and she'll get ratty with me and I'll hug her for the fright and we'll have hot milk together like Mother used to make even though we hated it as children but it's all right, I know it's all right, there's just been some creepy mistake, that's all . . .

But there was no mistake. Nula's bed had been made immaculately; the sheets folded tight and the quilt smoothed flat, like for an advert or photo shoot. On the pillow was an envelope with Kitty's name on it, only it just said, 'Kit', which was what Nula called her.

As Kitty's legs buckled beneath the leaden weight of her own body she lowered herself onto the floor rather than the bed, which Nula had obviously spent so long making perfect. As she read the note – which was really a letter, for it was four pages long – her skin seemed to cool and freeze and shrink and peel off her body like grape-skin.

A great gulf of emptiness opened up inside her and she started to vomit, though nothing came out of her mouth.

'Nula!' She read the words on the letter and suddenly the noise and the retching stopped and she was totally, utterly absorbed and lost in a new horror.

Two of the pages were handwritten, and two of them were typed. It was impossible to read them at first, she was looking too quickly for any of it to make sense. She stared at the typed sheets. They were formal, almost legal-looking. Nula had signed them at the bottom – a crazy, kid's sort of a signature that veered dangerously about the page.

Frustrated at her own lack of concentration, Kitty threw the typed pages down beside her and tried to focus on the handwritten ones.

Dear Kitty,

Sorry. Sorry for everything. no tears though because i can make you hate me more than you have ever hated anyone. I have killed myself because i can't live with any of it not what he did nor what i did either. This letter is a mess because so is my brain it was all going Kit, i wanted it as it was before we <u>were</u> happy weren't we? Remember with Burg when he and Chloe used to fight and we'd all laugh because the dog joined in too? Remember when mum and dad were so happy to and we used to have trust in the fact that that was the way it would be <u>forever</u>?

He cheated on her Kit he cheated us all he wasn't the man he told us he was the fine father the hero we had to admire and <u>trust</u>. He stole all our happiness Kit he knew i'd seen one day in the salon but god he didn't even care because i know he didn't stop because i had him followed. It didn't matter who he was with it just mattered that he wasn't with <u>us</u>.

This is what money does to you as a child Kit you were never spoilt but i grew up with everything and its amazing what you can fix if you go around with the right crowd. Raphael hated me i think. I saw the look on his face no guilt or remorse even though he knew i'd seen he must have told dad he must have mustn't he? What would mum have done if she knew? It would have killed her Kit how could he do that to us?

He was all i admired and to find out so much was wrong and so many lies means i can trust nothing and

471

never will. My head burst with it all Kit i couldn't stand it it wouldn't go away some days it actually <u>hurt</u>.

I'm sorry, Kit, I'm sorry, I'm sorry. I didn't want what happened. It was easier than you'd imagine – too easy. I just said to someone I know that he should die for what he'd done, for being unfaithful to Mother, and next they'd found a number for a detective agency in the *Yellow Pages* and then there were phone numbers given to me from then one minute it was a joke, like a movie and then the next this man phoned because the friend had given my number and he knew who I was and suddenly I got a call saying it had been done.

I was so crazy upset, Kit, but he didnt care about that or my age because he knew me and he knew I had the money because of my name. It was so funny but then suddenly it wasn't, and look what he did. I said I wanted dad dead but not really, I wanted him to love us and stay the father I thought he was, not leave us for Raphael . . . I didn't think it was real, Kit. It was all too much like the movies.

He kept phoning for the money, Kit. He said he'd kill me too if I didn't pay up and keep quiet. I just gave him the money. I didn't think it was real. How could it be? I'm just a kid, Kit. How could that sort of thing happen?

Sorry, Kitty, sorry sorry sorry sorry sorry sorry . . .

She barely heard the doorbell. It rang so many times she thought it was inside her head. Nula. Little Nules. Her own sister had murdered their father. The phrase ran around her

472

head like a trapped mouse and yet it made absolutely no sense to her.

All the people she had suspected. All the photos she'd laid out on her floor. All with grudges. Each one somehow capable of such a violent act. Of course it had been a contract killing. But her own baby sister? How could it have happened? This wasn't New York! How many kids *say* they want to kill their parents at some time in their lives? Yet how many are overheard by the sort of kids that had somehow helped Nula to commit such an act?

Kitty heard the answer loud in her own head. Rich kids, that's who. The only sort of kids people will arrange this sort of thing for. Celebrity children. The type who somehow get what they want. Kids who live in unreal worlds because their parents are famous.

There was a loud crack that made Kitty look up. Where the door had once been was now a hole. Kofteros stood framed inside that hole, bent double with pain and rubbing his right arm with his left hand. Kitty almost wanted to laugh at the sight. Nothing seemed real anymore.

'Kitty?' He was able to straighten up now.

'My door . . .' It was all she could think of. It was like being high on drugs. The door. Nicky's arm. Nula's suicide.

'I was worried,' he said, 'I heard about your sister.'

Kitty stared like an idiot, trying to make sense of it all. 'I thought it was you . . .' she began. She'd thought Kofteros had arranged the killing. Not all the time, sometimes. When she wasn't blaming Stephano or Burgess. Anyone but Nula, in fact. And yet all that time . . . in the end she held Nula's letter of confession out towards Kofteros. It was a family thing, she knew that. Perhaps he should never

473

have read it. But Kitty had carried enough by herself.

He took it and glanced at it. 'She's not dead, Kitty,' he said, grabbing her arm. 'Your sister's still alive. I've come to take you to the hospital.'

There are many ways to make your mark in life, and killing your wealthy father is one of them. Kofteros was right – Nula didn't die in the Underground, the wind from the train sucked her down onto the track and she fell between the wheels, rather than under them.

The press arrived at the hospital before Kitty got there. Kofteros was like a bodyguard, pushing her through the crush with one arm around her shoulders. She couldn't have been sure but she thought she felt him mash a few faces along the way, too.

When she walked into Nula's private room there was a celebrity PR already sitting at her bedside, planning her future.

Nula's injuries were ridiculously light but the PR had arranged for a few strategically-placed plasters to be stuck to her face for the photocall. The stricken expression came free of charge. Nula's poor mind had flown elsewhere, many miles away from any of them.

Kitty had to push past a posse of lawyers and PR assistants to get to her sister's bedside.

When she sat there softly crying nobody moved to allow her room or quiet. Nula's eyes only focused on Kitty's face once.

'I did it,' she whispered, 'I don't know how but I killed him. I'm sorry, Kit, I didn't mean it to happen. It was so terrible, too. I didn't know. I never thought.'

'God, Nules,' Kitty replied, 'how did this nightmare ever begin to happen?'

Once Nula was transferred to a nursing home of the sort used by royals and A-list celebs, Kitty felt a yearning to return to anything that resembled real life. She craved normality. The tragedy had been great enough to bring on a stifling numbness. She hadn't cried again since her hospital visit. Her shock had been too intense.

Nula had killed their father – almost by accident. Even after she'd read the note she hadn't believed it. Her sister had had a breakdown. Sweet little Nula would never have been capable of anything so unthinkable.

But it was Burgess who had suffered most at the news. It was Burgess who went to the courts every day and patiently and deliberately reported back to Kitty everything that happened or was going to happen.

It was Burgess who suddenly became human again, and supplied the strength Kitty and Hester needed to get through it all.

Hester had known it, all the time. She had been aware of Gabriel's affairs. What Nula and Kitty had failed to realize was that their parents were a product of the sixties, when behaviour like that was the norm. Hester knew, but she didn't mind. She loved her husband. She just shielded her children from it all. Maybe that had been her mistake.

It was when Kitty saw Nula's face on her television screen that she finally knew the time had come to repair her life. Her sister was speaking on something that looked suspiciously like Oprah Winfrey. She looked beautiful and she spoke well. Her cause had been taken up in the US, where a poor little rich child who has a hitman kill her father can receive sympathy and celebrity status.

Her mind had been unbalanced, that was the verdict in the UK. Now she had been asked to participate on a book and there was talk about film rights being sold, with Winona Ryder and Gwyneth Paltrow both up for the lead role.

And all this had happened so quickly. While Kitty's own life appeared to move in slow motion.

It was time to carry on planning the wedding. Gabriel was dead. Her sister had arranged his murder, more by accident than design, but what she had done had led to a terrible, violent death. Nothing would change those facts. They had all lived with the shock. Hester had survived better than most of them because her heart had flown out to her child.

'Do something good for the family, Kitty,' she'd said recently.

Would the wedding heal anything? Kitty doubted it but knew it gave them something else to focus on than grief. She went into the salon one night to try on the dress that Alain said was ready. They had the place to themselves. Nicky had given them free use of all the facilities. She'd lost weight. Alain tutted at the way her ribs poked through her flesh, ruining the even surface of the silk.

The dress looked wildly regal. Kitty turned in front of the mirror. Then she remembered the suit.

'Look at this,' she told Alain, placing the case she had brought with her onto the cutting-table. She pulled the wedding suit from its tissue and laid it out flat, smoothing the creases with her fingers.

'It's old,' Alain said, feigning indifference.

'Look at it closely,' Kitty told him.

Once he had walked over and touched the fabric she could tell he was hooked. She watched his back bend over the table as he inspected every detail, squinting at the fine embroidery and sniffing the pile of the fabric.

'It's my wedding suit, Alain,' Kitty told him, 'it's been passed down the family. My father wore the waistcoat, I think. It's for Freddy to wear at our wedding.'

Alain laughed. 'Is he going to diet?' he asked.

'Can it be altered?' Kitty asked him.

Alain shrugged. 'A pity,' he said. 'It would be easier to find a new groom. The fabric is delicate. This is a beautiful garment, Kitty, it belongs in a museum. Do you really want me to start ripping its seams so that your fiancé can cram himself into it?'

Kitty looked at him. 'Try it on,' she said. He looked doubtful, but she picked up the waistcoat and held it out towards him.

Alain slipped his own thick shirt off over his head and pulled the waistcoat around his body.

'It feels strange,' he said, 'dead man's clothes. Perhaps it is unlucky to wear it.'

She put her hand over his. 'Keep it on, Alain,' she told him, 'it has brought a lot of happiness since then. It has already been altered a couple of times – look.'

They stared at themselves in the mirror.

'It looks odd with jeans,' Alain said. She could tell he was bemused by what he saw.

'You could never wear this suit together with the dress I am making for you, Kitty,' he said quietly.

'No?' she asked.

'No. Absolutely not. The colours would be all wrong together. You need to complement the tones of the silks – look, here.' He went to the thread bin and pulled out a handful of delicate, faded-looking colours. 'You see what these would do with this?' he asked, holding them to his chest. 'You know Gabriel had one design already in these tones. Maybe he intended it to go with the suit . . .'

They pulled Gabriel's sketchbook out again and spread it on the table. Alain flicked through a few of the pages. 'Here,' he said, folding back the paper.

It was a subtle, clever dress, simple in shape but cut on the cross to come alive on the body. Attached to the paper were swatches of fabrics and pieces of thread that exactly complemented the colours in the suit.

'You didn't choose this?' Alain asked Kitty.

She shook her head. 'I liked it, but . . .'

'But what?' Alain asked.

'I don't know, Alain, maybe it's not right for the sort of wedding the Jacobs's are looking forward to. I kind of thought they'd want a few frills and frou-frou, you know? I think it sort of goes with the territory. You'd need to really know a thing or two about design and cut to appreciate this one properly. It's not exactly knock-their-eyes-out for the back rows of a crowded synagogue, is it?'

'I like it,' Alain said. 'It was your father's favourite, too.'

Kitty picked up the sketch. 'You mean you've had me here spending hours fitting this full-blown, belle-of-the-ball number, and now you start the emotional blackmail, telling me this was what my father would have wanted all along?' Kitty asked him. 'What are you, some kind of a workaholic nut or something?'

Alain lit a cigarette and shrugged. 'Telling a bride you don't like the dress she's chosen is like telling her you don't like her choice of husband,' he said. He turned his back and started sketching something on a pad.

'So?' Kitty asked him.

'So what?'

'So, does that mean you think Freddy's wrong for me too? Is that what you're saying?'

Alain kept his back turned towards her. 'I know this suit won't fit him,' he said.

'And for that I should call the wedding off?' Kitty asked.

'Don't you believe in omens?' Alain said.

'No.'

'Then marry your Freddy.'

'He's good-looking and kind.'

'So is the guy who sweeps the floor in the salon. I don't see you marrying him.'

'Freddy comes from a good family.'

'Good God, Kitty! I never knew you were such a snob. Is he good in bed?'

'What?'

'You heard.'

Alain stood and walked towards her. He was taller. He smelt good. It was his eyes that did it, though. They looked so weary, as though they had seen everything in the world. They were large and dark now.

He took her hand and placed it on his chest, on the waistcoat that Rosa's father had stitched for her, so many years before. His free hand found her chin and touched it carefully.

'Kiss me,' he whispered.

'No.'

'Kiss me,' he said.

Her chin tilted upward. His lips fell slowly towards her own. Then his eyes closed and the spell was broken.

'No,' she repeated, though even then there was very little conviction in her tone.

'Kitty?' Freddy stood in the doorway.

She looked at Alain. He was smiling.

'You knew he was coming,' she said to him.

'Of course,' he whispered, 'I took the call.'

He pressed his face against her hair. 'I owed it to your father, Kitty,' he said softly. 'Gabriel knew the marriage was wrong for you. He told me while we worked on the designs. You chose the wrong man and the wrong dress. Don't worry, you'll make the right choice . . . eventually.'

CHAPTER FIFTY-SIX

ZG

JACCONET
*Currently called nainsook, jacconet was a thin
cotton fabric, something between cambric and muslin in
texture and weave.*

Freddy waited for excuses but Kitty could find none to give him. It wasn't even a proper kiss that he had seen, but she knew, above all the anger she felt towards Alain, that he was right – she could never marry Freddy. He was wrong for her. So what could she tell him?

'I'm sorry,' she said, and she was. Sorry for the coldness and disappointment that came into his eyes. Sorry for cheating him but not cheating on him. Sorry that she couldn't be the person she had planned on being. If Gabriel hadn't died then she would have married Freddy and been happy. But now she was different. Someone else had been released inside her. There were things driving her now that she had no control over.

Freddy looked across at Alain, and Kitty knew he was considering punching him hard. She knew Freddy well enough to be aware of what was going on in his mind; how he was chewing the process over, where the punch would land, how much Alain would hurt. How he himself

481

would feel once the deed was done. In the end he settled for a quiet exit. No words, no punching, just a look and he was gone.

Kitty took a step to follow him but Alain held her by the arm.

'Are you going after him?' he asked.

She stared at him.

'To say what?' he said. 'To tell him you are sorry and that you love him and will marry him after all?' He smiled. 'Do you know what you are like when you are working, Kitty? You are happy and anxious and totally involved in the job that you are doing. Do you know how beautiful you look when that is happening? I saw this when we worked on the collection. Yet you would give it all up for a marriage you don't really want. The business is a passion for you, Kitty. Why do you let it all go so easily?'

The room was silent, lit only by the low ochre light from the desk-lamp. She watched Alain walk across to the cutting-table and she saw him lift up the giant metal shears that lay in one of the open drawers. The steel caught the light. They cut fabric like butter. Like an animal she stood stock-still, caught in a web of fear and indecision.

He came so close that his breath was upon her face. Still she was immobile, transfixed by the sight of the huge scissors.

He lifted the hem of her wedding dress with one hand. With the other he placed the open shears against the fabric, lifting them slowly but evenly so that the garment was swiftly sliced apart from the skirt to the waist. She closed her eyes. She could feel the cold metal on her bare stomach. Alain paused, staring all the while at her face, and then carried on cutting, up her ribs to her breasts and then to her throat.

Her flesh shrank in fear, but she was neither cut nor hurt. When the shears had stopped she opened her eyes and he was there in front of her, waiting for her move.

'Kitty, you know how much I want you,' he told her. His arms dropped to his sides and the shears fell to the floor with a deafening clatter.

She pulled the dress open and let it sink to the ground with a whisper. Then she began on the buttons of the waistcoat. They were small and difficult to open, but she worked on them carefully for she did not want to break the threads. All the time Alain watched her face and she could hear his breathing and smell the scent of his skin.

How many young wives had worked on these buttons? She saw Rosa on her wedding night, pulling each small fastening from its buttonhole, one by one, as careful as she was now. Did Richard wait as patiently as Alain, or would he have tried to rip at them in his haste to be with his bride? But then her mother had said the marriage was never consummated . . . Hester, too, would have folded the waistcoat for Gabriel. Did she love him on that day?

The last button fell open and Kitty looked up at Alain's face. His features were beautiful in the low light. The skin was pale nutmeg, with small violet smudges beneath each prune-dark eye. The shadows of his lashes formed a frieze along either cheek. His hair was like Nula's, cropped, dark and soft, like an animal pelt. On his chest was a down of similar hairs, though coarser and more curly. His flesh shone and pulsed with reflected colours in the half-light:

483

fly's wing, graphite, dioptase, moonstone and malachite.

She knew he ached to have her, yet she made him wait while she looked. She placed a finger to his lips and watched them form a kiss around it.

'Do you want me too, Kitty?' he asked.

She waited a while longer. 'Yes,' she told him.

He lifted her then, kissing her full on the mouth as she felt herself rise in his arms. He tasted fresh and sun-bleached like a pebble washed in the sea. Then he placed her gently and lovingly upon the high cutting-table, so that the bare wood was shock-cold against her back and buttocks.

The fat bolts of shantung and embroidered silks that lay beside her head emitted a warm and rich perfume that reminded her kindly of her childhood. Crushed beneath her skinny neck lay a pillow of dove-white velvet that should have formed the collar of her wedding gown.

Breathing carefully through her mouth like a child who senses Christmas, she watched Alain remove first the open waistcoat and then his jeans until they were naked together, moulded shroud-like in a parachute-sheet of fine pearl marocain.

He called her name inside her mouth many times as he kissed her and she pulled him close until their bodies merged into one like sodden clay. In the room there was silence, yet inside Kitty's head the ghosts of a thousand sounds kept her busily absorbed.

There was a woman's voice that sang a song she barely knew: 'I took a violet from my mother's grave . . .' the voice echoed high into the air until it faded and other voices took over. A chorus from a musical, sung in foreign voices, then fire-bells and shouting, followed by the sounds of children crying.

'Rosa?' It was her father's voice, and yet not her name. *For Rosa, the daughter I love.* There was the sound of stamping feet upon impacted snow and the smell of snow, too, and ivy and mistletoe, icy in her steaming nostrils.

'Kitty?' As Alain bored gently inside her she heard the name 'Max' called faintly in her head. Then she was lost in a tide of ancient longing that all but drowned her in its intensity. It was as though she had made love only once in her life. She felt herself open and empty, clinging to Alain like a straw in the wind, as much for safety as for lust.

As his face contorted and his back arched and became rigid in the eye of his orgasm she heard her own name roared at last like sea in a cave, and then she was gone – swept up in it totally, too lost in the stampede towards ecstasy, winced and wrinkled into her own everlasting pleasure, curling and squirming like a salt-coated slug until the pain of it had gone and she could straighten and hear normal noises again, like the tick of a wristwatch and the steady drip of her own droplets of sweat.

Wet and slippery as a pair of conger eels, Kitty and Alain lay entwined until they had cooled, then he slid back until he was spreadeagled alongside her and their mixed sweat evaporated to the point where she started to shiver. He covered her again with the fabric then, and held her until she was warm.

They left the building together and only parted once they had cabs. When Kitty got back to her apartment there was a message from Freddy on her answerphone, full of spite and slurred anger. She deleted it before the end. He was drunk. That wasn't Freddy. That was Vodka Absolut talking.

CHAPTER FIFTY-SEVEN

ZG

CHIFFON
Made from silk, wool or synthetics, chiffon is a gossamer-sheer fabric made from tightly twisted yarns.

When she woke it was late and her body felt flattened, like well-rolled filo pastry. She had to look in the mirror to make sure she wasn't pressed to an inch thick, like a cartoon character run over by a steamroller.

She walked about the place until body bits fell into place and she seemed less two-dimensional. Her spine felt bruised and her lips were sore. There was the trace of a rash on her cheeks and chin where his unshaven flesh had chaffed and burnt. She took some ice cubes from a tray in the freezer and pressed them to her temples and face.

When she emerged in her pyjamas to collect the post Kofteros was standing outside her door, immaculately dressed in a ghastly but expensive greige suit and cloud-white shirt.

'It's not your shade,' she told him.

'Good morning,' he said, handing her a styrofoam cup of very fresh and very bitter espresso.

'Sugar?' he asked, digging into his trouser pockets.

She allowed, rather than let him into her flat. When

she walked through a shard of gleaming daylight Kofteros raised an eyebrow at the sight of her face.

'I take it the wedding's off,' he said.

'You spoke to Freddy already?' she asked, sounding annoyed.

'No,' he told her, sipping his own coffee and wincing at the heat of it, 'only if you don't mind me saying so, he never made you look like you do right now.'

She slammed into the bathroom and poured water over her face.

'One last clue?' he shouted through the door.

Kitty sighed. 'I'm tired, Nicky.'

'But you are also curious,' Kofteros said.

'Why the hell are you doing this?' she asked when she came out. She had pulled on a sweater and a pair of faded jeans.

'Don't you have anything a bit more formal?' Kofteros asked her.

'Why, are you and Chloe getting married, or something?' Kitty asked. When he looked straight at her she remembered the dream and shuddered.

'Something more business-like would be appropriate,' he said quietly.

She changed into a trouser suit, kicking herself all the time that it was only her inquisitiveness stopping her from throwing him out on his ear.

'The last tiny piece of the puzzle,' he announced once she was beside him in the car.

'I take it there's no point asking where we're going?' Kitty said.

'You can know if you want,' he told her. She was

disappointed. Something inside her preferred the mystery of it all, like before. As much as she disliked Kofteros he had become something of a magician in her life, summoning up surprises: the photographer's studio, the insults hurled at Burgess. 'I'll wait,' she told him, sulking.

They pulled up outside a small building in a surprisingly seedy-looking street in Mayfair.

'More pictures?' Kitty asked.

'No,' Kofteros told her. He opened her door from the inside, leaning across so that his arm brushed her legs.

'I'm sorry,' he said, looking at her.

'What is this place?' she asked.

He sighed. 'If I do all the work for you, Kitty, you won't feel as though you've achieved anything. Just go inside and find out for yourself.'

She looked up at the building. 'Why are you doing these things?' she asked.

He smiled. 'Maybe I have plans to become your doting brother-in-law,' he said.

'No,' she told him evenly, 'we both know that's not it.'

His face became serious. 'One thing we share, Kitty, is a genuine interest in the business of fashion. My parents were immigrants and I was taught the importance of the continuity of history. Believe it or not, I don't enjoy breaking up your little family dynasty. I have a lot of respect for the traditional as well as the new and innovative.

'We both know that Zigo would never survive as it was, yet despite any pleasure I derive from my business manipulations – and, to be honest with you, Kitty, there have been many – I also suffer many pangs of regret that I should be the one to do the obligatory deed.'

'So you are helping me out of a sense of guilt?' Kitty asked.

'Maybe.' He shrugged. 'Although you should know that guilt has never been one of my prime emotions. I am a businessman, Kitty. And that's what I do – business. Who it affects and how it affects them is not my problem. I like to see things tidy, though, and the story of your family is beginning to fray around the edges.

'Burgess will stay in Zigo as long as the lawyers allow it, then he will reap his financial harvest from investing in virtual pornography. Chloe will continue as the masthead until her first bad facelift, but as she still has many years to go before the wrinkles start to appear I think we could consider her career a long and almost happy one. China is too obsessed with motherhood to be a worry and Nula . . .'

'Which just leaves me,' said Kitty. 'I'm not a charity case, Nicky. I can manage by myself.'

'And yet you have never visited this building before,' he told her. 'Why, Kitty? Do you have no curiosity or sense of history? Like I said, you are the only one of your siblings with a true taste for the business and yet you shuck the responsibility off like a snake sheds its skin. I would have thought the trail I've led you would have been enough to whet your appetite. It's *you* who has to carry on the family name, Kitty – don't you realize that?'

'How do you know so much?' Kitty asked him.

He smiled. 'Everything is there, Kitty – if you just know where to look for it.'

'Aren't you biting the hand that feeds you?' she asked.

He shrugged. 'There were many honourable men in my

own family's history – and many more crooks and scoundrels, too. It doesn't pay to be too straight, Kitty. Only losers reveal their entire hand of cards.'

She got out of the car. The building was an old one, in need of renovation. On the ground floor was a shop that was being re-fitted into some sort of a restaurant. She looked at the plaques on the wall near the stairway. None of the businesses sounded familiar, but one was a fashion firm, so she climbed to the first floor, where the company was sited.

There were heavy wooden doors with frosted glass inserts and a plastic sign above them: Seigfried and Sons, Fashion Importers. Kitty pressed a button on the intercom and the doors buzzed open.

Inside was a small showroom, unremarkable save for two massive and ornate windows that stretched the length of one end of the room. The place looked untidy. There were half-open packing boxes strewn about and half-empty rails with the odd hanging garment.

'Can I help you?' The elderly man who approached her looked polite but suspicious.

'Are you closing down?' Kitty asked.

'Selling up,' he told her. 'The overheads here are too great. We ran until the end of our lease and then – well, you can imagine property prices around here! Are you a buyer?'

'No,' Kitty said, 'I'm a manufacturer – well, I used to be. My father was Gabriel Zigofsky.'

The old man peered at her, his face a sudden mask of condolence. 'I knew I recognized your face!' he said. 'Please, sit down – look, I can clear a few of these boxes

491

away. Let me get tea – I'm sorry, we have had so many people come to look around . . .'

She touched his arm. 'Don't worry about the chair,' she said. 'I wonder – could I be another one of your visitors that comes to look around? Would you mind very much? A friend recommended I visit you.'

The man smiled. 'Of course, of course!' he said. 'I'm a little surprised you never came before. Look where you like – I'll carry on in my office, if you don't mind. Most of the stuff is packed away, I'm afraid. But the workrooms are still stuff-full. I collect too much, you see, I never could throw anything away. If there's anything you want to keep, just let me know, though I doubt it will interest a young lady like yourself very much. Still, enjoy!'

Kitty stared at him as he walked off. Help herself? She wandered across to the windows. They were so dusty the sunlight was diffused. The carpet she walked on was threadbare in places and the boards creaked painfully as she moved across the room.

He had given her the run of the place. She had no idea why, but curiosity drove her on. Did he think she might be buying the property? Maybe he was a little eccentric. Or perhaps her father's name opened more doors than she'd thought.

The workroom was long and narrow with a skylight in the ceiling. There was a handful of ancient machines and a cutting-table so gnarled and bent with age it would have defied even Alain's expert hand.

A woman eating lunch at the desk smiled as she approached. 'More like a museum, eh?' she asked Kitty. 'It's a shame these places have to close. They're all going now, though. Nobody wants couture these days, do they?'

Kitty returned the smile. 'I thought you were importers,' she said.

'Nooo . . .' the woman told her, 'agents for a German coat range, yes – but then there's this other side of the business, too. When the place was bought originally it was just couture. There's still a dressmaking service for the elderly ladies of Mayfair. Not a lucrative business, I must confess, but it's been running for donkey's years and the old man was rather loathe to knock it on the head. I think he rather likes the idea of the individually-made garment. He's always been proud of his little sideline and the ladies love it. I don't know what they'll do now it's closing – though most of them have kicked the bucket by now.'

She folded the wrapping from her lunch and threw it into a bin. 'Are you interested in fashion?' she asked. 'Would you like to see some of the old stuff that he's kept over the years?'

Kitty nodded. The woman led her into a large walk-in cupboard.

'All the old order books and sketchpads are here,' she said, pulling a lightswitch. 'Some of them date back to the last century. You can have a poke around if you like – I sometimes thumb through them while I'm taking a break, though the dust tends to set my asthma off if I'm not careful. There's a washroom over there if you need to scrub up when you're finished. Mind that nice suit – it's a Zigo, isn't it?'

Kitty barely heard the question. She had entered the cupboard and was staring at the workbooks. She didn't even hear the woman walk off. The sense of the place was overpowering enough to make her giddy.

The design books were coated with grey dust but still stacked in numerical order. The most recent was '96. Kitty pulled it off the pile and flicked through it. The dresses were mainly Hartnell rip-offs, designed for what Gabriel would have called 'the more mature client'.

Each drawing had been carefully executed in pen and a swatch of the fabric stapled to the side of the page. There was nothing exciting about either the styles or the colours. But then the sort of clients that these had been made for wouldn't have wanted anything more innovative.

Kitty put the book back with a sigh. She'd started at the end so she may as well finish at the beginning. She couldn't read the exact year on the spine of the first book on the shelves, as the numbers had faded, but it was compiled in the 1800s.

After an amount of tugging it fell out, bringing its own dust-cloud with it. Kitty coughed at the fumes and waved her hand about until the air cleared a little. There was a small table and a stool in the cupboard. She placed the book on the table and squatted down on the stool. There was a wad of tissues in her pocket and she used a couple as a duster to wipe the front of the book before opening it.

Maison Rosa, she read, in thin gold lettering. A thrill ran through her body like an electric current. She pulled the first page open. There was some spidery writing on the left and then an amateurish drawing of a woman's shape, with a floor-length garment sketched roughly on it. She barely made out the words that were scrawled beneath

494

it: *Princess dress of rose-pink foulard with striped pekin overskirt.*

A few pages on and the sketches were getting more assured, even though the proportions of the figures made Kitty smile. It was as though a child had done them. As she flicked the pages over, though, she realized that the artist was precocious – a very quick learner indeed. The lines became bolder and expressions even appeared on the models' faces.

An Empire dress of plain bengaline, she read from one page, *the panels of the skirt in jet crepe de Chine and the bodice stitched in embroidered flowers. Full sleeves of beaded lisse.*

The fabric swatches that accompanied each sketch were a deal less grand than the words, though. When 'fine woollen fabric' was described there was often a torn patch of dyed serge, or other cheap material.

'She was knocking off!' Kitty whispered, smiling. 'Rosa, you bad girl!'

She was in the cupboard for two hours without realizing. A mug of tea was placed at her elbow and she drank it without even wondering where it had come from.

Rosa Zigofsky. The books were her own personal diary – a complete record of her business as it was built up, and all in sketches and scrawled writing and little scraps of faded fabric and column upon column of figures.

There was a heart-stopping moment when she saw the first photograph. It was an old studio portrait of an awkward-looking young woman in a simple bridal gown. Kitty's fingers flew to her mouth with the shock of the change from sketches to photographs. So this was the beginning of the mail-order business that had built up and morphed into Zigo fashions.

There was a polite tap on the open door behind her. Kitty turned slowly, rubbing at her stiff and aching neck.

'Alain?'

He stood in the doorway, his expression as curious as Kitty's had been when she first arrived.

'I phoned you all morning,' he said, 'in the end I had to get the thumbscrews out on Mr Smoothie to find out where you were. I thought you'd vanished off the face of the earth, Kitty. Even your mobile's turned off. What the hell is all this?' He looked at the design books with mounting fascination.

She pulled him towards the small table. 'Look, Alain,' she said, 'this is like watching conception for me. This is a record of the founding of our fashion business.'

'*Your* business, Kitty,' Alain said, poring over the sketches and photographs. 'I was a little rude when Mr Smoothie refused to tell me where you were. He fired me.'

'I'm sorry,' Kitty said.

'Don't be,' he told her, sniffing at a small square of ancient brocade. 'How many of these are there?' he asked.

'One per year since the late 1800s,' she told him. 'This must have been Rosa's premises at some time, Alain. I had no idea. The only business I ever knew about was the one in Berkeley Square.' She stopped as a loose photograph fell out of the book and onto the floor.

'Look,' she said, 'it's her wedding shot again.' It was a larger version of the picture in the photographer's studio. Behind it, and slightly stuck to it, was another portrait, of a man standing by himself.

496

'Max Warkofski,' Kitty read from the back. 'It's the photographer, Alain, the one who did the wedding shot. She must have kept them both together.'

Alain stepped back. 'This place is too small for both of us, Kitty,' he said. 'You carry on looking. I'll wait outside.'

He was gone less than five minutes before Kitty heard him calling her. She walked out into the workroom, rubbing her eyes at the sudden light.

'Did you see these?' Alain asked her. He held out a couple of plain cotton blouses with the necklines turned inside-out. 'Look, Kitty,' he said, 'look at the label.'

Kitty read the heavily embroidered italics: 'Rosa Zigofsky Couture,' she said. She looked at the woman, who was now back at her desk. 'But these are new,' she said.

The woman nodded. 'It's a label that's been running since the old days. The couture house closed down but the old man kept the name going for his ladies, who liked to think they were getting something a bit special.'

'Didn't anyone question the copyright?' Kitty asked.

The woman shook her head. 'Search me,' she said.

Kitty took the blouses to the old man who ran the place.

'So you found your name!' he said, smiling.

'How did you manage to keep hold of it?' Kitty asked him. 'Surely someone at Zigo would have put a stop to this years ago!'

The old man nodded. 'It was a gentleman's agreement,' he said. 'Your father knew the name was being used, as did his father before him, but the place was started by Rosa Zigofsky and I think they allowed the name to stay as a little memorial to the woman. The business was her

497

whole life, I believe. Who would have dared to make it otherwise?'

'So this is legal?' Kitty asked.

'Talk to my legal eagles if you think it isn't!' the old man smiled.

Kitty's expression froze. Suddenly she turned and ran out of the building. Alain followed her down the stairs.

'Kitty!' he shouted. 'Where are you going?'

'To speak to my solicitors,' she replied.

CHAPTER FIFTY-EIGHT

ZG

SILISTRIENNE
A firm-textured wool and silk textile.

Dearest Kitty,

So now you know my story. And now that the world has turned full circle again, I shall watch with great pride as you work your way in the business that I founded.

Kitty, there were so many mistakes in my life that I should hate to see you make, yet your youth is all to advantage, whilst my own was a handicap, I believe.

While I arrived penniless in what is now your country my hardships and mean circumstances were as much an impediment to me as I believe your ease of life has been to you. My hurdle was starvation while yours has been apathy and an inability to survive alone.

I have done terrible things, Kitty, and I would not wish the same mistakes upon you. I have killed, dearest – for what would you call my treatment of Max, other than outright murder? How can I blame my own insecurities and lack of experience for such an outrage?

He loved me, Kitty, and I did not see it. Instead I sought to be as much the cynic as I thought him to be, even asking him to take my wedding photograph, for which final act of humiliation he took his own life. Look around you, Kitty. Never allow pride to blur your judgment. A gentleman is not always marked out by his manners and the cut of his suit. If such a man loves you, dearest, work hard to forgive his imperfections before dismissing him altogether.

And then, dear, as a punishment for all my sins my darling son David was taken from me, too. Even now the grief makes me ache with pain.

So what was I left with? A sham marriage, to be sure, for Richard hated me every bit as much as Max loved me. He treated me well enough, but his mind was elsewhere once David died. It was for that child's sake we had been joined and without him we had nothing. My marriage was never consummated, Kitty. Max was the only man I ever knew, save the monster in my homeland.

So the business became my life once again. With Richard's interest in the place all but gone, I worked day and night to make the money come in. And it worked, dearest. With Ruth's help I became famous in my own time. I was the one who persuaded her to marry my brother Gregory. When Max died, all her girlish hopes went with him and so a business-like union suited her very well. They were happy enough, Kitty. Their blood is in your veins along with my own.

Your wealth from the sale of the business enabled you to buy again the place that I sadly neglected, Kitty, and sold on the day of my marriage. My concern was to re-build my husband's business, for it was all I had aimed for, along with his love. Yet so much of me went into the small place you now have, Kitty. Your life is there, child, just as mine was at one time.

Now the name will not die and the family will own what I owned. Let other people do what they will with the main business – keep yourself small and exclusive, it is the only way to be true to the passion I know is inside you. You will find new clients, Kitty. Good quality is always in demand and as the old company begins to sell out to profit so yours can keep the name of which I was so proud.

Never lose the wedding suit, Kitty. It was my most cherished possession and should be yours, too. My marriage to Richard was the most splendid day of my life, for I had no way of knowing what lay ahead. How huge were my dreams then, Kitty! Yet you should make your own happiness and look to no others to achieve it, which is something I learnt at my cost.

Kitty, make no similar mistakes, I beg you. The business was my life, but love of cloth and cut is not all you will need. I died wealthy but I died alone, with only my pride to keep me company. You are young, Kitty, as I once was. Be generous with your love, child, and forgive those who appear to stray, for their love is no less strong. I discovered that only when it was too late. Max took his own life on account of me, Kitty. The memory of what he did has haunted me forever.

The new couture salon opened six months later, amid a welter of publicity that for once focused on the business, rather than Gabriel's murder.

Waika did all they could to prevent the launch, yet the pay-off they had given Kitty enabled her to afford the better legal team. They under-estimated her determination. In the end there was nothing they could do. When Zigofsky opened, it took with it all the traditions of quality and prestige that Waika had milked out of the Zigo name.

Kitty was proud, but Hester was prouder. She arrived at the opening in her odd stockings – a look which now had a cult following among women of a certain age who still wanted to appear innovative – with China's daughter clutched in her arms. Both were dressed in specially-made outfits from the Zigofsky 'Diffusion' range.

Alain's first collection was a masterpiece of exquisite understatement, making the garments at Zigo and Jacobs appear tacky and gaudy by contrast. Kitty had bought in an older Parisian couturier to add heavyweight experience to the designs and to give them the quality touches that would bring society names to their door.

Kofteros was not, of course, at the opening, though he phoned Kitty from his car once the main party was over.

'Are you coming over?' Kitty asked him.

'Me?' he laughed. 'Do you want to see me end up wearing a pair of cement boots in the Thames? No, Kitty, I don't think so. Waika are still going apeshit about all this as it is. Maybe later, under the cover of darkness, like a vampire.'

'You risked your job,' Kitty told him.

'No,' he said, 'nothing remotely as dramatic. All I did was give you a lift in the car. Nobody could ever blame a lowly chauffeur for what's happened. Anyway, there's no real damage done – only a dent to Waika's fragile ego. They can afford to ignore the problem. Just sit tight for a couple of years, Kitty, and they'll be buying you out ten times over.'

'But they must have blamed you for not checking out the legal implications?' Kitty asked.

'No,' Kofteros said, 'they blamed another guy in another suit. The man who was about to be given my job, in fact. I was going to be made redundant about the same time as you and your brother. It just happened that I noticed a small glitch in the paperwork which their newest blue-eyed boy failed to spot.'

'So you helped me in order to save your own skin?' Kitty asked.

'I never said you should say thank you,' Kofteros told her.

'Thanks anyway,' Kitty said.

There was an awkward pause.

'So I suppose you go off and marry your little swarthy Frenchman now?' he asked.

'Maybe,' Kitty told him, 'maybe not. Business comes first.'

'Well,' Kofteros began, 'if you ever need anything, you know . . .'

'There is one thing I still need to know,' Kitty said.

'Ask,' he told her.

'What exactly is it you do with jelly-cubes?'

'Chloe told you about that?' he asked.

'She did.'

There was a crackle of static before Kitty could hear him laughing.

'She was joking, Kitty, winding you up,' he said at last. 'Do you know, you are almost perfect – beautiful, talented, quite kind to people you like. There's only one thing that never got passed down in your genes, Kitty – a sense of humour.'

'I don't believe you,' Kitty said, smiling.

'You don't *want* to believe me,' Nicky replied. He sighed. 'Okay, if you really have to know. What I do with the jelly-cubes is I place them very carefully up . . .'

But Kitty had rung off.

'*Kitty*!'

The voice in her head again.

'*Kitty*!'

Sighing, she got his number on redial. He picked up after one ring.

'So will it be two years before I see you again? After the dust has settled?' she asked.

'Marry your Frenchman.' Nicky laughed. 'The suit fits him better.'

Kitty smiled. 'How about under the cover of darkness?' she asked.

'Maybe.'

This time it was he who hung up on her.

She waited until the phone rang again.

'Do you know a good tailor who can do alterations?' he said.

GLOSSARY

Pesach	Passover
Shiva	wake, the first week after the funeral
Chevra Kadisha	burial society
Talmud	fundamental code of Jewish law
Kichels	biscuits
Minyan	the required number – ten males over the age of thirteen – for parts of services or readings
Shtetle	Jewish village communities of Eastern Europe
Shema	a Jewish prayer declaring the oneness of God
Yamulkh	a man's skullcap
Simcha	celebration
Challah	bread
Schlemozzle	uproar